RAVE REVIEWS
FOR DOUGLAS CLEGG!

"One of horror's brightest lights."
—*Publishers Weekly*

"Douglas Clegg has become
the new star in horror fiction."
—Peter Straub

"Douglas Clegg is clearly and without any doubt
one of the best horror writers in the business."
—*Cinescape*

"Clegg gets high marks on the terror scale."
—*Daily News* (New York)

"Douglas Clegg is one of
horror's most captivating voices."
—*BookLovers*

"No one does lean, atmospheric, character-
driven, and damned eerie horror like Clegg."
—*Rue Morgue*

Other *Leisure* books by Douglas Clegg:

NIGHTMARE HOUSE
FOUR DARK NIGHTS (Anthology)
THE HOUR BEFORE DARK
THE INFINITE
NAOMI
MISCHIEF
YOU COME WHEN I CALL YOU
THE NIGHTMARE CHRONICLES
THE HALLOWEEN MAN

Writing as Andrew Harper:

NIGHT CAGE
RED ANGEL

DOUGLAS CLEGG

THE ABANDONED

LEISURE BOOKS   NEW YORK CITY

A LEISURE BOOK®

May 2005

Published by

Dorchester Publishing Co., Inc.
200 Madison Avenue
New York, NY 10016

ISBN 0-8439-5410-8

The name "Leisure Books" and the stylized "L" with design are trademarks of Dorchester Publishing Co., Inc.

Printed in the United States of America.

Visit us on the web at www.dorchesterpub.com.

*This novel is dedicated to Marty Shoushanian,
who won the dedication in a charity auction for
The American Heart Association.*

*Special thanks to Raul Silva;
to Don D'Auria, and the folks at Dorchester
Publishing; and to the readers of my novels.*

THE ABANDONED

AUTHOR'S NOTE

This is the fourth Harrow novel, following *Nightmare House*, *Mischief*, and *The Infinite*. None of the Harrow House novels need to be read in chronological order, but if you get a chance, you might pick up the ones you've missed to find out other aspects of its mystery.

If you'd like to receive special updates about past and future books of mine, please subscribe to my free online newsletter—just visit my website at www.DouglasClegg.com to sign up for it.

Through me you pass into the city of woe:
Through me you pass into eternal pain:
Through me among the people lost for aye.
—Dante Alighieri, *The Divine Comedy*

Prologue

You found the house because you knew of it from your dreams and you read of it in the ancient books.

It is a sacred place.

The ritual was simple.

You recited the words.

You made the sacrifice.

You called the thing back to the form of life.

You were only passing through then, in summer, but the house called to you.

The boy called to you, as well.

And even the blood, when it spilled, called out your name.

Maybe if you'd done it right that summer night, it would be under control.

Maybe there'd have been no leakage.

Spillage.

Seepage.

A shred of something—like ash—taken on the wind from a fire and spread out to others. It leaks and seeps,

1

slowly reaching out with whispered promises and the dreams that come from within its depths.

You cannot sacrifice the dead to bring the dead back.

Such sacrifice only makes the dead hunger for the living.

You intended to move on before morning; you meant to travel far away with life restored to the one you loved. The great gift was within you, but all of it called you back as if it owned you—as if you were slave to brick and stone and wood from the moment you recited the words and tasted the blood of the sacrifice.

You journeyed to distant places, but all the while, it called you.

Because the ash from your fire blew with the wind and entered homes and gardens and backyards and places where even the smallest insect moved—and it even reached you again, nearly a thousand miles away, tapping you on the shoulder, the hint of a whisper seeping into your mind. *"Do not abandon me, Nightwatchman."*

I

THE DARK PLACE

Chapter One

Summer Night at the House of Horrors

1

"I feel like we're lost," Lizzie said.

"How can we be lost?"

"If you told me we were about a ten-minute drive from my home, I'd say you must be crazy."

"Babe, I thought you knew where this place was."

"From the front I do. I know the main roads up here. Just not this back way. It's too dark. I can barely see the road sometimes. And we had to come the back way because . . . ?"

"Because we're breaking the law," the guy in back said.

"We're not breakin' any laws, dude."

"Try checking out one of these 'no trespassing— violators will be prosecuted' signs."

"Do people ever actually pay attention to those?" Alex, in the front seat, asked. He added with a snort, "Oh, I keep forgetting. You're a geek. Geeks never trespass."

Beyond the windshield, the haze of their headlights interrupted the absolute darkness along an indigo road

Douglas Clegg

curving through thick woods. A faint roll of distant thunder was met nearly a minute later with a brief flash of heat lightning far off in the moonless sky.

The breezeless dark breathed heat and damp down upon them; through a crack in the windshield it seemed to seep into the car's faulty air-conditioning and touch them with a wilting feeling—that sense of the hothouse river stink which sometimes passed through on steamy summer nights. It brought a drowsy peace to the night, like a déjà vu of other humid June nights when the crickets and the cicadas fell silent, when anything might happen and many things would.

The three teenagers rode in the slightly rundown '98 Chevy Malibu that Lizzie's twin sister had bought with money saved from a variety of odd jobs she'd had since the age of fourteen.

The car was on loan that night to Lizzie under oath that she wouldn't drive anywhere that might damage the car (like the bumpy road they were currently on), or let her lips touch a drop of alcohol (like the three six packs of lukewarm Budweiser in the trunk).

So far, Lizzie, who was nearly eighteen, had kept this promise, but she was fairly sure she'd break it once they reached the party.

She also had decided that she'd waited long enough, and this would be the night. Half of her friends had already done it with their boyfriends, and she was beginning to wonder whether something wasn't wrong with her for not having allowed much more than a grope and a feel to the two guys she'd dated so far. Lizzie was fairly certain that boys didn't want girls who put them off too long. She was fairly sure that Dan Favreau had dumped her sophomore year just because she wouldn't do more than make out.

I will become a woman tonight. I will give myself body and soul to him.

To Alex.

She had prepared herself. She had gone with her friend Bari right after their fifth-period class to the pharmacy three blocks from school in Parham and bought some condoms. Bari had said, "You know, they don't sell these things at our local drugstore."

"That's why half the village gets pregnant by sixteen." Lizzie laughed, then remembered something about her sister and just couldn't laugh about it.

But she was ready now.

She had waited long enough.

She knew that it might be a mistake to trust Alex, but she loved him and she just wanted to get it all over with as soon as possible. It wasn't like it would hurt her rep in school because Alex had already told his buddies they'd done it, and as much as it pissed her off that he'd be such a jerk, it at least meant that she wasn't doomed to be a virgin-by-legend forever.

Tonight, we'll make it real.

The guy she'd had to bring with them, the guy in the backseat, named Sam, was a logistical problem, but she figured she and Alex could find a private spot somewhere that night. She'd already figured out her alibi with her sister, Ronnie (although Ronnie had told them they'd get caught one way or another), and she wasn't expected home until the next day—probably not 'til noon.

But driving the car with Alex next to her, she began to wonder whether she really could go through with it. There he was, already stinking of his third beer, making fart jokes, blasting the music too loud, and now and then trying to feel her up when he thought she wouldn't notice.

"I guess we turn left here," Lizzie said, after switching off the car stereo.

"No, right," Alex said. "Right. *Right.* The right of righteousness. See?" He pointed to the hand-scrawled directions as if she could lean over and read them.

The car light was on inside, and it made Lizzie feel as if

they were being watched by the darkness around them.

"This is like one of those ghost stories," Alex said.

"*What?*" Lizzie asked, exasperation barely concealed in her voice.

"You know. I heard this story where people are driving on this kind of lone country road late at night. And they see someone by the side of the road."

"Nobody's by the side of the road here," Sam, the guy in back, said.

"I know, but it would creep me out if we saw somebody out here. Hey, favorite group?" Alex asked, after he'd made sure he correctly picked the right-hand curve of the road as their direction of choice.

"I love Smashing Pumpkins," Sam said. "My dad has these old CDs that just blow me away. I think the '90s are my favorite era. Musically."

"For me, The Strokes," Alex said. "For classics, Nirvana."

"The Yeah Yeah Yeahs," Sam said. "I love their stuff, too."

"I like some of their stuff," Alex said, and glanced at the road ahead, and then said, "It's like *Halloween* out here."

"Halloween in June," Lizzie said.

"I mean the movie." Alex reached up and flicked off the light within the car. "All this backwoods crap reminds me of *The Texas Chainsaw Massacre*."

"Shut up," Lizzie said.

"You ever see it?" Alex asked Sam.

"Sure."

"You like it?"

"I guess. I like the original one best."

"Not me. The chick in the second one's hot. Tell you what I'd do if I ever came across anybody like that."

"Don't tell me," Lizzie said. "You'd molest her."

"Ha. No. I mean the bad guy. Anybody with a chainsaw comin' after me," Alex said, "I'd kick out his frickin' legs and then I'd grab the chainsaw and cut him in two." He let out a throaty laugh dried out by too many cigarettes.

8

The twin high beams that captured the trees and the stretch of road only reached several feet ahead of the car.

"I didn't know it would be this dark out here," Lizzie said. "I mean, I knew it would be dark. But not like this."

"Dark side of the moon," Sam said.

"I love Pink Floyd," Alex said.

"Take the fork," said Sam. Nobody knew him well, but he was familiar with the roads up to the house, so they assumed he knew what he was talking about.

"What the hell does that mean?" Alex asked.

"Take it," he said, and pointed ahead to the left. "The fork in the road. Always means left. The other way is just straight."

"No," Lizzie said. "One way's left, and one way goes right. 'Taking the fork' means crap."

"You ever see *Wrong Turn*?" Alex asked, leaning into Lizzie, nuzzling her neck. "I wonder if inbred rednecks live out here. With hatchets and shit."

"I saw it," Sam said. "It was pretty good."

"Pretty good? It was frickin' awesome," Alex said. "What about *The Ring*?"

"I liked the Japanese version."

"It was stupid," Alex said. "A chick comes out of the TV all wonky. BFD, says me."

"It was brilliant," Sam said.

"Well . . ." Alex said, letting the word trail off. "I guess if you think a chick with lots of hair coming out of a TV is brilliant, then, yeah, it was a goddamn masterpiece. She wasn't very hot. Now, the chick in *The Grudge*. She was hot."

"Buffy," Lizzie said. "I love her."

"Sarah Michelle Gellar," Sam said. "She's great."

"Hot chicks are always great," Alex said. He reached over and touched the back of Lizzie's neck. "If we were in a movie right now, I'd play the hero, you'd be the hot babe, and the guy in back here would be the expendable one.

9

You know, the one who always gets killed because he's not a movie star."

"Or they'd make the movie and kill off the famous actor. Like in *Scream* where they killed Drew Barrymore in the first ten minutes," Sam said.

"Well," Alex said. "First off, you're wrong. They didn't kill her first. They killed the guy playing her boyfriend first, and he was just the guy in the backseat, basically. I mean, if you want to get all technical about it." Under his breath, Alex said, *"Geek."*

The car started churning up dust as soon as it hit the unpaved road to the left.

"Why'd we have to come out at midnight?" Lizzie asked.

"Why you think?" Alex asked.

"Because only stupid people go to haunted houses at night," Sam said.

"It's not haunted," Lizzie said. "I mean, nothing's haunted."

"You ever been there?"

"No way," she said. "But I've heard about it since I was a kid. Why aren't we having the party at the Point? It's always at the Point."

"The Point is old," Alex said. "The Point is for babies."

"I like the Point. You get to skinny dip. I thought you'd like that, too," Lizzie said. "And at the Point, you can make a big bonfire. And you can dance all night."

"We can dance all night here if you want, babe," Alex said. Looking to the guy behind him, he added, "You probably been here a few times, right? Keggers with the goths?"

"Maybe," Sam said. "It's creepy as hell, believe me. It has a rep for being a real house of horrors."

"House of whores, more like it. I bet you jack off there," Alex said, chuckling. "I bet you go to horror movies and jack off, too."

"Shut up," Lizzie whispered, and then barely audible, her teeth clenched and less than a whisper emerging from between her lips: *"He's my sister's friend."*

"Come on," Alex said. "Everybody does it. You do it. I do it. Your mom does it."

"Gross," Lizzie said, but she giggled a little. "Oh. Disgusting."

"Not much else to do in a dead place like this," Alex said. "Hey," he turned to glance at the guy. "What you do for fun out here? I mean, I guess you could hop a train and go somewhere else. But what do guys like you do for fun?"

Sam said, "I guess in Parham everything's hotter than a monkey in shit."

Alex snickered. "I'm just teasing you. I think your town's cool. I think even these back roads are cool. Hell, I once jacked off at *Alien Vs. Predator.*"

"Gross," Lizzie said. "Is that all guys talk about? Where they jacked off? Am I going to spend the rest of the summer hearing shit like this?"

"I did it in class one time," Alex said. "Right in front of Mrs. Armpit-Hair. She was going over the French Revolution. I had a little revolt of my own going on. I put my head in my guillotine and just made it go up and down a lot. I had my shirt-tails out, so nobody could really see anything. I just unzipped and—"

"Okay, enough," Lizzie said.

"No, it's a cool story," Alex said. "It was sort of uncontrollable and then Mrs. Armpit-Hair calls me up to the front to go over something about some French guy and I'm like, 'I can't come up there 'cause I already came up here.' "

"*That's* your cool story?" Lizzie asked. She pulled over the car, and put it in park. "That story is one of the grossest . . . I think you made it up. And it's offensive."

"Hey, being offended is so bogus, Lizzie."

"Funny how only people who are offensive think that."

"Well, Joe Davison laughed his ass off when I told him."

Lizzie started up the car again, cursing under her breath.

"Nobody's got a sense of humor anymore," Alex said. He drew a pack of cigarettes from his pocket. "Smokes?"

He offered the pack to Sam, who passed on them. Alex lit one, and it nodded up and down between his lips as he spoke. "I don't know how you guys don't smoke. It's like you have a little tension, you pop in a smoke, and before you can say 'jack-shit,' all tension's gone."

"Maybe it's the whole lung and heart problem," Sam said.

"Eh, I'll deal with it when I'm fifty. And that's a long time from now. Anyway, who wants to live that long? I want to go out fast and furious and with a smoke in my mouth and a mouth on my—"

"Window down, Alex," Lizzie said. "Alex. *Alex.*"

"But we lose the air-conditioning."

"Down," she said. "It's Ronnie's car. I don't want it smelling like an ashtray."

Alex brought the window down a bit. "My favorite horror movie of all time is probably *The Exorcist.* I begged my mom to let me see it when I was ten, and she wouldn't, but I snuck it out of the video store and watched it really late one night. I had nightmares for months. It was . . . oh damn . . . it was like a big fat boner of a movie."

"You jack off during *that* one?" Lizzie asked.

"Hardy-har-har. Baby, what's yours?"

"I don't know," Lizzie said, hesitating as she slowed the car down along a particularly bumpy patch. "I don't really like those kinds of movies much. I like that one with Nicole Kidman. The one where she was all uptight in a house back in a war, and there were things going on in the house. Come on, Alex, you know that movie. What's it called?"

"*The Others,*" Sam said.

"Thank you," Lizzie said, glancing in her rearview mirror at the guy.

"Hey, you," Alex turned around, cigarette bobbing. "What about you?"

"I don't know. *Alien* was pretty scary, I guess."

"Yeah, hmm, that's true." Alex turned back around and slipped his hand between Lizzie's legs. She reached down and flicked his hand away.

"I like a lot of John Carpenter's movies, too."

"*Halloween*?" Alex said. "My fave's *Halloween III*. With that song in it."

"Sure. But I meant more like *The Thing*."

"Holy mother of shit," Alex said, nearly spitting his cigarette out.

"What's wrong?" Lizzie asked.

"This guy and me, we got *way* too much in common," Alex said. He puffed the last of his cigarette, letting the ash fall on his jeans, then flicked it out the window. "I loved *The Thing*. I mean, loved it. I saw it like ten times. Kurt Russell. I mean, that Thing."

"I loved *The Shining*, too."

"Oh yeah. Classic Nicholson. 'Give me the frickin' bat!' " Alex said, chuckling. "Doesn't get much better than Nicholson. And that kid. Chillin', that kid. And those little bug-eyed girls. And that bitch in the tub. Holy crap. But here's the thing about horror movies. They always have these stupid people doing stupid things. I mean, ultimately. You don't go after your kitty cat if the alien is on the ship. I mean, screw the kitty. Right? You don't go doing the laundry when a damn killer's on the loose. That kind of stuff. *Texas Chainsaw*—you don't go to the rundown place with human teeth on the ground and stick around."

A passing moment of silence in the car while they heard the shriek of what must have been some kind of night bird. Then Alex pointed off to the left.

"You see that?"

"What?"

"A kid. Standing there," Alex said, "by the side of the road. He was just standing there. Staring at us. Staring."

"Yeah, right," Lizzie said.

Sam laughed. "I didn't see the kid, either."

"You guys are no fun," Alex said. Then, more quietly, "I'm sort of not joking. I thought I saw a kid standing back there."

"So, why are we going to this place?" Lizzie asked.

"Baby?"

"*We're* the stupid people. We're going to Harrow, the haunted house."

"Aw," Alex said. "Those are movies. This is real life. You know there's no boogeyman in real life, right? I mean, you don't believe in that kind of crap."

"There's people, though," Sam said.

"Huh?"

"Like Ed Gein. Or Dahmer."

"Who?"

"Dahmer's the guy who tortured and killed younger guys, then ate some of them," Sam said. "Ed Gein, he lived in Plainfield, Wisconsin. He used to dig up corpses of women and skin them and dress up in their skins."

"Like in *Silence of the Lambs*," Lizzie said, but had a slight clip to her voice as if she wished she hadn't uttered this.

"Baby, nobody's going *Silence of the Lambs* on us. You know there's no crazy chainsaw killer out here. You're not scared, right?"

"I don't know," she said. "But it's dark, there's no moon out, and this whole idea of getting together with people out here seems stupid at this point."

"I'm gonna protect you with my love, Lizzie," Alex said. "Come on, it's all fun. We get together with some of the guys from school, we party some, we stay out late and . . . well, we have fun."

"She's right," Sam said. "We're just like the stupid people in horror movies."

A momentary silence in the car.

"You know," Alex began, "In *Dawn of the Dead*, when—"

"That's it," Lizzie said. "No more horror movies. I don't want to hear about another one. If you bring up one more horror movie I'm going to put you out of the car and you can walk."

"You just a teensy-weensy bit scared, baby?"

"No," she said, but her voice was a little too soft.

2

"All these damn trees," Lizzie said, as she swerved around rocks in the road and narrowly avoided a ditch on the far left, only to hit a major bump in the middle of the road. The road kept turning and winding and bumping.

Then, they all felt it—a jolt beneath the tires.

"We hit something?"

"No way," Lizzie said. "I didn't see anything."

"Jesus, we hit something?" Alex asked again.

"Probably chains," Sam said. "There are chains up around here to keep people out, but they get pulled down all the time."

"It felt like more than that," Lizzie said, but somehow the idea of chains across the road made sense to her. "I guess maybe it could've been."

"Or we hit a rabbit," Alex said. "Lots of rabbits out here. And cats."

"I didn't hit a cat," Lizzie said.

"It was nothing," Sam said. "There's crap all over this road. I'm sure it was just a chain. It wasn't that big a bump."

"Isn't there a main road?" Alex asked, turning around to face the guy. Alex barely remembered his name—he wasn't someone who people really noticed at school, and it wasn't as if they ever hung out together.

"Yeah," Sam said. "But sometimes it gets patrolled."

Lizzie and Alex quickly exchanged a glance.

"It's because of break-ins," Sam said.

"We're not breaking in," Lizzie said, as if to confirm something.

"Look, I know this place. Don't worry. The back road's the best way in. The chains across the road are all over the place when you come in from the town side of things. They always forget to string 'em back up on this side."

"So says you," Lizzie said as they hit another bump. It felt like the frame of the car rose up while the axle stayed low to the ground. Alex got jostled around because he refused to wear a seatbelt.

"See? Look," Sam said, again pointing.

Lizzie glanced into the headlights, and there she saw what seemed to be a stone wall with a break in it. Not quite a gateway, but almost.

"This calls for a drink," Alex said, and drew the flask from his letterman's jacket. He took a swig and passed it to Lizzie.

"Get it out of my face," she said. She slowly drove the car up the last bit of unpaved road to the driveway.

3

They parked near the front porch, then got out.

Alex shouted, "Goddamn, when you said these people were rich, I didn't know you meant stinkin' *rich*. I mean, goddamn! How come we never got up here before? Who the hell owns this place? It's a frickin' palace is what it is."

"Quit yelling," Lizzie said. She looked from the turrets to the gables. It was so dark, and she had already turned off the headlights so it was as if the place were an inky angular shadow of darkness against a darker woods with sky on each side and above it.

Harrow loomed like a shadow that had grown in darkness. Night against a backdrop of endless night.

The place looked like a castle, and Lizzie felt less safe than she had in the car.

She had seen Harrow once or twice growing up, but never liked it. It had always reminded her of her dad when he lay dying in the road.

The car wrapped around a tree, and Ronnie kneeling over him, and Lizzie getting out of the car, a little eight-year-old running to her sister and her father's side, only to watch his last breath turn to mist in the chilly winter air.

The house reminded her of death like that.

The dread of death, coming.

Its silhouette, like dark fingers stretching into shadow.

Lizzie caught her breath and felt that strange shiver run through her that she remembered from childhood. The shiver both she and Ronnie had spoken of between them—as if something had touched them on the inside the moment their father had died.

Touched us and never let go.

"It looks like Bannerman's Castle, sort of," Alex said. "You know, that island in the river, and there's that castlelike thing there. Or the Vanderbilt Mansion in Hyde Park."

"Or a big fat mausoleum," Lizzie said. "I wish we hadn't come here. I don't know what I was thinking."

"You were thinking a wild time for Thirteenth Night. Where's the par-tay?" Alex asked.

Sam said, "The others said they'd be in the graveyard."

"Graveyard?" Lizzie asked. *"Graveyard?"*

"Cool," Alex said, taking another swig. "Frickin' cool. Partay with the dead."

"It's over there," Sam said, pointing off into a further darkness. "I bet the party's already started. There's a path up." He switched on a small flashlight. It barely lit more than a few feet in front of them. "So we all going now?"

17

"You sure it's empty?" Lizzie asked, glancing window to window, balcony to porch. "Why is it all boarded up? I mean, nobody lives here, right?"

"Not for a few years. It's practically condemned."

"Let's break in," Alex said, turning to Sam. "Come on. Please? Come on." He had a drunken, stretched-out plea to his words.

"I'm never going inside that place," Lizzie said.

But within a few minutes, she and Alex had slipped through a broken board at the back door, leaving the other teenager (of whom Alex whispered to Lizzie, "Why the hell did we bring the big loser along?" and she whispered back, "I promised my sister, and anyway, because you didn't want to come earlier, it's lucky we had him for directions or we'd just be driving all over the place") to trek up to the other party-goers on the hillside for some big drunkathon bonfire thirteen nights after the school year had ended.

Inside the house, Lizzie and Alex began making out. When Alex's flask fell from his back pocket, Lizzie pulled away from him and said, "Did you hear that? Jesus, how come you didn't bring a flashlight, too?"

Alex grinned, glancing around at the shadowed room they'd found. "Baby, it was just my flask. That's all. I dropped it."

"Shh," she said, and then tried to focus on the dark itself. But no matter how much she tried, it seemed to get darker by the second. She wasn't sure why this was happening. She had usually experienced the opposite—that if she was in the dark long enough, some slight light could be detected, her eyes would adjust to the darkness, and she'd at least be able to make out shadows.

But the room they were in seemed to be growing darker, like an ink stain seeping outward.

For just a moment, she thought she heard her sister's voice, and it scared the hell out of her.

Lizzie? You okay?

18

Ronnie? She felt as if she were talking to herself in her mind.

"Where's the door?" Lizzie asked the darkness.

"Huh?" Alex said.

"Is it behind you? Is that where we came from?"

"Maybe."

"Check."

"Okay. Okay. Hold your horses. Okay . . . Nope, no door here."

"Quiet. Shh. Just for a second," she said. She wasn't so scared that she trembled, but something in her mind had just begun thinking irrational thoughts about where they were and the stories about the house and about the kinds of people who had lived there in the past and what had happened to them. Within seconds, she had to swallow a sense of panic that seemed nearly natural to her—as if her body had decided that fear was its only response to this dark place.

And then she heard breathing.

Not Alex, not his wheezy breathing when he was trying to keep quiet. She held her breath to make sure it wasn't from her own nostrils.

Someone else was in the darkness with them.

She felt someone's breath on the back of her neck.

She froze, and was about to move toward Alex, but when she reached forward to touch him, he wasn't there.

"Alex?" she whispered, and realized it came out as a whimper. She felt a cool sweat break out on her forehead. *"Alex?"*

She reached around in the darkness, feeling as if she were completely blind. It was as if all light in existence had been doused, or as if she could not open her eyes at all, as if they'd been glued shut.

Her fingers touched something.

Just the tips—touched what felt like warm flesh.

Instinctively, she stepped forward, although part of her wanted to recoil from whomever this was.

Alex? Alex? Is it you? Please God, let it be Alex.

Her hands wrapped around arms. His arms. She was sure it was Alex.

"Alex," she whispered, wanting to scold him for scaring her in the dark.

She felt him, *thank God,* she felt him and he never felt so good. She leaned into him to hug him close to her, but he was wet all over and smelled coppery and dirty. As she felt his wetness clinging to her, she began to realize that the thick liquid on him was blood. All the horror movies he and the guy in the backseat had been talking about the whole damn trip suddenly came at her in a rush of images she wished she could forget. She let out a scream and would not stop screaming until somebody turned on the lights.

She closed her eyes, not wanting to see.

4

The guy who had been sitting in the backseat of the car the whole way was seventeen years old and was named Sam Pratt. He was chunky, with thick black hair that barely concealed a scar across his forehead from an accident he'd had when he was about four. He had a tongue-piercing and three piercings in his left ear. He had dreamed since nearly his birth that he would one day get out of Watch Point and head for New York City. He had applied to NYU for college, and he was hoping that would get him out soon enough. He tended to wear black, and although he didn't consider himself a "goth" by any stretch of the imagination, he knew that others at school thought he was. Many of them were sure he was into some mystical mumbo-jumbo and weirdo pursuits and that he might be one step away from going all Columbine. But in fact, he was just a fan of horror movies and rock music and couldn't really help being who he was—any more than Lizzie could help being a cheerleader and Alex could help being a pseudo-jock who cheated on his history tests.

And despite his sometimes off-putting exterior, Sam had been thrilled to think that he'd finally end up at a party with kids from his school because he'd never been to one before.

As Sam found his way along the side path through the straggly wooded area, he thought he heard some of the others from school up ahead, although it sounded less and less like guys and girls his age than it did some old guy cackling over some joke.

He saw the campfire somebody had started. Since it was the first time in all his school years that he finally felt included in something the "cool" kids generally did—get drunk, go a little wild, and pretend to have fun for a few hours—he jogged most of the way up the path, through the woods, until he reached the entrance to the old graveyard.

5

Back inside the house, the lights up, Lizzie felt a shock go through her.

But not from fear.

It was just the beginning of anger mixed with surprise mixed with a little pissed-offedness.

They were all there:

Bari, Mac, Andy, Nancy, Terry, Zack—all her friends from school who lived in Watch Point, a couple of guys from Parham, a girl she didn't know—and Alex, too. Of course Ronnie wasn't there. Ronnie never went out anymore. Lizzie had given up on dragging her sister to the parties.

She reined in her anger a bit and began laughing with them as they passed around a bottle of Boone's Farm

21

Strawberry Wine. They were laughing too hard to hear the scream of the other guy, the guy Lizzie only knew as a friend of her older sister's, and he needed a ride, and he'd show them the way to the house—the one who had gone up to the graveyard.

But when they stopped laughing, Lizzie heard it first and said, "What the hell is that?"

6

Sam's mouth was open as wide as he'd ever opened it. The noise was all around him, and he couldn't even tell that it was coming from his own throat.

He stood in the little graveyard, just beyond the small fire someone had started in a circle of old moss-covered stone markers. The feeble light of the flashlight pointed forward as he looked at the little boy who had been strung upside down and gutted like a deer.

The small fire behind him cast flickering yellow shadows.

The scream finally died in Sam's throat, which went dry—he felt parched and wasn't sure he could even speak after that scream.

He felt like a six-year-old again, stepping into a nightmare.

The smell of cool summer rain filled the air, just seconds before the downpour began.

Sam dropped the flashlight, and it rolled until it came to a dead stop at one of the stone markers.

He heard the distant rumble of thunder. Heat lightning played along the darkness above the trees, then cracked open into a great split of light that illuminated all the graveyard—the hanging boy, and a dark figure that stood back behind several stone markers, more shadow than human being.

7

Seven miles away in the village of Watch Point, three streets up from the railroad tracks, above the rocky ledges that curled over the Hudson River, Lizzie's twin sister, Veronica—or Ronnie, as she'd always been called—awoke from a deep sleep. The lightning beyond her bedroom window flashed white and made her mother's garden look as if it were covered with snow for a moment.

Ronnie rose up from bed, and went to look out the window as the storm broke above the village. Rain tapped at the window, and she lifted it up to smell the fresh air.

The lightning seemed green and blue as it danced among the dark clouds before it crashed into a white streak beyond the trees and houses of the village.

For a split second, she thought she saw the vague features of a child's face in the piercing light.

8

"Is that *Pratt?*" Alex asked, laughing. "Is that Pratt screaming like a bitch?"

The screaming beyond Harrow had stopped, replaced by the rumble of thunder and a *rickety-tickety* of rain on the house.

Alex kept laughing. "Oh frickin' hell, I remember in seventh grade when he wet his pants in gym and just stood there pretending he hadn't. Jesus, he's a little baby. A little teeny-tiny baby geek."

Zack joined. "Thou shalt not suffer a geek to live."

"I don't get it," Alex said. "That a joke?"

"It's biblical." Zack kept laughing at his own wit. "God said kill all the geeks."

"Maybe God's killing one right now up at that graveyard," Alex grinned.

"We better see what's happening up there," Lizzie said, moving toward the door. Alex grabbed her hand and pulled her back to him. She didn't resist much, and he wrapped his arms around her and planted a big wet sloppy kiss on her lips. He licked right up to her eyelid and kissed there, then slid his lips to her ear and whispered, "Come on. We can make out here. That's why we're here."

"He might be hurt," Lizzie said, and then realized the back of her head felt a little funny. *Too much wine.* The room had begun spinning a little bit.

"He's fine," Alex insisted. "He's fine. He probably just got freaked by the lightning."

Bari Love held up a nearly empty bottle of wine. She chugged the last of it down, giggling, and said, "I got the bottle. Who wants to play?"

9

"He's out there in the rain," Lizzie said, but even that came out a little slurred because she'd already had one beer.

They all sat in a circle, and it was Andy Harris's turn to spin the bottle in the center.

The bottle seemed to spin and spin, and it made Lizzie a little light-headed as she watched it go around and around.

Then it stopped.

Pointed directly at her.

Andy wore a big shit-eating grin on his face and nearly smacked his lips. Lizzie felt as if she were betraying Ronnie because her sister had briefly dated Andy during sophomore year and then had been dumped unceremoniously by him before he took up with Bari.

But it's the game. Stupid Spin the Bottle. We've been playing it since ninth grade, and for some reason the guys always like it just a little bit more than the girls do.

And still, we play it.

Andy crawled across the floor toward her. Lizzie glanced at Alex, who was so drunk it looked like he couldn't recognize anything let alone feel jealous that another guy was going to kiss her. She looked at Bari, but Bari was practically hanging off Zack after their last bottle-induced kiss.

When Andy got close, his breath all cigarette ash and warm beer, she drew back from him. She gave him a peck on the cheek. "Sorry," she whispered.

He pawed at her, but she managed to push him away.

"Bitch," he whispered under his breath.

"Bastard," Lizzie whispered back.

She stood up unsteadily. "I want to see what's going on with Sam."

"He screamed for his mommy," Zack said, laughing.

"Maybe he got hit with lightning," Nancy Withers said. "There must be a God after all!"

"I think someone's in love with Sam," Bari said. "Hey, Alex, Lizzie's got the hots for the geek."

Alex swung his head around slightly, his blond hair falling over his eyes. "What?" Then he swung around again to look at Lizzie. "Hey baby. *Bay-bay.*"

"Hey," she said. *What the hell am I doing with these jerks? Playing drinking games. Practically girlfriend-swapping. Ronnie's right about all of them. They think they're the winners of life, but they missed the boat completely.*

She ignored all the jeers, and went toward the door leading to the narrow corridor.

As she opened the door, she felt as if her heart froze.

A middle-aged man, scrawny and tall, stood there before her.

Naked.

His body covered with red paint as if he'd been drawing on himself—circles and lines and pictures.

His teeth were smeared with some brown-red color, and he parted his lips as if he were in the middle of saying something. His hands were down between his legs, furiously stroking himself.

She opened her mouth to curse, but felt as if the breath had been sucked out of her.

Lightning flashed outside, and the tall windows along the corridor seemed to light up so white it made her think of a nuclear explosion.

The light in the room flickered.

Then the entire house was plunged into darkness.

10

Lizzie stood still for a few seconds, catching her breath.

In the dark, there didn't seem to be a naked man at all.

Instead, she felt utterly alone, as if even those behind her in the room had vanished.

Someone struck a match.

She turned back around.

For just a second, she thought she saw her dead father's face—his features twisted, but she knew it was him—in the brief glow of the match.

The match extinguished.

"Who's there?" she asked.

But no one said a word.

Is this all a joke? Are they doing this to me? Are these people who are not my friends—not really, not the way friends really are—are they doing this?

Then, Alex near her. She felt his warmth. "It's all right, babe," he whispered. He struck another match, and it *was* Alex. *Thank God. Thank God.*

"I was scared," she whispered. "It got so quiet."

"Heh," he grinned. "I think they're all just taking advantage of the dark."

He blew the match out, and she felt his lips against hers. Her heart was pounding. She didn't want to kiss him at all,

26

but his mouth had a kind of suction that kept her there. She pushed him away, but his arms surrounded her.

She felt his arousal as he pressed against her, and she tried to draw back but could not. She felt his hands go around her back, stroking along her spinal column. It only made her shiver—she felt uncomfortable. *Even if they are all making out. Even if I only imagined seeing things. Even if that scream meant nothing. I want out. I want out now.*

Then she felt other hands, smaller hands, along her ankles, as if a little child were pulling at her.

Instinctively, she kicked out, then brought her knee up to what she estimated in the dark to be Alex's groin. As she drew back from him, she felt others touching her in the dark. She had to fight her way through them to move toward the one crack of light she saw in the doorway, the light from outside that came through the open window at the end of the corridor.

She ran blindly down the dark hall, found the open window onto the back porch of the house, and crawled out. She didn't know what had happened to the man, or to the others, but a primal fear had entered her, a sense of death and terror she had never before felt, and her heart thumped too rapidly in her chest. Once she made it to the car, she put her hand over her heart as if to calm it.

Breathe.

Breathe.

A flashlight shone in her face. She couldn't see who held it until Sam Pratt spoke.

"Something bad's going on here tonight," he said.

11

"You imagined it," Bari told her when the others all came out of the house, trooping out in the rain to get to their cars.

27

"No. I saw him. I saw him. He was . . . playing with himself . . . and then I saw . . . Alex . . . I . . . *saw* . . ."

"Jackin' off, was he?" Alex said, winking at her and wrapping his arms around her. "I'll protect you from the Jack-Off Monster. Should I kick him in the balls or just beat him off?"

She shrugged free of his arms. "And what about Sam? What about what he saw?"

Bari gave her an innocent look. "I have no idea. That's Sam's problem. Maybe he's a liar. You want to go up and check it out?"

Lizzie shook her head.

"Yeah, me neither. If Sam wants to call the cops, let him." She leaned into the car and glanced back at Sam Pratt, who stared straight ahead. "But if you decide to tell the cops anything, you're not going to include any of us in it. You're going to be the one who might get arrested for trespassing. Not me. Not the rest of us. You got that, geek?"

Sam looked up at her, but didn't say anything.

"It's okay, Sam," Lizzie said, sliding into the driver's seat. "It's all going to be okay. Maybe . . . maybe it was just some trick."

"Yeah," Bari said, opening the front passenger door to shove Alex inside the car. Alex fell in like a wet dog; he was too drunk to keep his head up. "It probably was some trick. Some asshole from school who didn't get invited tonight who's just being nasty and stupid."

Andy Harris, revving the engine of his Mustang, called out, "Come on, Bari! We can still party down at the Point."

Bari glanced back at him. "In the fucking rain? No fucking way." She grinned as she leaned back into the window. "Sometimes you see things in the dark when you're drunk and you have no idea what they really are, and sometimes they're just nothing."

Lizzie looked at Bari Love as if she didn't even know her.

What had gotten into her? As bitchy as Bari might get, she was handling all of this way too well, keeping her cool at a time when Lizzie felt like pitching a fit.

And yet something within Lizzie herself had changed. In some way she couldn't even fathom, she had begun to disbelieve herself. She wasn't sure ten minutes after she saw the naked middle-aged man with the markings on him that she hadn't just imagined it. Zack had told her he'd spiked her beer with something she'd never heard of, and she got all freaked out that it might be roofies or some other drug that might put her at risk in some way. She began to think that maybe she had imagined the man, and the more she tried to reimagine him, the less she could. She couldn't remember what he was doing with himself, and she wasn't even sure he was naked anymore. She had a sinking feeling that by morning she might not even remember seeing anyone other than her classmates at Harrow.

And worse, it felt all right to forget. It felt like a sedative to forget, to put aside the trembling fear she'd felt.

Glancing in the rear-view mirror, she was even beginning to wonder if Sam Pratt might not forget seeing a dead kid, strung up and cut open, up at the private graveyard on the property.

Or if everything they had seen might not just be some kind of hysteria, the way she'd learned in school that sometimes you can't even trust your own senses, sometimes you are prepared to see something that isn't there, out of fear or just a rush of adrenaline.

Part of her was happy to be losing the image of the man that had been put in her mind, as if it were some dreadful thing that she could've gone her whole life without witnessing.

As if her mind was settling now after going a little haywire.

"What'd Zack put in my beer?" she asked Bari, but Bari just grinned and went back over to Andy's Mustang and got in.

29

The rain continued its downpour as the lightning zapped a distant tree.

"You can't tell anyone," Lizzie said.

Sam just watched her from the backseat, and then told her which way to go to get back to the village.

When they got back to town, and Lizzie pulled over at Sam's front door, he said, "We should at least call the cops."

"No, we can do that," Lizzie said. "I'll call them when I get home."

"If you don't, I will," Sam said.

But the funny thing was, neither of them ever told anybody, and when the storm had run its course, the night itself seemed like a drunken brawl of a dream. Sam felt safer the less he thought about it.

12

When Lizzie snuck in through the back door of the small house, by way of the garden gate, her twin sister was waiting. The first thing Ronnie did was smell her breath and say, "You're never driving my car again."

The second thing Ronnie did was feel Lizzie's forehead. "You're a little warm. You're not much of a drinker."

"Yeah," Lizzie said. "I'm sorry."

"Forgiven. But you're still not driving my car again. At least not to any parties."

"Understood. Please, I just need to go lie down."

"You look *different*," Ronnie said, softly, but let the thought die as she spoke it out loud. She wasn't even sure what she meant by it.

13

That night, Lizzie Pond dreamt about opening the kitchen drawers at her home and wondering why she couldn't find a corkscrew and why the smell of bleach was in the air; Bari Love, when she finally hit the sack at four A.M., began dreaming almost immediately that she had walked into her father's workroom in the garage and found a hatchet that was soaked in red with bits of hair on it; Sam Pratt didn't sleep all night, but instead stared out the window as if half expecting someone to come for him; Alex Nordland, who had passed out on Andy Harris's bedroom floor, dreamt of screwing the Dallas Cowboys cheerleaders, although they all had the faces of the teachers—male and female—at Parham High; Andy Harris dreamed about driving a sports car nearly a thousand miles per hour down a long dark highway and feeling as if he owned the world; and Ronnie Pond simply dreamt of her father because she always dreamt of him when she was feeling a little sad.

Chapter Two

Summer Storms

1

Some said it arrived by water—because some basements flooded and the sewers overflowed that night.

Others thought it must've come in like germs, on people's fingers.

But it would be many months before anyone even knew what it was or where it had originated.

Things changed slowly, as they always do in small towns.

But in the case of Watch Point, a Hudson River whistle-stop in New York, things did not change for the better.

It began after a bad electrical storm late one night in June. The whisper of terror would stretch out that summer into a scream, but a scream that only a handful of people heard, mostly the teenagers at first. Fallen branches in yards; floods in basements; a live wire that shivered and spat sparks until the utility department shut down the power lines; the whispers among schoolchildren of weirdness and superstitious mumbo-jumbo, and fingers pointed at the unusual and different children among them; the screech of a car along the main thoroughfare, long after midnight, in the gasp of calm after the storm; the lights that came on all at once in the village at the precise hour of the early morning, it was rumored, when the act took place out on the bare plateau that overlooked the river far below it.

The child's body they found.

The small cemetery had moss-covered stones that went back to the early 1800s, was on a hillside surrounded by straggly trees, one of which recently had been felled by lightning.

The remains of a bonfire of some kind.

Marks on the corpse indicated someone had tied it up and strung it, and then had brought it down.

The boy's parents and the authorities were notified. The boy's name was Arnie Pierson, and he'd died of some gastrointestinal ailment just a day or so earlier. The body had been grabbed at the morgue in the county hospital just outside the village, so there was a freshness to the corpse disturbing to view.

Someone had torn the corpse open.

It was a ritual, many thought. A ritual of a sick and twisted mind.

The corpse-stealing episode brought further grief for his family and cast a new cloud upon the village to add to the others that were forming. The authorities did their half-assed version of an investigation and came up with the culprit—one of the lab assistants at the morgue had claimed he took the body home to work on it (which was as far-fetched an explanation as any) and that somehow, someone then stole it from him. But when horror novels and forensics books and videotapes of crime scenes were found in his apartment—along with sliced bits of human flesh in jars—it was assumed he was completely nuts, and he was thrown in jail until it all got sorted out. From jail he went up north to one of the hospitals for the criminally insane, but that would not be until the end of summer.

But all who knew of the stolen corpse suspected others were involved.

At the estate itself, authorities found evidence of drinking—broken bottles of cheap wine—and someone had scrawled words on some of the old gravestones using spray paint, in a strange language that looked as fake as it looked archaic. It was a well-known night among the high schoolers of the area—a special night of parties and mayhem, particularly for those about to enter their senior year. It was called Thirteenth Night, and the tradition had begun in the mid-twentieth century when the local high schools put on a series of celebrations thirteen nights after the last day of school. The police asked local high school kids questions, but no one had a reasonable answer as to what happened that night up at Harrow.

Most of the teenagers told of the wild parties out along the Point, a strand of dock and sand and rock that extended into the Hudson River—the usual place for the parties. Bari Love, the head cheerleader from Parham High, told the authorities nearly everyone she knew had been at the Point that night. "Why would anybody go up to that old house? That place gives me the creeps."

The incident had happened on Midsummer Night, and rumors quickly attributed it to a pagan rite associated with the equinox. The holy-rollers at Church of the Vale declared that devil-worshippers were back.

"What sickos would do this?" they asked. Well, they being Margaret Love and Norma Houseman, with Norma adding, "I think it's the occult. All these kids read about it. It's in children's books, for God's sake. I wish . . ."

"You wish what?" Margaret asked.

"I wish sometimes they'd just start burning these people. These kinds of people. Sometimes I think the olden days were right. You get rid of people who do this kind of thing.

You lock 'em up, ship 'em out, and burn 'em off the face of the earth. That poor little dead boy. Poor little dead thing. It's shameful is what it is."

"Disgraceful," Margaret Love added. "What kind of sicko would do a thing like this?"

"I'll tell you what kind," Norma said. "The same kind that's ruining this country and sending it to hell. The kind that's for marriage of . . . homosexuals . . . and the kind that's against everything America does . . . why, back in the early 1960s, things were so much nicer. I think the so-called civil rights movement started this trend. Believe me, no rights could have been less civil than those, and then things went downhill. I was only a girl then, a little girl, but I saw how the cities burned on TV, and I saw how the leftist media kept pushing their message the same time they were pushing drugs on my friends. Comedians on television using words I wouldn't even think let alone say. The Roman Empire fell because of things like this. We can't fall. We can't. God doesn't want us to fall. What this country needs is a good dose of old-fashioned stick-to-itiveness. We need to burn out everything that doesn't fit in right. If you don't burn them, they just keep multiplying and coming at you. What kind of sicko does this?" she asked again at the end of her tirade.

"Yes," Margaret Love repeated. "What kind of sicko does this?"

Although even as Margaret said this, she wondered if her friend's prescriptions had been adjusted lately. Norma was, after all, the Pharmaceutical Queen of the Block, besides being Mother of the Year and still looking like Miss Hudson Valley of 1980 all over again.

They both said all this in front of the journalist from the *Parham News Record*, a miniature tape recorder clutched in his hand, a grin on his face because he had been afraid there'd be no good quotes and no real story. He wrote up a half-baked article about the history of the house in Watch

Point and how eerie things happened there and how it had murders associated with it and now "devil worship."

If the journalist had not used the words "devil worship" it might not have gotten out to three other newspapers and the Internet. That summer a bunch of kooks and nuts might not have shown up in the village with their camcorders, looking to go all Blair Witch on the house and the village.

Finally, signs were posted, and a police patrol went around the property and did what they could to keep outsiders from trampling all over it in order to get their picture taken near what they were calling the House of Spirits.

By late June, a sixteen-year-old girl went missing in town. No one thought to find out that she'd simply run away from home to New York City to stay with her cousin. The legend grew that the house, once again, had begun to draw the unsavory elements of the world. A middle-aged man, a teacher at the local high school, went onto the property one night in the middle of July and shot himself in the face. The rumor mill went into full throttle with this one, and suddenly there were parents who claimed he had spent too much "alone time" with their children.

When the owner of the house—a young woman of twenty who had inherited it from the previous owner— died in a car accident in Manhattan in early September, and the news reached the village of Watch Point, there were those who said that the curse of Harrow could not be stopped simply by sealing the house.

"Someone should burn it," said some—Norma Houseman, in particular. While others (like Fitz, Mike Fitzgerald who ran a local construction company) said, "Someone should demolish it. Put a few sticks of kaboom around it and give it a lit fuse and then it's all blowed up in about less than a day."

There were those who felt the rumors were all a big nothing, exploited by a couple of journalists and "those kind of people who like to make it sound like we live in a world of spirits and demons," so said Army Vernon, who ran the florist shop and whose only employee was Norma Houseman, who had spent half the summer talking about the evil in town and how it should be torched. "Hogwash from the hogs," Army said.

Howard Boatwright, known by his friends as "Boaty," made the suggestion that they hire someone to check out the property now and then until the details of the will—and who inherited the house next—were settled. "It'll cost the village a little bit, but maybe it'll discourage all this crap," Boaty said at the meeting of the town council that was mainly concerned with the rezoning of the streets off Main Street. "Plus, we can charge it against the estate. Whoever inherits the place is bound to be rich. In the long run, it's gonna cost us nothin'."

A caretaker would be hired to patrol the grounds at night, to scare off any delinquents who might use the property for their drunken rituals. A police patrol was commissioned in town to drive out once a night, after midnight, to further the aim of keeping the badness away.

August was fairly quiet; the heat rose; the humidity soared; the trees thickened with deep green leaves; a little boy made news in town because he pulled his baby sister out of that big honkin' hole on Sycamore Boulevard that the village hadn't yet plugged up; and later, some supposed that if the dreams hadn't been taking them over—the bad dreams where people thought they were inside the house called Harrow—it might've turned out to be a fine summer.

The dreams were like wolves, howling through their sleep.

They dreamed of the windows and the floors, and of how the walls seemed to stretch for miles.

Most of the people who dreamed of Harrow had never set foot within it.

But some had.

2

Ronnie Pond awoke in the middle of the night, crying out from a dream. She had begun doing this far too often, and she knew that her sister Lizzie was growing tired of her nightly outbursts.

"What is it?" Lizzie asked, having rushed to the open door of her bedroom.

"Something's started."

"Ronnie? You were dreaming. That's all. Must've been a doozy."

"No, I feel it. Something's changed," Ronnie said, and though she was seventeen years old, she felt as if she were a little girl again, afraid of the dark, waiting for a far-off dawn to arrive. "That house. That night."

Her sister thought a moment and then nodded, but closed her eyes briefly, as if wishing a memory away.

Ronnie had promised not to ever tell anyone about that night.

"I was there, Lizzie. In this dream. I was in a long hallway. I heard . . . I heard someone screaming. And I kept moving toward the scream, and every time I opened one of the doors, I saw . . ."

"What? What did you see?"

"I saw people from town. In the rooms. As if they were waiting for me to find them. Only they weren't right. They looked the same as they always do, but something about them was different."

"Different—how?"

Ronnie looked at her twin sister and shook her head slightly. "It was as if it was Halloween night. And they all had masks on. Then they took the masks off."

"Were the masks scary?"

"No. The masks were their faces. It was what was beneath their faces. They had pulled the skin of their faces off and they showed me what was underneath," Ronnie said. "And then I found one room. Zack was there. And Bari. And Alex Nordland. Others from school. All in a room giggling like I'd walked in two seconds after a joke had been told about me. You were there, too. I went over to you. I said, 'Lizzie? You okay?' I didn't hear you say anything, but your lips were moving. It was as if you couldn't see me. And then, you took off your mask and showed me."

Lizzie tried to grin, but something in her sister's tone frightened her a little. Ronnie had a little bit of the bizarre lurking within her, and even though she and Lizzie were identical twins it was as if they saw things completely differently. Ronnie could creep her out sometimes with some of the things she said. "What'd I show you? Was I wearing a skull or something?"

Ronnie shook her head. "No. You were the same. Under the mask of your face. It was almost like you. Only I knew I didn't know you. I knew it was somebody else who had your skin. Somebody else was wearing your skin and they started giggling, only your lips didn't move and I knew it was another mask. So I reached up to grab it and pulled it off."

"Oh," Lizzie made a perplexed face. "What a dream. And underneath that mask, there was another one?"

"No," Ronnie said, unable to look her twin in the face. "It was a little boy. He was playing with the skin of your face. He had it in his hands. And when he looked up at me, *his eyes weren't there*. Just dark holes. His eyes stayed inside the mask. I had ripped his eyes out when I pulled the mask away."

3

You can just see it, sometimes, over the tops of the trees, if you're on one of the hillsides or if you're out on the river in a boat. Not the whole thing, but the spires and the turrets, and the way the treetops seem like fingers clutching its uppermost windows.

But few venture up the road to it, to the long private drive, overwhelmed with brambles and high grasses of summer and the fences and "no trespassing" and "hunting not allowed" signs posted along the way.

Some overcome the fears and the legends and the stories and the signs and the fences.

Some go there, because there are always those people—usually very few—who are called to places like this house.

The rooms of the house remained empty of life for the most part. Windows had been boarded up. The underground to the house had been sealed for several years. None of the local field mice had ventured within the place to make a nest; no wasp had spun a home of paper in its eaves; the local starlings did not huddle beneath its chimney; and it was said by those in the nearby village that someone had been poisoning the local cats that roamed too near the property.

Within the house, heavy curtains remained drawn tight in the rooms that still had furnishings. Unfurnished rooms had been closed off with plywood. Darkness was the only resident in the house, and although light might permeate a crack in a board or come under a doorway, it was quickly snuffed by the inky black of shadow.

With a house like this one, they say it is a shame: that such a beautiful mansion from the late nineteenth century should begin to fall, slowly, inexorably toward the earth, merely from neglect and the passing judgment of time over all that may die.

But the house has been known to others. It has a history of darkness, and like all houses of shadows, like a flytrap, it draws those to it who are most attracted to its petals, and upon whom it can most feed.

In the late 1800s, occult ceremonies took place in this

house; in the 1920s, sensational murders occurred here; over several years of the last century and into the twenty-first, it acquired the taint of bad things, more so than other houses of its age. Like a psychopath who begins slowly and picks up steam, the murders associated with this house began to be exposed to the world beyond its walls.

In the more than 100 years of its existence, the house had attracted spiritualists and investigators, the ordinary and the extraordinary. It had been a private home, a school, and a laboratory to a group of psychics. This particular summer, a teenage girl named Veronica Pond, a girl who had already begun to think of herself as a woman, had begun dreaming about it, imagining its slowly opening doors like gently smiling jaws.

It is called Harrow, and it waits, within the old brick and stone of its flesh, for what will come.

It is a castle on a sloping hillside overlooking the Hudson River. A man named Justin Gravesend, who allegedly had been a member of a cult of necromancers, built it in the late 1800s and had, himself, murdered spiritualists and buried them in the walls. There was a rumor, too, that he had walled up his own daughter alive in the house, but that she had lived for many years, wandering behind the walls in search of a way out before she finally died in that tomb.

But those things happened long ago.

Long before the summer and fall of this year, when something seeped from beneath the ground of Harrow itself.

Harrow waits with a hunger.

5

The village of Watch Point had not changed much in nearly a century, which is to say that it was very much like other towns and villages along the slender roads and byways that snake along the edges of the Hudson River north of Manhattan. The new train depot looked very much like the old one, although in recent years, two old and elegant train cars not in use since the 1950s sat side-by-side next to the tracks—one a small restaurant and the other a Visitor's Center. But once off the train, looking up the hill to the village, one might squint and imagine the same town a hundred years before.

The crossroads of Main and Macklin was called the Antique District, although there were only two antique shops to be had (one called Junks and Trunks, and the other called Timeless, Etc., and neither one open to the public very often, their windows cloudy with dust and grime). The bookstore, the florist, the shoe and dress shop, Erica's Steaks & Seafood Grill, The Apple Pie-Man, Caniglia Frame and Crafts Store, The River Roaster, the Ratty Dog Bar & Grille, and the usual suspects from the larger world, including McDonald's and Subway and a banner over a closed-up shop that read "Coming Soon! Starbucks to open here."

As the streets spread out, the shops continued and eventually bled into more residential areas. All the shops on Main, up to Macklin, looked as if they'd seen better days, but still there was something bright and shiny about these streets. The Boatwright Arts Center, which had once been the Majestic Theater, anchored Main Street up one side, and had a big banner over its marquee that read, "Watch Point Players in *A Midsummer Night's Dream*, Three Nights Only, To Benefit the Renovation of the Gaskill Creek Bottle Factory." The box office booth had a big hole in its glass where some teen had lobbed a brick at it many years earlier. Very little got fixed in town once it broke. The Watch Point Community Bank Building, a Georgian-looking brownstone on the opposite corner, held the south side of the street at bay. Other shops had squeezed into the streets, including the little psychic shop that some in town called "that witch store," although few said it with malice.

And on this particular day, the shop was open but empty of customers. Out front, a middle-aged woman sat in her rocking chair reading John Grisham's *A Time to Kill*, and was not sure why her toes and fingers had begun tingling.

One might imagine that the woman named Alice Kyeteler who sat upon the front porch of her shop had not dreamed that this day would one day come to pass. That the moment would come when she would whisper to herself, "You haven't been aware enough," as if whatever she was afraid of was like a teakettle left too long on the stove, and the whistle had just begun to blow with steam.

The autumn day when someone would come to her and ask about entering the dark place.

Chapter Three

1

In the early 1980s, a carnival had arrived at the village of Watch Point, New York. It was nothing special—the trucks brought the carnies and the rickety Ferris wheel, the Whirligig, the funhouse, the sideshow, the rows of arcade games that blew in on an October night and blew out a few nights later as if the wind had swept the village clean.

But the woman who had been the fortune teller at the carnival's seedy sideshow decided she liked the village, and she camped out there—first in a motel off the highway just outside of town, and then in a little apartment above a bookstore on the main drag of the village.

Her name was Alice Kyeteler, and she became both a massage therapist and owner of a small "Fortune & Tarot" shop down near the train station. Rumor went that she was a witch, but Watch Point was a sophisticated enough Hudson River town to deal with her little salon and its books on psychic phenomena, candles and perfumes. Although if she didn't have a background in Reiki and Reflexology massage, she might've gone out of business in her first year.

After the fire at the school called Harrow, and the bizarre circumstances of the psychic investigators and the murder that also went on at the house, she had all but closed her storefront and would just sit on the porch, people-watching. The village had lost some residents after the commotion and those seeking souvenirs of the house had left. Some who had the means to move decided that Peekskill and Ossining and Beacon might be a better place to live. A book or two had been written about the house, and an old diary had been published, written by a man who had lived in the house in the early part of the twentieth century. The house, whether truly haunted or not, had acquired an unpleasant reputation, and its only glamour was held by local kids who felt it was a proper place to scare each other on October nights or boring winter afternoons. Alice disliked the place intensely, and despite her lifelong devotion to the psychic and the spiritual, she had no interest in ever setting foot on the grounds of that place, which was just beyond the village itself, and yet distant enough to be forgotten on lazy afternoons.

Now and then she saw a ghost, but she preferred not to talk about it with strangers—and despite having lived in Watch Point for more than twenty years, most of the people there were still strangers to her.

One day, near noontime, a man with a soul like midnight walked up to her and said, "I'd like to know what's going to happen this fall."

2

The village had begun growing dark early with autumn, and the dusky winds blew along its leaf-littered streets; by the afternoon, any glow of the sun was gone, and daylight

Douglas Clegg

became tempered with the early twilight; along the trees, swarms of birds flew, telephone to tree to rooftop to tree, nearly ready to go farther south as the winds grew colder and the twilight seeped with a purple haze.

Alice glanced up from her sewing—she hand-repaired most of her clothes, and at that particular moment had been working on an old pair of jeans that had ripped right in the crotch not two days before when she'd been squatting to clean up some broken glass off the floor. She was so startled that she nearly pricked herself with the needle. She hadn't noticed the man a second before. She felt her heart beat a bit more rapidly, and she took a deep breath to calm down. He had the aura of death around him. It was a black, shrieking aura—that was the best Alice could describe it when she was asked later about it. "He had a head like a two-dollar avocado, all round at the top and narrow near the bottom, and it looked a little soft, too, and ripe," she told Thaddeus Allen, the part-time professor at Parham College who lived above her shop. "He had that darkness all around him. I could practically touch it. It was like black smoke, but it was heavy, too."

"But he wasn't dead?" Thad asked a little too blithely. Thad, in his mid-forties, the single most unambitious man of the entire Allen clan (from Albany), had spent most of his youth frittering, and so an afternoon with the local witch on her front shop porch seemed the right thing to do on a day when he had no classes to teach, and only a handful of papers to grade.

"No," Alice said. Again, she was sewing—this time, putting buttons on one of Thad's shirts for him as a favor for lifting some heavy boxes for her earlier in the week. "He wasn't dead. Not yet. But he had the beginnings of a ghost in him. It was . . . it was as if he had made a choice, and it had burned through him . . . like he was a photographic negative."

46

THE ABANDONED

"What did he want? Why did he ask about autumn?" Thad asked, a bit puzzled. He sipped his coffee—a buck twenty-five for a cup at the bookstore just a few doors down, and it never tasted as good as it looked. "I mean, who asks about the fall as if there's going to be a reasonable answer?"

"Oh," she said, softly. "I don't know. I barely heard him. I think it was all that aura around him that kept me confused. I got a bit light-headed. That happens sometimes when I'm near the dead."

"Or soon-to-be-dead," Thad said, trying not to grin. "Still, I'd love to know what he wanted. Who asks about fall like that? I mean, who?"

"He applied for the nightwatchman job, up at You-Know-Where," she said. "You know, he even called himself that. He said he was the Nightwatchman, as if it was a job like being mayor or king. But he said it softly. He spoke so softly, almost—and I know this is an odd thing to say—in a womanish way, not like me, but like those women who have small velvety voices."

Thad knew this about Alice—she avoided what she called Trouble Spots. In this case, the Trouble Spot was also called You-Know-Where. "I thought they hired someone."

"That guy quit," she said. "Sometime during the summer."

"Because of all that stuff?"

"That stuff. No. Because he found a better job in Beacon."

"All the good jobs are in Beacon these days." Thad grinned. He meant it as a slight joke, but Alice's emotions remained veiled. She was often flat and oh-so-serious like that, and it could annoy him to no end, unless he found her humorous.

"Lighten up," he said.

"You didn't see what I saw. He had a halo of night."

"But you think it's about You-Know-Where."

She retained that flatness of spirit as he took another sip

47

of the god-awful coffee. His love for the *idea* of coffee often overcame the taste of the stuff itself.

"Alice, it has always puzzled me. You come here to live and open shop. Yet you believe that house is haunted and you're too scared to go there."

"You should be, too."

"I'm sorry. I'm stuck in rational mode. I think anything that seems haunted is simply . . . well, some natural phenomena we can't quite pinpoint."

"I don't completely disagree," she said. "But that doesn't make it less haunted."

"Well, enough people believe it about that place. Just not me."

"You've never been there either."

"Of course I have. Once or twice. Wandering the property. It's quite beautiful. A bit falling apart lately. But after the fire and half-assed rebuilding, I can't expect much. And then the owner deciding to board it all up like that . . . well, it's no worse than some of the houses I've seen along the river that nobody really cares about anymore. Grande dames of houses from the gilded age. The one in Peekskill is a museum now. Maybe we should make Harrow a museum. Show off all the crocheting and crap like Norma Houseman's Mother of the Year trophies or Jack Templeton's Speedos. Or lack thereof."

"So I've heard." Alice smiled slightly. "You know, Thad, for a middle-aged man, you're quite the gossip."

"It's the only hobby I've got, besides all the others. But it may be a bit saner than yours. It's just a house. Every village along the river has one like it."

"It's hideous, that place," she said. She set down the shirt and the needle and thread, and brought her hands up to her eyes as if wiping them of an annoying memory. Her face was wide, yet with a certain long hangdog quality. Thad had always guessed she was about fiftyish, although she had let her hair—a bird's nest with a braid jutting out the back—just go gray so that she looked much older.

"How's the coffee?" Alice asked, when she glanced over at him again.

"Like the nastiest socks soaked in lukewarm water after having been left in a junior high gym bag for six weeks. How's the button coming?"

She glanced at his wrinkled shirt. "You know, when you sew for yourself it's fun and thrifty. When you do it for someone else, it makes you feel like a grandma."

"Is Grandma gonna leave anything to me in her will?"

Alice grinned. "You can always take my mind off my worries. For ten seconds."

"This Nightwatchman worry you?"

She nodded. "It was so quiet after. You know, when you teach, all that you teach, don't you see into it at all?"

"Mythology?" he asked. "I see the psychological significance."

"You don't see anything deeper?"

"Human psychology seems pretty damn deep to me. I know you feel there's more, Alice. If this all speaks to you about a deeper relationship to the universe, go for it. I see it as human irrationality. The part of us that can't face the way things are. Just as dreams aren't real, but are about the human brain and repression and desire. The idea of hauntings seems to me to be about those exact same things."

"I think you've just insulted me for the twentieth time this week," she said, on the edge of being irritated. "You love clinging to your so-called rationality. I wish I could."

"Give it a whirl some time," he said. "All you have to do is look things in the face and accept that there's logic to all of it."

"That's exactly what I do."

He began talking about myth and Jung and world beliefs and the idea of afterlife as a comfort for those who face death. After a few minutes, he realized he'd begun to drone.

"Look at Army," Alice said suddenly, as if she'd become bored with their talk.

I'm a windbag, Thad thought. *A forty-six-year-old greasy, graying, chubby windbag.*

Thad glanced out on the street—across the way, Army Vernon had begun rolling up his awning over the rows of flowers in white plastic pots. The first sign of fall on its way—the awnings would come down. Then the smell of beer in the air—for some reason, it wafted out of the Watch Point Pub during the cooler months. And finally, the young women in their smart raincoats when the skies turned dark; the men in sweatpants as they jogged by; the children dragging themselves home from the bus-stop on brisk afternoons. He loved fall in the village. "So?"

"What's he doing?"

"What he always does this time of day. The ritual flower murder." Thad chuckled.

"He was the first person I ever read. He was at the carnival, and he stood in line all eager just like he was one of the kids. I told him what I saw—not that I'm going to tell you now—and he laughed at me. Most people don't believe what I believe," Alice said. "I don't expect them to. But I do not expect to be laughed at."

"Did you read him at all? The Nightwatchman," Thad asked, saying the word "nightwatchman" as if it were a joke. "Was he easy?"

"You don't believe any of it."

"Well, I believe you believe. Did you?"

"He had a block, but somehow I got through some of it. Something about his son. Something about the girl in the car."

"There was a girl in a car?"

"More darkness. Nightwatchman. But his name came to

me. While we were talking. He has a German name, I think. But I'm not sure. It sounded like Spider."

"Spider?"

"Or Speeder. I'm not sure."

"Tell me about the girl. Are we talking over twenty or under?"

"Over, but not by much. She is tied to him in a way I don't understand."

"You read all this by being near him?"

She laughed lightly, breaking the dark mood that had descended. "No, I saw her. She was in the old station wagon, parked right in front here. She looked twenty-two. Maybe. I can't tell anymore."

"How old was he?"

"Fifty, easily. He looked almost like a farmer. Why did I think that, I wonder? He wasn't wearing any clothes that were like a farmer's."

"But he had the farmer's daughter with him. Maybe she's his daughter? Or else she's his son's girlfriend or wife."

"Oh. That never occurred to me. Maybe. She's pregnant. They've been running for awhile. Trying to find work."

"Okay, so a guy takes his pregnant daughter, whose boyfriend has run off, and tries to get a job for himself so he can support her. You think he'll be the caretaker?"

"I hope not," she said. "I suggested he leave. I told him about a job working for a church—as a janitor. In Poughkeepsie. Better pay, I'd guess. Free room."

" 'The Nightwatchman,' " Thad said, nodding. "I should put that in a book. I should write a book called *The Nightwatchman* and I bet everyone would want to read it."

"If only you could write a book."

"I tried once," he said. "You never know, I might try again. There's a new teacher in town who wrote a book. I met him the other day. Young and all full of himself. Still has the damn rose-colored glasses of life on him. That's who writes books about nightwatchmen. Men like me simply read them."

"Oh, I hate those kinds of people," Alice said, mildly. "Those happy-outlook people. I much prefer seeing shadowy, scowly people who drink bad coffee."

"I could not agree more," Thad said, and then closed his eyes, feeling a slight headache coming on. In the darkness behind his eyes, he saw a purplish-yellow image forming and then it became the mansion—Harrow, with its spires and towers and domed roof and many gables, not decayed and overgrown as he knew it to be, but with a shine to it. He opened his eyes, shot a sidelong glance to Alice, but didn't mention the thought that had come to him.

"Someone has to take care of that place," Thad said. "I think legally they have to. If someone fell in a hole over there or something, there'd be hell to pay. People sue all the time. And you know how kids go up there at Halloween."

"They're stupid, those children."

"Maybe, but someone needs to be there to chase them off."

"It's a terrible place," she said. "I was here through all that. When the school had its trouble. And a few years ago, those people. So crazy to go there."

"I heard a lot of it was just made up," Thad said. "Some writer blew it all out of proportion and made it sound like we were out of a Shirley Jackson story."

"Who?"

"You never read "The Lottery"? *The Haunting of Hill House*? She wrote a book about a haunted house. But it's all fiction. It's irrational to think it happened, simply because if it had happened, no human being could've stopped it. And supposedly it stopped."

"No," she said. "Nothing can stop it. Just a momentary end to an eternal struggle."

"Alice, come on. I've been at the house," Thad said. "I've never seen a ghost."

"That's how it tricks you, Thad. Someone has to spark it. Ignite it. That's how this is. I can't go there. I have a little bit of the ability. If I were to walk up to its door, it would devour me alive just to get that spark. The man who stepped up here. The Nightwatchman. The worst thing about him was I got the impression that he knew how frightened I was feeling of him. He had that darkness all around him. He was going to bring it to the house. He is a flint."

Then she turned to other topics, more pleasant, less bizarre, about the spring storms, about the politics of the world and of the village. Thad began to wonder if she might be a little unhinged simply because of what had happened to her as a little girl—as he too was unhinged a little by what had happened to him just a handful of years back when he let go of someone he loved.

Life is a doorway, you're the door, and sometimes you get unhinged. The longer you live, the more the hinges squeak and then begin to separate a little.

All of us, he thought. *Unhinged. Slightly broken. Grasping at anything that makes us feel the world still has wonder and mystery.*

And Thad Allen said, his voice a bit dry from the air and the coffee, "You know, Alice, you're probably my best friend in town."

"Feeling's mutual."

"Do you ever read me?"

"Impossible," she said. "You have the biggest block of all."

"Honest?"

"I thought you didn't believe in this."

"Well," he said, "I always believe in keeping the window open a crack to let the fresh air in."

"I know what you mean," she said. "Sometimes I wonder if I'm just crazy. But, Thad, I don't think so. Not about this. Something bad is brewing. I know it. It's like—well, you know how sometimes you smell a fire before you see it?

Douglas Clegg

Like there's smoke coming from somewhere and you can't quite figure out where and it's still kind of faint and you think maybe you're just imagining it? That's what it's like. Meeting that guy. And him asking about that place. It's like a little smoke and it's either nothing or it's going to become a fire when nobody's looking because it's too late if you ignored the smoke all along."

"So maybe he won't even get the job. He'll probably just take off again."

"Thad, it was weeks ago when he came by here. He got the job. They hired him. He's been there for at least three or four weeks. And I haven't seen him in the village at all. In all that time. Hasn't come to Mighty Mart for groceries, hasn't rented a DVD, hasn't grabbed a dinner anywhere, and hasn't even gone for a walk off that property. Nothing."

"He might just be going to Beacon for groceries. Or Parham. Their shopping district ain't too shabby."

"No, I don't think so. He's either dead or he struck a match over there."

"Oh," Thad said. "Gee, wonder if his daughter's had her baby yet?"

"Had to. That girl was so big she looked like she would've popped right then and there in the car," Alice said. She tried to push her fears out of her mind. She offered to make a fresh pot of coffee in the back of her shop so that he wouldn't have to suffer through another one of those dirty sock cups from the bookstore. As they got up from the porch chairs and turned to go into her shop, Alice glanced back to the street and the stores across the way.

She thought she saw some man who shouldn't be there. She said to Thad, "Who's that?"

Thad turned about, glancing to where she pointed her finger. "Ah. Well, I'll tell you about him once I get a little more caffeine in my system."

"A malingerer. I don't like him," Alice said, and as she

54

drew back the door to her shop, she wondered if it might not be time to leave this town.

3

Across the street, not looking over at the shops at all, Bert White leaned back against the Parham Bank, near the ATM machine by the front door, so as not to be noticed. Twenty years old, Bert was small and wiry and took on the odd jobs in town nobody else seemed to want, whether it was a storm drain cleanup, shoveling snow, laying asphalt or repairing a rooftop or two. He was a guy who just got by, and that was fine by him because it allowed him to pursue his favorite hobbies.

Watching and waiting.

He watched her pass by.

Ronnie Pond.

Veronica. He liked the name Veronica better. She was a twin. Twins were hot. Twins had all kinds of possibilities.

It was as if he were invisible to her, although he figured it probably was because she seemed to be in a hurry. She was headed toward the post office. She was lookin' good and she'd never understand how he liked her pretty hair so much when it swung back and forth like it did.

He liked to follow the teenager wherever she went, and when he could, he made himself as invisible as possible. He hid behind the columns at the post office, or he slipped into a shop like the bookstore and just watched her from the front window. Some nights, he went to her home and stood outside her window to watch her. Sometimes she'd just be reading in bed. Or she'd have headphones on, listening to some rock group on her CD player, and she'd dance around her room as if she'd forgotten where she was. Now and then, she seemed to look right at him through the window, and it would make him catch his breath—and then he'd remember that she probably couldn't see him at all out in the darkness. He would be just another inky shadow among the shadows of bushes and trees that were in the yard.

Back at his place, his mother had written him letters, and he flipped through them, hoping there'd be some money. By the third letter, he'd found just under a hundred bucks. It made him feel that his luck had changed a little. Things were going damn good, and only the thought that he might not get the girl alone anytime soon . . . well, that thought drove him a little wacko, and he realized that she was the one at fault because he had tried talking to her once upon a time about how it felt all over his insides, all runny and gooey for her and yet terrified that she'd say something to hurt him at the same time. She had pretended he hadn't even been there. That was worse than if she'd been mean.

How could she be such a bitch and still the love of his life?

After pocketing the money his mother sent him and tossing out her letters, he went outside again, down the back stairs of the house where he rented the room, then knocked on the back door.

His landlady eventually came to the door. "Glad to see you, Bert."

"Bathroom or kitchen?"

"Bathroom," she said.

His landlady let him into the house, and because she trusted him to work on the toilet that probably just needed a little handle-jiggling, she wouldn't even follow him down to the bathroom, which was right next to her daughters' rooms.

He would go in there and imagine the girl was with him. She was practically all grown up. As soon as she was ready—the right age was just around the corner, in less than a month she'd be eighteen and then he could have her legally—he intended to keep her quiet somewhere.

Maybe even in the apartment above her home. Maybe tied to the bed with duct tape on her mouth. Maybe, he thought.

Then he'd train her. She'd do what he wanted.

She'd love him.

In her bedroom, he would smell the things in her dresser drawers, then fold them neatly before putting them back.

He would rub himself on the bed until his mind went to the place where the girl also was, and in that imaginary place she'd be holding him, accepting him.

When he was done with Veronica's room, he'd go to her sister's room. Sometimes she slept in the bed in the late afternoons. Elizabeth had begun taking naps, and that made him happy to see her with her eyes closed, her breathing heavy and deep in a dream.

He would own them both someday, and they would love him.

He'd bet his life on it.

4

The Love house was not exactly like its name. The family was named Love, which led to many jokes at poor Bari's expense, as it had for her father years before, and as it always would for anyone with their last name. But the house they lived in was anything but loved. Jim Love didn't take great care of it because he'd been out of work too much—having been laid off from a plum job in Westchester County a year before, and having only picked up temporary work since then. His wife battled depression, his son seemed obsessed with religion, and his daughter demanded more and more from her father as a result of a distant mother. He still felt the meaning of his last name there—for he was a good man and had love for all of them—but one day in the fall, his daughter came down with a sudden illness and he wondered whether he could handle all that was about to befall him.

Jim pressed his hand against Bari's forehead. "No fever."

"I'm just sleeping. Maybe it's that sleeping illness," his daughter said. "I saw a show about it. Something bar."

"You're too young for Epstein-Barr." He grinned.

"I heard somebody had it," she said, and settled back against the pillow.

"Have you been feeling a little down?"

"No," she said.

"Is this about that boy?"

"What boy?"

"The one who called. The older boy."

"No, Dad. He's seventeen. He's not that much older."

"Too old to run around with a girl your age."

She made a lip-fart sound. He knew he wouldn't win this argument today—not the one about some seventeen-year-old hoodlum calling his daughter, who had only just finished her freshman year a few months before. Too young to date. Bari would not date until she was sixteen, and that was final. But he didn't want to harp on it too much. He had grown worried about her over the past few days.

"You weren't with him on Friday, were you?"

"Jesus."

"Do not talk to me like that, Bari. You know the rules."

She shot him a glare that probably was meant to be angry, but she just looked exhausted. Her normally bright eyes were encircled with dark smudges, bloodshot. Was she doing drugs? Is that what he had to worry about now? He had hoped by living in a small town and making sure they were in church every Sunday that his kids would avoid all that. Was it that boy? Drugs? Just insomnia?

So many things went through his mind, but he genuinely worried for her. She'd been too tired lately, and in bed too much on the weekend.

"I should never have let you go to that party in June."

"Nobody drank. It wasn't like that."

"I didn't say they did."

"Well, you thought it. We just talked. We had a campfire. It was so wholesome it might as well have been the church youth group," she said, her voice growing faint. "I'm just tired."

"How's your throat?"

"Not sore. Fine, Dad. Daddy, I'm not sick. I'm just . . . really sleepy."

"Maybe it's the humidity."

"I just want to sleep," she whispered, her eyes fluttering.

"Okay, honey. Tomorrow, if you're still feeling like this, we'll take you over to see Dr. Winters. Okay?"

"Sure, Daddy," Bari said, and then closed her eyes completely.

Jim glanced down at his teenage daughter, and then back to the hallway. His wife stood there, a slightly cross look on her face.

"We should take her to the hospital over in Parham," Margaret whispered. "When she was four and had scarlet fever . . ."

"She doesn't have a temperature," he said, and walked to the bedroom door and flicked the bedroom light off. "Look, I'll call the doctor and ask him."

Just as he'd stepped out of his daughter's bedroom, he heard her voice again. Mumbling. "Honey?" he glanced back at her sleeping figure.

Her lips were moving, and it was as if she was trying to say something.

"It's a fever," Margaret gasped. "She was tired all summer long. I told you there was something wrong. I told you it wasn't normal for a girl her age to sleep 'til noon so much. And she's had flu's and colds ever since the first of September. We need to take her in. No child sleeps for two days in a row. Not like this."

"Honey, can you turn the volume down a little?" Jim asked, using a hand motion that always drove his wife nuts.

"*Son of a . . .*" Margaret whispered under her breath. "She needs to see a doctor now. And what if she's really sick. Or . . . or . . ." As if the sun had come out from behind the clouds of her brain, his wife said, "Dear God, what if she's pregnant?"

Her husband shot her a harsh look.

"Well, you saw those condoms. It's not like we can pretend she's not active anymore," Margaret whispered, as if the neighbors might hear her.

"She's *not* pregnant," Jim said. He stepped back into his daughter's room, and turned on the light again.

Bari's eyes were closed, but her lips were moving rapidly.

"Bari?" He stepped over to her bed.

"Ga—Ga—Ga," she seemed to be saying.

Jim got down on his knees, and leaned in to try to understand her. He touched her shoulder, then gave it a slight shake. "Honey?" He turned back to his wife. "I guess it's a—" He was about to say, "bad dream," when he saw the strange look in his wife's face in the doorway, her eyes going wide. Jim felt goose bumps along the back of his neck even before he turned back to look at his fourteen-year-old daughter in her bed.

Her eyes were open, and she had somehow sat up without him even knowing she had moved.

"The rooms are filling up fast," his daughter said, her voice no longer her own. It reminded Jim of the one time he'd ever encountered a rabid dog—it had a snapping snarl to it. Her eyes burned with a fierce intensity.

"Hon? Bari?" Jim felt a strange trickle of fear along his spine as his daughter spoke, not looking at him, but through him.

It was as if she were going to strike at any moment.

"Gets me my hatchets," she whispered.

"Honey?" her father asked, softly, because he hadn't heard her well enough—she'd swallowed the last of the words. "What is it? Bari baby?"

"Gets me my hatchets . . ."

"Sweetie." Her father felt like crying, seeing his daughter so helpless and weak.

"Hatchets, hatchets . . ." she mumbled under her breath.

He leaned into her, wondering if he should take her down to the hospital emergency room to make sure this wasn't something life threatening. "Bari?"

"Hat-chets, rat shits," she said into his ear, and it seemed to him that she was shouting and his ear hurt from the sound. *"Pussy don't smell. Hat-chets, rat shits."*

He drew back from her again, and held his hands to the sides of her face, cupping her beautiful, pale, sweat-soaked face, looking into her lost eyes. "Oh dear God, Bari. Honey, are you all right?" Part of him felt sadness for his daughter, who went to church every Sunday and did not believe in using cuss words at all, and had even gotten after him for taking the Lord's name in vain; part of him felt as if he should make a joke about calling an exorcist before she went all Linda Blair on him; and a little scared part of him was afraid that it was not his daughter's face he held, but the muzzle of a rabid dog.

"Honey," he whispered. "Oh my poor little baby." Tears came to his eyes, and though he rarely wept over anything, the thought of his daughter being taken and ravaged by disease or some bacterial infection inside her made him think of the death of his mother and of all death and suffering. He wanted to call out to God Almighty for the reason for such suffering of the innocents.

"Daddy?" she whispered as if coming through a fevered moment. "Daddy, is that you?"

"Oh, baby," he said, his voice soft and gentle. "You're back. Oh, my precious little darlin'."

"Daddy?" she asked again, and it was as if she were blind, or somewhere else within her mind and unable to see him right in front of her face. "Daddy, is that *you?*"

"Yes, baby, it'll be okay. We'll get you down to a doctor and see what this is all about." He leaned forward and kissed her forehead. "It'll be all right. It's just a fever, sweetie. It's just a little touch of something."

"*Rat shit, rat shit,*" his daughter growled.

And then she went for his throat.

5

"I saw the little boy," the woman said, her voice weak and feeble, barely more than a whisper. "Right where you're standing. Right there."

"Oh," her husband said. "There's no one else here. Believe me. I'd know."

"He was. He was right there. He had something in his hands—cupped around it. Like it was a bird. He wanted me to see it. He opened up his little fingers slowly."

"What was it? What was in his hands?"

"I don't know. I just knew it was awful. That if I kept watching him while he showed me what he held I'd see something terrible. Something I could never take back. Never forget."

"It was a dream. Wasn't it?"

"No," the woman said, a bit of whimpering in her voice as if she were on the verge of tears. "But I closed my eyes. I pretended it was. He kept touching me. I wouldn't look. He touched me all over. That little boy. And he kept whispering something, and I wanted to cover my ears but I couldn't. I had to lie there and hear his vile words."

"It's only a dream," the man said, taking her hand in his. "You need to rest. It's all been too much, these days here. You'll see. A little rest and you won't see him again."

"Am I dying?" she rasped, her voice gone dry.

THE ABANDONED.

He pressed his finger to his lips and whispered, "Shhhh."

And then he refastened the restraints on the woman's wrists, and tightened them around the bedpost in the room in the old mansion where they lived, the one outside the village, the one called Harrow.

You are the Nightwatchman, he told himself.

II

OH, THE DREAMS YOU'LL DREAM

Chapter Four

1

The Church of the Vale was built first as a Dutch Reformed Church, and then it became, for a time, Catholic. It then transformed again in a whirl of madness—one year when most of the village's Catholics ended up going over to Parham to St. Anthony's after the priest at the Church of the Vale had an affair with one of the parishioners—into an Episcopal Church. Father Alan arrived on the scene. Some former Roman Catholics even attended, but none were as attentive as the acolyte who this very afternoon gazed up lovingly at the statue of Jesus and asked for direction. He was nearly eighteen, and had decided that it was time to think seriously about entering the priesthood. Or at least Divinity School of some kind.

His name, Roland Love. The elder child of the Love household, Roland had known from an early age that he would dedicate himself to his church and to the Lord. He'd spent much of his life preparing for this calling. His blond hair was kept short, almost in a military style. He was six foot one and had sinewy muscles and a strong frame. He'd been working out at the local gym after school because he had been feeling since summer that God was going to call him. He had slept nights in the church pews—having to sneak out from his bedroom window. Once, his dad had caught him and told him if he was going to sneak off to see some girl, to at least be up front about it. Roland couldn't tell his father that it was God who was his guide. His best friend. And he'd give everything he had to be with God as much as possible.

He felt as if he related more to people who had lived thousands of years in the past—those who had fought and died for the cross. Those who had carried out the orders of God without a second thought. Roland had felt the calling within him since he was a boy, but his parents, while perfectly good churchgoers, had never quite been the type to take it that one extra step further and dedicate their lives to Kingdom Come.

That's what Roland wanted—he wanted to be a knight of Kingdom Come.

He had trained for it, kept himself pure, and had forsworn the games of other boys his age. He had been dreaming of Kingdom Come since the summer, and had begun to imagine it as a vast cathedral, full of the Angelic Host. In his dream, when he walked across its floor, he could look below his feet and see the sinners in hell as they suffered. He had mercy on them in his dreams—he told the angels that he sought forgiveness, not for himself, but for those poor lost souls beneath him.

Roland was fairly sure his younger sister Bari was one of those lost souls.

He had caught her once in the backseat of Andy Harris's Mustang, and her bra had been completely taken off, the buttons of her blouse opened, and Andy's face had been buried against one of her peach-colored breasts like he was a baby sucking. (*Think of the baby Jesus,* Roland had thought then. *Think of the baby Jesus and the purity of Mary. Don't think of the awful fornication of those sinners. Pray for them. Beg God for His forgiveness so that their time in hell will be brief.*)

Roland did his best not to be the kind of person who told others about their own sins. He understood that this was between them and God, and had nothing to do with him. He wanted to be one of the soldiers of the New Temple of the Lord—for Kingdom Come to arise on this earth, for Heaven and Earth to combine. Although he couldn't quite remember when he'd first felt the touch of God on him, if you were to go back to his sixth year, when his Sunday School teacher had told him the story of Enoch, who had walked with God daily and who was the only man who did not experience death, for God took Enoch up with him—if you could get inside the mind of the little boy that Roland had been, you'd have understood that his religious feelings stemmed from his fear of death. He wanted to be a soldier of God primarily so that God would treat him like Enoch, and take him up without the pain of death.

But his devotion to God had been hard-won. Temptation was everywhere. Girls in school had been throwing themselves at him since he was fourteen. He knew it was his purity—they had a touch of the devil within them, and all that was evil wanted to taint purity. But he would never let the girls touch him. He paid no mind to them, and even when sexual thoughts arose within his body, he bit his hands at night rather than allow them to touch the filth down between his legs.

He was not going to mess this up just because of sex.

He knew the devil was always ready. He had argued with his mother about the devil once, telling her that the devil was real. "He is an angel who rebelled and didn't sub-

mit to God's word," he told her at fourteen. "And he sends
his demons to lie to men so we may become weak and not
enter the Kingdom."

"I am not going to raise some superstitious Jesus freak,"
his mother had said, and even though she had stomped
off, cursing under her breath, and they'd nearly dropped
out of the church altogether, Roland knew that God would
come through for them.

And for him.

God told him to lie to his mother. Roland was sure that
was the Lord's wish, for he didn't feel bad comforting his
mother later and telling her he had only been joking. A lie
for God was a lie for the good.

All other lies were demonic.

God filled him to the brim. God was his master. God
bent him to His will. God brought him to his knees. Roland
sought God's succor, and when he felt God's presence with
him, it was as if he had been opened up and entered by a
wondrous strange feeling.

He had always felt God's touch on his shoulder, and
God's voice spoke to him when all else was silent. What
perturbed him this day was that he had lost the feeling of
being called at all.

He closed his eyes as he knelt there, and prayed for
many things, including his little sister's recovery from
whatever ailed her, and for his mother's sadness, and his
father's stubborn nature. Then he began to list others in
town—the sinners and the saints and those in the world
fighting wars and those in heaven or hell who needed redemption. Roland intended to include every single human being in his prayers whenever possible.

He was sure that this would re-awaken the feeling that
God had called him to this church in particular.

That Jesus wanted him as a soldier in the Army of the
Righteous.

Dear Lord, please deliver me from the thoughts of night and from the devil's hands, deliver me from the nightly images of women who throw themselves around me, deliver me from the desires of the flesh.

Opened his eyes to see Jesus in the loincloth on the altar.

Jesus's body was like Roland's. It was sinewy yet strong, despite the pain and torture that had put Him on the cross.

Through your suffering, make me pure.

Then he sat back in the first pew and whispered to no one, "I just don't feel it."

He pressed his hands to his face, and began sobbing. *I want you in me. I want you in me.*

And that's when he got the strange vision in his head.

The impure one.

The one of tying up a girl he knew by the wrists, and tearing her clothes off, then taking his hands and . . .

Lord, help me. Get these thoughts out of me.

He closed his eyes to resume praying, and that's when Jesus spoke to him.

At first, he didn't open his eyes because he was afraid he imagined it. His heart beat rapidly; he felt as if he could barely breathe—the excitement at hearing Jesus was intense.

"Oh, my son, my precious son, you are the one who will bring about the great awakening."

"Lord?"

"You are the great architect of my cathedral on this earth," the voice said within him. "You will help lay the bricks and stain the windows. Your body will be scaffolding upon which my cathedral will reach the heavens themselves."

He opened his eyes.

The statue of Christ stared back at him with sad eyes. And the statue's lips moved. "You, before all men, will build the Cathedral of Kingdom Come."

The stone arms moved, and the feet pushed out the spikes

that held the statue in place. It climbed off the cross, pulling the large nails with it, and stepped forward to Roland. A halo of green lightning surrounded the statue's form.

"Do not be afraid, oh blessed boy," the statue said. "For I bring you great tidings of joy."

Shivering with fear but excited beyond reason, Roland nodded, tears streaming down his face.

"The enemy is near. Take up the instrument that I shall show you. Take it up, and plow the furrow that my seed might be planted. That you, Roland Love, true Love, eternal Love, will plow the field of blood and iniquity and plant the seeds of righteousness in the world. And on that field, you will erect the greatest monument to the infinite love, the most magnificent citadel since the Tower of Babel itself. It will climb higher than the ladder of Jacob, and you shall be wonderful in my sight."

A brilliant light seemed to explode from the center of the statue. As it grew and blossomed, it was a blinding light—a light beyond all light, and Roland felt a great wind accompany it as it spread toward him—and it knocked him backward.

He had passed out on the cold floor of the church.

When he awoke minutes later, he felt a terrible pain in the back of his head, and when he reached back to touch it, he felt the stickiness of blood. *St. Paul,* he thought. *On the road to Damascus. I have been visited, just as he was. I have been struck with a vision like lightning. I have heard the voice of the Lord call unto me.*

He glanced up at the altar. The statue was again on the cross.

And there, in front of him, was the instrument that the statue had bid him take up.

The plow for the field of blood and iniquity.

Still, his mind couldn't quite wrap around how this little instrument could plow a furrow, let alone begin the building of the greatest cathedral on heaven and earth.

It was a spike about as long as his own fist, and when he glanced back up at the statue on the cross, he saw the nail that had been thrust between the statue's feet was no more.

He got down on his knees and crawled to the spike. He touched it lightly with the palm of his hand. It was warm. It crackled with static electricity, and it made him jump slightly when he touched it.

Roland Love carefully picked up the spike and held it to his lips, kissing it in reverence of this miracle he had been brought—his calling back by all that was magnificent, his vision that surely meant he was destined for the life of a saint.

After a while, as he lay prostrate before the altar, the spike in his hands, praying for strength and wisdom and power and authority and the miracles that were known to the Almighty, he went out into the world to begin the work of heaven.

2

Dustin Moody, who ran the Coffee N Book Shoppe in the village, had already been checking flickering fluorescents half the afternoon. He called out to his lover, Nick, "You need to call electric."

"I am electric," Nick said, grinning. He was back behind the cappuccino machine that was once again coughing up brown foamy phlegm rather than its usual dark espresso. "You know this machine is like your grandma's plumbing—it's all broken down in the between parts."

Dusty never took well to jokes like that, and ignored Nick while still tapping the edge of the fluorescent lights with the spine of a book. They flickered in and out, all in a row above the Mystery and Romance shelves.

"You bought it all knowing it was crap," Nick added later, once he brought a hot mug of coffee over to Dusty. "Here, drink some of our brown sludge-a-chinno."

"What's it taste like?"

"If I told you, you'd never look at me the same again," Nick smirked, and then took a sip. "Naw, it's not that bad."

Dusty wanted some caffeine badly, so he reached over and took the mug. Sniffed it. A sip. He spat it back into the mug. "You've been serving this crap?"

"All day," Nick said, shrugging. "Hey, nobody told me how awful it was."

"We have to throw out that machine. You still have the Mr. Coffee?"

"Did Joe DiMaggio slam balls?" Nick nodded. He thumbed toward the storage room at the back of the store. "Packed away somewhere."

"It'll do 'til we can order another one."

"Serve regular coffee? Us? Half our customers will migrate to Starbucks up the road."

"They already have. And after drinking that brown shit, that little mystery is solved. You get the new shipment out on the shelves?"

"Some of them. All the new Nora Roberts and the new Cornwell. What time's Ronnie coming in?"

Dusty glanced at his wristwatch. "Whenever she feels like it, I guess."

"Well, that's about the time when I guess the books'll all be shelved," Nick said, "because I feel like a nap, and you know I'm owed at least one today."

3

Over at the Watch Point Free Library, a small, domed building at the center of a green that might've once been called a Commons but was now simply "Watch Point Park," Ronnie Pond sat on the stone steps out front, reading a copy of Chuck Palahniuk's *Fight Club*. She glanced up at some starlings that had begun swarming in the sky.

She then looked over at the red Mustang parked near the post office.

"You're stalking him," Lizzie said.

Startled by her sister's voice, Ronnie glanced around. Lizzie stood at the top step of the library, just behind her, nearly invisible by the statue of Athena, Greek goddess of wisdom and war. Lizzie, looking muscled and sweaty from an afternoon workout at the tennis courts, could've been a goddess of war herself. "Napoleonic shits," was all Ronnie said.

They had a secret language that they'd developed since they first learned to speak. As twins, they had been getting away with murder for years, and the language was just the smallest part of it. They looked nearly identical—although Ronnie had a rose tattoo on her shoulder, while Lizzie had opted for a Celtic circle tattoo around her wrist. Ronnie rarely saw herself in her sister—they had done everything in life to be very different in some ways. Whereas Lizzie had become a party girl and a jock in high school, Ronnie had opted for the pale life of books. Even though her glasses were only slightly necessary, they distinguished her further from her sister. Ronnie had begun dying her hair black by the age of thirteen—when her mother finally relented on her endless whines of not wanting to be so damn sandy brown—but had not yet progressed to the stage of wearing extremely different clothes from her sister, simply because it was easier and cheaper just to trade back and forth on shirts and slacks and jeans and skirts, although Ronnie was a jeans girl whereas Lizzie was partial to skirts. The language they'd developed over the years began with a twist on *baw-baw*, their word for "bottle" when they were toddlers. The term now encompassed anything they wanted so badly they were willing to fight for it (thus, at age seventeen, "baw-baw" also became any guy one of them lusted after, despite the other staking a claim). By the time they both entered high school, the secret language had progressed far beyond its childish beginnings and included parallels to history. "Huguenots in the Louvre" became their phrase for "I'm getting my period and it feels like a blood bath." "Stonehenged" might mean that a person or a sentence someone had uttered was completely unintelligible, or it might simply mean that whoever said it felt lost. "I'm completely stonehenged in Geometry," Lizzie might say. "Very Trianon" meant that a classmate was living in her own fantasyland. And "Napoleonic shits" was too simple—they'd heard that one of the theories as to why Napoleon lost at Waterloo was that he'd been eating sour green apples the morning of the battle and had to run to the latrine constantly. Thus weakened, he hadn't been up to snuff for his most important foe. "That's not the accepted understanding," their junior-year World History teacher had told them. But for Lizzie and Ronnie, it was enough. So when Ronnie said "Napoleonic shits" to her sister on the steps of the library that afternoon, what Lizzie heard was, "Okay, you caught me, I'm not winning this one, I've been going at this all wrong, and life just sucks and I think I'm going to be sick."

Beyond that, since Lizzie could easily identify the red Mustang, she also heard, "Andy Harris is already going with Bari Love and nobody's going to break them up, but I can't seem to stop obsessing about him when I really should be focusing on something important in life, like reading this book or developing my motor skills or even getting extra work at the bookshop."

"He's extremely H the Eighth," Lizzie said, trying to dissuade her sister. "The question's got to be, are you Anne Boleyn or Jane Seymour?"

"Bari's definitely Aragon."

"She's so Aragon, she's got an armada in her bra." Lizzie grinned, sitting down beside her.

"Why'd you and Alex break up? Was it . . ." Ronnie began, but then stopped herself. She wanted to say, *Was it that night when you changed just a little? Did he do something to you that night to hurt you so badly that you couldn't see him again? Did he . . . ?*

Ronnie didn't want to have to complete that thought.

"Naw. It was just regular break-up stuff. He freaked me out a little. He was a major perv. And, well, we just weren't suited. So whatcha reading?"

Ronnie showed her the book.

"Any good?"

"Very."

"The movie was great."

"Not as good as this."

"Want to go grab snacks?"

"No baw-baw," Ronnie said. "I have a knot in my stomach at this point. And I need to get to work."

"Napoleonic shits are the worst," Lizzie agreed, "but they're still better than Huguenots in the Louvre." She put her arm around her twin's shoulders, and they watched the red car until Andy came out of the post office a minute or so later. "You need to forget him."

"Yeah, I know," she said. "All boys are best forgotten. But I can dream, can't I?"

"You still having those dreams?"

They hadn't talked about the dreams for awhile. Ronnie had stopped telling her about them. They stopped being scary, and Ronnie felt they got boring, too.

It was always about rooms in a house.

Always about hearing footsteps outside the door.

"Not much anymore," Ronnie lied

She nodded slightly toward the post office. "He dumped you like garbage when you were sixteen. Don't forget that. You're just lonely. You'll meet some cool guy soon."

"I know," Ronnie said.

"Yeah, but life's rough," Lizzie said, leaning against her sister's neck. "Ooh, you know I'm a little sleepy. I wish we had naptime just like when we were little kids. I could use a nap right about now."

"You're a sleepaholic," Ronnie said, and was about to mention that it was weird that Lizzie never remembered her dreams anymore.

Just as Ronnie had been mulling all this over, sitting with her sister, something startled her—but it was just a little white-haired boy riding by on his bicycle as if he were hell on wheels.

5

There was nothing in the world like a bike if you were about eleven years old and feeling like the other kids in your new school hated your guts on sight. You had your jacket on and were running out the door before your mother could say anything about it, and you knew that once you were on that bike—as lousy as the bike could be—you were flying through it all. Flying through the beginnings of autumn, the leaves that already had been falling down on Macklin Street; flying past those boys who had tried to get you out on the blacktop for what they called the "New Kid Test," which was the strongest boy in sixth grade daring the new kid in school to a fight. Because other kids in the class—even the girls who had seemed meek and mild not five minutes before, playing games nearby—encircled the two of them, even teachers couldn't see what was going on in the two-minute ritual. Although in Kazi's case, it was a ten-second ritual because he knew enough to go down to the blacktop as soon as the big kid approached him. *I don't mind losing. I mind getting beat up,* he thought as he stared up at Mark Malanski, who stood over him. He had looked around at the girls and boys who had seemed so distinct in class before—now, in a circle above him, their faces watching him as if they were in a hypnotic trance, they no longer seemed like boys and girls. They seemed like one mob. One body joined together with many heads. Watching him be humiliated.

The New Kid Test.

Pass or fail didn't matter.

All that mattered was that they saw what you were made of.

At eleven, Kazi Vrabec was made of marshmallow. He even felt the marshmallow inside. His mother, who had come over from Czechoslovakia as a teenager, had told him that his name—Kazimir—meant "Great Destroyer," and sometimes she even tried to tell him the tales of his great-great grandfather, who was an adventurer and conqueror. She had been trying to teach him the language of her homeland, but he'd avoided it as much as possible because it made him stand out too much when she tried talking with him on the street. Everyone stared. He hated feeling like a foreigner. He was born on American soil, and he wasn't ever going to Prague if he could help it.

But sometimes being in a small town was awful.

And he didn't feel like a great destroyer—not ever.

He felt marshmallow all over, inside and out, and had not wanted to move to Watch Point, but his mother had insisted after his father had wandered off with the woman his mother called his "kurva" eight months before.

But on the bike, flying, he could throw it out into the wind, that memory, that school event he could never tell his mother about or his new teacher, or anyone. It was that level of childhood he hated, and being too good at math and science and English and social studies was not going to do him well at the sixth grade in Parham's public school. Even the bus ride home had sucked.

He could forget other days, too, like the time the kids all got him on the blacktop to play dodge ball, and he told them that they weren't supposed to.

"But that's another kind of dodge ball," Bobby Wofford

said, grinning. When Bobby Wofford grinned, Kazi had learned, you were screwed. And if he laughed, you might as well kiss it all goodbye. "This is a special game."

"Yep," Sandy Houseman chimed in. "This one's called Get the New Kid."

"Or Bounce the Czech," Bobby Wofford began laughing at his own joke, so Kazi thought, *Well, might as well get this over with*.

But luckily, Miss Aronson had come out at that moment and scolded the kids for having stolen the ball from the utility closet where they kept all the stuff for games and P. E. Whenever one of the kids slyly mentioned dodge ball around Kazi, he panicked. Just the sight of the ball made him want to run and hide somewhere rather than deal with those kids at that awful elementary school. And yet, he didn't feel he could run to his mother and whine about it. She had told him to toughen up each time they'd moved, and he was sure she'd just yell at him if he came back with another story of being bullied. "You need to fight back, Kazimir!" she'd shout as if he'd done something terrible and wrong. "You can't just keep taking things from people. You can't just be a big baby and come running back here expecting me to solve this. I worry that I'm turning you into a little coward. Your grandfather was a great soldier. It's your father. He's the coward. You take after him. You have to change this, Kazi. You have to. I didn't come all the way to America just to have a son who was a cowering dog!"

So he had learned to keep most of this to himself, even if it meant a little humiliation on the blacktops of life now and then.

All the New Kid tortures were getting to him.

But oh, the bicycle—his magic carpet away from the troubles. He could forget the dodge ball fear and the New Kid Test and Bobby Wofford's throw-up laugh and the way Sandy Houseman sniffed the air when he was around as if he smelled bad. On the bike, he was in another world.

He flew along the streets, avoiding the major traffic areas (of which there was only one, and even then it was only major for twenty minutes, between 4:45 P.M. and 5:05 P.M. weekdays), and finally finding zigzag roads that were full of pot-holes and dips and curves. Eventually it was all trees, and he thought he smelled a lake somewhere—that watery stink that lifted his spirits just with the thought of it—and he rode along a narrow road that went from paved to unpaved, until he came upon a sign that read:

NO TRESPASSING. ARMED RESPONSE.

He squeezed the hand brakes on his bike, nearly toppling over, but managed to steady himself. The dirt road had a thick chain across it and one at about the height of his shoulders. If he hadn't stopped, he would've been thrown.

There was a stone wall some distance beyond the posts that held the chains. And beyond that, he saw the beginnings of a driveway.

A man stood in the driveway. Or maybe it wasn't a man.

Kazi had the distinct impression that it was a scarecrow, positioned at the open gate between the ends of the rock wall to keep people out.

He dropped his bike near the chains. Then he walked around the posts, tapping the tops of them, touching one of the chains as if unsure whether it was real or not.

He wanted to see the scarecrow. Or the man who looked like a scarecrow.

He began walking up the dirt road until the pavement started again. He glanced back to his bike—it lay on its side, where he'd left it.

The main road he'd zigzagged off seemed a long way behind him. His mother would be calling him for supper soon, but he could be late. She'd live. She never got too mad at him anymore.

He glanced back up the driveway, to the gate at the stone wall. The trees along the edge of the wall were large and fat and thick with golden leaves.

The man who looked more and more like a scarecrow—with a funny straw hat and what looked like hay coming out from under it—waved his arms around, and for some reason this made Kazi grin and giggle a little.

People were friendly in Watch Point. He knew that much. The kids sucked, but grown-ups were all pretty nice to him.

Something inside Kazi made him want to turn around and get back on his bike and hightail it out of there. Something, almost like a little voice, whispered about how he wasn't supposed to talk to strangers, let alone walk up a lonesome road in the middle of nowhere to see if they were a man in costume as a scarecrow.

He knew about scarecrows. His mother had told him for years about a man and woman made of straw. They were named Dadko and Morena, and they brought disease and pestilence and must be burned. When his family had lived in the farmland when he was only five or six, he saw scarecrows in the field, and his mother had warned him they were images of Dadko. "They scare more than birds, Kazi," she warned him. "When I was a girl, we burned them, but I always was scared when I saw the man and woman made of straw."

The man in the driveway had started to come toward him a little, too.

Just a few steps beyond the gate.

Then a few more.

Chapter Five

1

Ronnie Pond usually stopped by home first before she went to work, but she was so late that she figured she better skedaddle and at least make a good show of being at the bookstore as close to the hour as she could. As soon as she went in the front door, Dusty called out from one of the shelves, "That better be Ronnie."

"Guilty," she said, and immediately went to the cash register to get to work.

"Well, look who's here. Veronica Pond. There's a pile of returns under there. Whenever Nick wakes up in the back, I want you to go and start getting the new shipment out on the shelves," Dustin called out without leaving the nonfiction section.

"Gotcha," Ronnie said as she crouched down to pick up some of the hardcovers that had to go back to the distributor. When she rose from the counter, Boaty Boatwright stood there.

"Mr. Boatwright," she said.

"Has it come yet?"

"It?" Quickly, she pulled up the accounts on the computer screen and tapped through the alphabet to his name. "Not yet."

"How hard is it to get a book that's been out for months?"

Ronnie glanced at the screen. Peter Straub's *In the Night Room* was listed. She'd read and loved that book. Part of her felt like just telling him she'd get him her copy from home at some point if he promised to return it. But that wasn't business. She'd done it once before and Dusty had been none too happy about it, although he and Nick had had a good laugh over it at the time. "The order's there. The book's available. Maybe the mail's slow this week."

"Ah," Boaty said. "Fear of terrorists."

"Sir?" Ronnie asked.

"They may be checking all packages. You know the way the world is now. Bad things come in small packages."

Ronnie grinned, "You mean good things." He had a blank look on his face, so she added, "You know, 'good things come in small packages.'"

"That's not always true," Boaty said. "Bad things do, too."

"Well, look, the book should be in by this weekend. Want me to just run it out to you when it's in? Save you a trip?"

Boaty nodded, but looked none too happy. Grudgingly, he said, "Thanks. Sure. That'd be great." Then, in a mousy voice that could barely be heard, he added, "I really wanted it tonight."

"Sir?"

"The book," he said, a bit more loudly. "I've been waiting for it. I really wanted to read it tonight. Nothing good's on TV. I have the place to myself for a few hours. All by my lonesome. I just wanted to start in on it."

"It's a good one," she said. Then she leaned over the counter. He drew closer to her. She mostly mouthed the words with the barest whisper accompanying her lip movements. "I'll get you a copy. After work. I'll drop it off."

Boaty grinned, glancing back toward Dusty, who had begun walking to the front counter with a stack of books. "Good. Goody. Thanks. You're a good egg, Ronnie. That's a compliment, even though it doesn't sound like one. It's amazing to see how you've grown into such a smart, beautiful woman."

Ronnie smiled. "Thank you."

Just as Boaty was stepping away, he drew back again. "You guys sell reading glasses?"

"Absolutely," she said, and took him over to the carousel of glasses near the magazine racks. "Getting a little blurry?"

"Well, you hit your forties and eye strain starts to take its toll," he said. He spun the carousel a bit and tried on a few pairs before buying one.

"Those look quite good on you," Ronnie said as he put on the smallish pair with a tortoiseshell rim. She passed him a paperback with particularly small print. "Try it. Read a few lines and see if they help."

Boaty flipped through the book a bit. "I guess these are the right ones. Thanks so much. I guess this'll have me reading a bit more."

"Well, they print such tiny fonts in some of these books," Ronnie said. "I'm about to tackle *Bleak House*, and let me tell you, I need to find the large-print edition myself."

Boaty grinned and gave her a little wink. "You're the best, Ronnie." He bought three hardcovers in stock that she recommended, and when he had left the store, Dusty said to her, "He doesn't bother you, does he?"

She gave him a quizzical look. "Bother?"

"Well, I think Boaty's hot for you, kid," Dusty said. "I don't like customers who seem to be hitting on high school kids."

"No." She grinned, shaking her head. "No way. He's just friendly."

"Gives me the creeps, sometimes. But hey, you got him to buy something. That's pretty amazing since he hasn't spent a dime in here since he found out about online bookstores."

"I'm a miracle worker," she said. "So how about that raise?"

"Soonish," Dusty said. "Okay now, let's go wake Nick up and tackle the stock in the back. How late can you stay?"

"Just 'til eight. I've got double-duty tonight."

"Baby-sitting on a school night?"

"Dusty," she said, nudging him slightly in the shoulder. "I do my homework when I baby-sit, don't worry."

"What brat are you with tonight?"

"Make that brats. The Housemans. And they drive me nuts, but she pays the best."

"Ugh." Dusty made a face at the mention of the name. "Those little monsters."

2

Two doors up, at the *Watch Point New Lady Style Shop*, a particular customer became annoyed with the girl trying to sell her the wrong pair of shoes.

"I want the one with the red straps," Norma Houseman said. She'd been feeling better ever since the Cadlomyx had kicked in. Cadlomyx was the new wonder drug her doctor in Parham had prescribed for her. It made her smarter, although that's not quite what the doctor had said about it. She had a pill to help her get to sleep, a pill to keep her asleep, a pill to wake her up, and a pill or two to keep her awake and alert during the day, to say nothing of her daily anxiety pills that kept away the cobwebs for her.

She wished she had a pill to make this sales clerk go away.

"They only come in blue," the sales clerk at the dress and shoe shop said, pointing out the three styles of elegant heels.

"I saw in the catalog that they have red straps, too."

"These are all we have in stock," the young sales clerk said.

"For three hundred dollars, I think I can have the color I want. Can you order the red straps?"

"It may take six weeks."

"I could drive to Manhattan tomorrow and be back by two P.M. with the ones with the red straps."

The sales clerk sighed and bit down into her smile. "Let me call our Ossining store. Maybe they'll have them."

"Please," Norma said. "And thank you."

She felt a gentle tug at her sweater, and glanced down at her youngest daughter, Cathy.

"Let's go."

"Mommy'll be just a few more minutes." Norma tried to keep an aspect of sweetness to her voice. The one thing about her new medication was it sometimes took away what was sweet and kept her a bit on edge. Part of her wanted to take her thumb and forefinger and flick little Cathy on the back of her head in hopes of jogging her daughter's brain a little. Maybe kickstart it for once.

"I'm bored," Cathy whined, ever so quietly, as if she were telling her mother she needed to go to the little girl's room.

"We'll go soon," Norma said, and reached down to brush her hand over her daughter's silky blond hair.

The sales clerk was on the phone, talking in a low voice, back toward the stock room door, stretching the phone cord as far as it would go.

Norma glanced at the shoes on the counter. *But could I just use the blue? No, it's for the family picture. I'll be in front, with my legs crossed. I need to have the red straps. My red dress, my red shoes, my red straps.*

Douglas Clegg

Norma Houseman was a shoe freak, and had been since she was a young woman training to be a ballet dancer. Instead she had ended up marrying an idiot and giving up on her dreams. She loved the way shoes made her legs look. She loved the rich feeling she had in a pair of Manolo Blahniks or Jimmy Choos. Most of her shopping was done by catalog or on her once-every-two-months trip to Manhattan when she got to leave the kids with Lizzie and Ronnie Pond for an overnight, and go down to check in to the Plaza Hotel for one heavenly night. She would spend two full days doing nothing but shopping and drinking—both of which were heaven to Norma, and her little secret from the village, who all seemed to think she was Maria Von Trapp or something.

But sometimes she was stuck having to buy a new pair of decent shoes in the only shop in town that ever got anything passable in.

Every three years, she took a family picture, and she had to look magnificent in it.

Or she'd just die.

The family picture meant that much to her—she intended to gather all five of her children around, from William who was nearly thirteen all the way to Cathy, who was barely four. A perfect family picture meant a perfect family.

It'll show that rat bastard who the winner is, she thought. *I'll be sexy and beautiful, surrounded by my loving children. And he'll get it two months before Christmas in his lonely little world where he sleeps with every other slut who likes Chivas, and he'll cry and hate me and hate himself and then I'll have won. I'll have the love of my children and my looks and my youth—I'm only thirty-five. I still look late twenties. He looks like a rat bastard of fifty if not more.*

Norma Houseman had to win in life, and it didn't matter whether it was winning the battle of wills with the stupid twenty-year-old sales clerk at the shoe store; or the surge of victory she felt when she'd gotten her problem child, Frankie, to finally admit that Mommy was always right on things like life and math, and that whatever Frankie thought was always wrong; or whether it was the charges she brought against her husband to make sure he'd never have custody of his kids again and would have to pay through the nose to clothe and feed them until the end of time. She won. That's all that she cared about, and she even won with Chuck, the man she saw sometimes, the man who gave her some pleasure in those brief lonely moments when the love for her family didn't quite cut it for her.

The sales clerk turned around again, and went to hang up the phone. "We can get them in by tomorrow."

"That's not good enough."

"Mrs. Houseman," the clerk said. "I'm very sorry." She still looked like she was biting down on her own smile. "That's really the best we can do."

"Your best is anyone else's not-so-good," Norma said. "I suppose I'll take my business elsewhere in this case."

"We're sorry," the clerk said.

"Oh, sorry, of course you are," Norma said. And then, she asked to see the girl's supervisor. After sitting with the supervisor for nearly half an hour, Norma realized she'd won again. The girl was going to get fired—after all, she'd been rude and insolent to a customer, and Norma had stretched the truth slightly and embellished a bit so that the sales clerk would have more to answer to once Norma and Cathy had left the store. Norma smiled politely as she left the shop, and thanked the sales clerk who had no idea that ten minutes later she wouldn't have a job.

"Let's go home," Cathy said.

"No, we have some errands to run."

"I'm bored," Cathy said.

Norma stopped, and let go of her daughter's hand. "Well, if you're so bored, why don't you go run into the street and get hit by a car?"

Douglas Clegg

"Mommy?" The little girl looked up at her.

"That's what bored little children do. They put them-selves in harm's way," Norma said. She turned Cathy around to face the street. Although traffic was fairly slow, a car passed by every few seconds in the shopkeepers' district. Norma nudged her daughter toward the curb. "Come on, you're bored. Why not give it a try?"

"Mommy," Cathy said, looking out at the street and then down at her feet.

"Well, it'll cure that boredom right away," Norma said. "And being bored is just so boring, isn't it? Being with your mother on a nice day out shopping is just the most boring thing in the world, isn't it?" She nudged her daughter be-tween her shoulder blades. "Little girls get hit by cars all the time. Nobody thinks anything of it. You land in the hos-pital with a broken pelvis, sweetie, believe me, you'll know real boredom."

"All right," Cathy said, her voice going soft and apolo-getic. "I'm not bored, Mommy. I promise I'm not."

"I once knew a little bored girl," Norma said. "She lived in a big city and the people who took her from her mommy put her in a teeny-tiny room, so small she couldn't move, and whenever they brought her out they hurt her every way they could. You don't want to get hurt do you?"

Cathy shook her little blond head.

"Then why don't you just put all the words you want to say into that piggy bank in the back of your mind and don't speak until someone speaks to you first," Norma said, and grabbed her hand again. "And when we get home, I want you to clean up your room. It's an absolute sty. First, Mommy needs to go to the post office to check the mail."

Norma Houseman made daily trips to the post office, even though the Watch Point mail delivery to homes was excellent. But she had a special post office box for her

90

maiden name, Spretz, which seemed to collect more mail than the usual. As little Cathy went and looked at the framed stamps on the wall, Norma retrieved her special key from her purse, and went to check the oversized box she rented each year, paying cash, under the name "N. Spretz."

Three letters were inside the box, and she drew them out. Each had return addresses. She opened the first one. It was from a Mrs. Marshall Allen of Eastbrook, New Jersey. A brief note within, and five crisp one hundred dollar bills. The second, from a Mr. Matthew Schwartz, also of New Jersey, held a total of three hundred and fifty dollars in cash. And the third had a money order from someone named B. Little in the amount of $2,300 with a note that read, "I'm sorry it's late."

She folded the money and the order in half and pressed them deep into her purse. Then she went to drag Cathy over to the bank before it closed.

Afterward, at home, whiney little Cathy had her mouth washed out with soap during which she cried the whole time and Norma had to ask her over and over again, "Is this boring? Do you think this is boring? You bored, Catherine? You bored? This boring to you?"

Once her boy William the Conqueror (as she called him because he was so responsible and smart and good-looking, like her side of the family) came in and made his mommy her favorite kind of apple martini to help take the edge off the day, she called Chuck at his place. Only he wasn't there. This was the third time this week, and it was beginning to piss her off. The last time she'd seen him was when they took a few days over on the New England coast, leaving William in charge of his brothers and sisters.

How Norma had loved those days on the Cape—long nights of wonderful passion, days spent walking barefoot on the beach, and lobster and clams and champagne for dinner, all courtesy of some of the people with whom she conducted her mail-order "business," which had very little to do with business, but much to do with mail.

"I want you to call me," Norma said in an annoyed tone, hoping that he checked his messages soon. "Norma's had a rough day and needs her Chuck."

Then she hung up the phone.

3

Chuck Waller was so deep inside Mindy Shackleford that he felt like he was diggin' for clams. Ah, he loved it, loved the feeling of banging her, the thumpity of the hump (he liked to make up words around "the slappy whap of the ugly tap," as he called sex) and she clung to him like a monkey on the bars of the zoo. He loved reaching the heights of pleasure as it all just ran away from him—the thudding, thumping drumbeat of lust pounding out against flesh.

Chuck was never happier than at these moments, and even though he didn't like Mindy too much in any other department, she was a vacuum cleaner of a lonely middle-aged housewife whose husband was always away, and whose kiddies never were around when she brought him into the house and had him make love on her teenage daughter's bed.

He had this whole routine of servicing some of the lonely and horny and sometimes single mothers in the village who were just a little bit older than he was and looking for a little fun when the kids were off somewhere else.

Slap, slam, thank you ma'am, you know baby I don't give a damn. He let it all out—a growl, a moan, a gruff deep "oh yeah," and then something happened that had never in his entire adult life happened before. He began to float a little. Not really him. Just something in him. His mind. His consciousness. He felt as if he were *whooshed* up behind himself, watching the lurches and jackrabbit *thwack* of his buttocks as he went with the old in-out, and he had never noticed how hairy his back had become over the years, now that he was in his thirties, and how he had a little bit of back fat and a spare tire, too. It all jiggled as he plunged into her depths. It was a sensation he didn't like. He should have been watching her face for that wonderful sign that she knew he had her pinned, like a butterfly in a little glass case, but instead he watched the back of himself—his round small bald spot almost like a monk's tonsure, the freckles on his shoulders, and even worse a bit fat zit on his rear end, which made him think he was ugly and kind of gross, not the king of the world as he had been feeling.

I am the king, he thought, and he still felt that buzzing pleasure in his loins, but looking at himself he felt nasty and dirty. Then he noticed her face, from the distance where his consciousness floated—she wasn't enjoying it. He saw her eyes—she was somewhere other than beneath him. She didn't love it. She wasn't an animal in heat. She was just some woman in her early fifties who dreamed of the past too much. She was just thinking she was a teenager again, thinking of another time and another bedroom where maybe she felt loved and taken care of.

But not under him.

Then *whoosh!* Again he felt a hammer crack his head as darkness enveloped his mind, and he was right back in his body again, looking down at her.

Only she was different.

She was dead.

A dead body.

For some reason, he remembered something that Mindy had told him once, something silly and affectionate when they'd been groping each other down at the multiplex in

Poughkeepsie, "My fuck place is a little bit worn out, sugar."
She still clung to that Southern accent even after twenty
years in New York State without one visit to Georgia since
her first child had been born. When she'd said it during a
showing of *The Ring*, he had laughed out loud because
he'd never heard her be quite so specific and blunt about
anything regarding sex, even though their relationship
mainly consisted of bouts of the old in-out.

And those words came to him as he looked down at her
corpse.

My fuck place is a little bit worn out, sugar.

He was sure of it.

Eyes were all blank and staring and her mouth was
agape, and her skin was somewhere between pale white
and light blue.

My fuck place is a little bit worn out, sugar.

In his memory, her voice was like pulled taffy from a
Deep South candyman in Savannah—*Mah fuck playice is a
leeddel bit who-wen ow-et, shu-gah.*

He felt different on the inside now, and something
about the way the room around him wavered a bit like a
flickering candle flame made him realize that he'd entered
a dream.

He drew back from Mindy's body, and lay on his side using his elbow to prop up his head.

Your fuck place, Mindy? Worn out?

Hell yeah, he thought. *What the hell, it's beyond worn out.
It's split up the middle.*

Shu-gah.

Mindy was definitely dead—her breasts had begun rotting, and half her torso was split up the middle as if someone had taken the Jaws of Life to her and just cut her
open. He held tight to the idea that this was a dream, but
as it went, he became more convinced that it was—for the
room was no longer Mindy Shackleford's daughter's bed-

room with its posters of Justin Timberlake and other boy band pop stars of the moment.

It was a much larger room, more elaborate, with a large gold harp in a far corner, and a door that looked as if it had been carved by master craftsmen in some Italian mansion; the four-poster bed they lay upon was long and wide and had a thick blanket of deep red over snow-white sheets. Above them, a canopy as blue as heaven itself.

Wake up, he said within himself. *Wake up. You're dreaming too much. Something might happen.*

What might happen?

Something. I'm afraid.

He hated admitting fear in real life, but in a dream Chuck Waller had no problem being scared shitless.

Narcolepsy, came the word. He hated the word. He suffered from it and he hated it and no matter what medication he tried, none of them worked. And he'd been trying them since he'd been nineteen, when he'd first begun experiencing the sudden sleepiness. The latest round of amphetamines he was using must've triggered this—this too-vivid vision. *That's it. It's the drugs. Too high a dose. I still fall asleep, but I get this bizarre psycho dream where Mindy's been cut open and I'm in some rich man's bedroom.* But usually he simply blacked out into sleep and awoke a few minutes later.

Now and then, he'd experience hypnogogia—that hallucinatory half-dreaming, half-waking state . . . but it was never like this.

His tongue felt dry in his mouth. His limbs, sore. He even felt sleepy in his own damn dream, which scared him, because how could he be a narcoleptic within the dream itself?

Yet his mind was trying to shut down—to sleep. He pushed himself up to a sitting position, feeling sick to his stomach. Half the bed was soaked with dark blood, and his thighs were covered with it. Not his blood, but hers.

It's a dream. Don't be afraid.

As he sat there, fighting sleep, feeling an urgency to wake up back in Mindy Shackleford's house and not in this place, he began to hear a *tap, tap* beyond the great wooden door. Not precisely a rapping at the door. But a tap that echoed slightly, as of someone walking.

Footsteps.

Light footsteps.

He stared at the door.

There was a key jutting out from the keyhole. An old-fashioned kind of mechanism.

If you turn the key, you lock the door, he thought.

The tap tap tap of little feet. Pitter patter. It's a child out there, running toward the door. Running down a long hall.

Fighting sleep, he rubbed his eyelids with his fingers. *Don't sleep, someone's coming.*

But he closed his eyes—within the dream itself—and for just a second saw blackness. Then he was beyond the bedroom door in a long hallway full of other doors. He ran like a young child down the hallway.

Pitter patter of feet. Coming for your door.

Opened his eyes again, and he was sitting up in the bed of blood next to dead Mindy Shackleford.

He looked at the door.

At the key in the lock.

If you get up now, you can lock the door before he comes in. Before that wicked little boy who is pittering and pattering toward you comes in. Get up, you oaf.

He leaned forward to stand, but the falling darkness in his head—that spiraling downward into the feather bed of sleep—kept him on the edge of the bed.

He looked down at his feet.

Just stand up. Put one foot on the floor and stand up.

Tap tap tap in the hallway as a little boy ran toward the door.

If you don't reach the door before he does, he will kill you.

That's ridiculous, he thought. *A little boy running to this room is not going to kill you.*

But the irrational belief had taken hold—that beyond this door, there was a malevolence—a boy who ran toward him, and who would have a great jagged cutting instrument in his hands. Giant scissors perhaps, or the Jaws of Life, or even giant teeth in his little round mouth that could cut into human flesh the way that Mindy had been sliced up her center like a big *V.*

V is for Vaginal Cutting.

Now that was a voice in his head he'd never heard before. It wasn't his own voice, but a variation of someone else's voice. He felt he knew that voice, the one that said the *V* word to him, but he couldn't quite place it.

Then the voice spoke again in his mind: *I know that voice. I do. It's somebody, oh, somebody on the tip of my tongue, but I swallowed it.*

His feet touched the floor. The floor was icy cold, and his feet, bare, felt like lead weights.

Chuckawalla, you ever swallow anybody on the tip of your tongue?

He felt a gentle thumping in the little blue vein above his right temple that always meant he was too tense and one of those big hammering headaches would come on.

They never come on in dreams, he thought. *All righty then, we're back to my own voice in my head. Yay for me. No strange voice that's disturbingly familiar. This is just a dream. A dream with an extra voice.*

This is no ordinary dream, Chuckawalla.

Don't call me that.

You are a Chuckawalla.

That's stupid. That's what kids called me. It's nothing.

Chuckawallas run on their hind legs through water. They bloat up and they run and if you grab their tails, the tails fall off and wriggle.

Shut up. Is this a dream about fourth grade? I haven't been called that since I was ten.

Hey, is that a lizard in your pants, or are you happy to see me? Oh, wait, damn, it's a lizard. Chuckawalla, don't let what's on the other side of the door in.

He just wanted to stop and sleep on the floor, but he saw the doorknob turn slightly.

That little bastard is testing. He wants to see if he can get in without you knowing. Go turn the key and lock the door.

He took another step forward.

He glanced at the doorknob. It slowly turned to the left. Then slowly to the right.

He stepped forward, but had to bend over, his hands clutching his knees. He wanted to drop right there and sleep.

The little bastard is coming. He's coming back to cut you open. He's coming back to tear you apart.

Took a deep breath. Better. Feel better.

Stood up again, stretching. Another step forward.

He heard the boy's voice in the hall. A high-pitched little voice. "Please. Hurry."

The little bastard wants you to come to the door, but the question is: Will you get there before he does?

That is the million dollar question, Chuckawalla. Will you race like the lizard that is your totem? Will you puff up and bloat and race across that floor and turn that key before he can turn the knob and push his way in?

Shut up, Chuck told his mind. *I don't want to be dreaming this anymore. And I'm not a damn lizard!*

Look, Lizard-Breath, you're not dreaming. This is where you are, and where you're gonna stay, and nobody's waking you up or kissing your cheek. She's really dead back there, and this little bastard in the hall has these cutters that are going to snicker-snack you up and down, the Vorpal Blade of the Jabberwock is in his grubby little pokey fingers, and you are gonna be meat on the floor in about ten sec-

onds if you can't find your reptilian way to that door and turn that key so that the little bugger can't get you.

Chuck Waller took another step to the door, and just as he reached it, he heard something behind him.

"Please," the little boy on the other side of the door said. "Hurry, hurry."

Chuck glanced behind him, but as he did, he felt all the little hairs on the back of his neck rise up, and even some hairs down below, on his balls.

He wasn't scared so much by the kid in the hall or the voice in his head or even the noise behind him that probably meant that Mindy Shackleford was rising up on the mattress and grinning at him with teeth black and grimy with blood.

He was scared because he knew where he was, and he had been there when he was a kid, and he'd sworn he'd never set foot in that place again.

It was the house.

The old one.

The one up on the hill beyond town.

Harrow.

Make it go away. Make this dream go away. I am in Mindy's house. I am not in this place.

Shu-gah, you're just in my special little fuck place. You're all worn out and you're a big old Chuckawalla lizard running around and I'm gonna have to tear your tail off and watch you run around without it, bleeding while that nasty little boy decides whether he wants to tie a string around your neck or stomp you with his little boy feet.

When he opened his eyes again, he was still sleepy and in the terrible house. He glanced back to see if Mindy Shackleford—the dead and torn open Mindy—might be standing on the mattress as he'd imagined she would.

Instead, it was his father.

His head was still caved in from that long-ago fall from the river cliff *(or was it a jump, Dad?)* that had killed the old guy, and he still had that bloodied suit on.

Even though his right leg was turned all the way around—as it had been in the accident—he dragged it forward, toward Chuck, and said, "Come here, Chuckawalla, come here my little sleepy boy. Let's tuck you in good, all right my little man? My little little man? My little shu-gah man?"

Chuck heard the boy at the door, behind him, crying out, "Please, hurry. You gotta! You gotta hurry!" and realized it was his voice, his own voice, that's why it had been familiar—and the door wasn't in need of locking.

You should've gone to it. Unlocked it for the boy. He knows how to save you. Only he knows.

"Come on, my little shu-gah man, let me tuck you in, I'll read you a sleepy-bye story, and you just lay there," his father's broken jaw wagged to the left and right as he spoke. "My little little man."

His father, using a hand that had been broken in twelve places, right at the moment of impact of that long-ago accident, began reaching for the zipper of his pants. "Let's make you nice and comfortable, my little man," and Chuck felt himself falling asleep—in the dream, he was going to sleepy-bye, to sleepies, to slumberland, and now he was more terrified than he'd been of anything else that the dream had offered him.

And the shame.

The shame that had been there in childhood that he'd choked down came back. The shame that made him want to shut down and sleep and just make sleep protect him from everything bad.

Dreams protected him.

But not in this place, shu-gah.

He dreaded falling asleep with the mangled corpse of his father coming to him to "whisper a secret to you, just a little secret for my little man," his father's words slurred, and his jaw waggled and the leg that was completely turned around backward dragged as he moved toward Chuck. "My little man who keeps secrets with his daddy."

4

Mindy Shackleford opened her eyes.

Chuck lay snoozing on top of her, as he sometimes did, even in the middle of making love.

He was problematic that way for her.

You fall in lust with a narcoleptic, you get used to it.

She shoved him away, sat up on her daughter's bed, and drew a cigarette from the pack in Chuck's shirt that hung on the chair by the bed.

Lit it up, took a few puffs, then glanced back at him.

Because she knew about his narcolepsy, she didn't want to wake him, but she hated him just lying there. Better that he sleep through it.

But a glance at the clock told her that she couldn't let him sleep much longer.

Particularly since her daughter Judy might be home in another hour, after staying late after school with the debate team. She wasn't sure when her eldest boy would be home, and she was fairly sure her youngest—who was fifteen—wouldn't be wandering in until after football practice ended.

But she never knew their exact schedules, and she hated taking the risk, particularly once the sex was over.

"Come on, Chuck," she said, tapping him lightly on the back of his head. "Hit the showers."

But forty minutes later, Chuck Waller still remained asleep on her daughter's bed. Mindy became too nervous to just let him stay there and sleep, so she began shaking him. "Come on, Chuck. You've got to wake up." Her voice was soft and sweet at first, but when she returned from a quick shower and had dressed in her slacks and sweater and was ready to go out and see her friends for drinks, she was pissed. She began yelling at him and slapping his face to try to wake him.

Finally he opened his eyes.

"It's about time," she said. "Get your clothes on and just get out, hon. Judy'll be home any minute and who knows what Pete's gonna do."

Chuck Waller looked up at her, and for just a second she felt as if it were not him at all.

"Hey there, shu-gah," Chuck said as he sat up on the bed.

Hell, Mindy thought. *Doesn't even sound like him.* "You makin' fun of the way I talk?" she asked, teasing a little, annoyed a little. "Back where I'm from, we don't take to Yankee ways."

"Come over here a second, okay, shu-gah?" Chuck said, patting his knee.

"You okay?" she asked. He'd told her more than once that if he zonked out to just let him sleep, but she hadn't assumed he'd be so . . . well, cold. That's what she felt from him. Something almost reptilian in it—as if he were not the warm, fun-loving Chuck she'd known the day he'd come over to work on the kitchen cabinets, the Chuck who had let her touch him while he was working, the Chuck who had taken her in his arms and told her that if she wanted him to, he could be there for her whenever she needed.

"Just come over here a sec, shu-gah honeylamb chile," Chuck said, a grin breaking across his face. He tapped his knee lightly. "Come on, I got something to show you. Maybe you can bust up a chivarobe for me."

"Chuck? A *chivarobe?*" The only time she'd heard the term "chivarobe" had been as a little girl, or when she saw the movie of *To Kill a Mockingbird*.

"Yeah, honey chile," he said. She hated the racist overtone of his voice. He was definitely making fun of her being Southern. He was adding a racist edge to it with his minstrel show accent. *The jerk.*

"Chuck? Stop it. What's this about?"

"Come on, my baby, come on my honey, come on my ragtime gal, it won't hurt," he said. "It's a secret. Only you and me will know what it is." Again, he patted his knee. "Pretty please with shu-gah on top?" he asked. "With co-coa buttah and mmm-mint jellaay and cah-reem cheese and grits and ham biscuits and pig's knuckles spread all over it?"

"You're being . . . silly. Chuck?"

"Just a sit down here with me, my little honey chile," Chuck said, and when she stepped away instead of com-ing toward him, he got up and began moving toward her in a funny way—as if he were shambling along, as if one of his legs was hurt. His jaw seemed to drop. "You woke me up, little shu-gah cube," Chuck said. "And now ah need to make y'all go sleepies so that weezuns can be all comfy-cozy and get tucked in good, tucked all tight and good, tucked really deep and warm. Shu-gah honey pie lamb."

Mindy Shackleford had never screamed before—never in her life. Well, perhaps when she'd given birth, but she'd never screamed from fear or as an alarm to others. But now she heard a scream, and surprise of surprises, it came from deep within her, rising up her throat into her mouth. Although it sounded distant to her, it was right there, com-ing from her, as she watched Chuck shambling toward her.

She stepped back toward the door, but something about Chuck's eyes didn't frighten her. She saw that warm lost lit-tle boy look in them, the same look she'd seen when he'd confessed what had happened with his father so many years before, and the mother instinct—that same instinct that might drive a woman to hell and back for her own flesh and blood—compelled her to move forward instead of back, to go hold this broken and sad and frightened lit-tle boy that she saw inside the thirty-year-old man.

She wrapped her arms around him, whispering, "It's okay. It's a dream you came out of, Chuck. That's all, it's just a terrible dream." She felt his fingers digging into her sides as if . . . as if he were trying to cut her open with his bare hands.

"Y'all's fuck play-ee-ice is awl wohen ow-et, shu-gah," he said.

5

Lizzie crawled into bed, feeling a little feverish. Her mother called out for her, but she was too sleepy to respond. "Bert's here, working on the plumbing!" her mother called down to her, but Lizzie was so tired the words made no sense to her.

She stared at the ceiling of her bedroom, trying to imagine emerald islands and diamond skies, images that helped her drift into a dream, but instead, she closed her eyes and she was out like a light.

Even when she felt the man's breath on her face, she remained in darkness.

Yet she felt him.

6

In the darkness behind her eyes, in what might have been sleep or might have been another reality that Lizzie visited too often when she felt sleepy, the man she had come to think of as the Nightwatchman took her by the hand and led her along the dark corridor.

The windows were boarded up, but cracks of light broke through at the edges, leaving a thin blue-white outline of a window.

She passed by room after room. Many of the doors were closed, but some were open.

She only had a moment to glance in one, and there was the man from town who ran the florist shop—a man old enough to be her grandfather, she thought—and he was down on his knees in front of Andy Harris, who sat naked in a large velvet chair, his arms lazily up behind his head, the whites of his eyes showing as the old florist spread Andy's legs apart, and then glanced back at Lizzie.

The old man winked at her, and she saw his chin ran with blood that soaked his shirt.

Andy's entire groin area was bloodied.

Behind Andy, Bari Love lay on a bed, her legs wrapped around a Doberman pinscher's thighs. Bari opened her mouth as if to scream, but instead she began barking like a little yappy dog.

And still, the man who tugged at her hand in the darkness, took her along the corridor, past other rooms.

7

Bert White leaned over the sleeping girl.

Elizabeth Pond.

So sweet.

She wasn't quite as intriguing as her sister, but this one would do. She slept through anything. He could kiss her lips, and she would barely wake up in the middle of it. She was that deep a sleeper, and since the beginning of summer, she'd taken nap after nap as if she couldn't get enough sleep.

Or maybe she's faking. Maybe she wants you to touch her, he thought. *Maybe she's just lying there with her eyes closed, too afraid to tell you how much she wants you to tear her clothes from her, to kiss her in every place she has, to taste the salt of her sweat running down the small of her back.*

This was the first he'd gone beyond just tapping her

105

lightly when he found her asleep. He felt an exquisite shiver as his lips brushed against hers.

Her breath was sweet and a little sour, and he longed to part her lips with his tongue, but he was too scared to do it.

If you do it, she might welcome your tongue. She might invite you into her. She might show you how much she appreciates you.

Being the local Peeping Tom had been no picnic for Bert, but the Ponds had presented him with a unique opportunity to go beyond staring through bedroom windows while he "played his fiddle" as his grandmother had called it when she'd caught him as a boy fiddling outside his cousin's bedroom window. *I'm gonna whip you so bad your fiddling days are through,* she'd said. But all the beatings he'd received made him want to fiddle more and more.

Until he'd reached this—the pinnacle.

Actually kissing a real live girl.

A real live sleeping girl.

Like a prince in a fairy tale, he thought. *Every girl dreams of a prince kissing her while she's asleep. Awakening her. Every girl.*

He sniffed around the girl's face. *Such aromatic loveliness—some cheap teen girl perfume, so simple and light and fruity.*

He watched her, his face so close that she was practically out of focus.

This is my dream come true. This is what I want. I want her like this. Sleeping. Unaware. I want her to not know what I might do to her.

Suddenly, the girl's eyes opened.

She reached up and grabbed him swiftly behind his head, holding him there with great strength while he tried to pull away. She brought his face closer to hers, and then moved her lips to his ear. He tried to shake her off, but she had a grip that overpowered him far too easily.

She whispered, her voice nearly like a four-year-old's, "Are you the Nightwatchman?"

Chapter Six

1

"Are you?" Lizzie Pond asked the man who stood before her. She wasn't in her bedroom at all. She was at the foot of a staircase up through what seemed to be a tower of some kind. The place stank like a swamp, and the man who stood there wore the kind of waistcoat she would've thought someone in Victorian times might have worn. His gray hair was badly parted near the middle, high on his forehead, and he had a fishy look to his eyes and mouth. He checked his gold pocket watch.

"Oh, my ears and whiskers," the man said. "I'm late."

Then he looked at her. "The Nightwatchman? I have a watch," he said, holding the pocket watch up to her as if for inspection. She noticed that the glass face of it was cracked. "But I am no watch-*man*. No, my dear. Hardly. If anything, I'm more of the watch-*maker*. My question is, what are you doing on the other side of the mirror?"

"I'm dreaming," Lizzie whispered, almost afraid to admit it. "This is the other side?"

"You go through a looking-glass and you come out here," he said. "I would've thought you'd have a room assignment. You've been a guest here before, haven't you?"

Lizzie shook her head, and looked up the staircase because she thought she heard a noise from above.

"Yes, I remember your face," the man said. "It was in June I think."

"No," Lizzie insisted. "I've never been here."

"Well, perhaps you weren't. But that would be very odd, because you're here now and the only reason you might be here right now is because you once were a guest. You can't be a guest if you've never been invited." He glanced down her body. "Do you always walk around like that?"

She looked down at herself. She was almost completely naked except for her panties. Yet because she felt that this was a dream, she didn't need to fear it. It seemed ordinary to some extent.

"Who are you?" she asked too softly. Then, "Who *are* you?"

"One of many," the man said. "But you're here for the child, I suspect. Everyone seems to know about him."

"I don't know any child."

"The boy. The one who's caused all this uproar here. The rooms are filling up fast, too fast. The door's closed to everyone, so once the rooms get too full, all kinds of bad things will start. It always leaks out if the rooms get too full. And then more come in."

"I'm sorry," she said. "I don't know what you mean."

"It's like a vacuum. Once you turn it on, it just sucks, doesn't it? It sucks and sucks and sucks and until someone kicks out the cord or shuts off the electricity, that vacuum will keep sucking." He shot her a knowing glance. "You still believe you're dreaming. You think that you're in your bed right now at home. But you're not. Since that night, you've always stayed here. You're forgetting too easily. Or you're blocking the dreams, Elizabeth. We've met here before, and you accompanied me upstairs each time."

She looked up the stairs. "Where do they go?"

"Up," he said.

He offered her his hand. "I won't bite."

She stepped over to him, and he clasped her fingers in his. When she saw his face again, he resembled her father, and the waistcoat and jacket were gone. Instead it was her father in the sweater and slacks he'd worn when he had the car wreck, his head still steaming from the fire, his face a mass of intersecting burns and wounds, but his eyes still gleaming with fatherly love.

"Daddy?" she asked, tears running down her face.

He squeezed her hand again. "We're going to have to do some butcher work. We have a piggy that needs to go."

"What?"

"It's in pain. You've got to put animals out of their misery, honey," her father said. "Come on, I'll show you. I'll take you up to the killing floor."

He let go of her hand. She stepped ahead of him and began walking up to the tower. *It's only a dream,* she thought. *It can't hurt me.*

2

A slight shivering of her vision seemed to overlay another face across his. The guy named Bert White who lived upstairs. The guy who always gave her the creeps whenever he did any of his handyman work around her home.

Bert's mouth seemed to open and close slowly, like a fish dying for air.

3

Bert White had tried to draw back from Lizzie as she rose from her bed, grabbing him so tightly around the waist that he could barely breathe. She sniffed like a dog around his face and neck, and it terrified and thrilled him at the same time as he felt his arousal—his fiddle—pressing against her lithe young body.

The pleasure warmth that arose at these times made him confused because she had begun to hurt him with her strength.

"What I'm going to do to you," Lizzie whispered, "well, it's a marvel, my love. It's a marvel of human engineering."

"Please," he whispered, feeling terrible pain and even worse pleasure as she held him.

"First, I'm going to incapacitate you. You'll pass out. While you're asleep, I will sever your vocal cords so no one can hear you, should you wake during the procedure."

The effect on him of her voice, a low guttural growl that sounded so little like the teenage girl and so much like a man, strangely did not diminish that pleasure that shot up and down his spine. It was as if he'd wanted this his whole life. His entire life, the fear of those he watched had given him pleasure.

But now, to be held, and told what would happen, it brought him nearly to a climax.

"Then I'm going to take a small sharp blade. Perhaps my mother's apple paring knife. And I'm going to make a series of twelve incisions along your body. I will pull your bones from your flesh, and you will be alive for as long as you can stand it," she whispered, and as she said the last word to him he felt her grip about his chest tightening and he began to black out.

4

Lizzie's mother Margie had just put a frozen dinner into the microwave when Lizzie came up from downstairs. "You looked tired, dear."

Lizzie smiled slightly, and then went past her mother to

the sink. Flatware soaked in a pan, and she rooted around in it for a small knife. She turned around and her mother said, "Just you and me tonight, dear. I figured we'd have those enchiladas I got at the grocery store. They're so good. You know, you think frozen food isn't very good, and then you find something like these enchiladas, and you think, why even cook when the microwaveable stuff is so good?"

Margie glanced between the microwave and Lizzie, and then looked out the window because it looked like the little Marshall boy was about to skateboard right into a truck that was barreling up the road. "Good Lord," she said, but as she watched, the boy and the car missed each other. The boy skateboarded down the street, and the truck swerved around the corner of Forsythia Avenue. She sighed a little and then checked the microwave again. "Two more minutes." Turned back to face her daughter, who had come closer. "You look a little flu-ish," Margie said, reaching over to put her hand on Lizzie's forehead. "Hmm. You don't feel feverish."

But Margie didn't mention what she did feel on her daughter's skin—a kind of slimy sweat that reminded her a little too much of fish skin.

Margie glanced at the knife in her daughter's hands. Then back to her daughter's face.

Lizzie also looked down at the knife in her hand, then at her mother. She started laughing and feeling a little nervous. Her mother began laughing, too.

"What's so funny?" her mother asked as she came down from the high of laughter.

"Oh, you," Lizzie grinned. "You were looking at me as if I were going to attack you or something."

"I know," her mother chortled. "I know. You looked like something out of *Psycho*. Just for a second. You know that scene? The one in the shower. When he parts the curtains."

Margie mimed stabbing her daughter as if she also had a knife in her hand.

"Oh, Mom," Lizzie laughed. "You have to stop watching those scary movies."

"I know, I know." Her mother grinned, turning back to the microwave to turn it off before the enchiladas over-cooked. "But you know I would've never gotten pregnant with you and Ronnie if your father hadn't taken me to a midnight show of—what was it—*Hellraiser*? Or *Hellraiser 2*. Well, I don't remember exactly. Your father and I weren't quite watching the movie. You looking for something?"

Lizzie squatted down by the sink and opened the cabinet doors. When she found the liquid bleach, she drew it out.

"Doing laundry, dear?" Margie asked.

Lizzie got back up, knife and bleach in hand. She set the knife down on the counter, and undid the lid of the bleach bottle. She sniffed it a little. "Can bleach go bad, Mom?"

Margie made a face. "I don't think so. I wasn't exactly a chemistry major, though."

"Here," Lizzie said. "Sniff. It smells funny."

"I'm sure it's fine," Margie said, opening the little door to the microwave. The spicy scent of enchiladas filled the air. "Target has some of the best frozen food," she said as if to no one. "You know, your sister loves these enchiladas. I should save her some for later."

"Come on," Lizzie said, bringing the bottle to her mother's face as Margie turned about again, holding the tray of food, the plastic cover still over it. A light steam rose up from the tray.

"Lizzie," Margie said, exasperation in her voice. "If that bleach isn't good enough for your gym socks, I'm sure there's another bottle down in the laundry room."

"I just want to make sure."

"Oh. All right." Margie leaned forward slightly, closed her eyes and sniffed at the bleach.

It smelled fine. Strong, but fine.

"Good grief," Margie said, as she opened her eyes, but as she did so she saw something that made no sense to her.

A fist coming for her face.

Lizzie slammed her fist into her mother's jaw.

5

Margie reeled backward.

Lizzie leapt upon her and brought her down to the linoleum floor. Lizzie had her pinned by the shoulders, and reached back for the bottle of bleach.

"Lizzie!" Margie cried out, but her voice was soon choked by the bleach gurgling down her throat as Lizzie pinched her mother's nose with her fingers and Margie felt burning in her throat and lungs.

"Get you clean inside and out," Lizzie said, and waited until her mother swallowed all of it.

6

Bert White awoke a minute or two after he'd blacked out, and he had to lay on the bed and catch his breath for another few minutes before he could sit up. He had a vague sense that he should get the hell out of that bedroom, but he also felt too disoriented to put the thought into action. He looked up at the ceiling. Then over at the window. At the bookshelf with its neat rows of books and photo albums and yearbooks.

His eyes went in and out of focus as he took a few deep breaths. His lungs actually hurt—and he wondered if some bones had been crushed. *What is she? A fuckin' bear? Jesus H, what the hell kind of bitch is she?*

Finally he sat up. The pain in his back and side was intense, and he had to hold his left side with both his hands, feeling around for the origin of the pain.

He heard a noise beyond the open door, and he

glanced into the hall. Besides her sister's bedroom, there was a small room with the washer and dryer in it, as well as a sink. On the floor were stacks of dirty clothes.

Lizzie was there, and she had her mother slung over her back. Her mother was moaning, and it wasn't the kind of moan that made Bert feel any safer.

Lizzie switched on the laundry room light, and dropped her mother onto the pile of the clothes.

Then she glanced over at him.

She pointed her finger at him.

You.

He saw the knife in her hand.

Adrenaline shot through him, and he pushed himself up from the bed, but immediately fell to the floor in pain. He cried out, "For the love of God! SOMEBODY HELP ME! HELP!" He kicked his legs out as she walked over to him. "GET THE FUCK AWAY FROM ME, PSYCHO BITCH! GET THE FUCK AWAY!"

She got down on her knees, and combed her fingers through his hair. "It's okay. It's okay. Don't worry."

She brought the knife up and showed it to him. His eyes went wide, and he whispered, "Please don't hurt me. Please. I can get you help. I can get you whatever you want. Whatever you need."

7

Lizzie Pond brought the knife just beneath his chin and made a quick incision to his throat. He grabbed her by the wrist, but that just made it worse as she cut into him, tearing at his Adam's apple and the surrounding area until she'd cleaned it all out.

And then she went to make the other incisions on his body so that she could pull the bones out from the meat of his flesh.

In another place in her mind, she and her father were in

the killing room, and there was a big piggy lying there.

"We have to debone this one completely," her father said.

"Won't it hurt him?" she asked.

"Ah," her father said. "Piggies like to get slaughtered."

He passed her a knife and she approached the piggy with it. "You pull the bones out, one by one," her father told her.

As Lizzie did it, cutting messily into the piggy, he guided her hand in finding all the sweet spots.

8

After she was all done, Lizzie dragged the piggy's bones and set them all in a pile near the skin and the meat.

"Time to clean up," her father told her, although he wasn't there with her anymore. Just in her head.

She stepped out into the hallway, taking off her clothes as she went. Completely naked, she walked upstairs to the bathroom. Went in, turned on the shower, glanced at herself in the mirror.

Red girl, she thought. *Red girl with the pretty eyes. Hello.*

Then, she pulled back the shower curtain, and got under the hot spray of water and washed the filth of the meat off her body and listened to what the voices were telling her.

Chapter Seven

1

The dog pound wasn't in the village precisely, but out in the unincorporated area near the dump. It consisted of a U-shaped, one-story cinder block mess, with a fenced in courtyard behind it. The dogcatcher, who also operated the bulldozer out on the dump piles, was a guy of sixty-two named Benny Marais. He had just gotten a call from a woman who claimed she'd be in to get the litter of kittens that had been found up at the old Harrow property two weeks before. "I'll take good care of them," the woman said. "My last three cats died this past year. I could use some kittens."

But she hadn't come to get them, and it was time to put them down. "I don't operate a damn cat charity," Benny said to his assistant, Dory Crampton. "I'm sorry for the kitties, and it's a damn shame, but there's not much to be done."

He went out to gather the four little kittens in the cages

117

off the main office, but when he got there, all the cages were open and the animals gone.

"What the hell?" he said, and then checked the chain-link runs in the courtyard—they too were empty.

Some delinquent had opened all the cages sometime during the day. "Dory!" he called to the back.

Moments later, a chunky, disheveled seventeen-year-old girl, her hair cut moppet short, her overhauls slung a bit low, with a baggy white T-shirt covering most of her frame, came out from the employee bathroom, a cigarette hanging out of her mouth. "Yeah?"

"You know anything about this?"

Dory Crampton glanced around at the dog runs. "Wow."

Benny glanced back into the dump dunes that rose and fell behind the pound. Not a sign of the animals.

"The great escape," Dory said. Her cigarette toggled up and down as if she were laughing a little.

"What you just say?"

She drew the cig from her lips. "I just can't believe they let themselves out. Must be some nut somewhere."

Benny felt his blood pressure shoot up. It had happened at least once before—a group of kids or idiots had let the animals out once, and he wasn't sure but that Dory had something to do with it. "Well," he said and went to bum a cigarette off her. "I guess we gotta get the truck and go round 'em up."

Dory put her hands on her hips and gave him the look he considered a little too insolent. "I didn't have nothin' to do with this, Mr. Marais. I can practically read your mind."

She drew her pack of Camels out, and offered him one. As she lit his cigarette, she said in that flat almost country way she had, "Them dogs done gone for good, you ask me. I think half of 'em knew their time was just about up." She looked at his face and squinted, cocking her head to the side as if trying to make out something. "That a mole on your face?" she asked, and then reached over to touch the protruding bump on Benny's cheek, near his left ear. "Oh, hell," she said, grinning. "It's a tick."

Benny swatted at her hand, and cursed and stomped a little as he plucked the offending bug from where it had nearly taken root in his skin. He held it between his thumb and forefinger, and grabbed Dory's lighter, flicked it up, sparked a little flame, and pressed it onto the round fat slightly bloated tick. "Goddamn dogs!" he shouted as he dropped the burning tick down on the pavement, and then stepped down hard on it to rub it out of existence.

2

Jack Templeton knew he had only a day or two left.

It was either today or wait 'til the spring, and even that might not be 'til May, and with the way the damn thing cracked on him the previous year, it might be half the summer before it got fixed and filled.

He took a sip of his Johnny Walker Red. Practically a ritual after a good work day. After the commute. After the train and the walk home and the feeling that the tie around his neck was a dead animal.

Just a sip of Scotch, and then the tie came off, the jacket, and the starched white shirt.

And it was on to paradise: the pool. He loved his swimming pool. He had worked his whole life so he could afford a place and put in a lap pool so he wouldn't have to drive an hour to a gym. So he could have it right there, all to himself.

But it was getting too cold. Some years, he had to close it down earlier—by mid-September. The weather had been fairly moderate for the fall, and even now, in October, it hadn't quite gotten so chilly that he couldn't stand getting in.

He stripped off his work clothes on the back patio, and got in naked. The fence in back gave him privacy. He loved being naked in his backyard and just swinging around free and easy. It was like paradise sometimes, and once winter had come on full force he wouldn't get a chance to do it again until late April, and only then if the ice had melted.

He needed that pool. It gave him solace from the world. It made him forget bad things and the people he had to screw over continually just to keep his business running.

Oh, that pool, it was the pool of his dreams and every time he got in, the temperature was perfect—so close to body temperature that it was like not being in water at all, but on a current of air as he did his fifty daily laps with some sadness, knowing that he'd have to cover the pool over for winter and drive to Poughkeepsie three days a week just to get some swimming in.

He leaned over the edge of the pool, slipping his legs in. A big smile spread across his face. Then he slid down, all the way in, and stood up so that the water came just above his navel. He set his swimming goggles in place, then dipped beneath the water. The pool was always such a relief that he often began dreaming as soon as he was submerged—he'd fantasize about traveling around the world, about beautiful women with enormous breasts, about swimming in the ocean or one of the Great Lakes—an endless beautiful swim.

But as he went under and pushed himself off from the back wall of the lap pool, he felt as if he were not alone in the pool.

As if there were others there. It was an irrational, stupid feeling, so he tried to shrug it off. He began his crawl, his head cocked to one side and then, after a stroke or so, the other.

But he still had that feeling. Not that there were people around the pool. But that beneath him, in that warm water, there were others, and that the pool was not a fairly shallow lap pool, but was instead a deep lake, and he was nearly sure that if he touched down for a second that his toes would graze reeds and water grasses.

And again, that feeling that there were others there, swimming beneath him. Creatures that were nearly human.

Nice imagination, Jack, he thought. *Some beautiful mermaid underwater touching you all over.*

It was as if someone were touching his thighs and the tips of his toes. And then, he felt that tingling in his penis that just made him feel stronger than strong whenever it happened. Despite his self-professed good looks and winning ways, Jack didn't get laid much anymore. He lived for that tingle. The tingle was everything to him on some lonely, horny evenings of porn DVDs and Pete's Wicked Ale. Some nights he couldn't even get himself excited watching the gorgeous and lascivious women of porn do unto others as they had done unto themselves. His God-given right to pop a boner had begun to diminish, and he wondered if he just needed some new sexual thrill to get it back—or if it was just the way things went when you lived alone and didn't make friends with women very easily.

But in the pool, that potent feeling came on strong, and he was happy he'd resisted slipping into his Speedos in favor of complete balls-out naked.

Ah, it was like a warm tongue down there.

The water.

The way it moved against him.

He could nearly imagine a long-haired beauty tasting him.

Yet he knew he was just imagining it, so he tried to focus on his breathing and his form. Roll and stretch, reach, stretch, kick. In seconds, he was able to put aside the notion that there were others swimming beneath him in some underwater deep.

Yet he still felt like the Rock of Gibraltar where it counted.

As he came up to the end of his first lap, tilting his head to the side to breathe, something thick and hairy touched his lips.

Startled, he stopped and stood up, drawing his swimming goggles from his face.

A dead rat floated near him.

And then he saw several of them, all at one end of the pool—and not just four or five. He counted nearly twenty dead rats floating around him at the far end of the lap pool.

Disgusted, and nearly on the edge of being sick, he got out of the pool fast, and stood there wondering whether to call the animal control center, or go next door where the teenager lived who kept a python as a pet—and fed it rats—and kick his ass all the way to the pool and make him clean it up.

Normally Jack Templeton wasn't a violent guy, and maybe it was because he'd had two sips of Scotch instead of one; or maybe it was because he'd been warned by the vice-president of his department that he needed to clean up his act at the office; or maybe it was because that pool was his holy place and some stupid teenage boy who was dumb enough to keep an enormous snake in his home—with stupid parents, to boot—had allowed an invasion.

Or maybe it was something else. Even Jack had felt the change when he'd first gotten into the water. It was as if the water had gotten into him. As if his ears got a little waterlogged and his mouth had taken some of it in.

But anger didn't cover what he was feeling.

He felt an enormous rage, and given how he usually never got angry, even he was amazed by what he felt as he went through the back gate to the neighbor's house.

The garage door was up, and he went around to it. The kid was there—a dumpy and sloppy kid with a black

122

T-shirt and hair that was too long for his round face and a little smelly because he must not wash much. Jack snarled, "Miss any rats lately?"

And then, Jack felt an impulse within him. It was almost as if he had not even come up from the pool, but was still underwater, and he was fighting for breath as he stood there in front of the teen.

The impulse was to kill the kid.

It was more than impulse, actually.

It was compulsion.

He raised his fist and brought it down on the top of the kid's head before the kid even knew what was coming.

Jack Templeton, naked and more erect than he'd ever felt in his life, began slamming his clenched fists into the kid every which way, and when the sloppy kid fell to the floor, covering his face with his hands, Jack began kicking him and only stopped when he saw the really beautiful woman lying in the big terrarium at the back of the garage.

He knew it was insane that a woman so beautiful could even fit into that terrarium, and he knew on some level that still remained rational within him that this might in fact be the big python that the sloppy kid raised and fed rats to, but Jack couldn't shake the image: She was there, circling around a long stick. Her breasts peach-colored and plump, her hips small but perfect as she arched her back toward him, and though there was the trace of a slithery snaky tongue coming from between her bee-stung red lips, it didn't bother him one bit.

He knew that she was there, waiting for him.

He knew that he would rescue her from this enormous terrarium, and they would make love like no man and no woman had ever made love before in all creation.

He would be Adam to her Eve, and if somewhere in there he felt the stirrings of a serpent, he'd accept whatever fate awaited him. His penis was his king now, and the garage itself seemed to fade away around him as he felt

Douglas Clegg

that he was in an enormous bedchamber, and the naked beauty lay there on the covers, her fingers lazily moving toward her epicenter with an effortless motion.

He went to her, and lifted the lid of the cage. She embraced him even while he embraced her.

3

Sam Pratt looked up from the garage floor, feeling weak and sick from being beaten up, and watched as the naked guy who lived next door began wrapping Sam's pet python all along his body and kissing it over and over again on the lips.

It looked like the guy was humping his snake.

4

The beautiful pale woman pressed her lips against Jack Templeton's mouth, and parted them using the longest tongue he'd ever felt in a chick. It got him so hard he felt he wouldn't be able to control himself.

Then she seemed to reach down to cup his balls in her hand and then squeeze them, at first lightly, and then so hard it nearly hurt. It got him all the more excited, and he played with her breasts and felt down her body to draw her legs apart, only her torso seemed to go on forever.

As he looked down at her, he saw that she was, after all, a mermaid, just as he had imagined there were mermaids in the world, and somehow she was able to stand on dry land as they embraced.

She started kissing him so deeply again that he felt it was like she had put her mouth completely within his, and her tongue extended farther down his throat, into his esophagus. Though he could barely breathe, he let the passion take him over, and they both fell to the cold garage floor, entwined about one another.

She tightened her grip on his balls and he felt that sexual pressure mounting within him—

And he knew at any moment—

Any moment—

It was building—

He was going to let it go.

He would break free and give her his great gift of seed.

He held his breath, waiting for the moment.

Waiting.

Holding.

And then Jack Templeton passed out, unable to breathe, the pain at his mouth and neck and balls too much to take.

Something between his legs burst like a tick, and he was afraid to look down and see what the beautiful mermaid had done to him.

Chapter Eight

1

From *The Gospel According to Luke, Being the Private Diary of Me So You Better Not Open This If You Know What's What:*

Certainly, when I came back to Watch Point at the age of twenty-six, it seemed the same place I had last seen at fifteen while visiting my aunt Danni. I had only one piece of luggage, an old American Tourister suitcase that had been my dad's, and it was mainly filled with enough clothes to get me through three days before doing laundry. Also, tucked into it was my laptop, so that I could write the Great American Novel while not preparing lesson plans for my work as the new eleventh- and twelfth-grade English teacher at a high school one town over from Watch Point, New York.

Rewinding a little: more about me. I was born in the hills of North Carolina, and as a result, was sure I'd become the next Thomas Wolfe, as if one wasn't enough.

But we'd hopscotched the US of A for too many years for me to call one state my home—I was just happy to keep it generally to one continent. I began to think I'd be Jack Kerouac by the time I was in high school, and after that, I just wanted to write something, though I'd never actually written a word outside of school assignments. We'd moved too much for me to find a place to write. My father being always between jobs and halfway to getting a new one— and the same went for wives. My mother had left him when I was three (did I tell you they were hippies?), and Dad took my brother and me all over. We lived in Brooklyn; then he and his new girlfriend woke me up to tell us we were moving to Mexico. Sometime after that we moved to Oregon, where I had to live in a cult-like ashram. One night I fell asleep in Taos, New Mexico, and the next day I woke up in a horse trailer in Montana. My brother's life and mine was not owned by either of us; we moved where Dad and his various girlfriends and wives moved. My aunt Danni was my only real stability. She had money, as they say, and lived a quiet life in Watch Point, all the while endowing the arts up and down the Hudson Valley. She was a "dyke," as my dad put it, but you'd never know by the insane stereotype made up by people about lesbians. She reminded me of Emily Dickinson— scribbling poetry, drinking orange pekoe tea, taking care of my grandfather while he suffered through illnesses of old age.

She was the most wonderful woman I had ever met as a boy, and I was relieved when my father would send my little brother Cody and me to stay with her for a summer or a holiday. At first, she kept her girlfriend a big fat secret, un- til finally I just told her that I wanted to meet "this Cynthia," and soon enough Cynthia Marchakis was produced—a sleek, handsome half-Greek half-WASP goddess of six foot one with silky dark hair and lips as juicy and thick and red as filet mignon, extra-rare. Cody and I were in awe of both of them—the bookish aunt who bird-watched and got us both out in the yard to identify the finches as accurately as possible; and that goddess whose kiss on our cheeks seemed to bestow a thrill as enormous as a roller-coaster ride. My grandfather died by my eleventh birthday, and then I didn't see Aunt Danni or Aunt Cynthia much. My father married what he called a good woman, and he cut his hair and stopped drinking. He and his fifth wife settled in Stoughton, Wisconsin, where we ate cheese and skated on silver, frozen ponds. Somewhere in all that, I managed to get a trip to Aunt Danni's when I was fifteen.

And that is when she told me the truth about all things related to the Smithsons, which was our family name. "Insanity," she said. "Depression. Two suicides on two branches. Fallen branches all over the damn lawn. Too many failed artists. No one with discernible talent." She listed all the failings of her own generation, including hers and even Cynthia's. Then she started in on my father's foolishnesses, and I managed to stop her since it was like reliving a very bad stomach ache on my part.

"But you're not like that," I insisted. "You live here. You have a beautiful house. Cynthia is wonderful. You're the only couple I know that's lasted this long. None of dad's friends have stayed married for more than a few years at a time. And now that dad has this good woman, maybe he'll stay married, but maybe he'll meet a middle-aged Swedish-descent waitress at the Stoughton Pancake House and that'll be it for the good woman and him."

"I've done some bad things in my life," she said.

"Like?"

"I mean being bad," she said. "There's a streak in our family tree that just doesn't work right."

"Why are you depressed?" I asked.

"I guess . . . I guess I miss my dad," she said.

I went over to my aunt Danni and wrapped my arms around her and told her that no matter what, I loved her, and she was not bad, and that if I could I would live with her all the time.

And I tried to—I spent that summer with her and got to know the village of Watch Point better than I ever had before. I didn't think I'd be coming back after that summer, though. I was wrong about my dad—he stayed in Stoughton, working at a local bank, and the good woman worked at the hospital in town. Cody loved her, although I never grew that attached. Instead, I wrote letter after letter to Aunt Danni, and ran to the post office, waiting to get her letters in return.

She died in a normal, everyday accident by the time I was entering college. The funeral was so fast, during my orientation week at school, that I didn't hear about any of it until after my first day of classes. I wept; I hid from the other students at college for the first few weeks, and skipped so many classes that I ended up with bad grades.

I wrote letters to Cynthia, but never heard back from her. My father told me when I asked him, "Danielle's in a better place, Luke. Think of it that way."

The good woman told me, "She's not in heaven, I know that much."

So when I saw an ad posted on the bulletin board of the craptacular little high school I got stuck teaching at in Riverview, New Jersey, the little notice about a position up at a town called Parham, not far from Poughkeepsie, I thought I would finally have a reason to be in Watch Point again.

A reason to see that village again that I had loved as a boy and remember the aunt who had been my rock during all those turbulent years.

When I got off the train the day I arrived, I walked straight up the sloping hill and took the first left, then the next right, then another right, all the while clutching the too-heavy suitcase, and wishing I'd just called for a cab at the train station.

But walking down Hibiscus Lane, I came upon the low white fence, overflowing with roses of all hues, and the slate path up to the two-bedroom house where my aunt Danni had lived her life—the belle of Watch Point—and where now her partner Cynthia waited for me.

She came to the door smelling of lavender and gin. She had lost much of her sensual allure—or what I had remembered of it when I had been a boy—and she had put on too many pounds for me to pretend that it was a temporary change of shape. Yet the goddess still shone through Cynthia Marchakis, and the lips were still big fat juicy steaks. "You got so tall! I bet you wow all the girls now. You were sort of scrawny before, but you filled out. You look like you turned out good." She laughed, her voice like a Long Island foghorn. Cigarettes had done a number on her vocal cords, and as she puffed away, offering me a drink from the largest display of liquor I'd seen on a kitchen counter since my college graduation party, she regaled me with stories about Danni and my grandfather and my dad and my other aunt (Francesca, who didn't talk to my father, my brother, or me because of a long-ago rift that was never spoken of among the family). We settled on the old spring-loaded couch, and as I took my third sip of a cooling gin and tonic, I said, "Have you met anybody yet?"

It came out of my mouth too easily and too innocently for her to take offense, and she grinned and puffed and said, "Why? Why? I've met a lot of people in life. I don't need to meet any more people from now 'til the day I die."

"I really appreciate your putting me up like this," I said.

"It's your house," she said. "Well, your grandpa's."

"It's yours now."

"Yeah, well, maybe I'll just give it to you. I wouldn't mind a change of scene."

After another drink between us, we were laughing about old times and talking about Cody (who was in the military and overseas, so we were worried for him and yet very proud of his decision, which reflected back to my rather ordinary cowardice and my father's unending anti-war sentiments). And then she dropped a bomb in my lap as we sat there: "There's something she wanted you to have. But I just couldn't send it to you. Not after she went. But it's important, and you should have it. You're old enough now."

Before I could ask what it was, she had leapt up and run into the kitchen, drawing open cabinets and drawers. I heard the metal clanks and clinks of forks and spoons as she searched for whatever she'd held back.

When she emerged from the kitchen, she had a piece of paper that had been folded into a square and seemed far older than six or seven years.

When I opened it, I knew immediately what it was.

A suicide note.

Dear Luke,

I love you. I hope we see each other again some-day. You were one of the great joys of my life. I hope you knew that. And I hope you know that what I'm do-ing today is not about my feelings for you or your brother (hi Cody! I love you, too.)

I talked to you once about all the bad things in our family. Unfortunately, I have at least one of those. No, not depression. Not insanity. Not even ordinary fucked-upedness. What I got is the Big C. And I'm go-ing. And I know I'm going. And Cynthia knows I'm go-ing. Your dad doesn't know, but I guess he will someday.

But I wanted you to know that I'm doing this not because I want to abandon you. I feel like you got abandoned a lot, even when you had a lot of family around. But if I could be here forever, just for you, I would. If I could turn to God and make a deal where He gives me another twenty-five years just so I could

131

be here for you when you came around, I would, believe me.

But I can't. And I'm going faster than fast. I'm not a coward at all. I just don't want the last month of my life in a hospital. You know me.

I don't like any of them. And I want this to be on my own terms. The doctors tell me (I've been to three) that there's a one-in-ten chance I'll lick this. But even when they tell me that, in their eyes they're really saying, "Yes, Danielle, you have a hope in hell, but only if you're one of the really lucky ones, and if you can feel that thing inside you growing, if you get those pains, you're not on the mainland with the rest of us. You're out on some strand, and the dark water's pouring in. And you're going to have to go to the outermost reach. You can't come back to the mainland."

And you know what, Luke? It's fine by me. I'm A-OK with it. Now Cynthia knows nothing about this, so don't blame her. Don't blame anyone but me. If you were in my shoes, I think you'd do what I'm doing, too. I'm not some big self-sacrificing martyr. I'm not a TV movie-of-the-week. I just am tired of this fight. I know where it's headed because I've worked as a nurse for twenty-five years, for God's sake. I've watched others go with exactly what I have. And I know how they go. And I refuse to do that to you or to Cynthia or to Cody or to your aunt Fran or your dad. I learned from taking care of Grandpa. When you're meant to go, you're meant to. When our old cat Wooster died, she went out in the woods and just lay down and waited for death to come. God, how I wish it were like that for me. Would that I were a cat!

But no, I have to overcomplicate things and buy a book on how to do this exactly right, and it's a big secret from Cynthia, although I'm guessing she'll know by the time you read this (Shh! Don't tell her, she's going to hate me enough as it is, but I can't stand to put her through what we're going to have to go through if I go to the hospital now.)

Okay, enough comedy. I love you, Luke. I want to see your face in heaven someday when you're an old man and you can tell me what your life was like, and we can have Grandpa over and play Parcheesi or Boggle. Just like we used to play in the attic, sometimes, when it was cool up there and Grandpa wanted to go through the old pictures and things. That to me would be heaven. It's where things go when everyone forgets the value of things. I think of it like our attic—when people are ready to die. When it's their time to only look back and not forward, they climb the stairs. They sit among the memories, and somehow, they're in a better place just sifting through the past. And then, they're somewhere else. They're beyond the attic.

That's how it's going to be. Please try to understand this. You've always thought beyond the normal idiocy of people, Luke. Don't fail me now. I chose life when I could. Now I have to choose to climb the stairs to the attic. To sit among the memories. And then to move beyond the attic of the past.

It hurts me to leave you more than you know. But I promise, I'll be one of the many friendly faces waiting for you when you get to the other side from here. I promise, if any promise in the universe could ever be made, I make that one and will keep it. And I can't wait (but don't rush over here. I want you to be about ninety years old or something. Okay?)

And don't put up with any crap from Cynthia. She is going to be pissed at me for years to come over this. If you get this note, don't drop out of college or anything, but plan on spending at least a summer with Cynthia. You can talk some sense into her, and you both have a lot of fun together.

Love you with all my heart and anything else that matters. Meet me in the next world, but only after you've had great-grandkids. Okay?

Danni

When I finished reading the note my aunt had written several years before, Cynthia said, "I was mad at first, but you can't stay mad at the dead too long. And I feel like she's here. Not like a ghost. But I just feel her with me sometimes."

I could barely see through the tears in my eyes. I set down the letter, folding it up again. I swiped at my eyes with the backs of my hands since I didn't have a tissue. "Why didn't you show this to me before?"

"Are you angry?"

"No," I said, but it was a lie. But what was the point of the truth? I couldn't take back the past few years that Cynthia had kept the note from me.

"I guess I was angry with her," Cynthia said, another puff on her endless cigarette. "I'm sorry."

"It's okay." Then, I had to ask. "How did she do it?"

Cynthia answered in a fairly off-the-cuff manner, as if she'd told the story a million times and now it was like saying that someone had gone to the store. "She went off by herself one day. She was supposed to be going in for another blood test. She just walked a little ways out of town, to a place nobody really goes. And then . . ."

"Like the cat," I said. "She went off by herself."

"Yep," Cynthia nodded. Took a sip of her drink. "Just like ol' Wooster. Went out to a lonely place and just gave it up. You know, once a couple of months had passed, I was a little afraid to show you the note. I was depressed. I was upset. Your aunt Fran came down on me like a ton of bricks. Tried to get me thrown out. Blamed me for everything, including your grandpa's death. She had lawyers figuring out how to shut down my bank accounts. It was pretty awful. And I just wanted to crawl into a hole and die. But finally, she called her dogs off. I think your dad got her to back down. By then, a year had gone by, and I was afraid to show you the letter. I was afraid you'd be angry. Everybody was angry with me for awhile. And I was still looking for that hole. The one to crawl in."

"I know. I understand. Can I ask one thing? What did she have?"

Cynthia placed her hand on her scalp. "Up here. Brain stuff. It was messing with her mind a little. Worse was, she knew how it would go. She said it was going to be bad. I guess now I don't blame her. But I did for a few years there."

"We were lucky to know her," I said.

"Yep," Cynthia said, finishing off her glass.

"I wish she hadn't killed herself," I said, suddenly, as if it had been on my mind for years and I could not shake the thought. "I wish she'd called me. I would've been there for her. I'd have come to the hospital and made it like a home."

Cynthia arched an eyebrow. "Luke, she didn't kill herself. She wanted to. That was her intention. She got out to this abandoned property and she just was about to set this thing in motion, but whatever was inside her got her. Right then. Nobody was around. She fell. She died. Her gun never went off."

I took a nap in the guestroom bed, a little drunk and a lot confused. When I woke up, feeling sweaty because Cynthia didn't like to turn on the air conditioner during the daytime, I had a headache to murder all other headaches. It was from a dream I'd had. And I wanted to write the dream down, so I pulled out my laptop and started writing, "The Nightwatchman looked into the hearts of the dreamers, and found their secrets."

It's because of Harrow. The house. They hired a night-watchman, and I saw him once. Briefly. In town. He was just getting into his car—an old dusty station wagon that looked a lot like the one my parents had when I was little. I guess that's why I noticed him. It was that Ford station wagon, so dusty I couldn't even see through the windows. I barely saw his face, but what I saw of him wasn't important. It was when Cynthia said, "Oh, that guy. He just got hired. He's the nightwatchman up at Harrow."

And I said to her, "You mean caretaker." A nightwatchman would imply that there was something to watch at night, but a caretaker—someone who'd fix the place or make sure everything ran that was supposed to run—made sense to me. She said, "Oh, of course. He's the caretaker."

But her word stuck with me.

Nightwatchman. It conjures so many thoughts, and makes me wonder what a nightwatchman does all night long.

So, I wrote, "The Nightwatchman looked into the hearts of the dreamers, and found their secrets."

It was just one sentence, but I knew it would be a novel someday. I felt better, just having gotten it down, even while the dream evaporated in my head. That will be the novel. *The Nightwatchman.* Sometimes it comes like that—inspiration from a dream. *The Nightwatchman* will be a story about a man who must take care of others, but he will find out too much about those he has to watch. Somehow I find this intriguing, and I'm hoping it's an up-beat tale of the human condition.

I went to take a shower, and afterward, being my normal snoop self, I opened the medicine cabinet. There was the dental floss I'd last used at fifteen. I could identify it by my initials on the side of the little plastic box (the good woman of Stoughton always marked my stuff). This meant, to me, that Cynthia just had not done much to change the house or her life since Aunt Danni's death. I felt the burden of death in the little house and decided to take a walk back into town, grab a sandwich or something, and just think about all this overload of information.

I didn't rent the little apartment until September, when I felt too uncomfortable staying with Cynthia—the cottage seemed heavy with something other than grief and remembrance. It seemed not to suit me, and I've always preferred living alone, anyway.

Besides, getting back to my novel is important, and it was hard to focus living at Cynthia's place. I want *The Nightwatchman* to be a really great novel—not the Great American Novel, but a novel like Wouk's *Youngbloode Hawk* or Styron's *Sophie's Choice*—a novel about everything, about the world. I want to encompass the world—the day and the night. I want the character of the Nightwatchman to be fascinating, and on the edge of something wonderful. The more I think about it, the more dreams I'm having that seem to be bits of what the novel might become. Sometimes a ten-minute nap will bring me the dreams—and I suddenly see the Nightwatchman himself, with his narrow lips and the way his eyes widen as he speaks, and I see the plaid shirt he wears beneath his uniform. The Nightwatchman must have a uniform—it's important for his sense of self. I see a green-gray uniform and a hat and in his belt I thought there'd be a gun, but in the dreams, I see a row of little knives, and I'm not sure what that means, but it seems to suit the Nightwatchman to have them.

Maybe this novel will be about murder. Maybe the Nightwatchman witnessed a murder on his rounds. His rounds? I still don't know what he's watching. What he's protecting. Is he looking through windows? I need to develop this novel further before I write too much in it.

Maybe he's watching a mansion, like Harrow. But I don't want to write about Harrow. I don't want even to think about that place. No, I think the Nightwatchman would be in a bustling city, but spending his nights in a lonely building—a factory perhaps. A factory of dreams—what would that be? A movie studio? A sweatshop? A department store? What does he watch? I'm still unsure.

If I didn't have my own place, I don't think I could be planning this novel out so much, and I bet it gets published. It feels so real. It feels as if it could happen.

I'd have worked on the novel more, but after doing some errands and helping out with a neighbor in slight trouble, I decided to go back and just look at the cottage again. Remember Aunt Danni. Wish I could recapture the past in that moment.

Why was it all lost? Why did time have to move forward?

I saw Cynthia inside with a few friends—probably enjoying life, even while I watched from the outside. I felt too much like a voyeur, as if all my life had become about watching and waiting and remembering the past, clinging to it and my childhood as if it could somehow fix all my dreams and desires in the present.

I turned, finally, and was walking back into the village center to grab a bite, with the early winds of October farting out leaves and leaf mold that made me sniffly and sleepy, when I saw the dead man.

Dead to me, anyway.

Or maybe I was dead to him.

His name was Bish—short for Bishop—McBride, and he and I had been friends on my summers and holidays to Watch Point. He wasn't officially dead, but he might as well have been because the last time I saw him he told me that I could go fuck myself and that if he ever saw me in this town again he'd make a point to get his gun and plow me down and no jury would convict him.

And maybe he was right.

I had hurt him in a way that I guess you're not supposed to hurt somebody, particularly when you're best friends and you're teenagers and you know the Rules of Friendship.

I had betrayed his friendship by stealing his girl, then telling him later that she had meant nothing to me.

But then, sometimes, when I tried to remember it, I think I got it wrong.

Sometimes I felt like Bish had a thing for me.

2

"Bish," Luke said, nodding slightly.

Bishop McBride had gotten a little chubby, but only in that frat boy way that meant he probably had too many beers and now and then forgot how many fries he'd scarfed down and how many ice cream cones he'd had in the summer. He looked like he'd been living the good life—his cheeks were rosy and round and his hair was a thick flop across his forehead and his untucked white shirt was starched and his jeans looked brand new.

All in all, he hadn't changed that much.

"Luke. I'd heard you'd moved here." His eyes lit up briefly, as if he expected a big hug and "Missed you, old fart!" from Luke, and then that little hope seemed to extinguish. Still, he kept the grin and added an arched eyebrow. "Been avoiding me?"

"Yeah, well. Not really."

"You should've dropped me a line, buddy."

"I figured I'd see you around."

"Want to get a beer?"

"Sure, but . . ."

"Us as kids? Don't be ridiculous," Bish McBride said. "Long time ago. I was stupid. I lost a good friendship over nothing. How dumb is that?" He stepped over to Luke Smithson and slapped his shoulder. "Goddamn, it's good to see you."

While Luke and his old buddy Bish wandered up and over to Macklin Street, to the Ratty Dog Bar & Grille, each feeling as if something great had just happened—a reunion that was long in the making, a new beginning for an old friendship that had nearly been like brotherhood once upon a time; and while Ronnie Pond started looking for the box cutters so she could start unpacking all the boxes of books in the back of the store; and while Jim Love tried to tear his daughter Bari away from chewing more of his face off; and while Chuck Waller pressed his weight down on Mindy Shackleford's neck so she couldn't scream and could barely even breathe and then turned around on her throat and leaned back over, trying to find a way to tear her lower half open with his bare hands; and while Thad Allen stripped to his boxers and laid down on Alice Kyeteler's massage table so that she could "relax the most uptight man in three counties," and as Alice rubbed scented oil on the palms of her hands and thought of that phrase from Shakespeare's *Macbeth*—"By the pricking of my thumbs, something wicked this way comes. Open locks, whoever knocks!"—and began to wonder why she was feeling so sleepy; eleven-year-old Kazi Vrabec walked up the driveway of the house called Harrow to see the man who looked like a scarecrow.

Chapter Nine

1

"Here's the thing," the man on the property said to Kazi Vrabec. "It's completely nuts, but I locked myself out of my own house and my wife is in some kind of trouble in there. I only just started on this job a few nights ago, and I can't really get on the cell and call my employer because they'd see me as completely incompetent and I'd get fired. Only I can't get fired, and I don't mean it's because they won't fire me, it's because I'm screwed if I get fired—you don't mind language like 'screwed' do you?"

"No," Kazi said.

"Good, well I'm fucked six ways to Sunday if I have to call my employer for the keys and I think a little boy like you—well, you might be able to help me out of this predicament," the man said, taking a breath.

Up close, he didn't look like a straw man at all—he had big dark circles around his eyes, and he definitely had some hay or something in his hair, under his hat, but that might've been from mowing—half the lawn beyond the stone wall looked like someone had been cutting grass, while piles of high weeds and sticker bushes that had been torn at the roots lay alongside the stones.

"I don't know if I can help," Kazi said.

"What's you're name, boy? Casey?"

"Kah-zee." Even as he said it, Kazi wondered how the man would have guessed "Casey," since that was what he was called sometimes by substitute teachers who didn't know any better.

Did I just tell him my name and not remember I did it?

"Well, look K-Z, all you need to do is crawl through a little gap. That's it. See, I can lift you up to this window on the second floor and there's this little gap for getting in. My wife, she's in some kind of trouble. I can't get in at all. Doors are locked, windows sealed up on the first floor. It's a goddamn fortress, and I dropped my damn key somewhere. The front door locks and the back door's all barred up and closed and padlocked, and it's because I either lost the fucking key or I left it inside although I don't know shit about how that could've happened," the man said. "Hey K-Z, am I mumbling?"

Kazi shook his head slightly. He knew to give grownups respect; his mother had told him to never give lip and always treat adults as his betters.

"If I'm not mumbling," the man said, leaning down toward him so that his face was nearly next to his, "then why in hell are you looking like you don't understand me. No habla een-gless? You a furrinor?"

"Mister?"

"A furrinor."

Then Kazi understood. He nodded. A foreigner. "I'm not. But my mother and father are from Czechoslovakia. They came over before I was born."

"Yeah," the man said, his eyes squinting a little, sniffing at the air. "You smell like one of them. You a Jew?"

Kazi wanted to tell the truth, but he was a little afraid. "Not really."

"What's that mean? Not really. Jew's a Jew, no questions asked."

"My grandfather is Jewish. But my mother and father think religion is made up to make people feel good about death."

"Worse than a Jew," the man said, straightening up. "A goddamn atheist unbaptized baby boy. You know what some folks do with the unbaptized, Mr. K-Z Slovak? Some people throw 'em in a pot and boil 'em down and use their fat to slick up their naked bodies and fly on broomsticks stuck up their twats to witch Sabbaths."

Kazi took a small step backward. The little voice in his head that he knew must be his conscience was telling him that something was wrong here. More than that, it was practically screaming inside him, SOMETHING'S WRONG HERE. And yet he was afraid to turn and run. He knew that dealing with the straw man might be the same as dealing with a snake, and you had to walk very carefully away from a snake. His mother had told him about irregular people—"They look like anybody else, but they got bad stuff inside them. You just keep away from them when you can."

Kazi took another step back.

"They slap all that little unbaptized boy fat on their bodies and slide it all over their tits," the man said as he stepped a little closer. "They look like greasy old hags with snatches like gumless grandmas. And then they fly off to the devil and dance for him and kiss his smelly *culo*, as they say in the Southern climes." Then the man roared with laughter.

Kazi would've liked to turn and run then, but instead, something really stupid happened inside him. He began to shut down a little—and he froze on the spot.

143

"It's a joke, K-Z. It's a joke. Nobody does that. People used to, maybe, but you don't believe in the devil, do you? I mean not if your Slovak mama and papa don't believe in God. You a commie?"

Kazi didn't even quite understand the question. "A what?"

"A comm-a-nist," the man said. "You believe in the Soviet dream? You a Havana buttboy? When I was a boy I used to know a lot of people who believed in it. All of them, godless. You godless like that? You taking calls from Castro and quoting Marx in the parks in the darks for the larks? What I mean to say, K-Z, is are you a patriot of the U.S. of A., or are you one of those immigrant leeches who comes over to take up all the welfare and medical suckage you can get and still you keep trying to knock ol' Liberty down and make sure that God stays good and buried under your red, red feet?"

Kazi stared at the man, but all the while he was wondering if he could run fast enough back to his bike and jump on and get the hell out of there before the man could go running after him. The straw man was old, after all, older than Kazi's mother, and Kazi could run really fast and he could bike faster.

The man seemed to leap forward—almost like a dog. He landed down on his haunches in front of Kazi so they were at eye level. Kazi held his breath and peed his pants when it happened.

"I told you my wife was in trouble and I need somebody to help. You gonna help?" the man said. Then he looked up at the sky. "You think it's gonna rain later? Looks like a storm up there. Up there in heaven."

2

"What kind of trouble?" Kazi asked. He hated the feeling in his underwear and trousers—that just-peed nasty stickiness and the smell. He hadn't done this since he'd been in kindergarten, so he found that troubling, too.

The man had grabbed him by the left arm and locked his hand around his wrist in such a way that it felt like a handcuff. A powerful grip—and though Kazi didn't struggle as much as he thought he should've, it would've been tough to pull away. Truth was, Kazi knew this from the schoolyard New Kid Test to any number of other tests that had been thrown at him in his eleven years, that sometimes struggling was worse than just playing along until you had a chance to run.

And something else, too. Something about the man, as soon as he touched Kazi, it scared him less. He didn't know why he was less frightened than he had been just seconds before, but the man drawing him onto the property by the arm—it took away some sense of fear for the boy.

It's not right. I should be running away. I should be screaming. But I feel . . . like I know him already. I feel like he's all talk.

"What do you mean?" the man asked.

"Your wife. Mrs. . . ."

"Mrs. Fly," he said.

"Mrs. Fly. Like a housefly?"

"A little different," the man said. "There are all kinds of flies in the world. Some sting. Some have big mandibles. You know what a mandible is?"

Kazi shook his head.

"Jaws, kid." The man grinned. "Mrs. Fly's jaws are so big she can't seem to keep 'em shut most of the time."

"You said she's in trouble," Kazi said, his voice a whisper. He had the twin feelings of fear and curiosity. There was something about the man that was like a tickle along his spine—scary, but somehow it felt as if Kazi needed to go with him, and he felt as if he were picking at a scab to see what was underneath. "Is she in bad trouble?"

"Ah yes. This time of day, she gets that way," the man said, still dragging Kazi along. They went up the long drive, with tall trees on each side of it, all full of gold and red and brown leaves, many of them having already fallen in drifts along the grass. As they rounded a corner, Kazi saw it at some distance.

The house.

Harrow.

He knew its name even though he'd never been there. All the kids told stories about it at one time or another. He had heard it was a castle. He had heard it was a fortress. One little girl told him that it was the biggest house, bigger than the Empire State Building; and a boy in school told him not to believe that girl. "She lies all the time," the boy had said. "It's not so big. It's like any other house. It's big. It's just not so big."

But Kazi's first view and reaction to the house was not that it was big or monstrous or even creepy.

But that it looked a little sad.

It was like the picture of his grandmother from Prague—a little bit bigger than normal, a little bit older than you'd think, and a little bit on the edge of falling apart if you looked at her the wrong way, and a little bit pissed off that that she was stuck where she was. That was the house. It didn't seem scary at all to him—any more than the image of his grandmother did—but it looked very sad and very much in need of fixing up.

It was bigger than any house he'd ever seen, and it looked like it had towers and windows that went off in the distance—as if it were as big as the village itself.

"See?" the man said, tugging him forward. "See the spires and the turrets? Oh, you little Commie boys probably don't know about turrets on houses. It's too budgie-wa. This is the kind of house rich people live in, K-Z. In America, if you work hard, you can own a place just like this."

146

"I'm an American," Kazi said too quietly.

"What's that? You're a what?"

"An American."

"Ha. You don't smell like an American, and you don't look like any Americans I know, kid. You look a hundred percent Russkie to me. I bet you can even speak the Old Tongue. Can you?"

Kazi didn't look up at him, but watched the house as they approached it. It began to loom as only old houses can—its dimensions seemed to grow from the pile of brick and stone and wood from the distance, into a mansion that looked as if it had been messed with by too many architects and too many people trying to tear it down.

"*Je pozdé litovat,*" the man said.

Kazi stopped in his tracks, and so did the man. The man grinned so broadly he was like a jack-o'lantern with all his teeth in place. "What?"

"You heard me," the man said. "What, you think I can't talk like your mama? I'm smarter than you'll ever be, K-Z, and smarter than your mama and smarter than your daddy and you stink like you peed yourself. Did you? Did you? *Chlapec je jako obrázek.*"

Kazi glanced up at him. "Who are you?"

"I'm the guy who takes care of this place. Also, handyman and sometimes the electrician and sometimes I get to pee my pants just like you did. Look at your crotch, K-Z, you really yellowed it. You get scared or something? It wasn't me, was it?" the man said, tightening his grip. "I bet it chafes down there. Peeing your panties is what girls do, you better hope none of your friends sees you on the blacktop like that, K-Z the Commie, because if they do, they're gonna laugh at you like there's no tomorrow and you're just gonna have to sit there in your own filth and take it. Little pissy panties boy. And just remember, milk, milk, lemonade, 'round the corner fudge is made."

Kazi tugged hard to get his wrist out of the man's hand, but he couldn't. The man just held tight, and he leaned over and slapped Kazi hard on the side of the face.

For a second Kazi was about to cry, but the man snarled, "And don't let me hear the big baby whimper, either. You pee your panties, don't start being a little girl about discipline, K-Z. Crybaby. You a crybaby? Crybaby K-Z. You're here to help. My wife's in trouble."

"Who are you?" Kazi whimpered, and as much as he hated to give the man the satisfaction, he couldn't control the tears that had begun streaming down his cheeks. He had begun moving from hurt and confused and feeling bullied to suddenly feeling as if he were going to get killed if he did anything wrong. His mother had told him about kidnapping. Had told him about how little boys get taken off in the woods by ogres and strangers and how he had to be careful. "If you go where you're not supposed to," she had warned him, generally if she'd had a bit too much to drink and he hadn't obeyed her, "I can't help you. Bad people are everywhere. There are bad men in the world. Little boys go missing. Little boys die sometimes."

Kazi had heard about the little boy they found up on this property.

Little boys go missing.

All the kids had been buzzing with it since school began—the story about the boy who was found all cut up at the graveyard near this house.

Little boys die sometimes.

Please, Mama, I won't do this again. I won't wander. I'll come home right after school. I'll say my prayers. I'll wash my hands and face. I won't wander ever again. Kazi thought the prayer out, hoping his mother or God or someone would hear him.

"Who am I?" the man said. "My boy, my little foreign spy, I am Mr. Speederman, but most of my friends call me Mr. Spider, and I want you to do that, too, K-Z. Or you can call me Dadko. That's my first name. You know Dadko? I bet you do, K-Z. I bet you know about how people burn the straw man and straw woman at harvest time. I hate that. It's so silly and pagan, and pagan things are devil things and devil things are atheist things. But call me Dadko. Or Mr. Spider."

"I have to go home. Now," Kazi said.

"Oh poor little Czechie got to go see the babushka who can make his peed little panties all right," Mr. Spider said. "And meanwhile, my wife is up there in pain and doubled over and all you think about is yourself, K-Z Slovak. I don't like that one bit. Not one bit. Mind your betters, you hear me? *Jsou lidé, kte˘rí neve˘rí—je pozdé litovat.*"

Kazi understood this Czech phrase too well:

There are people who do not believe—it is too late to lament.

He didn't know why Mr. Spider was saying this, but it was getting to the point where Kazi knew he had to either run or accept that Mr. Spider might never let go of his wrist and might, in fact, kill him. There are bad men in the world.

"I have to go," Kazi said. "Mr. Spider."

"Well, I understand you do, Kazi. Have I been scaring you? Lord knows, I don't mean to frighten you, you sweet little kind kid of a kid. Gah, don't listen to me. I'm an old man. I am. I'm older than I look. I look fifty. But I'm really fifty-seven. Fifty-seven is old, K-Z. And I guess I'm a little senile already. You know senile? It's when all the old farts start to lose it. I was just havin' you on, kid, really. Having fun. Sure, nobody gets my sense of humor," Mr. Spider said, but this time, he tightened his grip on Kazi's wrist and brought his other hand up behind the boy's neck. It felt icy as it touched him, and if Kazi had any pee left in him, he was fairly sure it would have leaked out right then.

Why isn't my mother here? he thought. *Why can't she protect me?*

Douglas Clegg

"Come on, it's okay. Lighten up, kid. I just need you to crawl up on this window sill. I'll be below you to catch you. You won't fall, but I mean if you did." Mr. Spider prattled on as he tugged and pushed at Kazi, and eventually they got up on the big front porch of the house. He said, "See, if I lift you up, you can reach that little balcony kind of thingy over there and you can just scramble up like a monkey and get to the window sill and slip in there—see how it's open a bit? And then you just run downstairs and unlock the door for me."

"Why can't Mrs. Fly come to open the door?"

"Gah, she's in pain, K-Z, now will you do it or not? I mean, you're free to go. You are free as a ˘cub˘cí syn—I promise. Oh Lord, I upset you. I'm sorry, dear boy. Dear one. You, who have always been so good to me," Mr. Spider said, and then with one swift swooping motion, he hefted Kazi up on his shoulders. Mr. Spider was taller than he'd seemed, and Kazi felt as if it would be a long fall to the ground. "What you do is you just stand up, use my shoulders, see, stand up, and then when you stand, you can just reach the balcony. See? It's not much of a balcony, but it's enough for you to stand on, and if you go on tippy-toes you can get to that window ledge. I know you can do it."

Kazi didn't want to do anything to help Mr. Spider, but he was a little scared and a little afraid to do anything to upset Mr. Spider. *If I just do it, he'll let me go. He's crazy but he hasn't hurt me. He's just crazy. He's like one of the teachers at school—they're kind of mean, but maybe they don't know how mean they sound. Maybe that's all. Maybe.*

150

Chapter Ten

"Two Guinness," Bish said, sliding onto a barstool at the Ratty Dog Bar & Grille.

"Just one," Luke said. "I'll have a boilermaker."

"Jeez, that sounds 1930s. Like Nick and Nora Charles."

"It is. I just like 'em."

"Alcoholism runs in your family."

"It better not run too fast or I'll never catch up."

The bartender, who was named Pete, leaned over and said, "We're out."

"Out?" Bish asked.

"Out of everything you want."

Bish and Luke glanced at each other; one shrugged, the other smirked; and then Luke said, "Out of beer?"

He looked at the bartender's face—hadn't seen him before in town. Looked sort of like several people in the village, most of whom were probably related. He had that inbred kind of chin—recessive and with a bit of an overhang of skin beneath it. His eyes were bloodshot and squinty, and the curl of his lip went down instead of up.

"We got nothing you want," the bartender said. "Couple-a-queers."

For a second or two, it was as if time froze, and Luke Smithson felt a little shiver of something inside. Not like a memory or anything, more like a nightmare that he might've once had. But even then, he wasn't sure of it.

Couple-a-queers.

The frozen moment broke into bits, and he looked at Bish.

"What the fuck," Luke said, laughing, and making an *I don't fucking believe this* face.

"Should I tell him?" Bish said, jokingly putting his hand on Luke's scalp and combing his fingers through his hair. But Luke pulled away. He didn't like that kind of joke. Didn't like it at all.

Luke felt his face flush; he felt as if he were peeing all over his own body. It was a strange heat inside him, and it felt closer to humiliation than he'd ever want to come.

He hated homophobes. He'd seen what his aunt had to put up with in her lifetime. Never liked it as a kid, didn't like it now.

"Neither one of us is gay. And what the hell does that mean, anyway?" Luke said, standing up too fast from his stool, nearly toppling it over behind him. "What the hell does that mean, anyway, bubba?"

Bubba was the best word he could come up with on short notice.

"Two pretty gayboys," Pete said, looking Luke in the eye. "We don't serve your kind."

"What century are we in?" Luke asked. He glanced at the couple at the end of the bar. "What century is this? This the nineteenth century? Eighteenth?" He laughed, but something in the sound of his own voice sounded hollow. "What the hell? Bish, is this guy for real?"

"Wait, Pete," Bish said, looking from Luke to the bartender. Bish grinned, shaking his head. He could not quite believe this. "This is a joke, right? It's gone far enough. Come on. Come on."

"I saw you two kissing and . . . fondling," Pete said, his face wrinkling with disgust. He stepped back from the bar. "I saw you with your ass in the air so your boyfriend here could poke you, gayboy."

"Pete?" Bish asked. "This is not funny. Not funny one bit."

"Funny as hell, gayboy." Pete shouted to the two other patrons at the end of the bar. "We saw 'em, didn't we?"

A guy and his girl sat sipping from highball glasses, and playing a video game on the bar counter. The guy looked over. "Yeah. Sure. Yeah."

"What the hell do you mean, 'yeah'?" Luke said. He felt as if he were burning up inside. It was insane and nasty—this kind of joke. To pick two people out and make a stupid comment. A stupid homophobic comment. Only ignorant morons did that. Backwater trash creeps who all should be shot for their ignorance.

"I mean, hell yeah," the guy said. He looked at his girl, then back to Pete. "Those two? Yeah. In love like two girl-friends." He grinned, and started chuckling; his girlfriend tried to shush him, but she had a big sloppy smile on her face, too.

Luke had a feeling he hadn't had since he'd been a kid—that somehow, his mind wasn't smart enough to un-tangle the confusion in his brain. He began recalling some memory—a time when he was in his teens. A time where he had heard somebody say something mean about some-one else, but it was as if his brain were blocked, and all he felt from this gasp of memory was confusion and shame.

And now, this was too weird.

Even for Watch Point, this was weird. It wasn't that much of a backwater. Nobody gay-bashed in Watch Point, not just a drive up from Manhattan. Not with the commuter

Douglas Clegg

train that ran through town. Not with two gay guys running the main bookstore in town. Watch Point had even tried to get gay marriage recognized. Despite a handful of ultra-backwards, it was a pretty liberal place, he thought. *Cynthia and Danni lived here together for years. We're just a couple of hours out of Manhattan. We're not in some redneck boondock.* Maybe he'd heard about some gay bashing once or twice, but usually it was the other towns in the Valley that had hate crimes and open-handed bigotry. Watch Point wasn't that bad, not these days. How could it be?

But this was something else.

And it made no sense.

None at all.

"Shame on you." The words entered his mind as if someone had spoken them. A taunting teenager in his brain. "Shame on you."

He tried to figure out every angle—was this a sick joke? Was it some setup Bish had made?

Bish.

Luke had a memory from high school about Bish.

He wasn't sure what it was.

Bish's anger at him. Inexplicable.

But that wasn't it. It couldn't be a big jokey setup because Bish would know how insensitive it was given Luke's aunt. Bish had always been cool with Danni and her girlfriend. Even when Luke had had some trouble with it . . . *I mean, it was hard for me to accept her being gay,* he thought. *But I was a kid. I didn't know any better.*

But this nastiness in the Ratty Dog Bar & Grille—this was something else. This stank of something awful that Luke didn't think happened in the world.

He liked girls. This was a nasty joke. He was in love with one particular of the female species and he had no intention of ever going gay.

Gay's bad.

The thought had never come to him before.

In his mind. A voice. It wasn't even his voice. It was just a voice.

You hate queers, the voice said. *You like girls who are pretty and who like you to look at them because they have all the right parts. Tits and pussy and all the in-between. You're healthy and well-adjusted and any dark secrets you have are the kind nobody ever finds out about because you write them in your diary. Men often write in diaries. It's a manly pursuit.*

Just because your aunt was a homo doesn't mean you can't hate all of 'em.

Hate the sinner, love the sin.

And nobody but nobody calls you a gayboy.

Nobody does it and lives.

Something was wrong, and it wasn't just this sick stupid joke that had gone on two minutes too long.

Luke felt as if his brain would not shut down with this voice. It kept going and going inside him, all the while he was pissed off at the bartender. Sometimes his brain did that late at night, just kept going and going, and that's what got him to start writing in a diary in the first place—the nights of no sleep, of wandering, of worrying and fretting and imagining and writing in the diary.

He had assumed it was a healthy outlet, but he now wondered if he hadn't been kidding himself.

The diary stops you from doing the things you want to do, the voice said. *You write in it so you don't have to live. So you don't have to do what needs to be done. You sublimate, my boy. You sublimate when you really want to lash out. You hide it in your diary when you really want to unzip it, take it out and swing it around.*

Luke said, "Okay, let's go, Bish. Something's fucked up here, but I'm not putting good money down in a place that would ever treat anyone like . . ."

"Oh you nanthy boy," Pete said, and to accompany his

lisp he added a limp wrist and a hand on his hips. He began walking to the left and right, swinging his hips too much. "You got your feelingth hurt by the big bad heterothexthual. Why don't we jutht run off and play rimjob poker? Or we could thucky thucky. You like that, pretty boy?"

"Okay, *enough,* Pete," Bish said. "What the hell are you doing? What the hell is this about? It's not even funny. It's nasty. It's stupid. What in hell do you think you're doing?"

"You wanna know?" Pete said, dropping the absurd nasty act. "You wanna know? You wanna know, gayboy?"

"I think the gayboys wanna know," the guy at the end of the bar said.

"Yeah, I wanna know!" Bish shouted.

Luke noticed that Bish's face was a bright red hue. He had never seen Bish this upset.

"I want to know what this nasty stupid joke is about and why it's so important to you to keep it going. I want to know why you're willing to stand there and be a goddamn homophobe and . . . shit, we're not even gay, so I don't even know why you're doing this. I want to know, you damn well better believe I want to know!"

"Okay," Pete said. "Look at this."

The guy with the girl at the end of the bar said, "I saw you two lovebirds going at it. It was . . . it was . . ." They both started snickering and then tried to hush each other.

The girl, a frowzy blond with a big rack, said, "It was disgusting. *Unnatural.* Unspeakable. And it looked like you were tearing that poor dude up. I mean, I can't take it in the backdoor, if you know what I'm sayin'. I like my action all normal and front door."

"Yeah, go in the front door," the bartender said. "Clean plumbing."

"We're moral people," her boyfriend said, and then chuckled to himself as if remembering a particularly funny joke. "But you. Well, shame on you. Shame on you."

Luke felt an icy finger along his spine when the guy said it.

Shame on you.

Bish glanced over at Luke, who had backed away from the bar, but met Bish's glance. *What the hell?* Seemed to be the expression on both of their faces.

In Luke's mind, the voice said, *Oh, the sights you will see. The passion, the drama, the bittersweet love.*

"Want to know what this is about?" Pete asked again, and he reached beneath the bar and pulled out a DVD. "Your kind disgusts me. You disgust anybody who's decent." He popped the DVD in the player that fed into the bar's video system.

On three TV sets—one over the bar, one back near the pinball machine, and one just over the front door of the bar—a porn scene came up, only, as Luke looked at it, he saw his own face—and it was not where it should've been.

It was buried between Bish's thighs.

"Oh my God, that's so gross," the blonde cried out. "That's like so gross. How can you do that shit?" She slapped the bar and started giggling into her "oh my God's."

"Wait for the part with the butt," her guy said, giving Luke a sly wink. "Naughty boys, you two."

"That's not me," Bish said, his voice raising an octave as if he suddenly were a little boy again. "That's not us. Who the hell made this thing?"

Luke reached into his jacket pocket and withdrew his cell phone. "Let's call the police. Something's too fucked up here."

"Cops?" Bish asked. "What the hell are they gonna do?"

"Give me another solution. It's either that or beat the crap out of everybody here. Bish? Bish?"

But when he looked over at Bish, his friend had become transfixed as he watched the images of the two men making love on the video. It was as if Bish could not take his eyes off of it.

Luke looked at the bartender—he too watched the video as if it was the most fascinating thing in the world, and only the blonde in the back kept shouting "Nast-ee! Oh, Jesus on a stick, who would do that to a man? Oh! Damn! That's gotta hurt. It's just gotta." She turned toward Luke, pointing her finger at him, laughing. "Oh my God, you got a little one, too. You got a teeny-tiny."

"What the fuck," Luke whispered under his breath. He felt a mix of confusion and a kind of fear he hadn't felt since he'd been a kid—the fear that brought shame with it. *But that's fucked,* he thought. *That's completely messed up.*

He flipped opened his cell phone, tapped in for the operator, got connected to the Watch Point police department and could not believe that the phone just rang and rang on the other end with no one picking up.

He looked up at the TV screen.

"Turn that off!" he shouted, but the others were watching the show—and when Luke looked up, he had just turned Bish over on his stomach and had begun licking down his back, all the way to the mounds of his buttocks.

Oh, the voice in his head whispered. *The things I will show you.*

Luke tapped off the phone on the eightieth ring to the local cops, and instead tapped in 911.

This time, after several rings, someone picked up.

"Hi. Look, I need some cops out here. There's something screwy." He gave the address of the bar.

"I know that place," the woman on the other end of the phone said. "I drink there sometimes. What's this about?"

"It's about something too strange to say over the phone. Maybe it's fraud. Or gay bashing."

"Wait—you're gay?" the woman asked.

"No, I'm not."

"Yeah, 'cause usually they sound a certain way. Funny like."

Luke could not believe her response. "Can we get a cop out here?"

"You might want to take a few deep breaths."

"What?"

"Calm down a little. Just take it slow and easy. Relax. Don't fight it. If you relax, you can take all of it."

Luke drew the phone back and stared at it, feeling disassociated from it. Then he put it back up to his ear. "I'm not sure what's going on."

"You know, when I'm not sure what's going on," the woman said, "the last thing I do is pick up the phone and dial 911. This is for serious emergencies only."

"I tried calling the local police. But nobody answered."

"Maybe you misdialed."

"Can you put me through to them?"

"What's the nature of the emergency?" the woman asked.

"I told you."

"Oh, right, people think you're gay or something. Is that a gay bar?"

"What?"

"That place. The Ratty Dog. I thought it was straight, but has it gone gay? 'Cause if it has, I don't want to drink there. Those homos who run the bookstore in the village—I mean, I can take their pansy ways in small doses, but if I'm in that place more than ten minutes I feel like I'm sucked into the homo underworld. And thinking about them— what they have to do to each other. And their toys. They all have toys. Ooh, that grosses me out. I mean, I have toys, too, but they're for all the right parts, you know what I mean." Then she seemed to be talking to someone else. "You know what? I can put you through. Hang on."

He waited. He heard a phone ringing. It rang six times. During those six rings, he saw Bish on screen with his lips slightly parted and his eyes rolled back beneath his eyelids as if he were in heavenly ecstasy. Luke glanced down at the floor.

At least the voice in his head seemed to be gone.

He looked at Bish, who had sat back down at the barstool and was watching the TV. Pete leaned against the bar and watched; and the blonde with her guy made noises and faces each time something new happened on screen. The blonde glanced his way and started giggling and pointing at him.

Then, someone picked up on the other end of the phone. A man. "Hello?"

"Hi. My name's Luke Smithson. I'm at the Ratty Dog."

"You're at a dog?"

"It's a bar. Off Macklin and Westmont Terrace."

"And . . ."

"Did she tell you anything?"

"Who?"

"That woman. From . . ." Luke couldn't think of what to call it. "From 911."

"Oh, you need to call emergency services," the man said.

And hung up the phone on his end.

Luke stared at the cell phone in his hand. He tapped it off and on again, and dialed 911.

A different woman answered. "I need help," he said. "It's an emergency." He gave the name and address of the bar.

"Yes, sir," the woman said. She added, "You're very calm for someone in an emergency, sir. If you don't mind my saying."

"Well," he said, but had nothing to add.

The woman said, "Oh. It's *you.*"

"Me?"

"The gay guy who called Deirdre just a second ago. Right?"

"No. That must be someone else," he said.

160

"I bet it's you," she said. "Hey, Deirdre, it's that homo."

"What do I have to do to get a cop out here?"

"Well, maybe in your world it might take a good throating, but here in the real world Mr. Fancy-Pants, we do just fine in the normal way. Missionary if you like. But where all the parts fit by nature's plan."

"Wait. What the—" Luke asked. He felt as if he had stepped into another reality. He listened to the woman—there was something hypnotic in her tone, and he had the déjà vu of having dreamed this on some level, although he could not for the life of him remember the dream. A mounting unnamed dread took him over, and he did not feel he could close the cell phone as he listened and watched the DVD play out the sex scene between the two young men who looked exactly like him and Bish.

"All I'm saying is if you meet a girl and fall in love with her, that's normal. I mean, even if you chase her down or something. You're a man, she's a woman. Even if she's sixteen. And you're older. Maybe much older. Even if you beat her up now and then. I know nice guys who do that. That's normal. What's not normal is that whole queer thing you're into," she said. Then she giggled. "I mean, your aunt, she was one of those perverts, too. She liked the whole girl-on-girl action. But that doesn't mean it's genetic. You can fix yourself. I heard about people who do that. They force themselves to do it with the opposite sex and if you do it enough with any hole, you get used to that hole. Women are a little squishier inside, so it makes it better for the guy. I mean, that's what I heard. I read about it. I think it was in some magazine."

"*Fuck you,*" Luke said, his voice faint as if something had just begun to dawn on him. Something about this cosmic joke. Something about Bish and him when they were teenagers and Bish had told him something so secret about himself.

161

"Exactly," the woman said, still giggling, and then she hung up the phone.

He shut his cell phone.

He looked up at the movie on the TV screen.

"Turn it off," he said.

The blonde shouted, "But it's not over. There's more! They do it with this other guy, too!"

"Turn it off," Luke repeated.

But Pete and Bish and the guy at the end of the bar with the girl all kept watching as if it were the most fascinating thing in the world.

"All right then," Luke said. He went first to the television set over the door, and pulled a wooden chair out from a table and stood on it. He flicked the TV off. Got down. Went over to the television by the pinball machine, and shut that one off, too. Then he stepped over to the end of the bar, around the guy and the blonde, and lifted the counter gate to get behind the bar. He walked over near Pete, and switched off that television set, too. He glanced beneath the bar, and there on one of the shelves was the DVD player. He crouched down and played with the buttons on it until the DVD popped out. He slipped it into his jacket pocket.

As he stood up again, Pete the bartender had what looked like a double-barrel shotgun nearly up against his nose.

The couple at the end of the bar were laughing at the TV screen again, and when Luke glanced up, only slightly, so as not to piss off the bartender, he saw a different movie that showed him making out with Bish against a tree. The laughter grew louder in the bar, and he felt his face burn from shame, even though it could not possibly be true. *This can't be happening*, he thought. *Rewind this world. Rewind it. This cannot be happening. This is not the world. Something's changed. Something broke here.*

And then the thought came to him.

THE ABANDONED

The Nightwatchman looked into the hearts of the dreamers, and found their secrets.

His cell phone sounded, and even with the gun pointed at him, he opened it and put it to his ear, all the while watching Bish.

On the phone, the voice that had been only in his head before was now talking to him on his cell phone.

"Oh, the things you'll do for me," the voice said.

Chapter Eleven

1

"Here comes the weirdo of Watch Point," Army Vernon said to his wife as they loaded up the van to deliver the last of the flowers to the funeral home that day. His wife, Brenda, glanced over the dozens of white roses to the street. "Benny's out."

Brenda watched the dogcatcher truck swing by and then turn up Macklin. "I saw some dogs running around," she said. "I wish people would just take care of their pets."

"That guy likes killing those animals too much," Army said, and then went to help his wife lift up one of the larger funeral arrangements. "You ask me, they should've kept him up at the hospital for observation."

"He's fine," Brenda said, shooting her husband a look. "Just stop that. He's fine."

"I don't know. I was up there a couple months ago to get rid of that old loveseat, and he and the weird girl who works with him were playing the soundtrack of *Oklahoma!* and dancing around with these big mastiffs on their hind

164

legs. A few bats in the belfry's all I'm saying." He noticed it was getting dark earlier, as it did each day, and he said to his wife, "After this run, let's go grab a bite out tonight. I feel like celebrating."

"What's the celebration for?"

Army shrugged a little as he crouched down to pick up a couple of fallen blooms by the back tire of the van. "I don't know. I've been feeling a little old lately."

"It's the routine," she said. "We're stuck in it."

"I've been dreaming a lot about winter. About a bad winter coming up." He said the words as if they carried a heavy weight for him. "As if a frost is covering me."

"It's our age." She smiled, fondly. "We're feeling it."

"Maybe," he said. "Smells like snow, doesn't it?"

Both of them took a couple of deep breaths, their nostrils flaring.

"Smells like October," she said. "Leaf mold and brisk winds."

"I smell snow," Army said. "Like winter's coming too fast. Or maybe it's me. I feel aches and pains now I never had before."

"We can take a little time off," Brenda said.

"Naw," Army said. "It's just a feeling. That's all. Maybe it is my age after all. We're entering winter."

"A few more months," his wife said, and went to touch him lightly on the shoulder.

"No, I mean in life. We're leaving fall behind now. Winter's coming," Army Vernon said, and he went over and shut the back of the van. "I don't want it to come. I don't want to feel that frost on my bones. I just don't want it. I want summer. I want nothing but summer."

2

As Alice Kyeteler finished the last of the massage with Thad on her table, she decided she'd try a little Reiki to help soothe him a bit. The process of Reiki was mysterious to her, and sometimes felt like a laying on of hands. Just by meditating over key spots on his body, she felt the heat and warmth of life between them. She heard his sighs as she cupped her hands just above his neck.

Then he began snoring.

She grinned. That was sometimes a side effect of the relaxation. She didn't love that he fell asleep when she'd like to lock up the shop and get home. But the truth was, Alice cared deeply for Thad, though she hated admitting it to herself. So she let him sleep on the massage table, his face poked through the round doughnut-hole at one end of it, his feet hanging over the other end, a towel around his middle.

She heard the light ring of her shop door opening. *Thought I locked it.*

She passed by the shelves and counters, and parted the bead curtain just before the shop's front door. There stood a very rough-and-tumble looking Goth teen. Alice began to wonder if it was Sam Pratt, who she had seen running around on his skateboard just a year or two previous, with his hair too long and too scrawny for his frame. He'd filled out since then, if this was him, but had begun moving toward the sloppy and dumpy side of things. Still, she saw that cherubic little boy face behind the too-black hair and the dark oversized T-shirt and remembered his mother, who used to talk to her a few years back, before some cloud had passed over the family.

"Miz Kyeteler," the young man said, nodding. "Just want to look around."

"We're closed," Alice said. "*Sam?* Sam Pratt?"

He nodded and glanced over her shoulder.

"Ye gods, what happened to you?" She barely recognized him because of his sunglasses and his demeanor, which seemed different than the previous times he'd dropped by the shop. He looked like he was hiding from the world and she was sure she saw a faint discoloration along the left side of his face, almost like a port-wine stain.

"Oh," he said, removing the sunglasses. She saw two black eyes and the purplish bruise became more prominent. "I got shit-canned by a neighbor."

She ushered him in the shop, and put her arms around him like he was her own child. "Who did this?"

Sam looked at her as if he were about to start crying. She hated seeing this. "Well, *who?*"

"Mr. Templeton."

"Jack?" She said this as if she could not possibly believe it in a million years. "Jack Templeton?"

"Yeah." Sam's voice was flat. He sounded exhausted, and his lower lip had a tremble to it. "He came running over to me. I was working on my bike. He was shouting about finding rats or something. He pushed me back and just started clobbering me. I mean, like he had gone crazy. He really knocked the wind outta me. And then he went over to get Cleopatra—my snake—and he started *kissing* her. And . . . he didn't have his clothes on. And he started rubbing himself all over her and sort of . . . well, doing things to her. When I got up, he looked at me funny and I just got scared shitless and started running the hell out of there. I came here because . . ."

"Because I'd believe you," Alice said, nodding.

"Because I didn't know who else to go to. I'm really worried about Cleo."

Alice cocked her head to the side slightly, trying to figure out how big a whopper of a lie it might be. It was so absurd, it didn't even sound made up. "Where's your father?"

"Someplace else this week."

"He's on a trip?"

Sam shrugged. "He leaves me home all the time now. I'm almost eighteen. I can keep it together."

"Be that as it may," Alice began, then cleared her throat.

"Be that as it may, let's get you over to the hospital. I can close up and drive you to Parham in ten minutes."

"I'm fine. Really."

"All right. I'm going to call somebody."

"Who?"

"The police. If Jack Templeton has gone crazy like this, who knows what he's doing."

"That's the weird part. I mean, on top of every other weird part," Sam said. "I called the police. On my cell phone. They told me . . . they told me . . . I can't say it."

"I'm a big girl," Alice said. "I used to be a carnie. I've heard it all."

Sam whispered, "They told me to go fuck myself."

3

Within ten minutes, Alice had tried to call the local police herself, but there was so much static on the line she couldn't understand a word that was said on the other end. She heated up some cocoa and took it over to Sam, who was slumped in the big Barcalounger she kept near her massage table. "This'll make you feel better."

He looked at the steaming mug, then up at her. He took a sip. Set the mug down. He looked over at Thaddeus Allen, who lay on the massage table, snoring lightly. "Who's that?"

"It's a friend. He needed some rest."

"He naked underneath the towel?"

"No." Alice grinned. "He's too modest for that. He has his boxers on."

"Whew. I'm not so fond of these naked guys running around town right now," Sam said. He nearly grinned, and she felt a little heartened from his slight joke. Then his face darkened again, and he looked so sad she wanted to mother him until he felt better again. "I think stuff is starting to happen because of what we did. On Thirteenth Night last summer. No, I know it is."

"At Harrow," Alice said, and she did not mean it as a question. She had already answered a question in her mind.

Sam nodded. "I'm the first one who saw that little kid. The one hanging upside down. The one that got torn open."

Alice tried to put the image of the dead boy out of her mind. "You did that?"

"No. No *way*. Only he wasn't put there like they found him. He was hung upside down. It was freaky. When I saw it, I knew they'd blame kids like me."

"Why? Why you?"

"Look at me. I like horror comics and I read Stephen King and Bentley Little and I listen to Marilyn Manson. My mom thinks I'm one of the signs of the Apocalypse. I know what people think. But I'm not like that. None of my friends are like that. That was some sick, warped creep. It was like a ceremony. It was like somebody really knew what they were doing. He was hung upside down and naked and they had opened him up."

Alice caught her breath. She closed her eyes briefly, not wanting to think about it. Not wanting to imagine the little boy, though dead, positioned that way. Cut open. She hadn't read any of that in the papers, but she knew they might keep it hushed up so as to protect the dead boy's family.

What was his name?

Arnie Pierson. That's right. She didn't know the Piersons, but she remembered the name because she had never known an Arnie before. She knew that some mentally ill person from the morgue had stolen the body, and had even been arrested for it. She didn't know much else about it.

"When I saw the dead kid like that, hanging from that upside-down cross, I screamed and eventually went running back toward the house. And even though it was dark I saw her. I saw a woman at one of the windows. She freaked me out. She had opened the window and was just pointing at me. The other kids all came out of the house wondering why I was yelling, and I'd peed my pants and they all went up and saw the dead kid, too, but I was already running like hell down the road to get out of that place. None of the other kids there told about it. We all saw that dead kid. We all saw it. Someone cut him down, I guess. Closed him up. And when they found the body with clothes on buried a little, I figured it must've been whoever strung the dead kid up in the first place."

"You didn't tell anyone? Not the police?"

He shook his head and shrugged. "I figured they'd find out who did it. Somewhere along the line."

"Is this the truth, Sam? I mean it. Is this the absolute truth?"

He nodded, looking her straight in the eye.

"And your friends didn't tell anybody?"

He squinted as if trying to hold back tears. "No. I don't think so. I've had nightmares since then. Nothing but bad dreams."

"That's understandable," she said. And then she added, "What sort of nightmares? Are they about the house?"

"If I told you," Sam said, "they'd put me away."

"What happens in them?"

"The boy."

"Arnie Pierson?" Alice said.

"Uh-huh. Yeah. The kid we saw hanging upside down. Only he's different. He has teeth like knives. Like sharp little shiny knives," Sam said. "And he makes you do horrible, horrible, awful," as he said this, his whole face crinkled up and it was as if she were watching him have to take foul poison down his throat, "nasty things to him. Over and over again. And his teeth start squeaking and making these sawing noises . . . he opens and closes his mouth . . .

he makes you put your hands . . . inside . . . where he's cut open . . ."

Alice felt her throat go dry as she listened. Sam told more about his nightmares, and then he told about how in his dreams he explored the house, even though he'd never been inside it. "I can see through these windows that are this green swirled glass and outside, there are people, I know there are even though I can't quite see them, and they're just waiting for me, but I don't know why. Someone—a man but I only see his shadow—is repeating these words over and over again, only they're in another language and it freaks me out every time. And then the kid, no matter how I opened him up, gets up and starts running down the halls and that squeaky scraping sound of his knives, I mean his teeth, gets louder and louder. And so I start going room by room through the house and see all this stuff. All this stuff that just makes me sick." He looked over at Thad, who still slept. "I think I saw him in one of the rooms there," he said, unwilling to meet Alice's gaze. "You, too."

"You dream about *me?*"

Sam nodded, looking at his shoes. "And others. Mrs. Houseman. That guy who delivers eggs and milk. The woman at the art studio. Jessie something. A lot of people. And they're in the rooms and they see me and I see them and they're doing terrible, awful things. And I pass by this one room and there's this girl I used to hang out with sometimes only she looks different and she starts coming after me with what looks like an axe, I mean a big axe and she's chopping at the walls and then sometimes she gets another guy and cuts off his fingers one by one and he just lets her, and sometime she catches me and holds me down and takes the axe and just presses it against my mouth and I can feel it going through my lips into my gums and deeper and I can't do anything about it and that's when . . ."

"You wake up?" Alice asked.

"No," he said. "That when it gets really, *really* bad."

4

Bari Love tore into her father.

First the throat.

Then the right shoulder.

Her mother felt frozen in place as she watched the bursts of blood spatter the walls and cover her daughter completely in brown-red.

Within her mother's mind, she felt as if she had stepped through to the other side of some mirror—into another place—as if she were dreaming all this, because she knew this could not possibly be happening, not in the real world, not in Watch Point, and not in her own home.

Bari dislodged three of her front teeth tearing at her father. Her mother had stopped screaming and slid in a heap on the floor near Bari's bedroom door.

Margaret Love's thoughts were a jumble, and she shivered while tears streamed down her face and small gurgles of moans and mewls came from her mouth. "Make it end," she whispered. "Make it end. Make it end. Make it end. Make it end."

When Bari was done tearing at her father, she stood up and went to her mother and crouched down beside her.

"Wake up," her mother said. "Wake up, Bari. Wake up. You're dreaming. Make it end. Make it end."

A ring of bright red stained Bari's lips and ran down her chin, down her throat, down her breasts—the entire front to her nightgown was soaked a rusty-brown crimson.

Bari stroked her mother's sweat-slick scalp lightly, like a cat cleaning its kitten. She looked into her mother's face, freckled with blood.

"Oh, Mommy," Bari whispered softly. "I can make it end if

you want. I'm gonna get me a hatchet and chop you up into teeny-tinies. But you wait right here, okay? Just you wait right here."

Her mother looked up at her and somewhere inside her body, she'd become paralyzed with the animal instinct of the trapped prey.

She stared at her daughter and just wished for it to be over.

For the nightmare of life to end.

Ten minutes later, after Bari had retrieved the hatchet from her father's work area in the garage, her mother got her wish.

5

Inside Bari Love's head, she was doing something very different. She was on top of Andy Harris, bouncing up and down, meeting his thrusts and arching her back and just riding him like he was the devil himself.

"This is for Daddy," Bari said. In some dream in her head, she swung the hatchet down against her mother's big toe. "This little piggy went to market!" She swung again, and cut three toes at once.

But in her head, she felt as if Andy Harris were going to explode inside her and give her the baby she'd always wanted. *Just a pretty baby. That's all. A baby for me to love. Give me the seed to plant in my garden, Andy. Gimme. Gimme. Me want a beautiful shiny baby to love forever. A pretty piggy baby. That's all. I wanna be the mama. I wanna love the piggy.*

In the vision in her head, they were on the floor of what looked like an old library, and Andy lay back on the swirling red and black patterns of a Persian rug, while she milked him so she could get pregnant. She knew it was all just a dream, that she wouldn't really get pregnant, but her desire for that baby was real. She had always wanted to be a mother. She wanted to be Mommy to some beautiful baby.

MOMMY! Here it comes, you ready? Fingers out. Fingers out, Mommy!

This little piggy had none! This little piggy stayed home.

And this little piggy went wee-wee-wee—and bled all over the place!

Chop. Chop. Chippity-chop.

Bari raised the hatchet—a dream within a dream to her—and she began slicing off her mother's ears as carefully as she could, but one time she grazed her scalp and that made her mother shriek.

WHERE'S MY BABY? she cried out. MY BABY NEEDS TO BE BORN! MY PIGGY BABY!

Bari began giggling as she decided to take her mother's lips next, but slowly, methodically, so that they'd remain intact. Her mother had big fat lips, and they'd cut nicely, she thought.

MY BABY NEEDS TO COME THROUGH! Bari screamed, as she finished with Andy, and then leaned forward toward his face. He looked up at her as if he wanted to kiss her, but instead she brought her hands to his neck and began choking him.

But in the other dream—she could switch channels now just like it was cable TV—only the colors came in really clear and it was practically HDTV and up-close so she felt as it were almost real—she skinned her mother's face clean off.

MY BABY NEEDS TO COME OUT NOW! the voice cried, and even though it felt like it was coming from Bari's mouth, it was some other woman's voice.

And when she looked at Andy's face—which melted into her mother's bloodied skinless meat face—she saw a man with a slightly crooked nose and small dark eyes and a grin that was as wide as a crescent moon.

6

When it was all over with, Bari licked the blood off the hatchet and went out in search of more piggies.

7

At the bookstore, Nick slept on, and Ronnie could not get him to open his eyes even when she snapped her fingers in front of his face.

"I tried to wake him up," Ronnie said, coming back from the storeroom. "He wouldn't budge. He's kicking his legs a little like a puppy dreaming."

Dusty got down off the stepladder, bringing down a handful of overstock hardcovers, and glanced back at her. "He never naps this long."

"Well, I did everything but pour cold water on him. Maybe we should let him sleep a little longer."

"Not with you leaving in a half hour and me having to do four thousand things at once," Dusty said. He went to the back of the store with her and pushed the door to the storeroom open.

Ronnie had never liked the storeroom much—it was nothing but boxes upon boxes of books, books that needed to be returned to the publisher and metal shelves filled with paperwork and files. But Nick had put in a little cot so that when they had inventory weeks any of the employees could take a catnap on a break.

Nick was curled up nearly in a ball. "Gone fetal," Dusty said, grinning. Dusty crouched down beside his boyfriend, nudging him lightly on the shoulder. "Hey, baby. Wake up."

Nick snorted a wheezy snore, and for just a second, Ronnie was sure he'd said something.

"He talks in his sleep now and then. It's sweet."

"What's he say?"

"Nothing interesting. Things like 'where's the dog?' and 'I can't go home right now.'"

Dusty gave a devilish grin. "I know how to get him up fast." Then he leaned down and pressed his thumb and forefinger over Nick's nose.

"That's so mean," Ronnie said.

"I know," Dusty chuckled. "He'll snarfle himself awake any second now."

Nick's eyes opened.

Dusty laughed, and let go of his nose.

"Motherfucker," Nick said.

Ronnie noticed that something was off about Nick. His eyes seemed a little yellowed and he opened them so wide that it was as if the lids were tucking up behind the eyebrow.

Nick sat up, scrunching his hands across his scalp.

"Sleeping beauty," Dusty said. "You have a foul mouth on you."

Nick glared at him, but said nothing. He reached back along the shelf next to the cot.

Ronnie had just turned to go back into the bookstore when she heard a guttural sound, and turned back to see—

Nick jabbing a pair of scissors into Dusty's chest.

Then Nick withdrew them. Jabbed again.

Dusty wheezed, and Ronnie ran forward, trying to make sense of what this was, and why it was happening, and glancing quickly around to see what she could do to stop this. The first thing to catch her eye was the cutting board they used to slice off the edge of book posters so they'd fit on the walls and shelves. She grabbed it up, figuring that she'd slam it into Nick—and still, her mind could not quite grasp this, but she went on instinct, and knew that she had to stop Nick, protect Dusty, and she had only seconds.

She rushed over with the board, holding the cutting

blade down so that it wouldn't fly up at her face when she slammed it into Nick's head—

Nick kept jabbing the scissors into Dusty, whose eyes had rolled back into his head. His shirt was a mess of blood and torn flesh.

As Ronnie slammed the board against Nick, she knew she had to run out of the store. The back alley gate would be locked, so she'd have to run back out of the storeroom, through the store, then out the front door.

She knocked Nick over, and he fell quickly.

She held the board up to slam it down on him again, but he seemed to be knocked out. She knelt down, pressing her hands against Dusty's chest and throat, trying to keep the blood from gushing out, but soon her arms were soaked, and she knew she had to get help or he'd be dead in minutes if not sooner.

She laid Dusty down as gently as she could. Stress tears poured from her, but she fought to keep her thoughts clear. Get help. Come back. Paramedics. 911.

She stood and moved quickly toward the storeroom door, but as she drew it back, she felt something ice cold and sharp in her shoulder.

The scissors.

Nick had risen up behind her, and withdrew the scissors from her, ready to stab her again.

She turned swiftly, fighting the pain in her left shoulder. She balled her right hand in a fist and swung, connecting perfectly with the side of Nick's face.

It threw him back a bit, and he teeter-tottered. He likely would have regained his balance, but the blood river from Dusty made him slip. He fell onto his back, and the scissors went skidding across the floor.

Ronnie decided it was better to disarm him than to risk fighting him again, so she slipped and slid over to the bloodied scissors, and brought them up. She held them in front of her. Tears nearly blinding her, but she fought the undertow of her fear. "I'll kill you," she spat at Nick. "I will. You just stay there. Stay there."

She backed out of the storeroom, and when she was all the way out, her shoes touching the carpet of the bookstore, she shut the storeroom door and then scrambled in her pockets for the keys. Her hand was shivering and shaking but she managed to get the keys out. She used both hands to hold them steady as she aimed the main key for the storeroom door.

The doorknob turned.

She began shivering, and the keys dropped from her fingers.

She grabbed them up again, quickly sorting through them to find the storeroom key.

The doorknob turned again.

She pressed her left shoulder against the door. The pain of the wound in her upper shoulder felt like pincers tearing at her; holding the key with her right hand, she pressed it into the lock beneath the doorknob, and turned it.

It locked.

The keys hung there.

She stared at the doorknob.

No movement.

"Let me out," Nick said, on the other side.

"No way in hell," she spat.

"Please. Oh God. What happened? There's so much blood, Ronnie? Blood! What did you do?"

Ronnie stood there, taking deep breaths.

"Please, Dusty needs a doctor, Ronnie," Nick said. "I don't know why you did this. I really don't. But please. Please, he's gonna die. His blood is everywhere. Blood! Ronnie! Blood!" Ronnie felt his fists beating against the other side of the door—the thuds sent vibrations through her that confused her even further.

Phone. Call. Get help.

On the other side of the door, Nick rattled the doorknob.

Ronnie dropped the scissors, and ran as fast as she could—but it seemed feeble and slow to her, until she reached the phone by the cash register. She picked it up.

Dead.

"He's dying back here!" Nick shouted from the storeroom, pounding on the door. "You killed him, you bitch! Blood! Everywhere! You killed him! Oh sweet mother of fuck! He's gushing. He's gushing all over the books! All over the bestsellers, Ronnie!"

Ronnie wiped her hands on her shirt, a thousand thoughts going through her mind at once, and she went around the counter and toward the front door of the shop. She drew back the front door—

Bari Love, a girl she couldn't stand from school, stood there, completely naked, soaked red, and in her hands, she held a hatchet.

"Let him out," Bari said, raising the hatchet up and pushing her way through the door, into the bookstore.

Ronnie fell backward, and a lightning bolt of pain shot through her shoulder. She began screaming uncontrollably, "Help! Help me! God! *Somebody!*"

Even as she screamed at the top of her lungs, Ronnie thought she heard gunshots going off somewhere out on Main Street, and the sounds of car alarms going off, and maybe even the shouts of other people—

But she had known instinctively in these moments since Nick had stabbed Dusty to death that she couldn't wait for someone else to help her.

"Chippity-chop, choppity-chop," Bari Love sang an off-key tune. "Okay, here's the deal, Veronica, I'm going to axe you a question. Now, don't say anything. Nothing at all. No answer need reply. But I need to know." Bari raised the axe up and sliced at the air just above Ronnie's face.

Ronnie thought she heard dogs barking and scratching at the front windows and door. For just a split second she looked between Bari's legs and saw a Rottweiler and two Chihuahuas at the door, their paws bloodied as they scraped at the glass door, trying to get in.

Then she heard the *whoosh* of the hatchet as it came down for her head.

Chapter Twelve

1

"Mrs. Boswell, please calm down," Benny Marais said into the phone.

"You—you get your truck out here now. You get this . . . these mongrels . . . and you get them now!" she shouted on the other end of the line.

"Mrs. Boswell, please. Are you sure you haven't been . . ." Benny Marais didn't want to say what he was thinking. *Hitting the sauce.* He was sure of it. Nancy Boswell was drinking again, and now she was hallucinating.

"If I have to, I'll have the police out here and after they shoot them, they can arrest you," the woman said on the phone.

"I'm not the dogcatcher."

"You run the pound," she said. "And these are yours. I got calls from half the neighborhood that wild dogs were roaming the streets. You tell me. Are you missing any dogs? Are you, Mr. Marais?"

Benny Marais decided it was best to shut up about anything that might incriminate him in some way—just in case something happened. He tried to keep his voice even. "Just do what you can to keep them safe. I'll be over. I'll take care of this."

"What the hell?" Benny Marais asked no one, although Dory Crampton stood right next to him. He scratched the back of his head and put the phone down. "That was Nancy Boswell, and she's up in arms because she said six mangy dogs are in her backyard growling at kids."

"I don't know her," Dory said.

"She runs a day care up on Macklin. In her backyard. You must've seen it. Her husband always dresses up as a clown when she's trying to get people to dump their brats with her."

"Oh." Dory grinned. "Yeah. We used to egg him sometimes. Me and my friends. We'd drive by and egg the clown."

Benny glared at her as if she were at the bottom of all this.

"You're acting like it's something *I* did wrong."

"She's got seven three- to four-year-olds over there on the playset in the backyard, scared shitless because a pack of wild dogs is terrorizing them. And just who left the damn cages open?" he said, his hands going to his hips, which made Dory snicker a little because Benny had wide hips and it reminded her of her grandmother when he got all high and mighty like this.

"I didn't let the dogs out. And how does Mrs. Boswell even know the mutts in her yard are from here?"

"All I know is I need to get my rifle."

"You're gonna *shoot* the dogs?"

"She said they're growling. If I can't bring 'em in, then yeah, I'm gonna shoot 'em."

"You are so not gonna shoot those dogs," Dory said, and by the time they'd gotten the rifle and some leashes and thrown them in the back of Benny's pickup, she had begun laughing at the whole thing and telling him that Mrs. Boswell probably was rabid herself.

But she stopped laughing when she opened the back gate at the Boswell place and saw the blood.

"Holy shit," she whispered.

The Boswell Clown-A-Round DayCare had a bright yellow and blue and red playset in back with a twisty slide and a rope ladder climb and what looked like plastic monkeybars and a ball pit full of plastic balls with a plastic window on one side. About six little tots were inside the ball pit, up to their necks in the blue and red plastic balls, looking out, bawling to high heaven for their mommies.

Surrounding the playset were six dogs—all of them she'd seen at the pound.

A Doberman, a pit bull mix, a collie, a German shepherd, a spotted mutt, and a pug.

All of them were digging in the dirt beneath the ball pit as if they could dig their way into where the little kids were.

As if they wanted to eat those kids.

That was the thought that came to her.

They want those kids. They want those kids the way they usually want a milkbone.

For a moment, she felt a strange tugging in her brain as if the world had just changed its rules and nobody had told her. As if she were confused and hallucinating and not completely sure that she really was seeing anything the right way.

Blood was spattered all over the backyard, and pooled in small round pits that made it look like the dogs had already been digging holes.

Already been burying something.

She didn't like to think it, but she was nearly certain that she saw a child's sneaker sticking up from one of the just-covered-over holes the dogs had dug.

Near one of the holes, a clump of what she had thought was hay . . . *but it couldn't be.*

Her mind fought what it tried to make sense of—that the clump was hair.

A child's scalp.

The pit bull started leaping up at the thick plastic that protected the children sitting in the ball pit.

Dory had never seen children's eyes go so wide.

What the hell is this? What could make them do this? You have to stop the dogs. You have to stop 'em.

Dory felt as if she were frozen to the spot. Staring at the children whose faces poked up from among the little blue and red plastic balls.

The rifle.

Benny had a rifle in the truck.

The dogs scratching at the play area. It's impossible. This can't be happening. Even a mad dog would leave those children alone. No dog would do this. Not like this.

As if a hundred miles away, she heard a *ding-dong* sound.

Benny.

He'll know what to do. He knows everything about dogs. He's even mean to them sometimes. He knows how to control them. He'll get the rifle. He'll stop these dogs. Must be rabid. Must be sick. Something must've gotten to them. Someone must've poisoned them.

Her mind spun a mile a minute as she tried to reason through what could be happening. As she tried to believe that she must be seeing things wrong, that she must be misinterpreting what was right in front of her face, that her own brain was going haywire.

She glanced to the right to see if she could signal Benny in some way.

Benny Marais rang the front doorbell not more than fifteen feet away from her, and an instinct within her wanted to step back from the open gate, and close it and latch it and then run the hell back to the truck.

2

Mrs. Boswell answered the front door, and when she glanced over to Benny again, he was already inside the house.

3

The six dogs kept scratching. One of the little girls inside the ball pit saw Dory and pointed toward her. The girl started jumping up and down and screaming, "Help! Help, lady! Help! Help!"

A little boy cried out, "I want Mommy! Mommy! I want Mommy!"

As if it understood, the pug glanced back, looking at Dory.

Dory felt goose bumps along her arms when it looked at her.

The other dogs kept digging to get down beneath the plastic shield of the ball pit. Dory wondered what the hell Benny was doing in the house, and the pug turned and trotted over to her.

Its muzzle, spattered with blood.

Gristle of some kind in its teeth.

When it reached her, it began growling.

Dory took a step back.

Then another.

The pug advanced toward her, down on its haunches as if getting ready for a full-on attack.

Dory reached for the gate. The dog lunged. Dory jumped backward as best she could, and began to slip on the grass—she kicked out and managed to shut the gate as the pug leapt for it.

She heard its *thud* as it hit the gate and fell back into the fenced-in area.

The kids inside the ball pit began shrieking even louder.

She lay there on the ground, staring at the wooden gate. She couldn't see anything beyond it, but she heard the pug digging in the dirt beneath the gate.

It's coming for me. It saw me. It wants me.

It knows you know about it.

That dog has your smell now. He's sighted you. He's not going to let you go.

The thoughts jumbled around her mind, and she felt as if she were reaching a short-circuit point.

She heard someone with a low pitched voice whisper, "Bitch."

You're imagining things now. You've been pushed. You're imagining the pug on the other side of the gate just said that.

Finally she pushed herself up and wiped her hands on her overalls. She went around to the front door, which was slightly ajar.

She pushed it open.

The front hallway had dark wood floor with a Persian carpet runner that stretched past the living room to another door at the end of it. To her left, a mirror and a high table, stacked with mail and two rolled-up newspapers. Beyond the table and mirror, a staircase up, and a staircase down.

"Hello?" she asked.

She could barely hear the shrieking children—it was quiet in the house.

As she stepped farther inside the house, other thoughts occurred to her: *Why wouldn't the neighbors be here? And the cops? Why wouldn't Mrs. Boswell simply have the cops and the fire department out here to help? Why wouldn't she have opened the back gate to let the dogs out? To try to shoo them away from the kids? Didn't she have a garden hose? She could've tried that.*

She called out to Benny, but only silence greeted her. She glanced in the living room. It was a perfect living

186

room, the kind that would be in a magazine layout, magazines like *Martha Stewart Living*, *House Beautiful*, *City Home*, *Modern Mansions*, or any number of magazines Dory flipped through on her twice-weekly trips to the public library when she dreamed of getting away and living in some more sophisticated place; where she imagined a better family than the one she had, and finer things, and a kind of homespun happiness that came from the perfection of the home environment. The Boswells had that kind of living room. The sofa was wide and inviting; the drapes, though drawn shut, were thick and a bright yellow; the rugs were tastefully laid overtop the dark floor; and there was an upright piano at one end with several unlit candles upon it.

It seemed curiously unsuitable for day care, and she wondered if Mrs. Boswell always kept the children from playing in the house.

And now they're trapped in the playset.

She passed by the living room, and as she glanced to her left, up the staircase to the second floor of the house, she saw the clown.

He was standing there with what might've been Benny Marais's head in its hands.

And the worst part was, Benny had a big goofy smile on his face as if he'd just heard the best joke of his life.

4

Norma Houseman went to the door as soon as the doorbell chimed. Opening it, she looked out onto the porch.

"Veronica?" she asked.

"Ronnie couldn't make it," Lizzie Pond said.

"Oh. You two look so much alike."

"Twinsies," Lizzie said, smiling. "She had an accident."

"Did she?" Norma said. "Well, this is unusual."

"I'm as good a sitter as she is," Lizzie said, glancing around to see behind Norma. "Where are the little rascals?"

"What kind of accident did she have?" Norma asked.

"Just an accident. Nothing bad," Lizzie said.

"What do you have behind your back?"

"Nothing."

"Elizabeth," Norma said as formally and snappishly as she could. "What are you hiding?"

"It's a secret."

"Something's wrong with you," Norma said suddenly, as if she had just sensed something by the unusual look in Lizzie's eyes. She tasted something bitter in the air. "Something's not right."

"Everything's fine," Lizzie said, rocking her head back and forth so that her ears nearly touched her shoulders. The effect was somewhat comical, but Norma began to wonder if Lizzie Pond wasn't disturbed in some way. Her hair was over her eyes too much, her skirt looked like it had rips in it, and her knees were smudged with dirt.

"Well, I appreciate your coming by to tell me," Norma said, nudging the door shut.

Lizzie's stepped up so that the door could not be completely closed. "I'm here to substitute."

"I'm sorry?"

"For Ronnie. I'll take her place. I can baby-sit."

"I think I'll just cancel my plans," Norma said.

"Oh please, Mrs. Houseman. Don't do anything drastic like that. I love your kids. You know I'm as responsible as Ronnie is. And she's hurt."

"What do you mean?"

"I mean, I love being around kids. We can play games like Tag and Hide and Go Seek. I can even help them with their homework," Lizzie said.

"No, I meant you said she's hurt. Did she fall?"

"Oh, no. She just had a little mishap. It's nothing serious. Really. It was at the bookstore. You know that awful place where those two . . . well, you know those two who run it . . . anything can happen in that place, and I bet it usually does."

"Look, dear," Norma said, and an icy feeling moved along her spine. She didn't like the way the Pond girl kept looking around her as if she were . . . *hunting*.

That's what Norma thought. It was as if the girl was hunting for the children.

"Look, I didn't want to tell you this," Lizzie said, looking up at her with the face of absolute sweetness. "But Ronnie sometimes drinks a little. Not enough where most people would notice it. But I do. And I think it's terrible. Just terrible. Our father was an alcoholic. You knew that, didn't you? An awful man. He used to do terrible things to Ronnie and me when we were just toddlers. I don't like the smell of liquor because of him. But Ronnie, well, she's a little too much like him."

Norma opened the door a bit. Now, the one thing about Norma Houseman was that she loved bad news about other people. And she loved the inner secrets of those around her. She had spent most of her life feeling happy at the misfortunes of others, and though she knew intellectually this wasn't the right way to be, she could not help herself, any more than the chocolate-lover could resist a ten-pound box from Godiva. She enjoyed hearing the failings of her neighbors, and she took special pleasure in knowing that there were local sinners of any kind. *Makes perfect sense*, she thought. *Veronica Pond always seemed so perfect, but there was that rumor about her. About her and that boy in town. About them being up to no good.*

"So," Lizzie said, her smile brightening.

"All right, dear," Norma said, opening the door a bit wider and stepping back.

Lizzie stepped in, and drew the small knife from behind her back.

She pointed it at Norma, even while she elbowed the front door shut.

Norma laughed. "Jesus, Lizzie, I don't know what kind of joke this is, but a knife like that?"

Lizzie quickly jabbed the knife into Norma's left shoulder. Twisted it slightly. Norma felt the stab of pain shoot out from her arm and up the back of her neck. Lizzie pressed the knife deeply into the doorframe.

"There, you're pinned," Lizzie said. Then she reached into her coat pocket and brought out a corkscrew. "Okay, try this." She brought the metal corkscrew up to Norma's mouth. "Suck it. Suck it like it's Chuck Waller's prick."

Norma stared at Lizzie as if she'd never seen her before. The pain in her right arm was intense, and she wasn't sure she could tug away from the doorframe at all without causing more tearing and more pain. "Please, Lizzie. I don't know . . . I don't know why you feel . . . why you're doing . . ." The pain was white-hot now, and Lizzie jiggled the corkscrew against her lips.

"Suck it. Suck it like a good girl. Well, a good bad girl."

Norma said nothing.

She tasted the cold metal against her lips as Lizzie pressed the corkscrew to her. The girl nudged her lips apart with it so that it clacked against her front teeth.

"Suck it like a whore," Lizzie said.

"Get out of my house," Norma with her teeth clenched, but tears streamed down her face. She was too frightened to move, fearing that this crazy Pond girl might stab her again if she moved too fast or did anything untoward. Her mind raced as she tried to figure a way out of this. *If I tear my arm away, it may hurt. But I need to. I need to face it. Face the pain. Face it.*

And somewhere in the pit of her stomach, Norma Houseman had begun to feel a strange excitement. Fear and pain all messed up with a tingling inside her, as if she were about to have an adventure the likes of which she'd never before experienced. It was as if she were getting an adrenaline high from all this—as if she could smell something sweet and rancid that somehow made her all tingly.

Like I'm dreaming.

It's my dream, she thought.

Norma had had the dream just weeks earlier, and had been unable to shake it. It didn't involve Lizzie Pond, but a handsome stranger who had taken his fingers and pried her lips apart to thrust them inside her mouth. *Oh,* she realized. *Not a stranger at all.* It was Chuck. She had a sex dream about him, and in it, he'd been forceful and overpowering—something she normally didn't like at all. But in that dream, he had taken her like some primitive male force. And she had sucked his fingers in the dream, feeling dread and excitement at the same time, while his other hand had explored her body.

It was just like this. The terrible fear. The tingling.

The thrill.

"You don't suck, your kids will die." Lizzie Pond said this with such conviction that Norma nearly believed her. "If you don't take this corkscrew into the back of your hot little throat, Mrs. Houseman, I will go upstairs and into your backyard and I will murder each of your children. But first, I will tie you up so that you watch each of them die. And I will prolong their deaths for as long as I can. I will play with their suffering for your entertainment. Well, really for my entertainment."

You're insane. This is insane. Insane but somehow . . . somehow it's what I dreamed of.

"Suck," Lizzie said. "I will kill your kids, Mrs. Houseman, if you do not. I've always hated you. And I've always hated them. And unless you want to see their little faces screaming in pain, you will take this in your mouth and give it a nice polishing."

"Why are you doing this?" Norma asked feebly. "Why?"

Then Norma parted her lips and felt the cold metal enter her mouth.

191

5

Elsewhere in the village, other boys and girls entered their parents' rooms. A boy named Zack Holmes grabbed the wheel of the car from his mother as she drove him and their father out to an early dinner. He twirled the wheel so that the car spun out, then aimed it right for the telephone pole at the intersection of Macklin and Main. Inside the supermarket, four little tow-headed kids, ranging in age from eight to thirteen, had begun running down people with shopping carts and then kicking them in the head. Roland Love might be seen with a large wooden cross that he'd begun dragging up the hill toward the mansion beyond the village. A school bus that was bringing Parham's sixth grade back home late after a field trip at the planetarium over in Wheatley was hijacked by two of the girls, who slammed the bus driver's face into the windshield until he passed out. Gunfire was heard if you listened for it; screams now and then let out, although those who wished to scream sometimes had been cut down well before the sound could make its way up from their throats. Wild dogs and feral cats ran along the side streets, sometimes dragging bits of human flesh. Still others awoke or went into dreams or lay down for naps and blamed overwork and the change in weather and the lack of good sleep as the reason for wanting to wander off into dreamland.

Yet there were still people in the village of Watch Point, well before nightfall, who had not really noticed how things had changed that day, of how whatever had been planted on a stormy summer night had reached its bloom and opened up, a carnivorous flower, its perfume wafting on the October air.

6

So, this was what you wanted—you wanted to dream about the village, bring them sleep and the monsters that roam in their dreams will come into their flesh. You wanted to wander through their rooms and open their doors and find that part of them that could put you in control.

You wanted to whisper among them, free at last from the brick and wood that had captured you for centuries.

This was why the ritual had changed you—you were able to escape from the trap that once had been set for you.

You are the Nightwatchman, and the night has already begun.

The man who thought all this opened his eyes.

I am Mr. Spider. I am the Nightwatchman.

The air tasted crisp and fresh, and he felt as if he breathed for the first time. He felt the opening within his heart, and the electric jangle along his ribcage as it traveled outward.

He watched the little boy named Kazi Vrabec crawl up along the balcony, sidling along the slender ledge, over toward the open window into Harrow.

When the boy slipped through the window, the pane slammed shut behind him with such force that it cracked the glass.

III

THE MIND OF

HARROW

Chapter Thirteen

1

Kazi Vrabec glanced back at the windowpane. From inside the house, the glass looked filthy and was covered with what might've been dead flies that had been squished and left in place, pasted by their own mush. He looked back out the window, but the world beyond it looked fuzzy and blurry, and he couldn't see much beyond the balcony directly to the left of the window. He looked along the edge of the lawn and the driveway for the man called Mr. Spider, but he couldn't see him. Then Kazi turned to look at the room. It was nearly in darkness, except for the last bit of daylight outside, and three candles that were lit on a table near the door. The room was empty, it seemed, and it smelled like a toilet. The stink began to get to him, so he started breathing through his mouth so he wouldn't smell it.

"You have to help his wife," he said aloud, hoping it made him sound a little braver than he was feeling. He stepped cautiously across the creaking floorboards, nearly tripping over a loose plank. As he reached the door, he looked over at the burning candles, and saw the source of the stink. It looked like a dead possum lying there. Beside it, two dead crows and tucked back next to the candles were several small dead rats and mice. He stood at the door, his hand nearly touching the knob.

He had stopped breathing through his mouth, and now felt the heaviness of the stench of these dead animals.

He took a deep breath and touched the doorknob, turning it. Opening the door, he looked at the dead animals rather than out into the hallway. He noticed that just behind the animals was torn wallpaper, and in the flickering candlelight he could see what looked like drawings of stick figure people doing awful things to each other.

He looked away and drew the door completely open. Beyond the doorway, he thought he heard someone wheezing. It reminded him too much of his grandmother when she was sick. That heavy inhaling and exhaling with the whistle of a balloon in it, too.

Kazi shot one more glance to the dead animals, then stepped into the hallway and shut the door behind him.

2

Votive candles in mason jars lined the hallway. Kazi glanced down one direction and saw what seemed to be an endless number of doors. At the very end of that hallway was a large, wide mirror with a golden frame and the indication of a stairway that went either up or down—he couldn't tell. In the opposite direction, the hallway seemed to twist a little and end sooner—as if it turned a corner onto another area. Here, the wallpaper looked perfect and the smell was not so bad. It smelled like cabbage cooking from somewhere, and there was a scent of mild cheese in the air.

You should run downstairs and open the door for Mr. Spider. You should. You should.

And yet, once in the house, Kazi Vrabec did not want to see the man outside again.

You should go get him. He'll be angry. He may hurt you.

"Hello?" he asked the hallway.

The wheezing sound had become so regular that he nearly had stopped hearing it. It was like a slow, steady thump, and then like moan and a murmur, and then it became a dry, raspy breath. Because he was a little worried about the light in the house, he squatted down and grasped one of the mason jar candles, and then got up again, using both hands to hold the jar before him.

He didn't realize that he trembled a little as he took step after step toward the big mirror. The air began to smell sweeter with each step he took, and when he reached the next door, he tucked the jar under his right arm, and pushed the door open without turning the knob.

The door flew back, slamming against the wall, and he looked in at a room that had a bare mattress in the far corner. The window was only partially boarded up. There was a table and a chair near the window. Regular electric lights were on—a bright overhead one and a small lamp next to the mattress—yet these did not fully light the far right side of the room.

Again, he got a whiff of that dead animal smell, and he didn't want to look in the corners of the room at all. He didn't want to have to step into the room to shut the door again, so he left it open.

In the hall, the wheezing sound continued. Kazi went to the next door. The door itself had been knocked in as if someone had kicked it over and over again from the hallway. He turned the knob, and it rattled a bit, but didn't open.

He pushed at the door, but it didn't budge. Because he

wanted to make sure that the wife was not in this room, he got down on his hands and knees and looked through the holes that had been made when someone had kicked at the door or rammed at it with something. The holes were tiny, little more than pinpricks, but he put his right eye up to one of them.

He couldn't see much, but again this room was fairly well lit, and he thought he saw a man's legs not far from the door. They were horizontal, so the man must've fallen down. He wore no shoes and possibly no pants either, although Kazi only saw to the man's kneecaps. A large bed was situated back beneath the window, which was shuttered, and it looked like someone lay sleeping in the bed.

Was this who he was supposed to help? Had someone gotten hurt and fallen? He tried the knob again, but the thing was definitely locked. Then he felt something cold on the back of his neck. He turned about, but no one was there. He counted the doors down the hall—at least twelve more doors to try.

He noticed that one door near the end of the hallway was now open, though it had been closed before. He stepped away from the door with the little holes in it, and decided to try that one next. He wanted to get out of the house quickly, and already was sure that he'd spent too much time in it. His mother would be furious with him for being late, and something even worse played through his mind: the fear about little boys who went missing. He knew about it, other kids his age knew about it, and it was on the news. Sometimes little boys just got lost and never turned up again.

Don't be afraid. It's only a house. It's not like those scary stories kids tell. It's just somebody's home.

At the next door, he saw a little water on the floorboards in the hall, and he looked in the room. It was a fairly large bathroom with a light on over the mirror. Once through the doorway, the floor was made of white tile. There was a sink and a claw-footed tub over in a corner. The water on the floor seemed to be coming from the sink, and Kazi wondered whether he should shut off the faucet. But when he stepped into the bathroom, he noticed that the source of the water was on the far side of the sink. As he took another step or two onto the water-soaked floor, he saw that the toilet had overflowed. He glanced around, half expecting someone to come up behind him, or even for someone to get out of the tub, but he was fairly sure nobody was around. His mother had always told him to use a plunger to stop the toilet from overflowing, or to turn a little knob to the side of the toilet that would shut off the water, but Kazi wasn't sure if he should do that here or not. And he hated standing there with the toilet water under his shoes.

To the right, within the bathroom, there was a narrow, locked door that Kazi figured led to the room next to it.

He went back into the hall and shut the door behind him. He went to the next room. This one had a door that was off its hinges and leaned against the doorframe. Kazi pushed it back a little so that he could scrunch himself up and look in.

At first, he wasn't sure what the piles of things in the room were. The smell was awful, even worse than the dead animals smelled. There were several lamps in this room turned up bright, and the room felt warm to him. But the piles of dark things—as he looked more carefully, he saw that they were . . . *poop. Somebody went to the bathroom in here. Over and over again.*

On the wallpaper, which peeled so much that some of it was half off the wall, there were big blotchy yellow stains.

Kazi tried to understand what he was seeing, and why someone had done this. Someone had gone into this room and . . . done what they were supposed to do in the bathroom. He tried not to imagine the person who would do this. *Mr. Spider?*

201

Douglas Clegg

Kazi drew himself out of the narrow passage of door and doorway, and glanced about the hall again. The wheezing continued, and he began to wonder if he shouldn't just find the stairs and run down and let Mr. Spider in. But something about doing that bothered him a little. He didn't like being in the house, but he was afraid Mr. Spider would be waiting for him, downstairs, just standing at the front door to catch him before he could get out.

A contrary kind of curiosity had gotten the better of Kazi. He wanted to see these rooms now. It was almost a hunger that had grown in the little boy, as if just seeing the first room had made his heart beat a little faster and caused his imagination to go into some kind of overdrive. He went across the hall to look at that room. The door opened easily, and it seemed to be a large closet, but as he peered around it, he saw that it was a fairly deep room—perhaps bigger than the others. Within it were stacks of old dusty books, and more stacks of magazines—piled so high some of them seemed to rise above the door's height. But stranger than the piles of books and magazines and even shoeboxes that bulged with papers, there were stacks of paper plates, and then another one of plastic forks and spoons, all in a pile. All with the remnants of food on them—a bit of sandwich sticking out of one, or some globs of gravy and potatoes. The smell in this room was a relief for him, as opposed to the shit-smell of the previous room, for while it had a mild stink to it, it mainly reminded Kazi of the smell of old boxes in an attic. He shut this door, then went to the next one.

Opening the door, the stench was unbearable. It was like sticking his face in someone's underwear, only it wasn't quite that—for the room was full of what looked at first like animal carcasses, but when he went into the room, he saw that they were half-eaten turkeys that had been roasted and were now rotting; a ham that looked as if

202

someone had chewed at it a while and then had left it out; what must've been a pig had been roasted, and its face half-eaten and half of its body also torn, with blackened ribs sticking out, but melted in some way by the rot. There were flies in this room, buzzing around, and the only windows were high in the room, small windows that were too hard to reach, and had been kept closed. The room's light came from three bulbs that hung down from nearly invisible wires.

To his left, Kazi saw what he assumed to be two large freezers that each looked big enough to hold a human body. Curiosity got the better of him, despite the thumping in his chest. He walked toward the freezers, around a pile of rotting pears and apples and wilted lettuce, stirring up some of the fruit flies and houseflies as he went. He reached the first freezer and tried to lift the lid, but could not. He went over to the other freezer, and this one had a latch, which he toggled back and forth until it clicked up. Then, huffing and puffing a bit, he managed to push the lid all the way up, causing him to lean over the freezer.

He wasn't sure what he saw then—it didn't register for him because he had been expecting something else. But quickly enough he realized what was in this freezer.

It was full of dead cats, their furry faces all frosted over.

He drew back quickly, and the freezer lid slammed shut, nearly taking with it his thumbs.

He stood there, taking deep breaths that hurt his ribs.

You have to get out. You have to get out.

But he said his wife needs help. She's hurt. You can't leave. You have to find her.

Mom? Where are you? Why aren't you here? he thought. Then he remembered the kids at school who made fun of him, and he straightened up. *You'll be okay. Something's wrong with Mr. Spider. That's all. Maybe he's like Grandfather before he died. Maybe that's all it is. Maybe.*

But still, as he stood in the room swatting at fruit flies that seemed to be everywhere, his throat went dry. If he had any pee in him, he was fairly sure it would've run down his leg yet again. He felt ice-cold, despite the fact that the room was fairly warm—even hot.

It's some kind of sickness. It's nothing bad. He's just a sick man. But his wife needs help.

The worst thing for Kazi Vrabec was not his fear, or what he'd seen in these rooms. It was that his thoughts had begun jumbling like they did when he didn't get enough sleep. He felt as if he had already started to accept something within this house. Something about it had begun to make sense to him.

The rooms, by themselves, had seemed creepy. But when he thought of all of them, it was like he could see inside somebody's head and listen to their thoughts.

Someone who had lost his mind lived here. Someone who lived upside-down and backward.

Someone who embraced the nightmare.

Kazi, you see? You went into the looking glass. Just like Alice. And you're here on the other side of it. But now you know the secret. The secret is that you've lived on the wrong side of things.

He tried to shake this voice out of his head and even held his breath for several seconds, thinking it would somehow make things right. But the voice was in his head, the voice of the someone who occupied these rooms. *It all makes sense if you watch. Each room is a special place. Each room is sacred. Each room contains the holiest of relics.*

"Stop it now," Kazi said aloud, just as his mother would.

He walked as quickly and yet as quietly as he could out of the room of the freezers and the food and the flies, and when he made it to the hall again, he shut the door behind him.

Yet he could not keep from checking out the next room over.

3

This room was completely bare.

In place of lamps and lights were more of the mason jars with their squat little candles wavering with light. The windows of this room were made of stained glass, like a church, but the designs were of beautiful birds with long legs and long beaks, and of fish, and water lilies; and it was all bright blue and gold and pale green. He went to the center of the room. The floorboards all needed work— there were nails that had come up from some of them, and many of the boards were mismatched.

Someone had torn off all the wallpaper and had written words on the bare white walls. Some of them were scrawled so small it was hard for him to read, but some were enormous.

Kazi read it aloud. "Dear Luke, I love you. I hope we see each other again someday. You were one of the great joys of my life. I hope you knew that. And I hope you know that what I'm doing today is not about my feelings for you or your brother (hi, Cody! I love you, too). I talked to you once about all the bad things in our family. Unfortunately, I have at least one of those. No, not depression. Not insanity. Not even ordinary fucked-upedness." Kazi giggled at this part, because while he knew that he could never say this word in real life, it sounded funny to say it in this room. As he read more of what was on the wall, he had the impression that a woman wrote this. *Not just a woman, but a crazy bitch, Kazi. A crazy-as-fuck bitch wrote this, and when she ran out of ink, she used her own shit, and when she ran out of shit, well, she used her own blood.*

The voice was back in his head. It sounded a lot like his own voice, only Kazi never talked like that.

He read more of the note, and did his best to quiet the voice in his head, and swallow the feeling of both fear and excitement as he discovered more and more about the person who had written this. She was somebody's aunt, and she loved her nephew, and she was going to kill.herself. Then she started writing about God and the devil and eternity and the infinite and portals and doorways and places that existed outside time and space and places that may never exist at all and might have other gods in them that nobody had yet worshipped. Some of her writing was a mass of squiggles and lines, and then she seemed to have written math equations on the wall, as well as drawings of people—but they looked almost like more squiggles and circles and lines, the kinds of drawing a four-year-old would make.

Some of the writing he couldn't read, and some of it was too high up on the wall. How did she reach it? he wondered. How had she written some of it on the ceiling?

As he turned around to read the bit about how someone named Luke should follow in her footsteps, Kazi noticed something in the room that he hadn't when he'd first walked in.

Next to the doorway, but back behind the open door itself, was a large wardrobe. Kazi thought of one of his favorite books, *The Lion, The Witch and the Wardrobe,* but it also reminded him of one of his favorite pictures of his grandmother and grandfather, where they were standing in their bedroom, and in the background was a wardrobe just like this one—not too tall, but long and deep.

He opened one of the wardrobe doors. Inside it were some blankets and a pillow, and on a shelf just above this, a small desk lamp.

Someone slept here, Kazi. Someone. Maybe the woman who wrote on the walls. Maybe she spent her days sleeping in here, and her nights scribbling away, the crazy bitch.

4

He opened other doors, or looked through keyholes, as he went down the long hall. In one room, he saw what he thought were statues of animals—birds like the one he'd seen in the stained glass window, herons or egrets, and dogs and cats, and even some monkeys. The room was fairly dark—the window had been boarded up, and the only light that came in was from the hall and the mason jar candle in his hand. He wondered what the statues were really like, and as he went into the room he saw they were not statues at all. They were like mummies he'd seen on the National Geographic channel and the History channel. They were all dried up and covered with thin bandages and oozed a little with some kind of glue. He touched a mummified monkey's head, then quickly brought his hand back, afraid of it. In the feeble light, he could only see a handful of these mummies, but he had the sense that there must be a hundred or more of them in the room.

He went across the hall and opened the next door onto a room that looked as if someone had set it on fire several days before. Its wallpaper was blackened and curled and peeled off in most places, and the room smelled of barbeque. There was no window, but it was lit with several small floor lamps. At the center of the room was what looked like a metal trash can. Kazi stepped in. He coughed a little because the air had a bit of smokiness to it. When he reached the trash can, he looked inside.

Just burnt stuff.

Probably trash.

Next to the trash can, he saw a small knapsack. It looked like the kind any kid in his school might have. But something inside it was moving. Something wriggled.

Or at least, he thought it did.

He looked more closely, but it stopped moving.

Maybe it never moved at all. Maybe you just imagined it. Maybe it's just some knapsack some kid had, and someone is going to burn it in this trash can.

He left this room and thought of Mr. Spider's wife. She

had to be somewhere in here. *Either up here, or downstairs. Or upstairs? How many rooms did this house have?* It seemed endless, but he was fairly sure there were three stories and he was on the second.

In the hall, that wheezing, groaning sound as if someone had fluid in their lungs. Or perhaps the person snored—his mother sometimes snored like that, so much that it seemed to Kazi that it rattled her bedroom door.

The noise echoed down the hallway.

It's the house. The house is breathing.

No, that's crazy. Crazy as the crazy bitch, kid.

5

Kazi looked in on a few more rooms, and although he saw things that seemed not quite right, he couldn't figure out why he felt it. In one room, four tricycles were in the center, and a mountain bike leaned against the wall near the window. In another room, there a large rubber ball. It reminded him a little of the kind they used in dodge ball at school, but he didn't go into this room to look at the ball. One of the rooms was like a perfect bedroom of the richest person he could imagine. The bed was curtained and canopied, and there was an antique table and beautiful chairs beside it. A vanity table with an old-fashioned mirror above a wash basin. There was even a fireplace, though the fire was out. Yet something made him not want to step into the room, and so he remained in the hallway.

Several of the rooms were locked. Some of them had large keyholes and he could look in, but they seemed empty. Some had keyholes plugged up with something. At one of these, he thought he heard scratching at the door. He tried the doorknob, but it wouldn't budge. Something was scratching at the base of the door, and the scratching became more frantic as Kazi stood there. Because his curiosity was overwhelming, he got down on his stomach and tried to look under the crack between the door and the floor, but all he saw was the shadow of something. He thought he heard whimpering, too, like a dog.

Someone's dog is trapped in that room.

Or is it a dog? Is it someone crazy trapped inside there? Trying to scratch his way out?

Kazi had begun to forget that there even was an outside world at all. He found the rooms fascinating and scary, but he had to try to look in each one. He thought of Mr. Spider's wife, and how she might need help. But he didn't feel in that much of a rush to find her anymore. He just wanted to know what was in the rooms of the house. His mind pored over what he had seen, even as he went to the next room.

He reached for the knob, but it was so hot he pulled his hand back fast. He touched the wood of the door. It felt like a stove that was getting warmer.

He looked at the door.

It's a burning room. Inside that room, it's a furnace.

He glanced down the hallway to the staircase and the big mirror at the end of the hall. For a fraction of a second, he had thought he saw some movement. Or a shadow.

He moved on to the next room, which was in complete darkness. Even when he put his arm in the room with the candle, the flame went out. He took one step in the room, and if it were not from the light of the hall, he would have thought he was standing on the edge of a cut-out floor, and all around him was a huge pit of blind night.

6

Out in the hall again, the wheezing sound had stopped, replaced by someone shouting from some distant place. Was it Mr. Spider, outside wondering what was taking him so long? But it didn't quite sound like him. It sounded like someone shouting something happily, as if he had good news to spread. Kazi passed a few of the doors, trying to find the source of the sound. As he approached one of the rooms near the end of the hall, he realized it was the sound of a television set.

A man on television was shouting: "It's the time of miracles! There are wars and rumors of war! And we need to rejoice in this! For we know of what comes next. We know the signs and the miracles at hand. That Babylon, that great harlot, will ride the beast, and the plagues will come down upon us! But are we afraid? No! We raise up a joyous song to the Almighty! For though the lost souls will be cast into the flames of perdition and torment, the righteous shall be taken up into the arms of the angels!"

Kazi knew these shows. They were sometimes on Sunday mornings when he got up early to have his Frosted Flakes, and he'd sit in his jammies and listen to the preachers on TV because they seemed as if they meant just what they said.

He followed the voice to a partially open door, and pushed it further in.

It was a small, narrow room. The television, at the far wall, faced Kazi and looked like no TV he'd ever seen—it was smaller and the picture was rounded and distorted, and had no color to it. The man on the TV looked like he was from some old movie, and the camera went to a closeup on his face as he shouted: "Faith is the only thing that will save you! Do not rely on the works of men, but on the abiding infinite glory that has always been and will always be. There will be those who live in shadows in these days, and they shall build churches of damnation and will call themselves Sons of God, but they are Princes of Lies and Lords of Flies and Priests of Hell!"

Facing the television was a tall round-back chair. Next to

it, a small round wooden table. On the table were prescription bottles and an ashtray. To the right of the chair, what looked to Kazi like a large green metal tube, but the voice in his head said, *Dumbshit, it's an oxygen tank.*

The wheezing sound began again, and then a brief blast as if someone had just farted very loudly.

The noises came from the chair.

Rising above the chair, a thin trail of smoke.

Someone sat in the chair, watching the television, smoking a cigarette.

As he stepped into the room, he noticed the ashes piled on the floor beneath the table, as if the person in the chair kept missing the ashtray through several cigarettes.

It's her, he thought. *She's very sick. She doesn't know her husband's locked out. She may need help.*

He took another few steps closer to the chair. To his right, he saw a folded wheelchair, and near its wheels, several hypodermic needles.

"Do you need some help?" he asked. Another step brought him nearly behind the chair. The wheezing grew louder, but the smoke had stopped floating up toward the ceiling.

He boldly went around the oxygen tank, and was all prepared to see an old or very crippled woman, but the chair was empty. A few cigarette butts were the only thing on its cushion. The plastic line from the oxygen tank lay stuffed behind the cushion itself.

On the TV the man said, "Miracles are everywhere! Anything can happen now, if you believe. You must have faith or you will burn eternally!"

7

Do you have faith? The voice in Kazi's head buzzed around somewhere just beneath his scalp. *Do you, little Kazimir?*

Douglas Clegg

Faith can move mountains. Faith can alter reality. Faith is like having me inside you all the time. Your imaginary friend. That's who. Yes, me. You think you've seen some weird shit, kid, let me tell you, there's more where that came from. You haven't even found the room of knives or the room with the wacky art. And it's truly wacky—some of this shit has boogers on it where the crayons and fingerpaints didn't get the green-yellow color right. You want to see more, don't you?

Kazi turned off the television, and chose to ignore the voice.

Then he flicked the TV back on, but changed the channels in a way he'd never had to at home—on a dial that had only six channels listed (2, 4, 5, 7, 9, and something called UHF/VHF). When he turned to one of the channels, he saw a girl with blond hair raise an axe over a girl with dark hair; when he turned to another one, he saw some kids he knew from school chewing on a boy whose face he couldn't quite see; he turned to another channel, and this time, he saw the outside of Harrow. Mr. Spider stood staring up at the house; on the fifth channel, he saw the first room he'd entered. There in the corner, the candles, and the dead possum and crows and rats and mice. The camera moved through the room, into the hallway, and then he saw a shot of the entire hall again, with the big mirror at the end.

When he turned to the last channel—the one marked UHF/VHF—he looked at the narrow room he was in, only this time from the doorway. He saw the chair and the oxygen tank on the TV set, and the prescription bottles on the small round table and the ashtray, as well as the ashes on the floor beneath the table.

And he saw himself there, the back of him, as he watched the TV set, and the camera was moving into the room toward him slowly.

Don't turn around, Kazi, the voice said. *You don't want to see what's coming for you.*

212

Kazi trembled a little, his fingers grazing the knob of the TV as he watched the camera that was taping him move low along the floor. It stopped near the small table, and something that was not quite fingers yet not quite claws touched each of the prescription bottles lightly, as if checking to see whether any pills remained in them.

Then the camera moved around the back of the high-backed chair.

Kazi felt frozen in place and yet entranced as he watched the television and saw the camera that must be behind him, move toward him.

Whoever was in the room with him stood so close that she could touch him.

Why she?

Why not he? Or it?

Some crazy bitch is coming for you, Kazi. Get ready. Come on. You ready? She's gonna getcha. She's gonna reach out and take you in her crazy arms and rub your face into those tits of hers and then you're gonna know what crazy tastes like. Don't look now, wussy, because what's on the other side of the TV looking at you is not entirely human.

Kazi watched the television screen.

Again the thin, clawlike fingers—as if it were a very old woman, so old that she'd have to be mummified—bone-thin, gnarled arthritic fingers touched the back of his neck.

It felt like a shock of warmth, and goose bumps rose along his neck and shoulders and arms and even in places he didn't think goose bumps could find.

He could not stop watching the television.

Behind him, he heard a strange sucking sound, as if someone were trying to make a kiss in the air, or someone who had no teeth might be . . . *trying to say something, little shit. She's mad I tells ya, mad. And getting madder by the minute.*

213

Douglas Clegg

Don't look.
Don't turn around.
You don't want to see.

His own voice mixed with the other voice (but it sounded like him all along) and his mind became crossed wires, but he knew not to turn around. Yet he wanted to. He had to see what was behind him.

He had to see what was there.

If I turn around, it will be all right. If I turn around, whatever is there will be gone.

If I turn around . . .

You gotta have faith, kid.

Like the guy on TV told you.

You believe, Kazimir Vrabec? You believe in the house? If you believe in the house, maybe the house will believe in you.

A series of images flashed through his mind, so fast that it went by in the blink of an eye. He saw himself crawling through the open window, and then the window shutting behind him. He saw himself pulling down his pants, and pooping in the room that was full of human excrement. Then he peed on the wall. He saw himself taking a live cat in his hands and wringing its neck while it clawed at him, and then opening the freezer to throw the dead animal in with the rest. He saw himself on a stepladder, writing a long letter to someone named Luke, using crayons and chalk, scribbling fast and sure. He saw himself lying among the blankets in the wardrobe, peering out from the door as if expecting someone to come into the room. He saw himself in the chair, the thin plastic tube tucked up around his nose, a cigarette in his hand. And then, worst of all these brief flickering visions, he saw himself approach himself, standing there, watching the television.

These images flickered through his mind, and then faded as he kept hearing the strange sucking and smacking sound behind him.

He reached forward and turned off the television.

Against his own will, he forced himself to turn around to look at whatever stood behind him. At the edge of his vision, he saw something yellow, and then as he swiveled around.

Sitting in the high-backed chair was what looked like a shriveled piece of meat, wrapped in gauzelike bandages.

Kazi glanced about the room, thinking that someone else might be there. But there was no one.

He went over to the thing on the chair, and as he got a little closer, he saw its eyes and its ears and the dessicated muzzle. It was the head of some kind of dog—maybe even a wolf? Or a coyote? Some kind of dog with slightly pointed ears. The head had been wrapped up and mummified.

And it had just been put in the chair.

No one else was around.

He was tempted to turn around again and turn on the television. *But if you do, what if something worse shows up? I mean, come on, kid, the mummified head of a dog ain't so bad. It could be worse. It could be the whole dog, alive, ready to tear you apart.*

Go ahead. Pick it up. It's a gift from the house. To you. Look at the handiwork. It's like ancient Egypt, kid. You don't know about the ancients? They'd take beloved pets or sacred animals, and when the head of the household died, they'd just slaughter 'em all because they believed they could take them to the afterlife with them. Didn't know that, Kazi? Well, welcome to the world of "history is fun." Stick with me, kid, and I'll show you the sights. You know, for all you know, this is Anubis, God of the Underworld. And maybe he's just gonna be your best friend from here on out.

Kazi knelt in front of the chair, and looked all around the dog head. It was grizzled and shriveled, with matted fur sticking out where the thin bandages had come loose. It almost looked like someone had used oatmeal to bind the gauze to the fur.

"You want to go for a walk?" Kazi asked the head. He

215

asked it as if the dog had already told him it wanted to explore the house a little.

8

As Kazi explored the rooms of Harrow, the mummy head stuck beneath his arm, a Mason jar candle in his hand, Ronnie Pond had just avoided the slice of Bari Love's hatchet.

Chapter Fourteen

1

Ronnie Pond had been dodging and kicking out at Bari Love for nearly an hour, rolling around on the floor, until she finally got hold of Bari's wrist and tightened her fingers around it until Bari dropped the hatchet. But the hatchet refused to simply drop—instead, it flew from Bari's hand and whizzed over the romance bookshelves and narrowly missed hitting a bust of Shakespeare on the Classics counter not far from the cash register.

"What the fuck are you doing!" Ronnie cried out, nearly breathless, but able to bring her knee up between Bari's legs and push hard there until she saw a grimace of pain on Bari's blood-spattered face.

Bari snarled at her in reply and smashed her left fist into the side of Ronnie's face.

Ronnie groaned in pain and fought the dizzying feeling that made her wonder if she would black out. She knew if she did, she'd be dead meat. She remembered her sister's excellent advice about backhand in tennis, and reached

217

over to a fallen hardcover—a Janet Evanovich novel—and brought it up, whapping Bari as hard as she could in the face with it.

"Fucking bitch!" Bari growled. She grabbed an omnibus edition of Dean Koontz novels off the shelf and brought it down against Ronnie's skull. Ronnie nearly yipped in pain, but used the moment to knock Bari to the side; and then she rolled over on top of her.

She pinned her to the ground with her knees to Bari's chest, then swiftly grabbed each of her wrists and held it down.

Bari's face was practically between Ronnie's knees as she tried to crawl under her to get out of the position.

Suddenly, Bari grinned and parted her lips. Her tongue darted out and touched the edge of Ronnie's left thigh. Ronnie recoiled in disgust, and Bari shoved her in a split-second body slam. Ronnie fell backward against the bestseller racks, which gave and crashed to the carpeted floor.

Ronnie quickly glanced at the lower shelves—the only thing approaching a weapon was a thin metal bookend. She grabbed it and swung wildly at Bari, who had just leapt toward her again. She cut Bari clean across the nose and face, taking out her left eye.

Bari screamed in pain, and rolled to the floor, covering her left eye—or what dangled from the socket—as blood rushed down her cheeks.

Ronnie scrambled to her feet and ran to get the hatchet. Then she picked up the phone by the register, but it was dead.

Outside, several dogs with bloody paws leapt at the floor-to-ceiling glass windows and door.

She thought she heard a scream from the apartment above the bookstore.

She grabbed some of the twine that Nick and Dusty used to tie up books at times. Using the hatchet, she cut off lengths of the twine. Just enough for wrists and ankles. Then, the hatchet held high, Ronnie, confused and terrified but completely prepared to use it to defend her life, went to tie up Bari Love.

Bari's face was nearly obliterated with the first gushes of blood. Bari lay there, curled up like a kitten, snoring lightly, little bubbles of blood popping at the gash just above her nostrils.

2

Ronnie sat beside the sleeping, bloodied girl, and first wrapped the twine around her ankles. The pain in Ronnie's shoulders—from where Nick had jabbed her with the scissors—now seemed like a distant thunder of hurt. *You will get through this. You will, Veronica Pond. You were a Girl Scout. You can handle wounded and wild animals.* Then she thought the most ridiculous thing, given the situation: *I want some peach tea.* She and Lizzie had a ritual on bad nights when everything seemed to be going wrong. They'd take showers and get in their big bathrobes and make a pot of peach or blueberry tea, and just sit and chat about the five or six things bugging them. Their silly language would come through most at those times. Even the phrase "peach tea" was something they'd say to each other in school if it was a particularly hellish day.

But nothing's as hellish as this.

Lizzie, where are you when I need you?

Where's anybody when I need them?

It's peach tea time, and I don't have a teapot to piss in. Ronnie giggled when she thought this. She said it aloud, as if to affirm that she still could talk. "Teapot to piss in."

She glanced at the fluorescent lights overhead, and then at the line of books—the bestseller shelves on one side, the romance section behind her, and somewhere beyond all this the occasional growl and scratch of a dog at

219

the door. It was as if they wanted to come in here and finish what Bari and Nick had begun.

She glanced at her watch—the face had gotten smashed in the fight and the watch had stopped at 5 P.M.

It would be dark outside; it felt dark inside to her, too.

She watched Bari's face. *Is she faking? How does she fall asleep with her face all gashed up? Why did Nick wake up and kill Dusty? Why?*

More questions came at her, and none of them had rational answers. It was as if they had rabies. *Can people get rabies fast, like this? Or maybe there was a truck full of toxic crap that overturned out on the highway. Or maybe it's one of those viruses that mosquitoes carry—even though there aren't any mosquitoes around anymore. Or maybe there's some kind of brain swelling going on. The water supply. Terrorists? Maybe they picked Watch Point to . . . No, that's bullshit.*

It's something awful. That's all you know. It's something terrible.

Ronnie could not express, even to herself, the way her conception of life had just changed in a matter of seconds. She had lived a fairly quiet, sheltered existence, and had never had to deal with a life-and-death situation except for when she watched her father die in a car wreck. But even that hadn't left her feeling unprotected. She knew about cars and how they could have accidents and somehow knowing that it happened in the world to other people had softened the idea of his death.

This is different. This is like . . . like a plague just came down.

The dogs. Bari. Nick.

God, who else? Are there others dealing with this?

She sifted through dozens of scenarios to explain why Nick would kill his life partner, and why mad dogs would be trying to break into the bookstore, and why Bari Love, who truly may have had the bitch gene in her but still—*a hatchet?*

"It's like they're possessed," she said aloud.

As soon as she said it, she wanted to take back the thought. The word.

The ridiculous word.

Possessed.

Like some gooney idea of devils and demons.

Possessed by some infernal agent of hell.

Witchcraft. Demons. Supernatural.

All crap. All ridiculous. All irrational.

Like those dreams you've been having. The ones that started the night Lizzie made you promise to tell no one that she had been at the house.

Harrow.

Beyond the village, up and down the streets that sank farther into the woods, beyond those "No Trespassing" signs.

Harrow. One of the oldest houses in Watch Point. Falling apart. Nearly abandoned.

You once knew some boys who went there when it was a prep school. You read about the murders that had happened there when a new owner bought it a few years back, but you didn't really believe many of those stories going around because . . .

Because it's all so fucking irrational.

Possessed. Ridiculous.

Possessed.

It seemed so medieval to even think it. And yet, it was the word that stuck with her as she wrapped twine around Bari's ankles. She knotted it up as tightly as she could get it without cutting off the circulation in Bari's legs. Then she took Bari's limp hands and bound them behind her back. To do this, Ronnie had to turn Bari to the side. She held her breath, certain that Bari would wake up at any moment.

In the impression in the carpet where Bari's head had lain, a spattering of more blood.

Ronnie felt sick to her stomach as she laid Bari's head back again.

Taking the hatchet with her, she rose and began walking back toward the storeroom.

Each step felt like an eternity, and she began to have a feeling of déjà vu, although she wasn't quite sure why. Somehow it reminded her of dreams she'd had in the summer, but she could not for the life of her remember the specifics of any one dream. Yet images flashed before her as she went, dreading the door itself. Like movie clips in her brain, she remembered masks coming off faces. And behind the masks, the face of a single child. Behind every mask, that little boy who had no eyes and whose teeth shone like metal.

Ronnie took a deep breath and held it for four seconds before letting it out. *Calm down. Calm down. You're alive. You have a cut in your shoulder, but you can get to the Emergency Room later. Worst thing that'll happen is you get a tetanus shot and some penicillin. You'll live. This will all turn out okay somehow. Somehow.*

She reached the door to the storeroom, and got out the keys. She put the key in the lock, her fingers trembling.

When she opened the door, the puddles of blood had become dark stains.

Dusty lay where he'd fallen, a mass of bones and blood and flesh and torn clothes. She quickly looked away.

Nick had gone back to the cot and lay down again.

Asleep.

When she went into the storeroom, she locked the door behind her. She walked through the room, feeling numb and gulping back a genuine need to scream which had begun growing within the pit of her being. She held the hatchet in midair, ready to bring it down on Nick's head as she looked down at him.

His nostrils flared slightly, then sank inward; his eyes

were closed but fluttering in sleep; his lips moved slightly as if he were talking in a dream.

She glanced around the shelves and boxes as if sure that someone else might be lurking there. Then she began walking toward the back door of the building, hoping that there were no dogs or girls with hatchets on the other side of that door.

3

Ronnie emerged into the dusky twilight—the sun had begun going down and a chilly dark had set in. She stood in the gated alleyway and for just a moment sent a prayer up to whatever god might be listening. *I don't care who you are. I don't care what you are. I don't care if you're going to own my soul. Just please keep my mother and sister safe. And my friends. And please let this have been just a hallucination on my part. Please don't let this be real. I don't want real.*

The silence of the moment was interrupted by the piercing shriek of a woman—*no, it's a man, he's just screaming like a girl*—from a building down the block.

She saw little boys up on a housetop, and they had a woman with them. It looked like they were holding her hands. There were four of them—and although she wasn't sure who they were, she was fairly certain that the house was the Moldens'. She babysat those boys all the time.

She watched as the boys pushed the woman—*their mother?*—off the roof.

Ronnie clutched the hatchet, and went through the back gate into the alley behind the shops. She glanced each way along the narrow street, noting its green plastic trash cans and cars parked on each side. Fences along the other side of the alley defined the beginning of a neighborhood.

She had to get home. She knew she had to get home and make sure her mother was okay. She began walking down the alley toward the side street that spilled into Main Street.

Ronnie held the hatchet above her head. She walked slowly at first. She glanced behind a pile of garbage, and wasn't sure but thought she saw a child's hand there among the discarded McDonald's bags and withering vegetables. But she didn't inspect it further—she just did not want to know.

Lizzie, are you okay? Lizzie?

"Please let me be crazy," she muttered to herself, as if it were a prayer. "Let me be insane. Let me be insane."

She began walking faster as a new fear took over—the fear that whatever had gotten into Bari and Nick would creep into her next. *Is it passed through blood? How? How does it go? What is it? Is it a plague that comes at you from getting bitten? Do the dogs have to bite you first?*

As she turned left, she saw a man in a business suit running between the buildings as if trying to escape from something. Seconds later, a pack of mutts followed him, snapping and growling.

Then her view of the street was empty except for Army Vernon's florist shop across the way.

She waited to see if it would be quiet on Main Street for at least a minute. She didn't want to venture out until she felt ready.

She heard the screeching of tires as someone sped along the streets of town, and then a sickening crash and the sound of glass breaking.

In the silence that followed the crash—during which time she tried not to think of her father dying—she began to hear children cheering and clapping. Incongruously, at least for October, she thought she heard the sing-song bells of the ice cream truck. As she thought of it, she said the words, "I scream truck," as if it could conjure a scene in her mind. Her impulses were in conflict—part of her wanted to run away from the sound of the crash and find some safe place to hide. *With my hatchet. Me and my hatchet.*

But the other impulse took over. One that she had never been completely sure she'd have, and perhaps no one ever knew they had until faced with it in an irrefutable reality: She wanted to help. She wanted to protect whomever was in that car wreck.

Like I couldn't protect you, Dad.

With that intention, she stepped out of the building's shadows into the streetlights. *Me and my hatchet.*

Just up by the Watch Point Community Bank Building, she saw how the car had overturned right after hitting a lamppost, which leaned near the ground after the accident.

The driver of the vehicle—Mr. Boatwright, who she'd just sold reading glasses to that afternoon—was upside down in the shoulder harness.

There was smoke coming out from the back of the car, and the smell in the air was of fire, although she couldn't see any.

The dogs that had been scratching at the bookstore windows ran to the accident. As soon as they got there, a girl who looked about eleven grabbed a Chihuahua and began shaking it mercilessly. When she dropped it, it ran off up the street. The other dogs followed, as if on to a new scent.

She recognized some of the little kids from town and a couple of the older ones—Mike Spears and Allie Cooney, who were juniors at her high school. They were trying to open the doors of Boaty's car.

Boaty was as wide-eyed as anyone could be, and he had kept the windows up and the doors locked. As Ronnie walked up Main Street toward the wreck, which was beautifully lit in the lamplight, she saw what might've been someone else in the seat next to the man. Who was it?

Then Mike Spears took a rock and broke the driver's side window. They all dragged Boaty out of the car, into the street. Something was funny about Mike—and she realized it was that he wore no pants or underwear at all. From the waist down he was naked.

Something rose within Ronnie and she let out what she would only later describe as a warrior's yelp. She ran up the street, swinging the hatchet as she went, her only goal to make sure that Mr. Boatwright did not get torn up by these maniacs. Without thinking twice, she swung the hatchet into the group of children, and while part of her mind was aware that she'd just lopped off little Mark Malanski's left arm (*the kid didn't even shriek, what the hell?*) the rest of her brain didn't seem to care. It was as if she'd switched into survival mode, and all she cared about was making sure Boaty didn't get what Dusty got.

She began to feel almost exalted—and she wasn't comfortable like that. *It wants you to be a god,* she thought as she threatened Mike Spears with the hatchet. His face was blackened with what she assumed was blood, and, naked except for his shirt, he sported an engorged erection.

She pushed her way through the toddlers, some of whom were chewing on Boaty's fingers; others had little butter knives and were trying to cut into his throat with them. She kicked them, swung at them, shoved them, and they all moved away from him.

Boaty looked up at her, trembling. He whispered words, but his throat sent up a dry rasp. She knelt beside him, her hatchet at the ready should anyone jump her, and she got closer to him. He whispered, "Make it fast. Make it fast."

She drew back. "I'm not going to hurt you, Mr. Boatwright. Please, try to stay calm. Please."

"Make it fast," he whispered. "Make it fast. End it. End it."

He reached up with his right hand, which had been gnawed at enough that two of his fingers were no more than bleeding nubs, and grasped her collar. He drew himself up slightly. "Please, Veronica. Do it." His feeble voice shivered with his body. "I killed one of 'em. In the car. My niece. She wanted a ride. But she started touching me. *Touching me.* I saw all the others. I saw Mary Thompson. I saw what they did to her. How they dragged her." His breathing became too rapid, and he was in danger of hyperventilating. She wanted to try to keep him quiet, but she felt as if she needed to know why all this had suddenly happened. She glanced back at the blood-spattered children. She saw Allie Cooney down on her knees in front of Mike. One of the little boys had a metal rake in his hands and was slowly advancing on Ronnie, but when she held up the hatchet, he backed off. Some of the others had begun tearing at the Malanski boy. *It's because I cut his arm off. They smelled the blood. They want the blood and meat.*

"I'll get help," Ronnie said.

"No, no help."

"You need help."

"THERE IS NO HELP!" Boaty screamed and the force of it sent a shock through her. "THEY GO TO SLEEP AND THEY DREAM AND YOU CAN'T DISTURB THEM OR THEY THINK THEY'RE STILL DREAMING!"

Exhausted, he sank back down to the road.

She thought she heard what might've been hoofbeats— as if horses were running wild through town. She glanced up the road, and noticed that the other children stopped what they were doing—dropping Mark Malanski's lifeless body to the ground, their mouths dripping—and also looked in the direction of the thudding and *clip-clop* sound.

Rounding the corner, people.

Not just more children.

Not more teenagers.

But people she recognized from the village.

They had come running. Was it the smell of smoke? Or of blood?

They had made the hoofbeat sounds in their heels and Rockports and boots and sneakers and dress shoes.

And they stopped when they saw her.

"Make it end," Boaty whispered again, his voice fading. "They go to sleep. They go to sleep. I want to sleep, too. Make it end."

With the shadows of twilight all around them, and the buildings of town seeming emptier than she'd ever noticed, Ronnie Pond looked at the men and women from the village. They stood there as if waiting for a traffic signal to change.

Watching her.

They're waiting to see what I'm going to do.

They want to see me kill Boaty.

"Wake me up when it's over," Boaty gasped, and then closed his eyes as if he were being drawn into sleep.

She tried to lift him, but he was too heavy. Her shoulder throbbed a little from pain.

"There's nothing I can do," she said as quietly as she could.

Boaty's eyes fluttered open. "Kill me. Kill me when I close my eyes."

"I can't."

"If you don't kill me, it might take me over. I've been inside it. I know what it is."

"What? What are you talking about?"

"Harrow," he said. He reached for her right arm—and the hatchet. "Just bring it down on me. It'll be fast. I won't feel it."

"I can't," she whispered and didn't even realize she'd begun crying.

"It's like you stepped into a nightmare," he said with a slight smile. "It's like maybe after you kill me, I'll wake up. And it'll be over. And I won't ever have to dream again. Please. Please. I've seen what they do. They're like wolves."

"How is this happening?"

"When I was a boy, I saw something up there. At Harrow. Something that might have been the devil himself for all I know. Somehow, it leaked out. Something in that house broke open and leaked out like toxic gas. I don't think there's any way to stop it. Please. Veronica. I don't mind dying. Everyone I loved is dead here. I think you will be, too. Soon. I'm sorry." Then he made a grab for the hatchet, knocking her off-balance, and she fell across him.

When she looked back up, he had the hatchet in both hands, its blade aimed for his head.

"Goodbye," he said and then slammed the hatchet down onto his face.

In the same moment, the people standing at the corner moved forward.

The little kid with the metal rake began running toward her, and Ronnie had no time—she grabbed the hatchet, pulling it up with a sucking sound from the middle of Boaty's face.

She rolled upward, standing on unsure feet. She nearly lost her balance, but she came up swinging the hatchet and caught the hand of a girl who worked at the A&P. The hand flew, and blood spurted. Ronnie had already begun running, and the people at the corner watched as the children around the car wreck began circling Howard Boatwright's lifeless body.

Several people began running after Ronnie. She decided to try to run back down toward the train station.

Run along the tracks. Get the hell out of here.

Lizzie? Lizzie are you okay?

Mom?

She had to pretend they were fine. Fear had gotten hold of her, as well as that primal survival sense, that jungle feeling that the leopards and jaguars would leap out from any branch and the snakes would bite and the insects would devour—that human reaction to severe danger that only clicks into place, if you're lucky, once before you die.

Douglas Clegg

5

In the Houseman home, Ronnie's twin, Lizzie, had just begun popping the metal corkscrew through Norma Houseman's cheek. "Don't cry out," Lizzie whispered, her right hand petting Norma's cheek as the point of the corkscrew poked through her skin. "It may hurt, but this is what you want, isn't it?"

Norma's eyes were wide and her face had gone pale as the first drop of blood slid like a tear down to her chin.

Lizzie kissed the drop of blood, then turned the corkscrew around and around allowing it to drill through Norma's cheek until there was a nice big hole. "I know your dreams, Norma. I know this is what you dream of. Of holes in your skin. Holes all over your body. You're not afraid, are you? Not really. Not in that deep place inside that knows what you want."

Norma's eyes still showed fear, watching Lizzie as if she were some kind of ravenous predator. But even in that fear, Lizzie could smell the need. Norma needed the pain. Norma needed to open herself.

The back door slammed, and Norma glanced past the stairs to the kitchen. Her eldest son, William, who was nearly fourteen years old, trooped into the room, carrying her gardening shears in his hands. Norma wanted to tell him to run away, but she felt a strange eroticism as Lizzie Pond drilled holes in her cheek, as the pain in her shoulder tore at her, pinned as it was to the doorframe by the small kitchen knife. She felt a moisture in the pit of her being—a lubrication as if this excited her.

Even with William cutting at the air in front of him with her gardening shears.

She felt an excitement, and realized that Lizzie was right—this was her dream coming true. A dream of cutting and slicing and drilling. A dream where something opened

230

her up so completely that it was as if her flesh were turned inside out and she was nothing but tingling pleasure, electrical impulses of feelings, feelings, and more feelings.

William, his face shiny and fresh as if he'd just had a bath, clicked the gardening shears like crab claws as he approached her. As Norma closed her eyes, she felt the dream coming on.

It's taking me. It's going to open me.

My children. My children are going to open me again, as they did when they were born.

6

In the Ratty Dog Bar & Grille, you could hear a pin drop.

Luke Smithson closed his cell phone after hearing the voice of his dead aunt Danni on it. She had spent nearly ten minutes regaling him with stories of the house where she lived. "It's beautiful, Luke. I want you to come stay with me. Oh, wait 'til I show you the room. Your room. You can write your novel in it. It's perfect for that. The inspiration is all there. The Nightwatchman's story can be written down, at last, and you can be the famous author that you've always dreamed of being, although I think it should be called *The Caretaker*, because that seems more true, doesn't it? He's not really watching anything; he's taking care of a marvelous home. You can even work on your diary. The room has a beautiful desk made out of mahogany—brought all the way from an estate in London. It was once owned by one of those famous sad writers who killed himself too young but wrote his masterpiece there. If you look closely at the wood, you can see the scratchings he made on it. Like he had already begun to go mad as he was writing his greatest work. You can be like that, Luke. I want you here with me. I have some rooms all ready for us—you can have an office, a bedroom, and your own bathroom. It's really wonderful."

He said nothing. He felt a curious numbness go through his body as he watched Pete the bartender keep the shotgun aimed at his face. He watched his old buddy Bish reach into his own jeans and fondle himself while watching the movie on the TV screen. At this point, he and Bish were no longer kissing or making love on the screen, but instead, Luke had begun biting Bish along his throat as if he were a vampire. He drew small drops of blood from Bish's skin while Bish—on-screen—thrust his arm toward Luke's mouth so that he might bite along that, as well.

The blonde with the guy kept laughing and now and then pointing over at Luke, until finally, the movie on the television ended with Luke completely devouring Bish, first the fingers and the hand, and then tearing at his lips, and then chewing his face, until the picture faded into black. On the cell phone, Aunt Danni said, "I'm so lonely here without you, Luke. I want you here, and I know you'll come. It's hard to describe because it's not a place like any other in the world, but you want to see all, don't you? You want to write about everything, from both sides of life and death, don't you? You could be the greatest writer that mankind has ever known."

Luke dropped his cell phone. As it clattered to the floor, shattering the momentary quiet, Bish got off the bar stool and came over to Luke. He put his hands up to both sides of Luke's face. "You want to know why our friendship ended, Luke? Maybe you don't remember how you humiliated me one day. One day when I told you I loved you. Not 'was in love' with you. But loved you. And you laughed at me. You laughed and told me to go to hell. It was the most devastating thing that had ever happened to me. I confided something to you. I was afraid how you'd react. And look at you. You don't even remember, do you? You wiped it out of your mind like shit off your shoe."

Bish let go of Luke, then turned to Pete. Pete nodded and passed him the shotgun.

Before Luke could make a move, Bish pointed the gun at Luke, and then swiveled around so that the shotgun came right up to Pete's head. Bish squeezed the trigger, and Luke closed his eyes before having to see what the blast did to Pete.

Luke staggered backward, some of Pete's blood having splashed him.

Bish stood there, grinning. "How about them? Those two?" He pointed the shotgun at the guy and the blonde in the corner, who were laughing as if they couldn't imagine anything funnier. "You want to see what I can do to them?"

"Bish?" Luke asked as if he'd get a reasonable answer. He was beyond the shock of watching the bartender fall to the floor, or hearing his dead aunt on the cell phone, or even imagining the porn movie they'd watched on the television. He just knew he had to survive, somehow, and get out of here. "Bish, calm down. Don't do it. Don't do it."

"You know that movie we watched?" Bish asked, glancing back at him even as he approached the two at the end of the bar. "You know, the one of you and me making love? It was funny, wasn't it. It was fucking hilarious. But it's what my dreams are, Luke. You ever dream about what you can never have?"

Luke glanced around the bar, and decided to grab a chair from one of the tables. He hefted it up and ran toward Bish, and then swung it out and back, catching Bish on the side of the head. As Bish fell the shotgun went off, then skidded across the floor. Luke looked at the couple—the blonde had gotten it in the stomach, and was either doubled over in pain . . . *or laughter?*

Luke looked from her to Bish, who had already scrambled up and gone for the shotgun. "I'm gonna take out everybody in this fuckin' town!" Bish screamed.

"You gotta get outta here!" Luke shouted to the guy and his girlfriend, but the guy had nudged his girlfriend off the stool. She dropped like a sack to the floor. She emitted a noise that was a cross between moaning in pain and giggling.

"Look at what you can do," the guy said to her, pointing at her as she twitched on the floor.

Bish had the shotgun again, and turned around to look at Luke. "I'm gonna kill everybody in this town, but I'm saving you for last, buddy."

Luke felt vomit rise in his throat; he began to feel chills of fear and wondered if he would even be able to stand much longer. He felt like a little boy and wanted to curl up in a ball and hold his stomach until the nausea went away.

Instead, he turned around and went running out of the Ratty Dog Bar & Grille.

7

In the street, he saw an old man in a wheelchair and a bunch of girls, who all looked about thirteen or fourteen, running behind him, pushing him too fast along the street. As he went by, the old man gave a look at Luke that could only indicate that he was terrified. The girls were screaming as if they were on a ride at some amusement park. Across the street, at the Boatwright Arts Center, the banner had been pulled down over the old marquee. Someone had hoisted a woman up by her left foot, and she hung upside down about six feet from the ground. She was completely naked, but her face was covered with what might've been a pillowcase that had been secured at her neck. She wasn't moving.

The sky had dimmed into twilight, and it cast a strangely beautiful light over her naked form.

Luke felt as if he had just stepped from one dream into another. He heard the shouts and cries of villagers on other streets, and when he looked up the road, he saw a fire at the restaurant called The Apple Pie-Man. Flames shot out from the first- and second-story windows, and although there was a firetruck pulled up beside the store, it looked as if the firemen were . . . *pouring gasoline on the flames.*

Luke Smithson felt a sudden overwhelming dread take him over, worse than what he'd felt inside the Ratty Dog. He felt as if some nightmare of his had come alive—some terrible dream he'd had since his aunt Danni had died, and that all these things he saw now had been in that dream, as well. Even the idea of *The Nightwatchman* had come from a dream, and in his plans for his novel he had thought of a woman hanging upside down from some scaffolding on a building, naked, head covered with a pillowcase, at twilight.

The dread that arose within him made his entire body tense. As he heard more gunshots back in the Ratty Dog, he realized that if he did not start running right that second, he was going to die.

As the memory of that nightmare returned, he remembered a further development. In the nightmare, someone he had never met—a little boy—eviscerated Luke while he looked down at his body and watched his insides twist like steamy snakes as they fell out at his feet.

He ran up and down the streets of Watch Point, thinking that if he ran hard enough and fast enough he would get back to sanity. The dream would evaporate and he'd be in the real world again. But he passed the smoke of the dream at every corner—a pile of dead, burnt bodies in front of the Watch Point Community Bank building. Several shops along the Antique District had their windows busted. Yet there was no sound but the distant squealing of a baby. As he ran, Luke saw a baby stroller near one of the bus stop benches. Worried about the abandoned child, he went over to the stroller and lifted the canopy and thin blanket that covered it. But the stroller was empty, and the baby kept squealing from somewhere nearby. On the side of a building, someone had spray-painted:

The Nightwatchman looked into the hearts of the dreamers, and found their secrets.

This one sentence, scrawled on the side of the Watch Point Pharmacy, made him feel as if he were losing his balance completely.

"Shit," Luke said.

It's from my diary. I wrote that in my diary. I know I did. Who could've seen it? Who?

"Cynthia," he said, and glanced up the block. It was two blocks to Hibiscus Lane, and the cottage where Danni had lived. Where Cynthia now lived.

Terrified for her safety, Luke set off in that direction, passing blurs of human beings who stood on street corners, just staring at him. He stopped twice—once when he thought some children had fallen down in the street, but when he slowed to get a look at them, he realized that they were gathered around another child, chewing on his fingers and at his toes. One little boy had nearly gnawed the child's ear off. The child was dead, and his features had been obliterated so that part of Luke even wondered if it had ever been a boy. At another point, he saw an elderly woman in her front yard. She lifted a shovel and jabbed it down into the neck of a boy of about fourteen. When she had severed the head completely with the shovel, she looked over at him and shouted, "He tried to fucking kill me, the little bastard!" She turned and threw the shovel down and hobbled toward her front door as if she'd sustained some injuries that evening.

Luke ran around the corner of the next street and came to Hibiscus Lane. When he got to the little white picket fence, he pushed his way through the front gate. The door was ajar.

He stopped in the doorway and glanced down the narrow hall. To the left was the living room. On the beige carpeting that ran down the hall were muddy footprints. *A child's footprints*.

The smell of lavender and gin that always seemed to accompany Cynthia Marchakis since Luke had known her as a boy. The vague smell of cigarette smoke in the air.

He went into the cottage, and was relieved to see Cynthia lying on the overstuffed sofa beneath the picture window. One arm was behind her head, against a pillow, and the other crossed her chest.

As he got closer, he saw the end of a cigarette between her fingertips, with a thin line of smoke coming up from it and a pile of ash on the carpet. He took the cigarette from her fingers and tamped it out in the glass ashtray on the nearby coffee table.

He listened to her light snores. Relieved that she was asleep, he went to get a blanket to cover her. In her bedroom, he saw muddy little footprints up to the bed. A pile of something dark on the bed. When he went to it, he wrinkled his nose. It was human feces. As if a child had walked in barefoot from the garden, then pulled down his pants and squatted on the bedspread.

The muddy footprints went from the pillow to the open window behind the bed. The screen of the window had been torn open.

Luke decided to get a blanket from the guest bedroom. When he did, he took it back to the living room and covered Cynthia with it. She turned and whispered something inaudible in her sleep. He wanted to wake her, but as he leaned into her, he heard what she was saying in her sleep: "Fucking kill him. Tear his throat out. Save me his bladder. I want to eat his bladder." She whispered all this as if she were wandering through a happy dream.

He stepped away from the couch. Tried to make sense of any of this. He could not. But he was sure it had something to do with the nightmare he vaguely remembered.

He decided to let her sleep. *She's better off sleeping. Maybe they don't hurt you when you're sleeping.*

They.

Who is they?

What is they?

Maybe when you're sleeping, you're safe. Like you're in someone else's dream, if you're awake.

Like you're in someone else's . . . nightmare.

He went to try the telephone. When he picked up the receiver, he heard someone talking as if it were a party line. It was a woman, and she kept talking about "if we open up all the rooms, we can have all the guests stay here, but who's going to keep it all running? So much of the place is run down at this point." It was hard to hear her, and she sounded elderly. He tried to break in on her monologue, but she ignored him. He hung up, hoping to get a dial tone, but when he lifted it again, she was still there.

Luke locked all the windows and doors to Cynthia's cottage on his way out. He didn't know how he'd get help, but he knew he had to try something.

Outside, just beyond the low picket fence, a man in a suit was running as fast as he could away from a woman dressed in jeans and a white T-shirt holding a pitchfork in the air as she went after him. Following close behind her, a little girl with blond locks tried to keep up. She had a trowel in her hands, and was jabbing it at the air. When she got just beyond the front gate to the cottage, the little blond girl looked at Luke and stopped running. She was panting so hard, he was sure she was going to collapse. But then she looked up the road at the woman with the pitchfork and went running off after her again.

He glanced about among the roses for a weapon of some kind, and saw a metal rake lying just beyond the flower beds. He picked it up and hefted it between his hands to get a feel for it.

Then he took off running again.

He saw a pack of dogs fighting over what looked like a human arm, but he was running so fast he couldn't be sure.

As he ran along the more deserted streets, just beyond town, he began to slow a bit and catch his breath. There was a low stone wall just up the way a bit. When he went to rest upon it and try to comprehend what he'd witnessed, he noticed the dead birds.

8

There were hundreds of them, mostly starlings and crows. They looked as if they'd just fallen from the nearby trees, all at once. Poisoned, perhaps. He didn't know, but he'd never seen anything like this. There were even a few still flopping around.

Poison in the air? Could that be?

Just beyond the stone wall, still at some distance, he saw the house where his aunt had gone to kill herself.

It looked as it had when he'd seen it once or twice before. A mansion like many others he'd seen—castle-like to some extent, but certainly not as grand as places he had seen in his childhood, crossing the country. This was a crumbling mess of styles and alternated between brownstone and granite and some kind of whitestone, and its towers looked as if they might come off in a good strong wind.

When he closed his eyes for a moment, he saw her again in his mind.

Aunt Danni. Where are you?

What is all this? Is the insanity in the family getting to me, too? Is this the beginning of my brain getting ready to explode like yours did?

And that's when a voice popped into his head—the same one he was sure he'd heard on the cell phone in the Ratty Dog.

You know, Luke, you may be on to something. Maybe your brain is being eaten alive right now.

Or maybe you just want to see the house where she did it. Where she keeled over, gun in her hand.

I told you I'd show you some sights, bucko. You want to find out about that crazy aunt of yours, why don't you just go look at the place. It's a nice enough house. I bet it's not even locked.

Why, I betcha the Nightwatchman won't even stop you.

9

Luke wanted to believe that in a day or two, when this had somehow passed, this war that had erupted in the village between people like himself, who expected the normal in life and only accepted the nightmare logic when the lights were out and the eyes were closed, and the people who had become the "Others," for lack of a better word—he wanted to believe that when it had all passed on into daylight again, that somehow it could be understood. Perhaps even laughed about, after grief and shock and sorrow held sway. After it was over.

But part of him didn't believe it could ever be over, any more than the death of his beloved aunt could be over. It would replay in his mind, again and again. A movie that had no beginning, no ending, just this middle of murderous beings and horrible things. An existence that would never go back to what it had seemed earlier in the day. There would be no normal. There would be no balance. All was helter-skelter and skewed and twisted and exposed like the live wires—the hum of barbarity among them—all of it was scraped raw of that veneer of niceness and neighborliness.

It was an open wound, this world. Open and picked at so that it would never close.

Still, he felt it was a pretty thought: that later, he and Cynthia and maybe anybody else who survived the night might talk about how they should've taken a trip that day, or should've just stayed in bed and locked the doors. For some people, surely that had happened. They were out of town or out of touch. They could still wake up to normal.

He felt old as he sat there at the stone wall and gazed at the house in the darkening twilight. Someone must have had the fireplaces all going, for a white gray smoke rose from the various chimneys of the house as he watched it.

The world changed today. Voices in my head. My brain breaking down. Maybe I saw what I saw. Maybe none of it is real. Maybe there was no gay porn movie on the DVD player. Maybe Bish didn't shoot the bartender and the couple in the bar. Maybe there was no woman hanging upside down from the theater. Maybe there were no firemen splashing cans of gasoline on a burning restaurant.

He hated thinking how he could no longer put on the rose-colored glasses when he looked at the world. He would always see those children gnawing at bodies. Always see the elderly woman cutting down the boy with the sharp edge of a shovel.

There would be no redemption from this night. Hell had spilled over. And this house had somehow brought it forth.

He didn't like Harrow. He didn't like to look at it and think of Aunt Danni, alone in this lonely place, her brain about to go *kaboom*.

10

As Luke had written in his diary just a handful of days previous to the outbreak of madness that had taken over the village:

No one is meant to live in a house like this. No one with any shred of reality.

Only those whose worlds are out of kilter should go

there, for it is a house of mirrors and a house of smoke, and when I first saw it as a boy, I thought it a violation against the normal and the sane and the human.

11

The Gospel According to Luke

I had spied the house now and then as a boy, but returning to Watch Point, I needed to get a fresh look at the place that had acquired a small reputation as haunted. Aunt Danni had hated it and often said that it should be torn down. And yet on her last day, it was to Harrow that she traveled in order to end her life. So here I am again, and I wander the place. I think of this novel I want to write called *The Nightwatchman*, and I suspect this Nightwatchman would watch a house like Harrow. It is one of these Hudson Valley messes—part Victorian shambles, part Georgian crapfest, part Romanesque, part Greek Revival. If you took it and placed it in a city like Manhattan, it would be some museum to an antique age with no logic whatsoever.

Upon seeing Harrow, one expects a flight of doves in the air; or a grand pool in place of a driveway, with a fountain at one end. It seems as if it was made for grandeur, and has gradually slid into the mere hope of revival. And yet its soul is ugly. Houses acquire souls, I think, after years of incidents. Houses like this one—remnants of a gilded age, a manufactured Machu Picchu for those handful of robber barons of the nineteenth century with too much money and too little sense of the practical—were meant to decay and be abandoned over time, for they are absurd. They are not homes. They are edifices to vanity. Human vanity. Ridiculous consumption of wealth. The architectural equivalent of the empty boast.

I read in the local library about Justin Gravesend, the

man who built Harrow. He had searched the world for occult artifacts to raise the dead or call demons or do some such Faustian activity. His delusions knew no bounds. He brought tragedy to his family, to his children, to his grandson, who inherited the property. All inheritors are doomed (so says the part of me that wished Aunt Danni had left me something tangible of our bond with each other).

As with all tales of haunts, Harrow's legend grew as accidents happened or as murders occurred over the twentieth century. To detail them here would be unnecessary, as other writers of occult history have mentioned them in books such as *The Necromancers of the 19th Century: An Illustrated History of Spiritualism and the Rise of the Occult* and *The Infinite Ones*, a particularly hard-to-find volume by a spiritualist named Isis Claviger who had lived—and apparently died—within Harrow itself.

Despite these tales of the place, when I have gone to it, as I have done nearly every day for the past week or so, what I see is a fallen woman of a house. A whore past her glory, who no longer beckons, but simply lies and waits for the end. The windows are mostly boarded up. The doors are similarly locked.

I met the man who calls himself The Nightwatchman, a man named Speederman, who does not seem anything more than a nervous husband to an undoubtedly nervous wife. "My wife's having our firstborn," he said. "Soon. Perhaps tonight. Perhaps next week. Who can say for certain? I hate being this far away from the village when she's like this."

I glanced over at his car, a station wagon that looked like it hadn't seen a good day since 1972. He must've understood why I looked at it. "Oh, sure, we can drive places. She's just feeling isolated and lonely. I hear women get cranky in their last month."

I asked him what it was like there, if the place seemed strange at all. He grinned and shook his head. "One of the nicest houses I ever worked at. Sure, there's a plumbing problem now and then. We got some leakage, and the basement's flooded half the time with all these storms that are going through. But it's a pretty nice place. Want to see it?"

And so Mr. Speederman took me in through one of the side doors that led to the kitchen. This was in the late afternoon, a Saturday, and the autumn light had just reached a warm golden glow as it hit the white patchy walls in the kitchen. I must've made some comment (probably "Shit!") because he laughed and told me that people expected it to be as rundown on the inside as on the outside. The kitchen was magnificent—old-fashioned in some respects, but beautifully furnished and with an excellent grill and stove, as well as two large steel refrigerators, side-by-side. "The lady who bought it a few years back was fixing it up," he said. "She didn't finish, but what she managed to get done makes it pretty damn nice."

"I guess I expected cobwebs and broken floorboards," I told him, and then followed him down a hallway to the door to a bedroom.

"The wife sometimes naps," he said. "Let me check on her first."

He gently nudged the bedroom door open and stepped inside, blocking my way. In a soft voice, he said, "Honey? We have a guest. A local teacher. New to the area. You feeling up for a visit?"

I could not hear her response beyond a muffled murmur. A moment later, he came out again, closing the door behind him. "I'm sorry. She's not at her best right now. A little testy. It's exhausting I guess, the last weeks. Waiting for the babies to come."

"Babies?"

He nodded. "Might be twins."

This seemed odd to me. Surely he had taken his wife to see a doctor somewhat regularly, and surely he'd know if they were going to have twins or just one child. But I let that go, and I wondered how I would re-imagine the Nightwatchman for the book. How I would take Speederman with his rather plain demeanor reminding me more of an old-time farmhand instead of a nightwatchman and caretaker to a decrepit mansion, and how I'd transform him into someone larger than life. Someone who understood the inner workings of others. Someone who watched the night.

As he escorted me about the house, again by that slim kitchen doorway, I had the unsettling feeling that someone else watched the two of us. His wife? Or another companion who lived with them? Or perhaps it was just my imagination from having read too much about the house and thought too much about who the Nightwatchman of this place would be.

I went back again a few days later—right after my last class—and was able to see the sun go down over Harrow. I had the uncanny feeling that the house changed nearly imperceptibly at dusk. It was not just the shadows that cloaked it and showed depth, or a slant of the last bit of daylight in some latticework or on the curve of its dome—it looked as if I had stepped into another time and another country. Harrow looked like a medieval fortress to me then, with the dying light. Remembering the reports I'd heard of teenagers and something about the corpse of a boy stolen from the hospital morgue, I wondered about places like this. Do they attract us to them because of the mystery and the beauty? Or are they some kind of organic creature, perhaps not something that moves on feet and hands, but like a Venus flytrap that opens in a kind of spired glory, only to have a hapless fly crawl into its velvet pit and those jaws—those towers and domes and gabled rooftops—closing around whomever had entered. Certainly that was the history of the house.

What if there is an organic life to stone and wood? What if Justin Gravesend had really built a sort of repository of spiritual matter? It was alleged that he murdered psychics in the house at one point, simply to keep their energy in the walls. It is the stuff of fiction to think this, so I only write here toward researching the novel I want to create. *The Nightwatchman*, about a man like Mr. Speederman, who perhaps sees into the hearts of those who enter a house. I would set my story somewhere else so that I could include all the eccentric small town Hudson River rats I see in Watch Point and not risk offending them. I might even set the novel in a large city, but I like this idea that a building might become organic when it has devoured enough life force from others. When it has closed its tendrils about victim after victim, year after year, only to have grown a heart, as it were, a soul, perhaps. A life of its own, independent of the lives it has taken.

And what does life want to do once it has its own being? That really is the existential question I'd ask. To write this novel, I need to explore this. What does Harrow represent, after all? What of Mr. Speederman? His wife, pregnant and ready to bring forth a child unto the great palace on the verge of decay?

Thinking about this house and this man, I've had nearly lucid dreams for several nights. In them, there's a kind of nightmarish logic to the village. I see some terrible things. Murder, fires, children doing unnatural things to each other. Truly disturbing. But I think it's my mind's way of exploring what Harrow suggests to me.

It is a rich environment for the imagination, I'll give it that, and I've now spent many sleepless nights turning the idea of Harrow over and over again in my mind, and Mr. Speederman himself, who seems not to have noticed how the house changes and turns. Perhaps this is simply because he lives within it and knows its boredom. Whereas I see its possibilities. And its impossibilities.

This brings me to yet another line of thought. Aunt Danni. Coming out to this property to end her life. She, of course, knew its status as the local haunt, and she must've seen her going there as an overly dramatic gesture—almost a message to me. Perhaps this is why the house really fascinates me. Perhaps it's because I want to know what Aunt Danni was thinking. I want to know her last day.

Why had she chosen a place of purported haunting in order to end her life? Did she wish to remain in Harrow so that I might one day see her again?

Is that why I go there every few days at dusk, to watch how the house changes in the dark? It seems to be molten for a few seconds, shifting its form before me (hallucinations perhaps, brought on by the tears I can't stop when I see the house and when I think of Danni and how much I loved her).

I need to work on the novel. I don't know when. I think maybe in a week or two, once I've settled more into the routine of lesson plans and grading tests and teachers' meetings. I need to fully explore what Harrow and Mr. Speederman suggest to me—I need to come up with just what the Nightwatchman watches—is it the house, or the village itself?

Chapter Fifteen

1

Back in the village, Ronnie ran past horrific scenes beyond imagining. The street lamps seemed brighter than usual, and the sun, falling across some distant westerly place, still shed last light on it all. Some of it was a blur as she ran—the dogs dragging a little girl by the hair; the woman who, gun in hand, began picking off children from her rooftop; the burnt bodies in a pile, still smoking, as if someone had tied them up and set them ablaze not twenty minutes earlier; the old woman sipping tea from a dainty china teacup as she sat on her front porch, her feet resting on a human head. Some of what Ronnie saw made her stop in her tracks—but only for a brief moment before she heard the yapping of dogs or the screeching of a new kill or the "Yi-yi-yi" of the gangs of children and the thunderbeat of those strange people running in a mob around the village. She saw what must've been a man skinned alive and still wriggling in a mass of blood and gunk, hung like

248

a human dartboard from the church steps of the Church of the Vale, while four middle-aged women who looked like members of the Altar Guild *(Mrs. Calhoun? Is that you? My third-grade teacher?)* threw knives at the hapless man in the last moments of his tortured life. Three cars had crashed in front of Junks and Trunks, the antique shop just up from the old train depot. The Saturn had piled up onto the Jeep Grand Cherokee, and somewhere beneath it was an old Ford Festiva. Steam and smoke came up from the cars, but no one was in sight. Yet clothes were heaped up next to the accident site, and what might've been bones also had been thrown in a pile.

Just ahead was the old depot. When Ronnie heard the screech of brakes, she quickly moved up to the sidewalk, mindful of any mad dogs that might be running around.

What came around the corner had no effect on her, other than to numb her a little further and nudge her into a part of her brain that accepted far too much horror to process.

A pickup truck nearly spun out of control as it came up onto Main Street. In the flatbed, Mark Beauchamp and his wife Paula had chains dragging off the back of the truck. Ronnie knew them both—Paula was just two years older than she was and had dropped out of college to come back and marry Mark. She was seven months pregnant with their first kid. They were hanging on to the back of a truck while some crazy driver in a hooded sweatshirt drove. Wrapped up in the chains that dragged along the road behind the truck: two young women whose features were so torn up by the pavement that Ronnie could not clearly identify them. They were also pregnant, and the thought occurred to her that these young expectant mothers were close friends of Paula's—and might even be in her Lamaze or yoga classes. Paula had been very health-conscious since getting pregnant. Ronnie could even remember Paula coming in the bookstore to get information on natural childbirth and midwifery.

The truck sped on, narrowly avoiding the three-car wreck halfway up Main Street.

Ronnie kept running. *Put it out of your head. Put it out of your head. It can't be real. It can't be real.* She swung the hatchet out as she ran in case anyone should leap out at her, and when she made it to the depot, she turned north toward Parham.

She ran to the train tracks, too scared to look back to see if anyone pursued her. Ronnie ran along the tracks, and felt comforted by the darkness of the woods on either side. She kept heaving for deeper breaths; she tried to block everything she'd just witnessed out of her mind; she tried not to think of her sister or her mother. *Maybe they're safe. Maybe they made it out. Maybe they're waiting somewhere else. Maybe they went to Parham for supper. Maybe . . .*

But she knew it was all wishful thinking.

They're probably dead. There's nothing you can do.

She finally stopped running a quarter-mile out of Watch Point, and she leaned forward, her hands on her knees as she took great whooping breaths. She then lost it—and vomited over the tracks. Nausea overcame her senses, and she stepped off the tracks and went to lie down in the grass at the edge of the woods. Lying back, looking up at the darkening sky, she wondered if she should just go to sleep. Just like Boaty had wanted to do. Just like Nick had done. Just fall into a deep sleep and maybe when she woke up, it would all be some kind of dream.

Sleep.

Sleep is the enemy.

You sleep, you will die. There's no way around it. You sleep, they come for you. Or . . .

She remembered Nick in the store room, and how Bari had fallen asleep with her nose torn open.

THE ABANDONED

If you sleep, you become one of them. They're dreaming. They don't wake up.

"I have to," she whispered as she pushed herself up out of the grass. She picked up the hatchet. "I have to."

She cut through a section of the woods to get back to the village. The darkened woods were at peace. No children running with growling mutts to tear up some old lady. No one dying in the woods. The trees felt safe.

Trees don't dream.

Yet even the straggly trees were too silent. She wondered why she couldn't hear the chatter of squirrels or the night calls of birds.

She used flat stones to step across a brook that ran alongside some dying berry vines, and then up a low hill. Finally, she saw the backyard of a house, with its chain-link fence and its barbeque pit and an above-ground pool and the house lights up bright as if they'd been set automatically. She wasn't sure whose house it was, but she knew that children lived there, for there was a tricycle and a scooter leaning against the house.

Wonder if they're still alive.

Is anybody?

She walked unsteadily over to the fence. She felt the absurdity of how she looked. How unreal she herself must seem. If the homeowner looked out his back window and saw in the floodlights a teenage girl with a hatchet and her shirt stained black and red with blood, her hair a bird's-nest tangle, her face smudged and her eyes wild with both fear and fury.

But when she looked up at each window, no one was there.

All gone.

Ronnie Pond cut through the backyard next to the house with the chain-link fence, and went up onto the side streets of the village to find out if her mother and sister had survived this ordeal.

251

Once home, she found the remains of Bert White—although she could not possibly identify him by the pile of bones and meat—and she found her mother's body in the kitchen.

Standing over her dead mother, whose eyes stared up at her, and whose throat was slit, with an empty bleach bottle lying next to her, something in Ronnie began to switch over, from absolute fear and shock to a different horror than even what she saw before her.

She had dreamed it in the summer. It was one of her many dreams that she'd had.

Ever since Lizzie had gone with her friends to that house.

Ever since that night when Ronnie began having the terrible dreams about things to come.

2

Others in the village had been dealing with their own gauntlets while Ronnie Pond had been either running from or returning to Watch Point. About the time that Ronnie had been wrestling with Bari over who got the hatchet, Dory Crampton was looking up a staircase at the Boswell home and seeing a clown carrying Benny Marais's head.

Dory knew she was up shit's creek and the only paddle she had was in the back of Benny Marais's truck. *The rifle. You get the rifle, and maybe you make it out of here. You get the damn rifle and you blow these fuckers away.*

But she'd felt frozen to the spot.

There stood the clown. Not eight feet away from her. Just Mr. Boswell in his Happy Clown DayCare uniform that he entertained the kids with on their birthdays or on special holidays. *Gee, what holiday is it today? Rabid dog day?*

Here was the thing about Dory, and she could admit it to herself and she had right then and there: *You are one tough bitch. But are you tough enough for this gonzofuck of a crapmare? Are you, Dor? Are you? Or are you just little*

THE ABANDONED

Dorothy from the back of the classroom who doesn't raise her hand for fear of being noticed. You got a psycho clown staring at you with your boss's head in his mitts. Red nose. Big red and blue smile. Little funky hat with a wilted flower in it. The classic clown collar and the big baggy bright-colored clothes and the long floppy shoes. What does a tough bitch do with a psycho clown draggin' a human head by the scalp?

Dory Crampton did the only thing she could figure out to do. The only thing that had ever worked for her when the kids all ganged up on her in school, before she learned how to use her fists.

The only way to beat this is to out-psycho the psycho.

So she started laughing. Laughing and pointing. "Hey, Benny, how's it going? Man, I love clowns. You're a cool clown!"

Even she thought it sounded ridiculous, but Mr. Boswell-the-Psycho-Clown-from-Hell cocked his head to the left as if trying to figure her out. Then the makeup on his face wrinkled up a bit and she saw his teeth. He was smiling. Or grimacing, she wasn't sure.

"We're making soup," the Mr. Boswell clown said. He stepped down the stairs one at a time as if he were afraid of falling.

She kept giggling, and the worst thing about it was that she wondered if she was starting to lose it as he got closer to her. Wondered if she was going a little nuts after seeing what had gone on in the backyard with the dogs that had escaped from the pound. She was damn sure she saw what must've been remnants of kids' bodies. And she knew those little kids in the ball pit of the playset were scared shitless, wondering when those dogs were going to break down the see-through divider.

Dory wondered if her plan to giggle and laugh and sound as psycho as the clown must be feeling inside was just a cover up because she was headed for the looney bin

253

herself and might be dressing up as a clown pretty soon, too. It all hit her again and again—*this is not real. It can't be real. This is the world turned upside down. This is your brain on drugs. This is the world on drugs.*

The clown got to the bottom step and was just a foot or so from her. He smelled like rotting shit with a fart thrown in for good measure. Dory got that funny feeling that she sometimes did when she was smoking pot with her friends—that paranoid sense that her own brain was short-circuiting on her and that she somehow had begun to lose track of the ground beneath her feet. She had that floating sensation as the clown glanced her way.

Clearly, it was Mr. Boswell. Yet she had begun to think of him as Stinky the Clown. And this made her giggle even more.

"You like soup?" Stinky asked. Mr. Boswell seemed to have developed an aristocratic English accent in his clown outfit.

Dory shrugged. "Depends," she said, her voice softer than she wanted it to be. *Don't show him any weakness. Be a tough bitch. Tough as nails. Out-psycho the psycho.*

"My wife makes an excellent soup. A young, vibrant soup. Greasy. Fatty. But delicious." He said this in a wistful way, as if he hadn't had her soup in quite some time. He brushed against Dory's right elbow as he continued down the hallway toward what Dory could only guess might be the kitchen.

As soon as the kitchen door opened, Dory thought she saw Mrs. Boswell completely naked, bent over what might've been Benny Marais's headless body. But then the door swung back and shut after Stinky the Clown took the head into the kitchen.

She held her breath as she stood there. Glanced up the staircase, and down the other one.

Then Dory Crampton ran like hell out of that house.

3

She got the rifle out of the truck. It was a hunting rifle, and Benny used it both for shooting deer in the off-season and for shooting mad dogs. In her time working for him—two years part-time so far—he never had hit anything with it.

But she knew about guns. She knew how to aim and shoot.

All she thought about were those kids trapped out in the ball pit in the backyard, surrounded by rottweilers and corgis and chihuahuas and mutts of all kinds.

She loaded the rifle.

She looked at the houses across the street and thought she saw a man taking his lawn mower and going over and over some kind of stump in the middle of his yard. It was getting shadowy, and she wasn't quite sure why he kept going back and forth over the spot. It was a lump. It was something other than the stump of a tree. It moved. Her mind had not quite wrapped around the idea that it might be . . . it might be . . . a very, very, very small person.

Don't think baby.

Then she heard the children wailing in the backyard.

Took the rifle up. Turned.

"What the hell," she said. "Kill or be killed."

4

Dory unlatched and drew back the high wooden gate. A small yorkie lay dead near it, having bashed its head against the wood one too many times. She glanced toward the ball pit.

It was empty.

No kids at all.

Maybe they're hiding in all the balls.

Stranger still, no dogs to be seen.

She went into the backyard, pointing the rifle at what she considered strategic targets—the trash cans, the play-set, the back door to the screened-in porch.

The dogs had been digging holes all over the yard. She watched each step as she went, turning to the right and then left to make sure she did not miss a dog's hiding place. She glanced in each hole in the ground, but there was nothing. She reached the ball pit, but the red and blue balls definitely hid nothing. The children had somehow gotten out.

Although there was some blood and a few pieces of torn shirts and a shoe, she was fairly sure she had seen those in place when she'd been out there earlier.

She glanced around at the fence—and saw a large gap in the back fence.

They got in that way. And out.

Good.

But the kids? Where are the toddlers?

Then she began to suspect. She thought of the time it had taken her to close the gate behind her. To see Benny step into the house. To go into the house herself after he'd been in there awhile. To see Stinky the Clown with Benny's head.

A young, vibrant soup. Greasy. Fatty. But delicious.

The image of Mrs. Boswell naked, her pendulous breasts hanging down, and she was doing something to Benny's corpse.

Something nasty.

Then she saw the clothes of the children piled by the back door. Little red sweatshirts. Little tiny shoes for little tiny feet. Socks. Jumpers. A blue jacket like the one she had seen a little red-headed boy wearing.

Greasy.

Fatty.

A young, vibrant soup.

Dory took a deep breath.

THE ABANDONED

Hang on. It can't be happening. This doesn't happen. It wouldn't happen. Benny Marais is alive. Mr. and Mrs. Boswell are not psychos from hell who cook children in soup.

Those dogs. They don't corner children.

They don't.

But they did.

You can't leave this to fate, Dory. Can't. Better to die right here than to risk those kids.

5

She went in through the screened-in porch. The back door was unlocked, and then she stepped into a little alcove that had been used to hang up the children's coats. The smell of that soup was fragrant and meaty.

She pointed the rifle directly ahead to meet whoever might be coming for her.

As she stepped into the kitchen, she heard a slurping sound. On the stove were three large pots. She assumed they were like her mother's lobster pots. Steam came up from them, and Mrs. Boswell stirred one with a long wooden spoon. She glanced at Dory and smiled slightly. Over at a kitchen table beyond the stovetop, Stinky the Clown was slurping the soup back and sucking on some kind of marrowbone when he wasn't slurping.

The kitchen looked as if it had been sprayed with blood.

"They're so delicious when they're young," Mrs. Boswell said.

It was all Dory needed.

She pressed the butt of the rifle beneath her left armpit; her elbow went to her hip for support; she was used to shooting when it came to hunting season. She preferred getting some kind of mount for this kind of shooting, but the rules of the world had ended sometime between that afternoon when she and Benny had discovered that the

257

dogs had gotten loose and the moment she had first opened the back gate to the Boswells' property.

I guess it's open season now. If this is a dream, more power to it.

If it's not, well, fuck me twenty ways to Saturday.

Mrs. Boswell leaned over the bubbling pot.

Dory slowly squeezed the trigger.

When Mrs. Boswell fell, she went over and finished Stinky off, too.

When Dory had done her job, she turned off the stove.

And that's when the little kids in their underwear came running into the kitchen, whooping and hollering, and knocked her completely off her feet. The red-headed kid leapt on top of her and began smashing his fists against her face, while a little girl with blond locks kicked her in the ribs; two other anklebiters actually got down at her ankles and began biting. Dory thrashed out at them; the rifle slid across the slick, wet floor. She had to do something she could not have imagined doing in a thousand years—she began kicking at the kids and when she managed to get up to her hands and knees, she pushed them away from her. Must've been six of them all told, and she crawled through and around them trying to get her rifle, but then one of them grabbed it just as she had grazed her fingers against the butt of it.

A blind panic had begun taking her over. She got to her feet and went running across the bloodied floor, through the kitchen door, out the front door. As she went, she heard the blast of the rifle. *Those four-year-olds can shoot that thing?*

Running out onto the front lawn, she was sure she'd trip or slide or stumble, but somehow she made it out to the truck. She swung back the front door of the truck—lucky for her, as per usual, Benny had left the keys on the seat. She struggled with the keys and the damn rabbit's foot he had dangling off the keychain. Then she got the truck started, and as she did she revved it up and tore out of there so fast she nearly hit another car coming in the opposite direction. Although the other vehicle went by in a flash, she was certain the man driving had his eyes closed as if he were sleeping.

She drove through the winding streets along the split-levels and the ranch houses and even though she noticed something was wrong every time she passed by a yard with people gathered in the driveway or near the front door, she didn't look at them. She let the adrenaline keep pumping inside her. All she knew was that she wanted to get the hell out of the village, out of this place, and drive, drive, drive.

She switched on the headlights as she went, and when she got down near the Riverview Pass, a slim road that ducked out of the suburbs of the village and into a spot of wilderness, she actually began to believe that somehow she had eaten a bad mushroom or someone had slipped her an acid-laced sugar cube for her to have actually believed she'd experienced what she'd gone through at the Boswells' house.

The highway was dark as she turned onto it, but she didn't mind. She turned up the radio—playing classic rock—and let Led Zeppelin and then Todd Rundgren and finally some group she'd never heard of called Scorpion Queen take her mind away as she drove, hoping to make it to Beacon if she could, and from there, she'd get police. She'd get help. She'd do something.

She just didn't want to be in Watch Point that night, and didn't give a damn if her parents would throw a fit.

She figured that somehow, they'd understand.

As she drove down the highway, she began to feel a little sleepy. *Must be all this. Exhausting. Too much to take. Too much.*

Without even realizing it was happening, her eyes closed as if rocks weighed them down. But the dream she entered as she fell asleep was that she was driving in the truck down the highway toward the next town over.

Someone whispered, "You have to wake up, Dory. Wake up. WAKE UP!"

When she opened her eyes, the headlights lit up a large oak tree not more than six feet away. Her hands were barely on the steering wheel, but her foot had come off the accelerator so that the truck drifted lazily toward the tree. She fought back the need to sleep in time to grasp the wheel firmly and turn it to the right. She felt a bump against the truck, and realized she'd gone into a ditch on the side of the road.

At this point, she could not have been more awake. "Jesus," she gasped. She stomped down on the emergency break and turned the keys, drawing them out of the ignition.

She looked out the windshield. The headlights illuminated nothing but brambles and bushes. When she finally opened the truck's door, she realized she'd driven well off the road, into the woods themselves.

6

She wandered through the thin woods, trying to find out where she'd been driving *from* without actually having crashed the truck. She saw a light coming from somewhere across the brambles, and she followed this until she reached the edge of a stone wall.

The light came from several windows in a house she had never seen, although she'd heard of it.

It was undoubtedly the grandest house she'd ever seen, and it wasn't quite the way some of the kids at school had described it. It didn't look as if it were falling apart at all.

It was a beautiful mansion with towers and enormous

windows, columns along its porch and several rooftops along its uppermost ridge.

Harrow.

7

Roland Love had spent his twilight making a big wooden cross down at Harmon Prives' Village Hardware, just across from the Dairy Queen near the highway. He had to first incapacitate Harmon himself, who at fifty was still as strong as a bull. But Roland had his miracle spike with him, and when Harmon came at him waving his hands in the air, "What the hell are you doing, Roland?" he asked the young man he knew so well from church. "What in God's name?"

Roland simply blessed him and spiked him in the side of the neck. Since it was near closing time, nobody else interrupted Roland's work. He went out back to the pathetic pile of planks that Harmon had the nerve to call a lumber yard, and managed to find some heavier wood that looked almost like railroad ties. He went and got some more spikes and nails and hammers from the store, and sat down to make himself a cross to bear.

He listened to the angels all around him as they commanded and spake at him, and when an hour or so had gone by, he had a fine crucifix.

When he dragged it out of Harmon's store, he felt the weight of guilt and pain upon him.

Roland felt better than good as he carried the cross, dragging the back bit of it as he went along the streets. He felt medieval, and pure. He felt as if flagellants surrounded him, whipping themselves in a frenzy; and incense in the air, sweet smothering incense; and as he went through the village toward the great cathedral that rose up above the treetops, he bore witness to the demons that ran through the village, tormenting the damned before dragging them to hell.

"Iniquities!" he shouted, kicking at the child who crossed his path. "Fornicators!" He felt the impurity of that great world as it sank to the devil. He knew what was coming. *The end of days. The Apocalypse.*

Roland was the first to see the white-gray ash as it came down from the darkening sky, like first snow. He opened his mouth to taste of it—and the ash sizzled on his tongue. The wind picked up and the ashes fell as if someone, somewhere were burning trash. Or as if some volcano had erupted far from the village.

First, the plagues come, Roland thought. *The days of the martyrs are upon us. The plagues, and the fire from heaven and the release from hell of its minions.*

"The fire from heaven rains upon us in white ash!" he shouted at those who would listen as he shambled along with his heavy cross. "The blood of the martyrs shall spill! The Great Angel of the Pit will arise and call those who are weak and unholy to its army! But the mighty and the righteous shall not perish, but shall live in the House of Holiness!" His voice no longer seemed like that of a nineteen-year-old. He felt as if he had truly become a man, and he boomed when he spoke as a preacher might, a Man of God who would take away the sins of creation in one magnificent act.

A man by the name of Roland Love—*all Love was he, all Charity and Goodness!*

The damnable side effect of this infusion of glory that Roland had begun feeling seemed to manifest itself in a bulging and uncontrollable erection his trousers, and a sense that he had the Divine Creator within him now.

"Multiply across the land," he said to the ashen air. "Multiply the forces of the righteous, of the Ancient of Days, who have slept so long under the thighs of that Great Whore, Babylon, Mystery, the Bitch of a Thousand Vaginas, who brings forth her children from her mouth!"

He stopped and glanced around him.

There in the dark, others had gathered. They watched him as if he had special gifts.

They know.

They are my followers.

Followers.

Even Harmon Prives, whom he'd bashed to hell back at the hardware store, stood there among the others, his face nothing more than a pasty wasp's nest of flesh, his right leg turned completely backward. Harmon raised his arms and praised the God of the House, who had brought salvation to the believers of Watch Point.

Only Harmon's voice was a little messed up on account of the spike that had gone into his throat. It sounded like he was crying out, "Tek-ah-ny-lee-tho-soth!"

A chorus arose around Roland, of these broken and battered people, both the Quick and the Dead, following him, their knight of Righteousness, to the Great Cathedral of the Divine that grew in the woods like the fingers of a hand.

As he moved toward it, his followers all around, light came up within the woods and brambles, and he saw torches lit up and down the driveway of the grand estate.

The House of the Divine, he thought. He brought the cross up the drive, feeling the terrible weight of it, and his followers brought out electrical cords and ropes and began to whip him as he proceeded on his path to the magnificent place, the seat of all that was holy.

Upon his head, one of his followers (who looked suspiciously like Paula Beauchamp, although he wasn't sure because she had a mask made of human skin pressed across half her face) put a crown of barbed wire upon his head to complete his move toward martyrdom.

When he reached the front porch of the house, he hefted the cross from his back and shoulders and laid it down.

With the help of his followers, he brought the cross up and pressed it into the earth, leaning it a bit against the porch to support its weight.

Roland drew back, admiring his work.

Knowing that it was the word of the Infinite Knowledge that had brought him here and had commanded this erection of the wood.

The cross was in the exact configuration that had been in his mind when he'd witnessed the glory of the Most High at the Church of the Vale.

It was upside down, pointing toward earth. Roland announced to the gathered throng, "All the treasures that are in Heaven will be here now with us. And all that was in hell will arise to greet the angels."

If he could've moved outside of his own body as he wished to—for the flesh was notorious for error and sin, and the spirit pure—Roland Love would have seen himself and his followers in a way that would have surprised him. For he stood in the torchlight, shining with the blood that had dripped from cuts in his scalp from the barbed-wire crown, his shirt nearly stripped from the whipping of cords at his back and sides, his body long and thinly muscled and yet somehow gaunt and skeletal as if just the walk from the hardware store to Harrow had taken some element of a thriving spirit from him. His face was nearly snow-white from the ashes that had fallen upon him, a whiteness that was only interrupted by the streaks of black-red blood that glistened in the nearby fires.

His followers were a good twelve or so from the village—some children among them. All had been beaten or torn or mangled. Some were nearly dead and seemed to have the translucent glow of the grave to their skin; others looked as if they had never truly been alive.

And yet from behind Roland's eyes, they were the chosen of the Divine, to come witness Roland's ascension into the house that contained the essence of all that was both holy and unholy, in a marriage that would produce a new Earth and end the wars between angels and demons.

All around them, bonfires had been lit in the driveway and great torches had been erected, but these were not merely long thick sticks with fire at their tips.

The torches were the trees themselves, and in the trees, what had once been human beings were wrapped with rope and cloth to the heavier branches, or had been nailed to the trunks of the trees. They looked like beautiful fingers of a hand—the bound people who had been smeared with some kind of black tar and set ablaze. Beautiful burning fingers.

Their screams arose and died out as the fires overtook these human torches, as many from the village hoisted up their neighbors and their wives and their children to light the way for all.

It reminded Roland so much of the angel with the sword of fire who protected the garden of Paradise.

The gates of Heaven will open. This is the hour of my becoming, he thought.

It was from this fire that the white ash had come, spreading across the village, and with each person set ablaze, the trees themselves seemed to sing the praises of the angels to Roland.

He watched the torches burn and wept with happiness.

Even the stench of the burning bodies brought a holiness to the spot.

Chapter Sixteen

1

Alice Kyeteler had not been idle during those hours between late afternoon and early twilight. Alice, though hardly the witch those in town thought her to be, did believe she had a touch of psychic ability. So when Sam Pratt told her the tale of Jack Templeton's madness—involving the humping of Sam's pet python—and when Thad Allen slept so deeply even while Sam and she had been chattering away, Alice had taken it as seriously as if someone had told her that he had a life-threatening disease.

When Sam heard the commotion out on the street, he and Alice had rushed out of the store to the porch of the shop, and had seen much of what had begun to overtake the village. Packs of dogs ran up and down the street. They saw children running, holding up a man who lay on his back trying to turn over and push the children's hands away from him. They saw others at their windows, too, including Army Vernon above the florist shop. It looked to Alice like he had some kind of gun in his hands, and was ready to pick off anyone who came by. After seeing all this, they had retreated back into Alice's shop and Alice had locked the door behind them. Thad was still asleep, whispering to himself.

She went back to try to rouse him, but Thad merely shifted position and continued whispering. She squatted down a bit to hear him, but all he said was, "The rooms are filling up."

She glanced over to Sam. "That's not normal sleep. He's dreaming. In his dreams, he's somewhere else."

Sam said to her, "It's Harrow. It's because of the dead boy I saw there."

Alice, who took matters of the spirit world quite seriously, wanted to dismiss this. But Harrow was one of the reasons she had decided to live in Watch Point. She had felt that the village was on a magnetic pull toward the property. Her psychic understanding seemed to decrease a bit, living there, and she preferred that to other towns she'd visited, where she had been overwhelmed by the sense of those from the other side trying to communicate with the living. It had nearly driven her mad as a younger woman, and so she had chosen Watch Point because of what she thought of as a "dead area" where she felt comparatively fewer psychic rumblings than elsewhere.

And yet she had always known that she lived in the shadow of a haunt. She had read all the books on Harrow, had followed the career of the young psychic who had died at the house—along with several others in the early 1900s. She had tried to warn a man named Jack Fleetwood who, with his daughter and a woman named Ivy Martin, had opened the house just a few years previous in order to study its psychic field. She had written him several letters to keep any psychics away from Harrow, but they had come anyway, and there had been hell to pay at the house.

But now, she thought. *It has leaked out. Somehow. That nightwatchman. Spider. Speeder. I knew he was wrong for this place.*

She accepted within her mind what she had been prepared for since moving to the village. "I don't know what to do," she told Sam Pratt.

She closed her eyes briefly, thinking of Harrow. Thinking of what she knew of it. What she had felt when she'd had the twinges of intuition give her the little shocks she sometimes got when she saw a person or a place that was off-kilter. She got so few of them in Watch Point that they seemed that much sharper here. She tried to call out to the darkness she felt to see if she could find a guide of some kind—whether spirit or other.

She took Sam aside, at some distance from Thad Allen. "You came to me because you think I'm a witch."

He nodded, looking more scared and more brave than anyone she'd ever known.

"I can't do anything about this. I'm not a witch. Not like you think. I don't have magical powers. I get feelings sometimes, Sam. I've known about the house. I didn't know it could leak out like this. But I've stayed away from that property because . . . it would devour me."

"If it's leaking, maybe it needs to be plugged up," Sam said, his dark hair falling over one side of his face, obscuring his right eye for a moment. Suddenly, he looked too young and vulnerable to have to face this.

Alice Kyeteler, at fifty, felt more chickenshit than she'd ever imagined she could be in her whole life. It hit her right there—she had moved to the village at the edge of a dark place to escape the voices in her head that sometimes led her to believe she was slowly going mad. And she had done it because she was in awe of that terrible house. She felt its suction. She felt its pull.

Seeing the streets of the village, as they were now, scared the shit out of her.

"I don't know what we can do. I can't work miracles. I'm only someone who *believes* this can happen. I don't have any ability to fix it."

"All I know is someone started this," Sam said. "At that house. I was there that night. We all dreamed about it. All of us who went there. I dreamed about it. I dreamed about rooms in the house. I dreamed about that boy. Arnie Pierson. The one who was dead and cut open. I think I know why it's leaking. I think someone sacrificed a dead boy, and they should've sacrificed a live one." Sam said it as if he had been keeping a secret from the world that had overwhelmed him with anxiety and guilt, and now it was free. He was free from it.

Alice wanted to hug him, and weep against him as if she were the child and he the grown-up. "I can't go there, Sam. I know you want me to do it. I know you think I have some power. I don't. That place eats psychic ability. It was safe since the last time. They shut it down, I thought. Even if the man who lives there now performed some ritual, it wouldn't start it up again, I don't think. I don't believe the house is turned on."

"But you saw what happened in the street!" he shouted. "You saw! How can it not be turned on? You tell me that what we saw on the street is not—"

"I can't go there. I can't," she said back, just as vehemently. "I can't go there because if I do, this just gets worse. Whatever is here in this village, right now, it gets worse if I go there!"

"It can't get worse," Sam said. "It can only—"

In the middle of his sentence, Sam stopped talking. His eyes went wide.

Alice turned about to look in the same direction as Sam.

Behind her, Thad Allen, in his boxer shorts, had sat up on the massage table. "You don't have to go there, Alice," he said, his voice a monotone as if he were still asleep. "It'll come for you."

"Thad?" Alice went to him, and was about to put her hand on his forehead to check for a temperature because his face was shiny with sweat. Before her hand reached his face, he had closed his hands around her neck and began strangling her.

2

At Norma Houseman's place, Lizzie Pond and Norma's own children had spent nearly an hour cutting Norma open in ways that bled her as slowly as possible. Yet Norma did not seem to mind—her eyes fluttered open and closed, as she dreamed of making love to Chuck Waller in a lavish bedroom with a great frosted mirror on the ceiling. Even the floor had a mirror, and she could see herself riding Chuck's reptilian phallus, riding it and plunging up and down on it, while Mindy Shackleford stood in a corner of the room, watching them as if she were afraid of sex altogether. Norma smiled in the dream that played behind her eyes, and every time her eyes opened, briefly, she saw another one of her children hammering at her kneecap, or twisting a fork into her hand. But the dream was more powerful, and she rode Chuck Waller like she was in the rodeo. Even after he had transformed into an enormous scaly lizard, she continued to buck against him and open up further so that he could fit inside her and grow.

3

As the darkness fell across Watch Point, more and more people moved in small herds away from the village. Sure, they'd grab up anyone they happened to see, or throw themselves at the cars that drove along as a handful of what might be called "survivors of twilight" tried to get out of town. But still, their movements were slow and shambling as they went toward those least-taken roads, up Jack-

son Avenue, along a narrow winding road through the un-
kempt brambles of woods that led out to Harrow. Some
walked on nearly broken legs; others crawled, dragging
themselves with the weapons they'd gathered—knives,
trowels, hatchets, or rakes—and still others walked on
their hands, for their bodies had been so ravaged by their
companions that there was very little to drag behind them.
It almost looked like a carnival leaving town, a freak show
from some nineteenth-century idea of what a freak might
be, as they went with their knives in their mouths, their
guns stuffed into their trousers. Even some of the local
cops were there, moving slowly forward on their knees as
if in prayer. Jeff Funk, who had moved up from deputy to
sheriff in a matter of months, pushed a wheelbarrow full of
corpses. It was as if he—and the others—were off to plant
a special garden in the woods.

If you were alive and watching from your upper floor
window, as Army Vernon was, it might look like the most
bizarre parade. The lamplight in the street caught the
shadowy figures as they dragged and hobbled and walked
away from the village.

Army glanced back at his beautiful wife, who had fallen
asleep with a terrible fever. She lay on some blankets he'd
piled up nearby.

She murmured a word over and over again in her dream.
"Winter."

IV

REBORN

Chapter Seventeen

1

Kazi Vrabec had spent time wandering the rooms with the mummified dog's head tucked beneath his arm as if it were one of his beloved stuffed toys.

"I don't know," he said aloud.

Kazi stopped walking, as if listening to the dog's head.

"I guess so."

Another pause and a listen.

"If she's in pain, I want to get her help. Where is she?"

Kazi went up one of the staircases. Its banister was a rich, deep wood, carved into shapes of pineapples and grapes with a garland of wood flowers running along it, too. At a landing halfway up, there was a marble-topped table with a vase of dried flowers in it. Above this, an empty faded space as if there had once been a painting there but it had been taken down.

He looked to his left, up the rest of the steps. It looked a long way up, and had no candles along the floor at the top so that it seemed too dark to him. He held the dog's head up near his ear and cocked his head slightly to the side. Kazi nodded, and began walking to the dark at the top of the steps.

2

Inside his head, the voice of Dog told him all:

This is your house now, Kazi. I know all about how the kids have treated you. But I'm your friend. I'm a boy's best friend. I know about how you're feeling, but there's nothing to be scared of. Can you give me your loyalty, like I'm giving you mine? Because I know what great power you have in you—power you don't even know. That babushka of yours knew, didn't she? Didn't she pull you aside when you were three years old and tell your mother that she thought you had the Sight? Didn't she? If I'm lying, I might as well be dead. She knew, and maybe you don't even know that it's going to erupt in you in another year when your body changes and you start moving toward manhood. It doesn't come when you're a kid. It arrives full-blown when you're twelve or thirteen, when your voice changes, when you grow hair in places you didn't think you'd ever grow hair, Kazi. That's when it jumps out at you and suddenly you start understanding things that you would not have understood a week before. That's when you start seeing things that might happen, or dreaming them, and then when they happen, you gradually understand you have this ability.

You aren't even feeling it yet, but your journey has already begun. We like to call it a Hunch. You have a Hunch, don't you? You came into this house not because you really were scared of Mr. Spider outside with his funny way of talking—he was nervous around you, kid. Nervous as hell. Because your coming here makes him wonder how much value he offers any of us here. You have more potential Hunch in your little finger than he has in his entire body. Hell, he has to raise demons sometimes to get his power, and you and I know there ain't no such thing as demons or angels or all that imaginary friend baloney.

You got the Hunch big, my boy. It'll hit you hard soon enough, but it's already started coming through. We knew it the moment we saw you. You got a big talent on the way, and it goes back centuries in your clan, maybe back to when people lived in caves and worshipped bears and bulls. Your mama don't got it. Your daddy definitely was running on empty. But babushka had it and babushka's grandpa and you got the talent coming your way like a piano player has it or a singer has it or a one-trick pony has it.

Even you and me talking right now. It means you have it, because I don't just talk to anybody. Only my best friend. My pal.

You.

And your Hunch led you here, and into those rooms where you saw what crazy people do when they stay here too long. But you won't end up like that. Your best bud won't let it happen, Kazi. I see big things in your future. I see you maybe taking on a whole new life once we get this engine going.

Did I say engine? You can take the dog out of the pound, but you can't take the pound out of the dog. I meant to say, this machinery. It's vast here. Your being here helps grease the wheel a bit and get things moving. And that's all for the good.

Okay, see how it's all dark up here? Let's hang a louie. You know, take a left. You want to meet Mrs. Fly—that's her name, honest—she's down this way, and she probably is in a pickle right about now.

You may be afraid of what you'll see. Don't be. There are tricks of the eye and of the mind here, but you just keep on track. Listen to me if you need guidance. I'll make sure you navigate the rooms here.

When you see Mrs. Fly, I want you to ignore anything she says that might make you think she's afraid of you as well.

3

Kazi took one cautious step after another. The floor was slick, and his footsteps echoed as he went. He passed several closed doors, following the suggestion of the dog's head about where to go. He stopped and listened to the dog's head every few feet, and as he continued walking, he began to see better in the dark and it scared him less and less.

Finally, he came to the one room on this floor that still had a closed door.

He brought the dog's head up to his face and kissed it on top of the nose. "Okay," he said. "I will."

Then he opened the door.

4

The room was lit the way a doctor's office was lit—bright, with flickering fluorescent tubes in the overhead ceiling lamps, and with other long wiry lamps that stood near the two small windows. It was a fairly small room compared to others he'd seen in the house.

Inside was a narrow bed with four posts and a headboard. The mattress was stripped bare, and Kazi could see dark stains along it.

Mrs. Fly lay in the bed, her wrists strapped to the posts at the headboard, and her legs strapped to the lower posts.

She was completely naked, and shiny with sweat.

He had never seen a naked woman before, and it nearly scared him, but as he listened to the dog's head, he felt a little better.

There was dried blood along her stomach, and a strange incision running from her lower belly down to a thatch of hair at the place where her legs met.

Her mouth had a strip of cloth tied fast, and he could see her teeth over it.

A blindfold, wrapped around her eyes.

He heard a gentle humming as he stepped into the room, clutching the dog's head a little too tightly. He looked up at the lights—they might've caused the humming, but he wasn't sure.

He went over to help her. He thought of Mr. Spider, and wondered if he had done this terrible thing to his wife. Kazi didn't understand why Mrs. Fly was tied up like this, but he wanted to undo her blindfold and her gag and try to help her.

He went over to her, setting the dog's head on the floor near his feet. First, he tugged at the cloth in her mouth— she nearly bit off his fingers as she felt him touching her lips. He decided to try to get it off from the side instead, but it was all knotted and twisted and damp from her spit sliding down her face.

He listened to the dog's head, which seemed to know where things were.

Kazi followed the dog's instructions and went over to a metal table near the window. On it were a small saw that had hair on it, a little mallet, a little metal pick with a wooden handle, a box cutter, and a small tube of some kind of glue with its cap off.

He picked up the box cutter.

Returning to Mrs. Fly's side, he sliced the cutter through the gag, and it fell away.

Her lips looked parched and her teeth were scummy as she rasped, "Please. Hurry. Please. Another one. Another one. Coming." Her voice was like a rattle from her throat, but he could understand her well enough.

Then he took the box cutter and sliced the blindfold down the side, also, being careful not to cut her.

He drew the blindfold off.

Her eyes were closed in a way that looked as if someone had glued them shut. She made efforts to open them, but there seemed to be a thin seam of glue between the upper and lower lids.

"Stay still," he whispered. "You have to stay still. I can help you."

She nodded.

"I can cut your eyes open so you can see. But you have to stay still. If you don't, I might hurt you. By accident. I don't want to. I'm here to help you."

The humming he'd heard before grew a little louder, and it sounded like someone was in the next room humming—it droned and droned, and he didn't know what to make of it, nor did the dog's head tell him what the humming might be.

He knew he had to be very careful with the box cutter, or he might slice into Mrs. Fly's eyes. He grasped the box cutter close to the razor edge of it. He brought it to her right eye, which was nearest to him. It looked as if she was still trying to force her eyes open.

"Stop it," he said.

Her right eye still twitched beneath the glued lids.

"I mean it," he said. "I can't help you unless you stay still."

She swallowed, groaning a little. She nodded again.

He brought the box cutter blade to the edge of her eye. He sliced a little above the lid, and a tiny trickle of blood appeared, but she remained still.

He put his face as close to her eyelid as possible so he could see exactly where the lids met. He pressed the blade there, and drew it across the eyelid.

Her eyelids parted.

Kazi gasped, stepping back and dropping the box cutter to the floor.

It clattered as it hit the floor.

She doesn't have any eyes.

Where her right eye should've been, he saw a small pit. The flesh from around her eye socket had sunken and formed around the hole that had been left when her eye had been extracted.

Her lips parted. "There are other ones," she said, her voice as dry as a desert wind.

"Other ones?" Kazi asked.

"Other Mrs. Flies," she said.

5

After he cut through her restraints, Mrs. Fly touched his face with her hands. "I have a baby," she whispered. "Here. Somewhere. He took my baby."

Kazi backed up and bent down to pick up the dog's head.

6

In the hall again, listening to the dog's voice, Kazi went room to room, opening doors, and in each one, there was another woman blindfolded, gagged, her wrists tied in some manner, her clothes either torn from her, or ripped on her. Some of them seemed asleep; others seemed dead; they all had the cut down their lower belly that he could not bring himself to look at. There were perhaps seven of them that he saw, but there might have been more.

The humming sound grew louder. It sounded like locusts.

7

Don't be afraid, Dog told him. *Mrs. Fly is not in any real pain. She signed on for this.*

"How can there be so many?"

Mr. Spider catches them. He had one original Mrs. Fly, but

281

he went out some nights to catch more of them. He likes to wrap them up in his web. But he loves them all. He really does.

"But they're in pain."

All life is pain. You have to somehow change the pain into something else, Kazi. When you were born, you gave your mother great pain. She spent three days in pain and felt as if a bayonet were being shoved out of her body. But she changed the pain to something purposeful. You understand that, don't you? Mrs. Fly—all the Mrs. Flies—they are here for good reason. The same good reason you're here.

"What's the sound?"

Sound?

"It's like people are humming."

I don't hear it. Maybe it's only in your head, kid.

"It's here. It's like it's in the walls."

Well, maybe you're imagining it. Sometimes, we can imagine things that aren't real, the dog's head told him.

"No, it's real. It's getting louder. It sounds like those locusts. The kinds that come out in the summer and you can hear them all night."

Ah. Cicadas. Well, I doubt there are many of them in here, not this time of year. It's getting too chilly for the little buggers.

"I think it's coming from down there," Kazi said, pointing with his free hand to the end of the hall.

Ah, the tower room. Sure. I bet there's some cool stuff up there. Want to go?

8

Kazi went up a winding staircase, lit by the Mason jar candles he'd seen on the floor below. As he went, the humming increased and it tickled his ears a little.

At the top, an open door. As soon as he stepped through the doorway, the humming stopped.

THE ABANDONED

Inside the curved room of the tower, there were piles of small brown sacks. Kazi remembered a sack like this in one of the rooms. *Where?* he thought. Then, he remembered—the room that looked as if someone had set it on fire. There had been a trash can, and near it had been a brown sack that was tied shut and wriggled slightly.

He went to one of the piles and lifted one of the sacks. It moved, as if a kitten was inside it.

When he opened it, he couldn't see it clearly, but it looked like a large hairless rabbit at first.

He drew it from the sack, and held it in his hands.

Kazi had seen maggots before, in trash cans behind the school and once inside the torn open body of a dead squirrel.

But he had never seen one quite like this.

Its face was almost like a human baby, but its eyes were large and shiny white. It reminded him of a doll's face, all shiny and slick and unpainted. The baby's body was white-pink, and he could see through the skin a little to the pumping blood and what might've been the heart of the baby. It didn't quite have arms, but had several bumps and ridges along what should've been its shoulders and side, and its body ended without any legs at all, just a stump. On its back, what looked like shriveled fly wings, with little veins in them, but not separate from its knobby spine—the wings were coated with the slick white of the body, and seemed to be melted into its back.

It wriggled in his hands and felt to him as if it moved more beneath its skin than on it. It began humming, and as it did, all the sacks around him began humming, too, and wriggling again as the children tried to get out of their sacks.

All those Mrs. Flies have been busy, said the dog's head, on the floor near the empty sack. *Are you scared of them?*

Kazi shook his head, looking at the baby's round white eyes that seemed to not see anything.

You're part of them, Kazi. Your mind can control them, if you want. You have the ability to speak the language of the flies, my boy. All the Mrs. Flies gave birth—I watched them. Mr. Spider put me on the metal table as he helped their labors. He cut them open to make the passage easier, so that the Mrs. Flies wouldn't feel pain at all. And they gave birth to multitudes, kid. They brought forth Harrow's true children.

"Why?" Kazi asked, as the baby slipped from his fingers, and fell with a thud to the floor. The maggoty thing landed on its back and tried to roll side to side to right itself, but could not.

Because what exists in this place, Kazi, wants to live in the flesh. It is the will of all that have being—to come through into flesh and blood and bring forth its offspring. Like Mr. Spider, you will help, won't you? You can midwife the entrance into this world with what's inside you. Don't hide your light under a bushel, kid. Light your little candle in the dark and let it glow. This may seem like a nightmare, but it's really a wonderful dream made flesh, isn't it? The marvel of life coming through those Mrs. Flies, coming from their wombs, their souls, mingled with the seed of Harrow itself, with the rituals of Mr. Spider and of all who have ever given their light to the house.

Will you give your light to the house, Kazi? If you do, you will be opening yourself to another world that is more fun than the one you live in outside these walls. If you do, you will be a god here, and all doors will be opened unto you.

Others will come tonight. Some will join you. Some will not.

"Who?"

A witch. A girl who sees truth in her dreams. A man who is called here by the dead.

They will be fuel for you. For us. But Harrow is ready. Go to the window. Go. You can see the light of others.

Kazi crossed the room, careful to avoid the wriggling,

humming sacks. At the curved window, he pushed the panes back, and they opened onto what seemed at first to him to be daylight.

But the sky was dark.

The light came from the trees that lined the driveway—they were ablaze. And when he looked closer, he saw what seemed to be people in the trees, bound to them with rope and cloth, painted black, burning.

They are the dreamers set afire, the dog's head told him from across the round room. *Their dreams continue, even while they light the way for others.*

Along the edges of the driveway, he saw people from town—even some classmates he hated were there—all of them were on their knees as if praying to the burning people in the trees.

Are you one of us? the dog asked.

Now, further inside Kazi's head, deeper than even Dog could dig, he felt as if he were at home in his bed, sleeping, and all of this was some nightmare that had turned wonderful after it began very scary for him. It felt to that inner little boy that he was now in a dream that, as strange as it got, didn't really frighten him. It excited him a little, actually. And that dreaming boy in his head didn't mind that Kazi Vrabec, standing at the tower window of Harrow, nodded to the dog's head that was back by the doorway, on the floor.

Didn't mind watching people burning as torches in the thick branches of trees.

Didn't mind seeing what looked like kids he knew from school on their knees along the long driveway up to the house.

"Who are they praying to?"

You, the dog's head told him.

Chapter Eighteen

1

In her shop on Main Street, Alice struggled to break free from Thad Allen's chokehold on her. Sam had rushed over and jumped on Thad's back, wrapping his arms around his neck, but Thad would not let go of Alice's throat. Alice brought her knee up to his groin in one quick motion, and even though she felt it smush right into his balls—the force so hard she had pushed one of them back up inside his body—his grip was like a vise, closing ever more tightly. She fought for breath. Sam dropped off Thad's back, and she hoped that he was going to find another way to knock Thad out.

But as she lost breath, a vision came to her in a way that hadn't happened in years:

She was inside Thad's head.

It had never happened like this before. She had touched objects people had held and had seen things that told her what the objects meant. She had even had a sense of spirits that could communicate their emotions to her—in the past.

But she had never felt as if she had just wandered into someone else's mind. And yet, there she was—looking out from his eyes. But he was not there with her, his hands at her throat.

He was in a house.

She knew it had to be Harrow. She even heard his thoughts.

Seventeen times twenty-seven equals four hundred fifty-nine.

Behind his eyes, she saw that she was in a long room with a large fireplace that had a marble inlay with a dark wood exterior that was beautifully carved with the faces of children.

A fire burned away within it, and there were charred rounded shapes in it. Stacked along the walls, piles of clothes disturbed Alice to see them. Just piles of clothes. He went to one of the piles, and lifted a man's briefs, and pressed them up to his face.

She smelled the underwear just as Thad did, in his dreams. It made her gag. Then he dropped the underwear onto the pile. She saw a woman's blue dress, torn down the back. A white shirt with a large blotchy brown-red stain on it.

He glanced toward a bed opposite the fireplace. As his vision swept the room, Alice saw the piles of bodies in the corner of the bedroom.

On the bed, a young woman who looked almost exactly like the girl in town that Alice knew of as Lizzie, one of the Pond twins. Her sister Veronica sometimes came by the store because she had an interest in books on lucid dreaming and on dream interpretation. Lizzie sat up on the bed and thrust her arms toward Thad.

Thad went over to her.

Seventeen times twenty-eight equals four hundred seventy-six, he thought.

Alice hadn't seen the bloodied axe that leaned against the bed until he picked it up.

Lizzie Pond looked up at him and said, "When you get to thirty, that should be enough."

Thad Allen swung the axe, and lopped off Lizzie's forearm.

She fell back on the sheets, while blood flowed from the stump that was left.

Seventeen times twenty-nine, Thad said in his dream, *equals four hundred ninety-three.*

Alice was jolted back to her store, as Thad's grip tightened around her throat.

His eyes were still closed in a dream as he strangled her, and finally, she blacked out.

2

When she came to, she didn't recognize the man standing over here with the handgun.

When her vision came back into focus, she saw Army Vernon, from across the street, crouching beside her. "Alice? You all right? Alice?"

3

After a minute or so, Alice could sit up. Army had been chattering nonstop since she returned to consciousness.

"I saw him take off. I saw him," Army said. "I saw him. He had blood all over him, and I couldn't stay upstairs at my place no more. I had to see if you were okay."

"Sam?"

Army glanced around the store. "Alice, you need to just rest a little now."

"Where's Sam? Army, have you seen Sam? He was a here. A teenager. He was . . ."

"That must be who I saw," Army said. "He was taking off. He looked like he was mad as hell. But everybody in this town just went crazy tonight, didn't they? Everybody's either dead or sleeping. My wife, she's sleeping."

Alice said the first thing that came to her mind. "Don't wake her up, Army. Don't wake anybody up who's sleeping." Then, "Where's Thad?"

"Mr. Allen?" Army asked. "I guess somebody got to him."

Army helped Alice sit up, and that's when Alice saw Thad Allen lying against a broken display case. Shards of glass studded his body, and his throat had been slit with a large piece of glass.

"That kid Sam. He must be one of them," Army said.

"No," Alice shook her head. "He saved my life. I wish there had been another way, Army." She could not hold back what she felt any longer, and she grasped for Army's shoulder and buried her face against his neck and began sobbing as if she would never stop.

4

When she had wept herself out, Alice said to Army Vernon: "Sam went to the house. To Harrow. He thinks it can be stopped."

"Is everyone nuts in this town?" Army asked. "Are you?"

"Maybe I am," she said.

"Is it really Harrow doing this? I mean, a house can make this all happen?"

"I think so," she said.

"Maybe we should go burn it down then," Army said, and Alice felt relief at his simple determination.

She knew that despite any fear she felt, she had to try to end this.

5

Out on the street, Watch Point seemed deserted.

"It's like a ghost town," Army said when he and Alice emerged from her shop.

"Maybe it is."

"Maybe we need to get the hell out of here and get help."

"I know you think I'm the psychic nut of the world, Army, but after anything you've seen tonight, do you really think this is something you—or anyone—can run from? I'm telling you, it's that house. It's . . ."

"Haunted?"

She shook her head. "No. It's not haunted the way you think. Everything I've read about it leads me to believe it's an opening. A portal. It has things that come through it. And it needs the . . . well, the energies . . . of certain people at particular times . . . to open it."

"You really think you're psychic?"

"Not as much as you probably think I am," she said.

"You really think that house is at the base of all this?"

Alice nodded.

"I've been dreaming about winter," he said. "Haven't really talked about it much. But in my dreams, I've seen the house, too. Like it's in a snow globe of winter. Like it's been waiting for me."

"I think a lot of people here in town have been having dreams about Harrow."

"Since that kid. That dead kid was found up there."

"Maybe. Or maybe before."

"I don't believe it's the devil or anything like that. Some people might think it is. But I don't believe crap like that. Do you?"

"Not the way they mean," she said.

Army gave her a sidelong glance that made her think he

thought she was full of it. "Okay," he sighed. "How we gonna close it?"

"I have no fucking idea," she said, and it nearly made both of them laugh the way she'd said it.

6

When Army and Alice went out onto the street again, feeling both determined and filled with dread, they saw the lone figure of a young woman walking along with a slight limp. Dangling from her hand, a hatchet.

It was dark out, but the streetlamps cast halos of light around, and Army had just raised his gun, pointing it at the young woman as she approached.

"Sure," Ronnie Pond said, dropping the hatchet to the sidewalk, glaring up at him. She looked like hell—her dark hair nearly covered her face. Her shirt was torn and there was a dark blotchy stain of blood on her left shoulder. Army recognized her, of course, but at the same time he wasn't really sure it was still *her* on the inside. Not in her mind. "Shoot me," she said. "Come on. Do it. I don't mind. Take me out now before I start chopping up every damn kid in this town."

Chapter Nineteen

1

Mr. Spider, through all the drifting evening hours, had spent much of his time on the front steps of Harrow's grand, if dilapidated, entrance. He had fallen asleep so that he, too, could be part of the great dream that the house had made for him. In his dream, he was surrounded by Mrs. Fly—and all the Mrs. Flies—and was twisted among their flesh in an orgy. Their bodies crawled with small winged insects, and he, too, had transformed into a great spider that spun around Mrs. Fly and Mrs. Fly and Mrs. Fly, and they gave birth to their children who held the mind of another world within their maggoty forms.

When he opened his eyes again, the followers had arrived—those who had been touched in the great dreaming that he had begun when he performed the ritual with the dead boy during the summer.

He welcomed them and helped organize the human torches. Then he went inside the house and headed for the kitchen to make himself a sandwich. After his snack, he returned to the front hallway, and the young man named Roland Love stood there, a crown of barbed wire on his scalp, a spike in his hand.

He went and embraced him and whispered against his ear, "The one you called God is coming in the flesh tonight. You have brought this about with your worship. I want you to close your eyes now. Dream. Bring the dream into flesh."

2

Roland drew back from the Nightwatchman and looked the kindly man in the face. He reminded Roland a little of a priest—he had that godly look in his face. He had the countenance of glory upon him.

"I want Kingdom Come to come through," Roland said, looking the Nightwatchman in the eyes.

"There's one way," the Nightwatchman said. He led Roland by the hand into a large, wide room. It was as if Roland had stepped inside a great European cathedral— the vaulted ceilings were hundreds of feet in the air. Along the walls great murals were painted. Blue skies filled with angels that had golden wings, and they were naked with both male and female genitals; in their hands, they carried spikes just as Roland did. Intertwined with them were demons of the air—great dragon-winged creatures with scaly bodies and ram and goat horns on their heads. They held small innocents in their arms—little children—and as Roland watched the mural, they seemed to move along it, among the angels. "Heaven and hell are the same place," the Nightwatchman told him as he saw an angel in the mural bend over so that a demon might fornicate with it. As the angel's wings spread, the demon grinned and its enormous phallus plunged into the angel's buttocks. Then all the creatures of heaven and hell began intermingling, as the Nightwatchman began speak-

Douglas Clegg

ing in Roland's head: *All of heaven and all of hell embrace at this spot, Roland. God and devil are here. They love each other. They love you. They called you here to be their greatest achievement.*

"Why me?"

There is no why in this place, the Nightwatchman said. *All that there is, is.*

"How can I serve two masters?" Roland asked as he watched an angel press its member down a demon's throat.

The mating of the Infinite is here. There are no two. There is only one. The Holy-Unholy.

"What am I to do?" he asked, and looked from the moving murals to the great stone pillars and, ahead of them, a magnificent alter made of gold.

Suffer them, the Nightwatchman said. *Suffer the little children.*

Beneath the altar, on a marble staircase, there were several wriggling sacks. As Roland approached the altar, feeling the presence of the divine, the warmth and the burning cold of it, he knelt down before one of these sacks and opened it.

He saw the wriggly angel within its membrane. Part of his mind thought it was a maggot the size of a newborn baby, but the part that was moving toward a new understanding of what this sacred place might be saw it as the offspring of demons and angels and man.

He brought the spike up, and pressed it at the neck of the baby angel, slicing through the thick milky outer membrane. A dark, slick, wet creature began to emerge from within, and he brought the spike further down on the outer covering until he had ripped the creature cleanly from its larval pouch.

As the jelly of the creature quivered, being born from the maggoty outer skin, it opened its eyes.

It had the eyes of Roland's sister Bari. The small face,

though dark and lumpy, was like hers as well. Thin strands of blond hair grew from its scalp. Its body lengthened as he took it up in his hands.

The thing opened its mouth, and a gasp of air came out.

He set it down again, and took his spike and went to open the many sacks, the many angel babies who needed to be free of their birth skins.

3

Luke, who had been watching Harrow from his perch on the stone wall, thought for sure he saw Aunt Danni's face at one of the upper windows of Harrow. While he knew it was an impossibility that she could there, that she could be alive, something deep within him awoke to the impossible.

It's the Nightwatchman, he thought. *He looks into your heart and sees your innermost dream. He saw Bish's dream. That was the movie. Bish was in love with me, but I'd hurt him. That was what the Nightwatchman saw in his heart. The others in town, from the hanging woman to the children gnawing at the child—they had all of this in their hearts, and the Nightwatchman had simply brought out what was inside them. Out, like a nightmare that nobody could admit to themselves.*

Aunt Danni opened the window on the second floor of Harrow and called out to him.

He felt tears stream down his face as he looked up at her.

Don't do this to me. Don't do it. I know you're dead. I know this can't be.

Despite these thoughts, despite seeing human torches in the trees, Luke stood and began walking toward the house, all the while watching the woman at the open window.

4

Dory Crampton had decided to enter Harrow from the back of the house and avoid all the weird people she saw along the front of it. Some of them had been tearing at each other, and it reminded her of zombie movies that she had never liked and never wished to see again as long as she lived. But in the back of the house, there was a boarded-up door that was easy enough to break through using the butt of the rifle. She had more rounds to shoot off. She had decided—in that insane way that only a teenage girl might who had watched a clown carrying a severed head and a bunch of little kids try to kill her—that she was going to take out whomever crossed her path at this point until she found out what kept all this madness going. She sniffed at the air a bit. The house smelled funny, as if something—*some gas leak?*—was in the air. Yet she didn't smell gas exactly—it was more a smell she associated with the dog pound.

The smell of the killing room.

That's what it is.

It smelled like the little room with the metal table where the dogs went when their time was up.

Something about the smell made her think of other things, as if it had associations for her, and she remembered how her boss, Benny Marais, would snicker at the hapless dogs sometimes and say, "This mutt's too ugly to ever get adopted out. I think we just need to off him right now." She had hated Benny at those times, and just that smell had taken her back to a moment when she had managed to snatch an old dog from him before he could take the animal into the killing room. Instead, she took it home and eventually found a home for it out at a no-kill shelter up the river a bit.

With the smell in the house, she began to forget why she was there. *Dory, don't get off-track. This place wants you to forget. Don't. You're here because somehow monsters came outta here.*

As soon as she went down the back hallway of Harrow, a little boy came around from a room off to the side. She braced herself against a doorframe and pressed the rifle's butt against her hip, raising it up so that she'd get him right in the face.

He had dark circles under his eyes, and looked sad to her. His hair was dampened along his scalp, and he wore a striped T-shirt and underwear that looked like it had teddy bears on it. He looked up at her, and at the gun, and kept walking.

She was about to squeeze the trigger, but something overwhelmed her about the boy. He didn't look as if he was about to hurt her. If anything, he reminded her of images she'd seen on news shows about abused and neglected children. This little guy looked as if he'd been starved and tortured in some way, and she felt terrible enough to lower the rifle.

"Are you okay?"

The boy glanced back at her as he passed by, and then turned left into a room.

Dory took a breath. There didn't seem to be any threat nearby.

She followed the boy into the room. It was a small room and had nothing in it but a pile of blankets and a pillow in the corner beneath a shuttered window. A single bulb hung overhead, giving off enough light so that she could see the walls of the room. They were covered with shit that someone had wiped along them as if trying to paint a scene. She could make out stick figures of a man and a woman and a house, and maybe there was a dog and a big shit sun in the wall-sky.

297

The little boy had crawled beneath the blanket, and she immediately felt that she should help him in some way. She went over, and sat down, and touched the boy's forehead.

Fever.

She reached to the blankets, which he'd drawn up over himself, and drew them back. The boy's shirt was open, and she saw an open, festering wound running down the front of his chest.

A memory came back to her: *Arnie Pierson.*

The boy who had been stolen from the morgue. His corpse had been sliced down the middle by the sicko who had done it.

The little boy lay there, and grinned broadly at her, and she saw what looked like little sharp ends of knives thrust into his gums where his teeth had once been.

He reached down and fingered the gap that divided his chest and stomach. He drew back the flaps of skin.

She felt her tongue go dry in her throat.

Dory thought she could hear her own heartbeat.

Arnie Pierson.

The dead boy.

As he opened the wound, it began to look like some-thing more than a wound, and she hated to think of it, but it looked vaginal. It looked like it had little lips within it, at its edges, and as he opened it she had the awful feeling that somehow she was going to reach inside him, inside that *gap*, she was going to put her hand inside him be-cause her mind had already begun to wonder what he wanted to show her and what secret thing he could be hid-ing. Dory Crampton glanced at the rifle that lay nearby and her short-circuiting mind began wondering if she shouldn't just suck on that thing and blow her brains out rather than dig deep into this opening chasm within the boy's chest.

She felt as if she were watching herself at a distance as

she leaned over him and lowered her hands to press them into the dead boy's body.

When she did, the pleasure that came over her was intense, as if she had never known that tingling sensation before. He was wet and warm in a way she'd never felt anything, and her hands found his beating heart that throbbed as she squished at it with her fingers.

It has you. The house has you. You have to stop. You have to just leave. Just get the hell out, she thought.

But part of her liked milking the dead boy's innards, and as she found other organs, and little tiny bits of mushy yellow fat, she wanted to put her face inside his open stomach and smell what the insides were like and maybe she would find out why he had this power over her, to make her do this. To make her do this nasty, humiliating act.

This dead boy with his knife teeth.

She played with the dead boy for a long time, and perhaps she dreamed of less repugnant things, but you could not tell it by looking at her.

The Nightwatchman stood in the doorway, and when he felt Dory had reached a pinnacle of unadulterated pleasure at the touching of the dead, he went and took her up in his arms and whispered, "Mrs. Fly. We have a place for you upstairs."

5

Sam Pratt had been nearly out of breath the whole time he'd been running toward Harrow. He thought of Thad, and Jack Templeton, and the people he saw lying dead in the street. He couldn't take it anymore—he had to stop all of it from happening. He felt the pressure of guilt for having been there the night that the boy's corpse had been torn open by someone to start a ritual from hell that launched this night.

As he went, he saw others along the roadside—he saw kids he went to school with, and women who had been his elementary school teachers, and he saw men and women who lived on his block, people he avoided normally, people he ran into at the drugstore, the postman who always had a quick hello for him whenever Sam had to sign for a package . . . and they were part of it.

Somehow, they had gotten taken over.

Somehow, Harrow had gotten into them.

Possessed.

He ran between all the praying people and the burning trees, screaming that he was going to stop this once and for all.

But just as he got to the door of Harrow—it was open and he could see an incredible yellow and red light from within as if it were lit with a thousand candles—a little girl with a pitchfork jabbed him in the chest.

Sam looked down at her. He wasn't sure, but it looked like the little sister of a friend of his from down the block. He had seen her playing jump rope with some of the other kids now and then.

The girl looked up at him, her black braids swinging side to side and her grin nearly an infection as she twisted the pitchfork deep into his chest.

Sam fell to the ground, struggling to breathe. He saw the little feet—the feet of other children gathered around him. He turned over on his back, and the little girl drew the pitchfork back out of his chest.

Sam looked up at the children. One boy had a metal rake, and he pressed this down onto Sam's stomach until it punctured the skin. Two other boys began spitting in Sam's face as he fought to stay awake.

He felt his life flowing from him, and knew he had perhaps only minutes, left.

And during those minutes, these children who played on the front porch of Harrow were going to tear him apart.

6

"Put your gun down, Army," Alice Kyeteler said, reaching over to touch Army Vernon lightly on the shoulder. "That's Ronnie Pond, from up the way."

"No," Ronnie said, tossing her hatchet onto the road. Its clatter echoed in the curious quiet of the night. "Shoot me. Take me out."

"Stop that," Army said. "Life's sacred. Even if it doesn't seem like it right now." He lowered his arm, and tucked his gun into his jacket pocket.

"All right then. If you're not killing me, I'm going up to that house," Ronnie said wearily. She squatted down and picked up the hatchet, hefting it between her hands.

Alice was amazed, looking at her. It was as if she had seen the exact moment when a teenage girl had become a young woman.

Not just a young woman.

A young warrior.

"We're coming with you," Alice said.

7

It took them nearly forty minutes to get to Harrow. They walked slowly, cautiously, along the streets of the village. It was so empty and silent that it seemed to keep the three of them from talking at all. Dead bodies lay in piles along the shop doors. Houses down the little lanes looked as if they'd been abandoned.

"The lost colony," Alice said.

"What?" Ronnie asked.

"In Roanoke. It just disappeared."

"People didn't disappear here," Army said. "But I get your drift."

"Is everyone dead?"

Douglas Clegg

Alice shook her head. "From what I can tell, if they're sleeping, they're alive. If they haven't woken up."

"How come? How come they're sleeping?"

"Who knows," Alice said. "Maybe the ones who wake up from sleep are living their nightmares in some way. Maybe the ones who sleep are . . ."

"They're in Harrow," Ronnie said. "That's what Mr. Boatwright said. He said . . ." But she let the thought die in her throat. She closed her eyes, and Alice put her arm around her. Ronnie shrugged her away. "I saw my mother dead. I haven't found my sister. She must be dead, too. I think I'd know. A girl I know—Bari Love—attacked me. She went back to sleep after she did it, but she was bleeding bad. I'm sure she's dead now, too. And Dusty. And Nick. People I cared about. Everybody's gone. What's the point in living?"

Alice exchanged a glance with Army, who shrugged. "I don't have answers."

"I dreamed I was in that house," Ronnie said. "All summer I've had dreams. My sister was there. And others. A little boy who seemed to be behind everyone's face. Like they were masks. A little boy who seemed . . . the . . . well, the absolute evil of anything I've seen. I hate that word evil. It seems stupid. But whatever this is, it's utterly evil."

"When you dreamed of the house," Alice began, "what was unusual? Besides the strangeness. Was there some quality to the dream that you hadn't noticed in any dream before?"

Ronnie stopped in her tracks. "Yeah. There was. It was more real than real. That's what bothered me about the dreams. They were hard. Around the edges. The rooms in Harrow were . . . how can I put it? They were . . . solid. The floor was solid. I felt the floor. I never feel myself on a floor in a dream."

"It had the same quality as real life," Alice said, nodding.

302

"More than that. It was like real life was the dream. And the dream was more real."

Finally, they left the last of the buildings in the village and stepped out onto the narrow road that would be the beginning of their travel into the woods to find the house. They grew silent again as they saw the distant fires in the trees.

They thought they heard chanting in the chilly air, as if some ceremony were taking place outside the house—a revival of some kind, with the ecstatic cries of participants and that kind of nonmelodic singing that reminded Alice of her studies of ancient religions, where bloodthirst was the rule.

Yet when they reached the stone wall that marked the entrance to the property, the place had gone silent. And though the trees still burned, the three of them saw no one in front of the Harrow at all.

"Shit," Ronnie said, when she looked up the drive to the house.

Alice could not even find the words to say it, but Army had no problem. "It's . . . grown. *Jesus Christ*, has it grown."

Chapter Twenty

1

Ronnie glanced at Alice. "How could it happen?"

"Don't ask me," Alice said.

Harrow was no longer the Victorian monstrosity of the Romanesque and the Greek and the Georgian and its other influences. It had reached higher into the sky—its towers were now buttressed and it had arches coming off them. At the top, in the smoky darkness, it almost look like they were minarets.

"It looks like Constantinople, Jesus H.," Army said.

"Or Notre Dame," Alice added. "They've turned it into a cathedral."

"We're dreaming this," Ronnie said. "Somehow, it's making us see this. 'Cause this can't happen. It can't."

Alice whispered, "Anything can happen here. Tonight. I don't think we've seen the worst of this yet. Somehow, it's gotten its fuel. Somehow, those with sparks of psychic ability have given themselves to Harrow."

"We could just run away," Army said, but it didn't sound like he meant it.

"Those in the village who are still dreaming, are dreaming all this for us," Alice said. "Somehow, Harrow has crossed over from dreams into reality. This reality. Like Ronnie's dream. Hard reality, within a dream."

"But how?"

Alice reached pressed her hand lightly on Ronnie's scalp. She closed her eyes and tried to summon what she called "the stream," which was something she felt between other psychics whenever she met them. She felt a faint tingling along her hand. Alice opened her eyes again. "You have a little something, Ronnie. I think most people do but don't necessarily know it. Maybe they have more powerful dreams than others. Maybe they make good guessers, and aren't aware that maybe other people can't guess that well."

"If I have some kind of psychic ability, it sure as hell is buried deep," Ronnie said.

"Why us?" Army asked. "Why aren't we either dreaming or asleep?"

Alice shrugged. "I wish I had the answers."

"Some psychic." He said it to try and lighten her mood, but somehow Army knew it didn't come out right.

"I'm supposed to be. But it hasn't really been working much lately." She said this last bit as if she didn't care if they heard her or not. In a slightly more audible tone, she said, "Harrow collects souls. But it needs that psychic spark for fuel. It must already have one or two with the ability. Sometimes I feel it in the village—a slight tension in the air. Like a static charge. And then I get the sense that someone who has it is nearby—maybe just passing by on their way to school, or work, or out for a walk with a dog. I was attracted to this village. Until tonight, I thought it was because it had a certain pull that reduced my abilities a bit. I liked that. It's not always fun and games to see things others can't. But after tonight, I think I came here the same way that others with the ability, or the genetic disposition to it, might come to Watch Point. Harrow is the pull. It's not anything but this house. It was consecrated for evil, and it will always remain so. But I was sure it had been turned off. Yes, hauntings can be shut down, and it was . . . for awhile."

"I wish I could've figured out something in my dreams then," Ronnie said with a slight shiver to her voice. "I wish something in them had prepared me better for this night. My sister Lizzie went in there," Ronnie whispered. "That night. Last summer. She came home and I felt it. I started dreaming then. I started dreaming about this place then. She was with friends, and they broke into the house and partied a little. Sam was there, I guess, because I made her promise to give him a ride, even though he wouldn't talk to me afterward. Bari Love was at that party, too."

"Sam thinks it started that night," Alice said. "Maybe it did. Maybe that electrical storm we had didn't help, either. Maybe. It couldn't have been just the party that set this in motion. But maybe it was that dead boy that Sam saw. The one they found."

"We're too scared to go up to the door, aren't we?" Army asked. "The world is upside down right now and we have watched this town lose its marbles in less than a few hours, and . . . well, what isn't sleeping is murdered. Except for us, I guess. And whoever is in that house."

"We're all numb. All of us. But we have to get through this. We'll turn off whatever got turned on in Harrow," Alice said.

"Or die trying," Ronnie said.

"Come on," Alice said. She held up the gun she'd taken off the body of the sheriff. "Maybe we stop this. Or maybe we don't."

"Okay, you two go," Army said.

"Army?"

"I can't do it," Army said. "I can't. Can't. Can't. Can't. Christ, I'm an old man and I've seen some war in my time, but I can't go in a goddamn house."

Ronnie and Alice exchanged glances, but Army just started laughing as if he were losing his sanity a little. "We already saw what happens. This is like the meltdown of hell right here in this little piss-ant burg. You try and wake people up, they kill you. You try to talk to people, they try to kill you. How many nine-year-olds did I see chewing on some poor guy in the middle of Main Street? I mean, what's it gonna take before we all figure out that, yep, that house is gonna eat us all and spit us out, or else everyone we can't seem to see right now is gonna jump us from behind the trees. But I ain't walkin' in to that place. Somebody's gonna have to drag me. I think it's a living thing. I think that house," he pointed at Harrow, "is some kind of organic being with a big fat digesting stomach of the damned or something, and Army Vernon is not about to jump into the belly of the beast. Can't do it. Can't. Can't. Can't."

"If we wait here, we're probably doomed," Alice said.

"Yeah, well, which is more doomed—over there, or over here? I would rather take my chances and stay right here. We can wait 'til morning. We can stand guard right here. Look, nobody's bothered us. Nobody cares that we're standing here, right? Why not wait 'til morning? That's the reasonable thing to do. It's beyond insane to go into that place."

"I think it's afraid of us," Ronnie said.

"What? Why would *it* be afraid of *us?*"

"We dreamed about what's inside it."

"Others did, too."

"But they got taken over by the dreams. We didn't. Why is that?"

Alice nodded. "Ronnie, maybe that's it. Maybe Harrow is afraid of us."

"And yet, we end up right here. If it was afraid of us, wouldn't it chase us the hell away?" Army asked.

"Wouldn't it off us right away? Makes no sense. None whatsoever."

"It wants us. And it's afraid of us," Alice said. "Maybe we're the only ones it can't kill. Maybe we're the only ones who can defeat it."

"Maybe we're the only ones it really wants," Ronnie said.

"How the hell do you defeat . . . how in hell do you fight a place like *that*? It's a monster. It's not even a building. Look how it's changed. How it's grown. Shifted. We don't even know how much of this we're hallucinating and how much is real. What do we do to kill a house? Can we burn it? Blow it up? I don't think guns will do it."

"I suppose it's like any other living thing," Alice said. "You find its heart." She paused and thought a little more. "And then you rip it out."

Just a second after she'd said this, they heard a scream come from the house. It sounded as if someone's heart had, in fact, just been ripped from him.

2

Luke Smithson had climbed the stairs and had found the room with the writing on the walls. Candles were everywhere in the room, and their flickering light seemed to make the words dance along the walls. He saw the open window where the spectre of his aunt had stood. He even saw what looked like her wet footprints—as if she'd just gotten out of the bath, and had walked to the window to call to him.

The words on the walls were from his diary and his notes, and he wasn't sure what to make of them. Even while he looked at the words scrawled all over the walls of the room, they shifted and changed slightly, and then they became the words he'd written to her in his many letters as a boy, and the ones she'd written back to him.

Dear Luke,
Of course I want you to come stay with me here in Watch Point this summer. We can take a little boat out on the river if you want, or even take the train down to Manhattan if you want some big city living . . .

Dear Aunt Danni,
Well, things are worse here at home and I can't stand these people I have to live with. The Good Woman of Stoughton wants me to stay home this summer and I just want to run away . . .

Dear Luke,
Did you get the apples we sent? We're hoping they arrived fresh—the farm over in Woodstock certainly assured us they would . . .

Among these letters that he had never shown anyone, now scrawled and scrambled on the walls of the room, new words formed in a blank area, as if someone stood there, some invisible being was still writing out words:

Luke, I can't ever leave this place, but I'm so lonely here. I want you to stay with me. I came here to kill myself, but when I arrived I got a sense of this place. Of what it could be. It's like a trapdoor, Luke. It's a trapdoor to other worlds, and you can go back and forth here. I'm not even really dead. My body fell, but I was a sacrifice to Harrow. I want you to stay here with me. I'm lonely. I can't see anyone else here. I wander room to room, and I know others come and go.

Luke moved close to the words as they wrote themselves furiously on the wall, and waved his hand near where he estimated the "writer" must be. The scrawl was large and then went smaller and smaller, and there was something about it—a total effect of it—that seemed to him that a mad person was in this room writing. He began to doubt it could possibly be the ghost of his aunt. Something about the words that were being written didn't seem right for her.

I am so lonely here, Luke. If you could only join me. We could be so happy together. We know about true friendship, and real family, don't we? I can't be alone anymore. Not here. It is a lonely place, even when I see shadows of others and forms of those who come and go.

Then the writing stopped.

He hadn't noticed the wardrobe in the room because he'd been so focused on reading the walls. But once he saw that its door was ajar, he went over to it. Again, he saw the small wet footprints, too small to be his aunt's footprints.

He swung the wardrobe door back.

Lying under a blanket was his aunt Danni—her hair disheveled, circles under her eyes as if she had not slept in days. She lay there curled up nearly in a ball, looking up at him, completely naked beneath the blanket.

Slowly, she seemed to evaporate like steam—even particles of mist seemed to remain in the air. The blanket was flat, as if no one had ever been there.

In that second or two of seeing her, he had a sense that she truly had gone mad. Even when she looked up at him, there was no recognition in her eyes.

It can't be her.

He felt something along his belt. He glanced downward.

Something was moving the tongue of his belt slightly.

Some invisible hands unbuckled it, then unzipped his fly.

He held his breath, wanting to pull back and run, but wondering what this was.

What could be doing it?

He felt a hand run along his briefs, feeling his penis and cupping his testicles. On the wall to the left of the wardrobe, the ghost began writing,

Let me take you in my mouth.
Aunt Danni loves her nephew.
Let me take you in my mouth.
Let me.
Let me.

And that was when he let out the bloodcurdling scream that went out through the open window, into the night air, and made Alice Kyeteler wonder who had just been killed.

3

Luke drew back from the invisible hands that grasped at him, but it was more than one spirit. He felt someone behind him, pressing him forward—an unseen presence licked at his neck. He felt the hands again as they reached under his briefs, feeling along his pubic hair, grazing the edge of his dick with warm fingers.

"No," he gasped, but his voice had gone hoarse from the scream. He pushed at the invisibility all around him, but he felt as if it was a press of flesh at his back and his crotch, at his shoulders and his sides as he felt hands moving up and down his hips. "Please. No."

Someone was rubbing just beneath his balls, and his jacket ripped off as if someone had a razor behind him and had cut right through it to pull it apart. He looked down at his shirt, and it too became shredded. He felt fingers along his chest, and then a sucking at his nipples. He squirmed to pull away, but could not. On the wall others were writing words—it was not just notes from his aunt.

We want to tear you open.
I am hungry for you.
Take my love. Take it. Take it now.

He squinted as he tried to make sense of what they were writing. The unseen drew his pants down around his ankles, and then that razor feeling of cutting at his briefs, so that he was completely naked.

311

He felt sucking at his balls and just under them, and the pleasure was too much for him to resist, and yet his terror grew as he struggled against the invisible ghosts. He felt more lips sucking his nipples and under his arms, and when the ministrations to his dick became intense, his mind snapped just a little more, and he began to imagine that they did truly love him, the spirits in this room, they passed him around among them and they kissed his lips. He felt their rough, sour tongues press between his lips, and a gentle whispering at his ear.

He got so hard, and yet he hated every second of it, so he kept fighting them. Yet he kept feeling the love and the tender touching all over his body, in every crevice, every opening, he felt their tongues and their fingers and their breath and then he felt something press against his mouth that seemed all wrong to him, but he opened his mouth to it, and took it in the back of his throat.

Something crawled down inside him through his mouth, and he felt it move along, like an undulating snake, into the pit of his stomach, while all around him, the invisible dead took him every way imaginable.

Even when his skin began ripping—along his chest, just above his nipples—he experienced the complete smothering pleasure of it and his mouth, full of whatever had traveled within it, he was unable to cry out even if he was aware of pain.

4

After the scream, the silence outside the house seemed worse.

But the three of them—Alice, Army, and Ronnie—walked along the driveway, surrounded by trees that seemed to burn without burning up, and when they got to the open door in the front, they did their best to enter Harrow together.

But as soon as they were inside, it was as if they'd each stepped into a separate place.

5

Ronnie Pond held her hatchet up when she saw that the others were no longer beside her.

What she saw in the front entrance within the house:

Her sister Lizzie, sitting on a staircase at the end of the foyer.

Or was it Lizzie?

The girl looked like Lizzie, but her hair obscured her face. She wore the same shirt and skirt that Lizzie had on last time Ronnie had seen her—seemed like a year before, but it had just been that afternoon, on the library steps.

Ronnie took a step toward her sister.

She glanced to the left, and saw an arched doorway with the wooden door slightly ajar. A reddish light came from beyond the door. To the right, there was a brief hall that opened up into a wider area. *Perhaps some kind of living area?*

Or dead area.

"Lizzie?" she asked as she took another two steps toward her sister.

The girl on the stairs looked up at her. It was Lizzie, but it was not Lizzie. Ronnie was sure that it was a copy of her sister, and not really her sister. It wasn't that she didn't look exactly like Lizzie. In fact, it looked so much like her twin that it bothered Ronnie that she was sure it wasn't her twin.

Something was missing. Was she drugged?

But it wasn't like that—Ronnie didn't feel as if anything was fundamentally wrong with this person who resembled her sister in nearly every particular. The soft cast to the eyes. The full lips. The slightly tanned skin.

And she was fairly sure it wasn't some robot of her sister.

Yet it seemed like a copy. As if something around the edges of her being was a little bit faint. A run-off from a printer where the toner ink needed changing.

"It's so Huguenots in the Louvre here," the Lizzie thing said, using the mixed-up code language that the real Lizzie would use.

As Ronnie watched the Lizzie thing stand up from the stairs, she realized that what was missing from her sister was a certain *aura*, for lack of a better word. It was as if something about her sister's life force could not be duplicated, even if every mole and freckle and defect was there.

"But you're here now," the Lizzie thing said, and she smiled sweetly but sadly, as if she had bad news to tell. "Where are your friends?"

Ronnie didn't respond. She was watching this copy to see if she could find seams or if she'd see through her like a ghost at some point. And yet this Lizzie was in the flesh, moving toward her as relaxed and normal as her sister might.

Still, when the Lizzie thing got close enough that she reached over to try to touch Ronnie on the side of the face, Ronnie drew her hatchet up and tore into her sister as if she were a creature from hell.

6

Alice clung to Army Vernon's hand, even though she could not longer see him. "Are you still there?" she said as she squeezed what were now invisible fingers.

He squeezed back.

Alice saw the great cathedral entrance, with its gargoyles and statues of martyrs at its doorway. "Somehow, it's separated us. I suppose it has the power over our minds. I suppose that's the penalty for stepping into its mouth."

Then she felt Army's fingers tug away from hers, and she wondered if they'd ever find each other again. It was as if he had just slipped through a veil of mist—and had faded, a ghost, into Harrow.

THE ABANDONED

7

Army Vernon had not told Alice or anyone other than his wife that he had been dreaming about winter, about an icy death on some frozen tundra. Army was the kind of guy who kept it to himself.

When he let go of Alice's hand, it was because of the cold. Not just cold—the kind of bone-chilling cold that reminded him of the worst winter of his life. The mother of all snowstorms that had come down on Watch Point in the fall of 1957, as if out of the blue. He had been a young man then and had run through the village wondering why no one was taking shelter. And then, he'd known: He had somehow been the only one to see the snowdrifts and feel the icy winds. It had been his mental state, and although he spent his next year at the VA hospital a few hours away, in the psych ward, he still believed he had seen the snow and ice.

As he walked down what he assumed to be a hallway, he wondered if he hadn't gotten a little bit of Harrow in him. If the house had not reached out and touched him without his knowing about it.

If the madness that had taken him over that day was not just a preview of the madness he walked among at this very moment. The entire house, which looked just as it had when he'd once gone there as a young man, had a layer of ice and frost over the walls and along the floors. Up the staircase, there were snow drifts as if it were February and the place had no rooftop.

You went here around then. Before your insane day when you thought snow and ice had smothered the village. You came over here to the house. It was a school in those days. You had someone you wanted to see here, and you shouldn't have been seeing her. She wasn't the woman you'd married just a few years earlier. She was a teacher named Betsy who you'd seen at the Frostee Freeze one summer night, and you'd chased her like a greyhound after a rabbit. You couldn't not chase her. She was young and happy and beautiful, and she was the opposite of that wife of yours, who had begun to nag and annoy you in those first years of marriage, after the honeymoon had crystallized into rock. Betsy was not like the other women in Watch Point—she was from Boston, and had come down to the boys' prep school to teach for a few years but wanted to finish her master's degree and maybe get a job at Vassar or even Parham College in history. She was better than you. You even knew that then. Smarter, more witty. She had talent and loveliness, and she would reach into your unbuttoned shirt and slide her arms around your back and your chest would rub against her bra before it came off, and you felt free again.

And one day, after Harrow Academy had let out, and her classroom was empty with its blinds drawn, you had taken her there. Even though she had tried to stop you, you fulfilled that childhood fantasy of making love to a beautiful teacher on one of the student desks.

And you thought you were a clever young man, Army. Clever and sexy and ahead of the game.

You returned to your wife, and you forgot about Betsy, once you had her, but Harrow was watching you. Harrow had entered your mind.

And when you saw the snowstorm in the middle of September, in the late 1950s, you didn't even know that somewhere, laughter could be heard.

Somewhere, the house had begun to make ready for you to return to it.

Beneath his feet, a thickening glaze of ice and frost, as if he were not on a floor but on a frozen river. He squatted down and reached to the ice floor to rub away some of the frost. He thought he saw something beneath it.

Something moving.

He had brushed away a bit of the frost—beneath the layer of ice, he saw faces looking up at him.

People from the village he had known most of his life—the face closest to the surface was Jeff Baer, a contractor who had cleaned out the rot along Army's old house, and then when work needed to be done on the kitchen, Baer had been the one to spend days there. Another face near Baer's—the Mitchell girl, who lived two doors down. At thirteen, she had been like a granddaughter to him, coming over and helping out when Army had been laid up with back problems. Edna Loniker had her mouth open in a frozen scream, but he was almost positive her eyes had life in them. Then he checked the Mitchell girl—was her name Alison? Or Alicia?—and her wide-eyed stare seemed not to be that of a dead girl. Other people, too, some he had known, some he had spoken with now and again, some who were occasional customers who came into his shop for Christmas and Easter floral arrangements, and they all looked up at him, their eyes open, frozen in that frozen river beneath his feet.

When he rubbed away more of the frost, he thought he saw a tongue moving slightly at the edge of one of their open mouths.

Jesus. They're still alive.

It's an illusion. It has to be. Harrow can't change like this. It can't. It's a trick it's playing on you, just like the trick it played on you as a young man. It's a trickster place, this house. It's a shapeshifter. It gets inside your mind and fucks with you.

Still, he reached into the inner pocket of his jacket and withdrew a Swiss Army knife. Popped a blade up, and began scratching at the surface of the ice. After a few seconds, he'd cut down to what seemed to be slush, and when he thrust his finger into this tiny hole, it touched ice-cold water.

Then the Mitchell girl moved the pinky of her left hand.

So slightly he wasn't sure if he had just imagined it.

It's insanity. It's madness. This house is madness. It's not real. They can't be alive. They're not even here. There's no river. No ice. It's in your mind. You know them because it's using your mind to make the pictures. It's making you insane, and when it has you, it's going to open you up like a gutted fish.

Army felt compelled to keep scratching at the small tear in the ice that he'd made, and after widening it a bit, the blade of his Swiss Army knife broke off. But it had done enough damage to the ice that a crack began running out from it on the ice. Then another and another. Small cracks, but they opened the hole further to the slush of water.

Army pressed his hand into the slush and reached beneath it into the water. As chilling as the temperature was—his hand swelled up a bit with hives as it went beneath the surface—he wanted to reach the little Mitchell girl. He wanted to make sure she was really moving. As his fingers touched the palm of her hand, she closed her fingers around his, quickly. It felt as if a fish of some kind had grabbed at a line when she did it. And then he felt a heavy tug on him. She was heavy, and more hands closed around his wrist. When he looked down, he saw the frozen people all moving toward him beneath the ice, all pressing their mouths to his wrist or to each other like . . . *like thick heavy eels . . . trying to pull him down.*

He used all his strength to draw his hand back up, and nearly fell backward on the ice when they let go of him.

He looked down at the little Mitchell girl—her hands had broken the surface, and others began beating against the ice above them.

Army began shivering as much from terror as from the cold. He pushed himself up using the icy wall for balance. He glanced down the hallway, back where he'd entered the house. He was sure he heard some kind of heavy breathing from the front door, which was frost-covered and closed. The breathing seemed to be moving closer, as if there were a dragon of some kind moving down a long hallway in another part of Harrow.

When he looked down at the ice, the Mitchell girl had her head above it, and other hands were pushing at the cracks that Army had begun with his knife.

They're coming for you. They're coming. They have winter in their souls. They're gonna kiss you with permafrost. They're gonna drag you beneath the ice. Flash frozen and eyes wide open.

He moved back along the wall, careful not to slip on the ice. He could not take his eyes off them.

The Mitchell girl had come up above the cracked ice, though some below seemed to be trying to drag her back down. Her skin was blue, and her damp hair was filled with crystals of ice. She crawled toward him slowly, and the ice beneath her began to give way, but she kept moving forward. And the others there—Jeff Baer, his dark hair falling over his eyes, a woman named Kathy Swanson who sometimes stopped in for the yellow roses at his shop, a young man named Sebastien Pharand who had worked summers sometimes mowing lawns, whose taut, muscled body seemed to ripple as he moved, snakelike, alongside the others coming up from the cold water.

They all broke more of the ice as they came, and Army Vernon began backing down the hall. The sound of the ice cracking echoed, and he could still hear the breathing of someone or something as if they were just around the corner.

He passed by the open door of a room where men and women had been stripped naked and were hanging by meat-hooks from the ceiling. The ice seemed to be growing along the walls as if it were getting colder and colder by the second. As if winter itself, the mind of winter, moved along the corridors of Harrow. All memory of any other life became blocked for him, just as it had when he'd

319

gone crazy for a time as a young man. It took over his thoughts. He no longer felt as if he could escape the temperature drop headed his way, like a fine mist of frost moving in a nearly invisible wind toward him.

That's what's breathing.

Harrow itself.

It's breathing winter here.

The rooms to the left and right of him were blocked at their doorways by ice.

The frozen people from beneath the ice floor crawled toward him, some of them moving up to scale the ice walls. Even the Mitchell girl scrambled along the walls and then to the ceiling, moving toward him like a predator that had cornered its prey.

This is not happening. It can't be happening. It is your mind. Focus your mind, Army. Just do it. Focus. Frozen people do not hunt humans. It's psychological warfare from Harrow. It's your brain sputtering and spitting out this, because you had gone over the edge once before.

Yet fear clutched at him as he looked behind him at his possible escape route—the end of the hall was sealed with ice.

He shivered, thrusting his hands in the pockets of his coat. He felt the gun, and he put his hand around it as if to keep from losing it.

He didn't like standing there, waiting.

He glanced back to the doorway that went into the room full of the hanging people.

Might be a window. Might not. But you're never gonna know unless you try.

Army Vernon drew out his gun, pointing it at the Mitchell girl who, on the ceiling above him, was about to drop on him like a spider.

He shot the gun, and the bullet got her in the jaw. But just after he shot, the the gun became too cold in his hand, and he had to drop it. Looking up at the Mitchell girl, her jaw waggled and drooped as if the bullet had just knocked it out of joint. No blood came down, and the girl glared at him, but didn't seem worse for it.

Make it quick, Army. You're old, but you're not weak.

He ran for the open doorway, and would've made it if Sebastien Pharand hadn't reached out, leaping from a crawling position, and caught his ankle in his hands.

Army fell, and felt enormous pain in his spine and a burning in his left ankle. When he looked down at his feet, Pharand and Baer were twisting his ankles. He heard the pop that he dreaded, as his feet seemed to break like twigs. He felt ice there, and saw the frost that crawled up his body. He lay back and looked into the room of the people hanging from the meat-hooks, and among them, he saw a little boy and he wasn't sure but that he'd seen that boy many times before. *Kid's from Prague or something. Seen him on his bike, riding around. Sweet kid. Sweet kid.*

The kid had some kind of messed-up skull in his hands and although the kid seemed to be talking to him, Army began to feel as if the kid were talking to the skull.

8

Dory Crampton awoke in a smelly bed, her wrists and ankles tied to the posts. Her clothes had been ripped from her, and there was a tight cloth across her mouth. It smelled like a filthy toilet.

A man with strawlike hair and a pockmarked face who looked middle-aged and undernourished stood at the bedside. He wore a long white shirt with red stripes, and she noticed that he was naked from the waist down. Worse, he seemed aroused.

She kicked her legs to loosen the restraints, but they only seemed to tighten.

He had what looked to her like a small tube of glue in his right hand. He leaned over her, his breath smelling like he'd

Douglas Clegg

been gargling with shit, and said, "We have to make sure you don't see any of it, Mrs. Fly. The glory of the Beyond is too much for you. The sight of its triple phallus is enough to kill even the most jaded slut, and although I find its face so handsome, I'm afraid Mrs. Fly never seems to agree with me. This is just to make sure that you don't see the Great One when He comes to give you His seed. Don't be afraid. You're the chosen among all women, Mrs. Fly. Among all Mrs. Flies. You are going to be mother to radiance."

Then he brought up the tube of glue, and pressed a little onto her left eyelid. Dory moved her head rapidly, side to side, so that the glue would come out, but some of it went down into her eye and burned. More than anything she'd seen all day, this terrified her because she knew that no one was ever going to find her. No one was going to rescue her.

"Don't look at your husband like that. I love you. I really do. I wouldn't be able to put you through this if I didn't have complete and utter love. You are so wonderful for being the vessel for the Great One, Mrs. Fly. You are beloved of all who exist here. Your hole is the doorway from that world to this, and your child, born from a divine union, will have eternal life in this realm. Your hole with its arches and its door pressed backward will be the entry for the most magnificent, the most radiant of . . ."

He droned on and on. His words seemed to run together and had a nearly hypnotic effect upon her. Dory glanced to the left and the right to try to see what there might be in the room to help her, but the place was mostly bare. A table by a shuttered window.

She glanced over to the doorway.

A little boy who she had seen once in the newspapers but had forgotten, stood there. The same one she had seen when she entered the house. Arnie Pierson. The dead boy who had been found eviscerated at Harrow in the summer, just a few days after he'd died.

The dead boy with the tiny knifepoints in his gums in place of teeth, and that hollow look to his eyes as if he were always hungry.

She watched him reach to his chest and peel back the layers of flesh. Something black and shiny and coated with a gummy liquid that dripped to the floor began emerging from the little boy's open chest.

Mr. Spider had just managed to get the glue on her left eyelid, and then he reached down and shut it.

With only the vision in her right eye, she couldn't quite see what had come out of Arnie Pierson's body, but she heard it. It was a humming and buzzing sound like a swarm of bees, and then a gloppy thump-thump on the floor. A squishy sliding along as it moved toward the bed where she lay.

The buzzing grew louder, and Mr. Spider pressed the glue onto her right eyelid. She blinked to try to let her tears wash the glue away, but he reached up with his fingers and closed her eyelids shut. Though she tried to force her eyelids open, within a few seconds, she could not see more than shadows and light through them, and mainly she saw the edges of her eyelashes.

She had a sense of a warm red glow beyond her eyelids. A slick wet thing slapped down on her left ankle, and she felt its weight as the bed creaked beneath it.

It began slobbering, this thing that moved up to her knees, gently trying to part them.

"Oh, you should see this, Mrs. Fly, why it loves you. I think you're the most beautiful Mrs. Fly it's ever seen. It's growing so large now, it's going to be able to fill every part of you, Mrs. Fly, and it will hook itself from one phallus to another through your body for you to become the vessel. Oh, you must be very, very special, Mrs. Fly, for it to want you this much. Its excitement is extraordinary." Mr. Spider's voice began to go up an octave, and he sounded like an excitable little child. "Do not be afraid of the tentacles.

They're just to hold you and keep you steady while it vibrates through you. They may seem sticky and hot, but they won't scald your skin, and it doesn't hurt very long, and once you get beyond the pain of the way it pierces, I think you'll quite enjoy the ride, Mrs. Fly, as other Mrs. Flies have done before you."

Dory Crampton, unable to see, unable to scream, swallowed bile in the back of her throat as she felt the faintest of pinpricks along her inner thigh, and she felt welts forming where the thing touched her.

Please just let me die. Let me die. God, let me die right now. Don't make me go through this. Don't make it happen to me. Make it be somebody else. Don't make it be me. Make me be back at the dog pound with Benny Marais, not with this thing. This thing.

The unseen creature moved slowly, as if it had to undulate along her flesh to get anywhere.

Please, take my mind away. Make me insane now. I don't want to come back from this. I want this to be the exit from the world. I don't want this to be.

And then Dory Crampton got her wish.

The human mind is frail in even the best circumstances, but being faced with the terror of physical horror, or knowing that the body will be taken and destroyed while the consciousness will have to continue for a time, can send anyone into madness. But what Dory's mind did—besides pushing her into the world of dream instead of reality—was awaken a part of her brain she didn't even know existed before. It was as if something went *crack* inside her, and suddenly, she saw an intense blue-white light within the darkness of her mind. She saw the dog pound that she herself had been living in as she grew to womanhood—that she had a special ability that might be of some help to her. Within her mind's shadows, it came by way of Benny Marais's head, which just appeared, chopped under the chin as it had been at the Boswells' house in the village, with a bit of spinal column pushed out from the meat near the cut. He had that goofy grin, and he floated there in the dog pound of her mind with all the howling animals in their cages, and said, "You know, there's a reason you're not dead yet, Dory. We all are, but you're not. Why would that be?"

Dory, as mute in the dream as she was in real life *(and don't you think about those thousand little prickly feelers that are moving in strangle circles around your hips right now, and that feeling that something is drooling all over your stomach because, Dory, that's going to pull you right out of your head and put you smack dab in your physical body and that'll really fuck you up)*, shook her head and shrugged as only someone living in her mind could.

"Maybe it's because you are one of the few that Harrow's afraid of. You know it has to be afraid of someone, Dory. Why do you think it let you through its doors? Do you know how few people can get in here? Perfectly nice people have been trying, but they usually get axed or gutted before they get their hands on the front door. You don't see them yet, but there's even an Alice and a Ronnie here, too. Even another kid—not Tooth-boy out there with his rat face and chest of miracles—but another kid who has something in him, too, that the house has been so afraid of. Name of Kazi. Funny name for a funny kid, but you knew that, in this brain pound we're in, somehow, you knew that. Because what's inside you—the thing the house is afraid of—wasn't scheduled to make an appearance until you had some traumatic accident. They figured—they being those beings in this hell-hole—that if they gobbled you up first, you'd never be able to gobble them down a few years down the road. Same with those others—that Alice thinks she's psychic, but she's not even as psychic as that wunderkind Kazi. Only, the house got him before he could grow up and get down with the whole psychic shit and maybe take this house out once and for all and lock down the pathway."

The whole time Benny Marais spoke, Dory tried to ignore a tickling feeling at her buttocks and some thick, warm wet prong of some kind that moved along her earlobe. The buzzing seemed to be about twenty miles away, but she knew that it was probably just all around her as she lay in that bed.

I'm not going back to that bed, she thought, and her thoughts became words as she spoke to Benny.

"You have to, I'm sorry to say. But I'm not here just to blow smoke up your ass, although someone might end up doing that tonight. Dory, I'm not even Benny Marais. I'm that part of you that just got woken up. And I want you to fight. I don't want you insane. That won't help you. Even insanity has reality in it, and you'll never get out of here if you don't get back to your body and fight like a bitch from hell. I can't even tell you how to fight. And I can't even give you some magic power to fight. All I can tell you is, Harrow ain't happy. This place is scared of you. And of the others here. Harrow wants you to go into your happy place in your mind so that you won't turn around and bitch-slap it to kingdom come. You and these others are the only thing keeping the doorway to the ancient sorcery blocked."

I don't believe you. I don't believe in this. I think this is my insanity talking, Dory thought.

"Which is more insane? Trapped inside a dark dog pound in your mind with the severed head of your boss— or strapped jaybird naked to a bed while an unspeakable horror with three or more dicks tries to open you up?" Benny asked.

Dory felt like grinning. It sounded like just the kind of language Benny would use. *How the hell do I fight this? My eyes are glued shut. My wrists and ankles are tied. I have a gag over my mouth. What can I do? I mean, do I get a magic sword or something?*

"I don't have the answers. I'm just part of why that little boy with the teeth like knives is so damn hungry for you, sweetie. There's the horny squid from hell crawling up to your snatch, and you don't have time to sit here and talk to me about it. Understood?"

And then she was sane again. More than sane. She was in her body, feeling all the terrible wet fingers of the thing on her, the thing that was going to rape her if she didn't figure out a way to get out of this.

Tied to the bed.

Creaky bed.

The creature now sat over her, its tongues licking near her breasts.

The fucker's heavy.

Okay. Okay. Out of distressed-damsel mode. Into kick 'im in the nuts mode, even if monsterboy has twelve balls.

Dory took a couple of deep breaths. She drew her wrists up so that the restraints were taut; she spread her legs wide, despite the fear and revulsion she felt, just so her ankles would also pull tight at the restraints.

Then she swung her buttocks a little to the left.

Tiny damp feelers with feathery edges that seemed to be dripping some kind of goo on her that ran all over her ass like little bugs.

Then she swung to the right.

Again she felt the undulating movements of the creature upon her, and suction cups at the end of what she could only assume were tentacles.

Benny Marais, you better not have been lying to me.

She swung again, back and forth, and the creature clung to her with a thousand feelers.

Mr. Spider kept jabbering away about "glorious light," and "magnificent love" and "midwifing the infinite," and she thought she heard the metallic clanking of the little boy with the knifepoint teeth in the doorway.

But she tensed her muscles and then swung again to the left, and this time the bed tipped.

Over, come on, son of a bitch. Over. Tip the hell over!

And that's when Dory felt a shift in the fabric of reality. Even in the blindness of her glued eyelids, she thought she saw a yellow light like a brilliant sunrise.

Remembering the words from her mind: *What's inside you—the thing the house is afraid of—wasn't scheduled to make an appearance until you had some traumatic accident. They figured—they being those beings in this hellhole—that if they gobbled you up first, you'd never be able to gobble them down a few years down the road.*

In that split-second shift, when the bed tipped up with her swinging off it, and when she heard those words again and saw the golden light—

She felt it.

It was like a biting in her brain. Something bit down, and it hurt in her head, but she knew that it was what the severed head of Benny Marais had been telling her.

Traumatic accident. This is it.

She smelled something she hadn't caught a whiff of since she'd been three or four, and a memory came with the smell: of being a little girl taking her mother's hand as they walked along the street, and having that smell, then, too. Like something on the wind that had an element of something she had never before smelled, as a girl, or since—until now. It was neither sweet nor sour, but did have a bitter edge to it. Even as a girl, it had caused her nose to bleed a little.

This time, it caused her nose to bleed a lot.

Trauma. Bite in the brain. This is it.

As the golden light in the darkness of her mind shattered, the bed tipped all the way over. She and the mucky creature that had crawled up her naked body to force itself into her went over onto the floor.

Half a second later, she heard a strange splat against one of the walls.

One of her wrist restraints had torn as the post went, and she quickly went to untie the other one.

The creature buzzed and hummed, and sounded angry to her. Mr. Spider starting cussing, and the Tooth-boy, as Benny Marais had called him, began grinding his teeth into a series of high pitched squeals.

She still couldn't open her eyes, but she felt along her ankles and undid the restraints there. She crawled off a ways, trying to feel her way to the door. She rubbed her eyes over and over again to try to wear down the glue, but it was doing no good.

"You fucking little bitch, Mrs. Fly. You think you're too good to put out for our friends from the other side, do you? Do you?" Mr. Spider began ranting. "You think you're not good enough for bringing forth the children of miracles? Your pussy is beautiful, but that doesn't mean you're beautiful on the inside, does it? Well, we're just going to have to make it hard on you. Very hard. I suppose it's going to hurt this time. I was hoping you'd take it easy. But no, you have to listen to your imaginary voices in your head, don't you? You believe you have some special calling, some insane ability that makes you attractive to us here. Well, the only attractive thing about you, little miss, is your ability to provide a mass of eggs so that the seed of radiance can take hold inside you. You're not even good enough to have the name Mrs. Fly. You're Mrs. Flyshit, in my opinion, little miss."

The buzzing and humming seemed to follow her, and she wiped at her eyes, tears pressing out from them. *Please help me. Somebody help me. I can't do this on my own. If I have some power, keep me safe. Keep me safe.*

"He told you we're going to gobble you up? Well, that's just right, little miss," Mr. Spider said. "We're going to chew you up and spit you out and you're gonna love every minute of it. You don't have anything this house wants, believe you me, other than the mass of eggs inside that womb of yours. And it better be a womb with a view, little miss, because our friend is very, very horny at the moment and has a lot of sprayin' to do."

Dory hated girls that cried over anything, but she couldn't help it. As she wiped her eyes, trying to peel back the glue that had nearly sealed her eyelids, she could not stop weeping. She felt like that little girl, holding her mother's hand again, and that unusual bitter smell was in the air. And tears flowed.

But as she sobbed, now in a corner, balled up to protect herself, she began to see a little from her left eyelid.

The tears.

Between wiping at her eyes and crying, the glue had unsealed a little. Taking her sharpest fingernail, she put it between the lids of her left eye and further separated it. She had her left eye open.

It was enough.

9

Ronnie felt exhausted after she finished chopping up the last of the thing that had not been her sister Lizzie but had been a perfect imitation of her. Blood soaked her clothes and her face, and she clung to the hatchet like it was an amulet protecting her in all things.

Ronnie felt as if she had changed in the past several hours, from everything she had seen in the village until now.

She felt like a warrior, and even her arms felt muscled and tight. She glanced back at the corpse of the Lizzie thing. When she'd split it open, it had been nearly hollow inside. It reminded her of a cicada she'd seen cut open once—where it was all black and ridged on the inside, but nearly hollow. This thing was like that, too—it was an exoskeleton, with no interior, although a black bilelike substance oozed from what had been the Lizzie-thing's head.

When she crouched down to examine it more closely, she saw tiny, feathery feelers on the inside of the flesh. And she couldn't help herself—she had to see the rest. She looked at the Lizzie-thing's genitalia—it had two thin black spurs coming from an opening that was neither anus nor vagina. Just above this, on her lower belly, there were two red points that dripped with a viscous liquid.

Like a spider. Holy shit.

She glanced up the stairs and back toward the front door. The door had changed, and Ronnie had come to fully expect that whatever was in the house was going to fuck with her mind. But the door had shimmering white silky strands across it.

As she touched the banister of the staircase, she felt something sticky, and drew her hand back. It didn't budge—and the silky strands roped across the banister as well. She had to jerk her hand away from the banister, and even then the stickiness tore the thinnest layer of skin from the palm of her hand.

Spider's web.

Ronnie heard a high-pitched squeal from up the stairs, as if someone were scratching a nail along a blackboard. She stepped back from the stairs, clutching the hatchet. She held it up, but took another step back, over the dead Lizzie-thing.

She saw the shadow of something huge moving— almost flitting—along the walls.

Coming for you.

Coming.

She glanced back over at the web that covered the door. *If I chop through it, I can get out. I can get out and come in another way.*

She looked down the hall to her left. It was pitch black that direction. *Not sure I have many choices. Upstairs, something's coming down for me. The web—could try to chop my way through, but I could get caught in it, and then I'm screwed.*

Ronnie looked into the darkness, hoping she'd distinguish some movement or get some sense of how far the corridor went.

"Shit," she said. She kept her back to the wall as she went and held the hatchet up defensively. She moved slowly along the wall, down the corridor, into darkness.

At first, she felt a tickling along her ankles. She glanced down but couldn't see anything. She looked back to the entryway and thought she saw various shadows moving there near the door.

She looked ahead into the dark.

Held her breath for a second, dispelling fears.

You can get through this. You have strength. You'll kill them all if you have to.

She moved farther along and felt the tickling again.

Ignore it. It's nothing. It's not hurting you. It's not stopping you. Just go.

She swung the hatchet into the air, hoping to keep anything that might be coming after her at bay.

You'll get through this. You'll get through it.

As she moved along the wall, she saw that the windows of this hallway were all covered with the webbing, but they began to let in a speck of light. It was just enough for her eyes to adjust to the dark and see a little bit.

She went rigid, and pressed herself to the wall when she saw the forms moving in the dark.

They were clumps of movement, as if small children—impossibly small—moved in groups together and then separated and reformed other groups.

Behind her, as she moved along, she felt a doorframe.

Thank God. I'll get through this. Nothing's hurt me yet. Nothing can. Nothing will.

She brought one arm behind her back, while she chopped the hatchet through the air in front of her. The dark things moved along by the webbed windows and scurried down the hall; others regrouped, then split off from their groups. She still could not make them out, but she assumed they must be like the Lizzie-thing in some way.

She turned the doorknob, and the door opened behind her.

Light from this room flooded the corridor.

She stood there, the rectangle of light from the room illuminating the dark things.

No longer dark.

Jesus.

They were beetles with iridescent green backs, moving along dead bodies—six or seven bodies that lay there. Beetles as large as human fists were scurrying all over them, covering them and making Ronnie believe the bodies had moved slightly. But the beetles were quickly devouring the flesh of the corpses so that ribs stuck out from the torso of a woman, and a man's skeletal hand thrust from his fleshy wrist.

The light seemed to get the insects' attention, however, and although she felt it was the height of madness, Ronnie was nearly certain that they had turned their attention away from the flesh feast to look at her. Their antennae moved, and she saw some of their wings lift as if they were about to take flight.

They're going to eat me alive.

They're flesh-eaters, and I'm next.

Behind her, in the room, she heard a noise that sounded like a *sh-sh-sh-sh*.

She felt the small hairs at the nape of her neck rise up, and she swore that she could've peed standing up right then—

Ronnie Pond turned to see her dead father standing

there, in his boxer shorts, his face as smashed from the car wreck as she had remembered it being that day so many years ago.

Beneath his feet, the floor seemed to be covered with a dark, thick liquid, almost like moist asphalt, that rippled like the surface of a just-disturbed pond.

No. No.

Something within her mind snapped, as if it hadn't been snapping all day. Something snapped big, and she began shouting inside her head. *YOU ARE NOT GOING TO FUCK WITH ME, HARROW. YOU ARE NOT GOING TO DRIVE ME INSANE WITH DREAMS AND THEN PUT ME DOWN IN SOME WASP NEST AND SHOW ME EVERYONE I EVER LOVED WHO DIED.*

"Fuck this," she said, and pulled the door shut again, stepping back into the darkness as the beetles flew at her and began tearing at her skin. She swung the hatchet out, and ran as fast as she could toward a feeble glow of light she saw. As she reached it, she saw it was the beginning of more stairs up, lit by jars full of candles.

In the flickering candlelight, the beetles had vanished. Glancing back from where she'd come, Ronnie saw them moving in their thick swarms, heading back to the piles of corpses.

Under the stairs, a doorway.

Locked.

And that's when she heard Dory Crampton's ear-piercing scream in an upstairs room.

10

Alice Kyeteler had entered the glorious cathedral that was Harrow. She saw the altar up ahead, and the bodies that had been split open and pinned back along the great pillars. She decided that it was going to be easier to ignore the trappings of this place—that the glamour Harrow projected was simply another way of trapping souls within it.

You didn't live this long to get caught like this.

Yet part of her said to herself, *You stupid, stupid woman. You lived here for years and knew never to come to this one spot. This one place. This is the only thing that will destroy you for what you have.*

A man stepped out from behind one of the pillars. He wore a wide red cape, and for a moment she thought he was dressed as a cardinal.

Cardinal of Hell, of course.

She didn't recognize Roland Love, but that was because the house had changed him since entering it. He had been tearing open the birth sacs of the reborn ones, and had shepherded them along in their pupal stages of growth. But during this process, their claws and pincers had torn at him—for even though he used his spike to tear at the outer white maggot, the dark creatures within still had to pull their way out into the world and feed upon something. Roland had been that feeder, and the marks of the creatures were upon him in gashes and gouges. His face, though still strikingly handsome, was now sliced along the cheek and forehead. The barbed wire crown had been pressed farther down into his skull until his own flesh had covered over it, marrying to the barbed wire so that the barbs thrust out of his now-bald head. His eyes had sunken back a bit so they seemed smaller and darker, and the insanity of the house had pulsed in his blood long enough that he as much resembled a nightmare as he did a dream. His bloodred cap flowed over him, hiding the more obvious scourges to his body, but he had come through it all, a servant to Kingdom Come.

Alice saw all this—feeling the gentle fever of her psychic ability on the surface of her skin as she touched him. She had not felt such a strong charge since she'd first come to Watch Point.

The house owns this one, she thought.

"We can hear your thoughts here," Roland said. "No need to hide them with your mind."

"I suppose you speak for Harrow."

He nodded. He swung his arm out to suggest that they walk farther along the ancient stones toward the altar. "The Kingdom is at hand."

Alice showed no fear. She walked with Roland Love toward the great golden altar that looked as bright as the sun. As they neared it, she saw the worshippers on their knees, gazing up at the statues around the altar.

Roland stopped, and smiled. "Do you see what we can accomplish? If all are here?"

She reached over and touched his wounded hand, lightly pressing against the large gash just beneath his thumb. "You had visions, once."

"I am a visionary."

"No, you believe God spoke to you. But this is no god here. This has perverted your belief and twisted it so that it could devour you."

He shook his head lightly. "I was told you were a scorpion in our midst. I was told that no matter how you seemed like someone's mother with your graying hair and your granny braid and your granola charm, that you had a stinger waiting to come out."

She gazed up at him, at his eyes. "You're in a dream. You're sleepwalking through it. This place has done it to you. But you and I, we're just electricity for it. That's all. It'll use me, and use you, and then the lights will go out again."

"Do you see the reborn?" Roland said, taking her over to the worshippers.

There may have been forty of them in the first pews and along the altar, and when they turned to look back at Alice, her fear finally returned. "How could you be part of this?"

"I will be reborn, as well," he said.

She looked at the others there. Ordinary people from the village.

She had already known that some of them were dead. But these were not the dead.

These had vestigial wings in their backs, and the women's breasts had fine dark hairs all over them. She gasped at one of the men because she was sure it was Army Vernon, but not really him. *It's a second one of him. He's dead. The house got him.*

She also saw Thad Allen, big as day, naked, squatting near the altar, looking at her . . . *the way an insect would. As if there's nothing to be seen. A praying mantis, a cockroach.* His eyes were not yet fully formed and had a milky discharge in them.

Beyond all these worshippers were maggot creatures that wriggled and hummed, and some of them had begun tearing with pincers through their larval covering.

A young man with a beautiful face and a flop of sandy brown hair, as naked as all the rest of them, got up from a pew and began bounding toward them.

It was Roland himself, but not exactly him. The imitation's eyes were more human than the real Roland's eyes had become. His skin was flawless, and his sinewy muscles showed off a vibrant, strong physique. Only his penis would've betrayed a difference, for there were three prongs hanging downward that looked almost like a fly's proboscis.

"It's a nightmare," she said. "That's all."

"The village has sacrificed much to the marriage of the Holy and Unholy tonight," Roland said, raising his arms to embrace his other self. The naked Roland went to the caped Roland, and they held each other for several seconds. The caped Roland began squirming in the other's arms, and Alice gasped when she saw that his other self had begun chewing at his neck, taking away a thin strand of skin.

The other Roland looked at her, sniffing, but returned to the throat of his origin.

"It is beautiful," the real Roland said, his voice turning to a rasp as his other sucked at his earlobe, taking a shred of his ear and part of his scalp down its throat.

Roland opened his cape, and others came to him—children with their teeth gnashing and the fine hairs on their stomachs quivering, old women Alice had passed every day in the village, recreated but for a change or two in their bodies or the discharge from their eyes and mouth.

Beneath Roland's red cape, he, too, was naked. They came to him, and he covered them with his cape. His eyes rolled up into the back of his head as their ministrations to his body sent him into a state of delirium. He gasped and moaned as if he were climaxing, but Alice watched in horror as the others tore at his flesh, and then began to draw the flesh apart.

They were turning him inside out.

The noise itself was unbearable. She covered her ears to block it out, but the slurps and the squishes seemed to reach her, and she cried out because Alice Kyeteler, at last, had given up.

She fell to her knees, not in worship, but in the utmost terror she'd ever felt.

The others continued to draw and quarter Roland Love, and he groaned and grunted as the doorways and passages of his flesh and organs were pried apart until the meat and bones and blood of him was all on the outside.

11

Trying to follow the source of the scream, Ronnie Pond raced along the upper hallway, looking in the open rooms as she went. All the lights were on bright, and she passed rooms in which she saw a man who looked like he had somehow transformed into a large lizard, tearing a woman apart between her legs, while she laughed; in another room, she saw a man with a bloodied crotch with what looked like a python halfway down his throat, its head poking from within the skin at his collarbone; passing another, she saw a mass of blood and bones and organs, like a man skinned alive, writing madly on the walls of a room, talking to himself; in others, she saw more of what she'd seen in the village—the madness of human beings possessed by malevolence. She followed a second stairway up, and found room after room of dead, torn women. It was purely by luck that she found a very naked Dory Crampton in a room, fighting a man in a long striped shirt who needed to find a good set of trousers himself, while a strange-looking little boy jumped up and down and kept making a strange whistling sound.

12

Ronnie didn't hesitate, despite the green scum all over the floor. She raced into the room, and brought the hatchet against the guy's right arm. The little boy went running out of the room making yet another weird sound, like a clacking.

The man she'd hit fell over onto the floor, moaning and screeching about "The days of judgment are at hand! You can't stop it! It's a force to be reckoned with!"

Ronnie shouted at the other girl, whom she recognized from school. "Dory! Get the hell up! Now!"

Dory Crampton looked up at her and said, "Holy shit. You're not another one of them."

"No time to talk. Those yours?" She pointed to the overalls and shirt that lay in a clump by the door. "Get dressed and let's get the hell out of here. We need to find the others."

"Who?"

"We'll know when we see 'em," Ronnie said.

13

When Ronnie reached out to pull Dory up, they both felt it at once. It was like a play of lightning between them. A recognition went through both of them. Before Mr. Spider could get up, Ronnie slammed the hatchet into his thigh, and again he fell. Blood spurted from him this time, and it splattered on her already blood-stained clothes.

Once out of the room, Ronnie began pulling Dory down the hallway.

"It's us," Ronnie said, nearly out of breath. "You know that."

"Us?"

"Harrow wants to keep us separate. You have it. I have it. Alice has it. Army must have it. It killed everyone else."

"Did you see the monster?" Dory asked.

"What?"

"There was this *thing*. I didn't get a good look at it. It sort of was all smushy and had tentacles and . . ."

"No." *Don't be afraid,* Ronnie thought.

Her voice passed into Dory's mind. She nodded.

We have to destroy this place, Ronnie told her in her mind.

They thought they both heard something moving toward them from the far end of the corridor, so Dory and Ronnie raced to the staircase at the large mirror. Dory stopped suddenly, seeing something in the mirror.

When Ronnie looked up at it, she too saw it—wisps of what might've been people they'd never seen before, like ghosts trapped in the mirror, reaching out for them.

She remembered the words Alice told her about the place.

Harrow traps souls. It harvests those with psychic ability and it uses them up. It sucks at them.

Ronnie hauled back and swung the hatchet at the mirror, breaking it. "Well, if any souls are trapped there, we just set 'em free."

But when the mirror shattered, they both saw it:

Behind the glass and the frame, it looked like there was an entrance to an entirely different house.

"You want to go see what's there?" Ronnie asked.

"No fuckin' way," Dory said. "Let's just find your friends and get the hell out."

Dory nearly tripped down the stairs getting to the first floor. When the front door was in sight, a naked blond girl with stringy hair stood in her path. The hair nearly obscured her face and was all damp and matted. When Ronnie came up behind her, she gasped. "Shit. It's Bari Love. I thought I'd killed her. Or at least put her out for awhile."

Ronnie raised her hatchet as if to attack, but stopped.

Bari Love's eyes were milky white and dripping a substance like cottage cheese down her face. Her blond hair was too thin, and showed her scalp in places. She opened and closed her mouth as if trying to say something, but there was no sound.

"It's like the Lizzie-thing," Ronnie said. "She's all hollow on the inside."

She swung the hatchet and caught Bari just above the jaw. The hatchet got stuck there, and flew out of Ronnie's fingers. The Bari-thing fell to the floor, the hatchet still caught from her ear to her mouth.

And that's when the little boy with the dog's head came out into the foyer.

"Who the hell are you?" Dory asked.

"Kazi?" Ronnie asked. "Kazi Vrabec?"

The boy nodded.

"I babysit him sometimes," Ronnie said. "We're friends, aren't we? Are you okay?"

Kazi nodded, and held the dog's head up for her to see.

"How do we know it's really him?"

"I just know," Ronnie said.

Ronnie took the dog's head from him, and grimaced as she looked at it with its pasty gauze and bits of fur and leathery skin at the muzzle and around the ears.

"He's my friend," Kazi said. "My only friend." Then he pointed down the dark hallway behind him. "Mr. Vernon died down there. Of fright."

14

The three of them stood in the empty room and looked down at Army Vernon. His eyes were open so wide they nearly had burst out. His mouth was stretched in a final scream to the point that it looked like he had a dislocated jaw.

Ronnie was the first to see the gun, lying a few feet away from him. "Know how to shoot?"

Dory nodded, and went to retrieve the gun.

Kazi Vrabec said, "There's another little boy who lives here."

Ronnie and Dory looked back at him.

"His name is Arnie. He can't talk with his mouth. His tongue got tore out. And his teeth got pulled one by one. And his insides all went on the outside. But he can talk in here." Kazi tapped the edge of his head. "Arnie's one of the doorways."

"Doorways?" Dory asked.

"You know, like a door. He lets them in. He told me with his mind that I can start to let them in, too."

"Who?"

"Others," Kazi said, almost as if it were an embarrassing thing to admit. "But I bet you can be doorways, too. He said people like us keep the doorway clear and the door open and unlocked. He talks to me in my head, just like my buddy does." He went and took the head back from Ronnie, and cradled it in his arms.

I can talk to you in your head, too, Ronnie said, hoping he'd hear her.

Kazi nearly dropped the dog's head, and looked up at her.

15

Don't trust them, kiddo. They're bitches. I can smell a bitch a mile away, and they even hurt Mr. Spider, which was really mean, the dog's head told him.

"But they seem nice," Kazi said aloud, still watching the two young women.

Nice? Hell, kiddo, one's covered with blood and one was a Mrs. Fly only now she's Mrs. Flyshit. You can't trust those types, Kazi. They're not like you. Sure, maybe they could be doorways, but what kind of doorway are we talkin'? The kind that that creaks and makes you trip and the door's locked just because they feel like locking it. They're like the old man. You saw what was in his heart. You saw it. He was ice cold inside and he would've shot you if he'd had half a chance, you know that, kiddo. We hated him. All of us.

Kazi cocked his head to the side, listening to the voice of the dog.

But tell you what kid, let's take them to see Arnie. Arnie'll know what to do with them. Maybe the two of you—Arnie and you together—you'll come up with a way to incapacitate the bitches.

"I don't like when you call them that," Kazi said, looking up at both Ronnie and Dory. In his mind, he asked the dog, *Can they hear what we're saying?*

Only when you open your mouth, kiddo. They're not the power source that you are. They're like little candles. You're our pint-sized nuclear power plant, Kazi.

Ronnie Pond watched him as if she knew what the dog

was telling him, but all she said was, "Well, let's go find Alice. If she's still alive."

Then she went to pull the hatchet out of the Bari-thing's skull.

16

Alice lay down on the cathedral stones and looked up at the great murals that moved with the demons and angels, and the dome above that had strange creatures painted upon it, with tentacles and wings like dragonflies, wrapped around women. From the women's bodies came other creatures of varying weirdness.

Harrow can create all this from the dormant psychic spark in a handful of people.

Harrow can draw even from me to create this.

Can draw from anyone—from Ronnie Pond and Army, who probably didn't even know he had some ability, however slight.

Why now? Why here?

She thought of the dead boy who had been found mutilated on the grounds, and she knew that had been the point of awakening. Even the dead boy—freshly dead—had something within him that Harrow had wanted.

And the Nightwatchman.

Why destroy the village? Why leak out like that?

She heard the humming of the worshippers, and felt safe from their rabid hungers. *The house wants me. That much I know. It will take me dead, but it won't kill me. It wants me, but it's scared of me.*

And then, Alice Kyteler knew. She knew with a conviction that could not be shaken.

The ones in town still sleep. Their dreams are fueling this. We're fueling this. The house without us is nothing. It doesn't want us to die, but we're frail. We may die. It wants our awe. Our allegiance.

It wants to convert us to . . . opening the portal.
Where is my ability? What can I bring to this to shut down this house? Where is its heart that I might rip it out?

17

And that's when Alice heard Army Vernon's voice. He wasn't speaking to her in her head. He said, "It doesn't have a heart, Alice."

18

Alice sat up and glanced around. The cathedral had grown fuzzy around her as if it were a watercolor melting in the rain. But as it shimmered, she saw the bare walls of the house again. Still, the great cathedral came back into focus, and she saw the worshippers as they strung the meat and bones and sliver of face of Roland Love up to a makeshift cross at the altar.

There, sitting in a pew not more that six feet from her was Army Vernon.

19

He was as insubstantial as morning mist, but his face moved as it would have in life, and unlike flesh and blood, it gave off no aura for her to see.

"You're dead," she said, no longer afraid of the idea of death because she had already begun assuming that death would come for her.

"Be that as it may," Army said, "the house has no heart, Alice. You can't kill what isn't mortal."

"How do I know you're not just part of the house now?"

"I guess you don't," he said. "I guess I am part of the house at this point."

"Is it bad?"

345

Douglas Clegg

"Being dead? Not as bad as being alive, let me tell you. Now here's all I know. There's a kid here."

"Arnie Pierson. His spirit?"

"He didn't tell me his name. But this kid, well, he has power you can't even imagine. He showed me something pretty damn bad, Alice. I watched a real horror show in that kid's face. I don't know how he did it, but it was like he was reaching inside my chest and giving a good juicing to my heart. Those girls found me."

"Ronnie?"

The spirit nodded, with wisps of evaporating particles of his flesh moving in the wake of the nod. "Her and some other girl. The one who works with Benny down at the pound. They found me and they can probably tell you that it didn't look like I had a good time in my last seconds. But I will tell you that it's worse than that. When that kid shows you what he has inside him, believe me, you can't live past that point. It will stop anybody's heart."

Alice watched as he raised his hand slightly, and then bits of his misty fingers slowly drifted away from his form like milkweed floating in the air. "All this," he said. "This cathedral nonsense. It's just a distraction. There's a . . ." As he spoke he looked to his left as if he'd just heard a noise. "Oh shit. It's coming again."

"What? Army?"

"I think of it as the cosmic vacuum cleaner. It's going down the halls of this place sucking up the dead. Listen, I'd better go. All I can tell you is I'm stuck here. Nothing you or I can do about that. But that kid has to be stopped. He has something bigger than you or anyone here has ever had, and I can't even call it psychic ability. It's not that minor. The house gave him a big gift, and it's the gift of madness. All I can tell you about it is it's bad. Mean bad." And then, his eyes still glancing to the left, he rose and his particles spread apart until they were a fine mist

346

on the air. Then there was nothing to be seen other than the pews and the great stone pillars.

Alice felt a desert hot breeze pass by her, almost as if there were a fire just beyond the walls and a blast of its heat had burst through.

Then where the wind had come through—what Army must've meant by the "cosmic vacuum cleaner"—a gap in the stone wall of the cathedral.

It was about as tall as a man and wide enough to fit through, but as she got up to go look at it, she noticed it was shrinking as if filling with sand.

She rushed over to it and squeezed her way through the gap before it closed.

20

Alice nearly lost her balance in the next room—it was a small, plain room with a mattress in a corner and several jars full of lit candles around its walls. She first noticed the stench—it was a smothering belch of human gas in her face.

On the mattress, the corpse of a little boy wearing the kind of suit that a little boy might be buried in—the dark tie and gray suit with shorts and black socks that went nearly to his knees.

She went over to the corpse, covering her face with her hands and trying to breathe through her mouth.

His face was rotted nearly to the bone. His teeth had been pulled by someone, and lay beside the corpse.

She knew who it was without having to think twice.

Arnie Pierson.

She went over to the window near the body, and peeled back the shutters that had been badly nailed in place. Then she opened the window to let in the chilly air. She looked out at the night—it was simply darkness with no lights to be seen whatsoever. And yet above she saw the pinprick of stars in the fabric of night and she thought, briefly, of things other than Harrow and death.

When she turned around from the window, she saw the closed door behind her and the peeling wallpaper of the area from which she'd come. *A dream of a cathedral. Someone else's dream. Stolen by Harrow. The mind of Harrow. The devouring soul of this place.*

A dead boy, his soul still inside his body, sacrificed to this house.

Stealing dreams from sleepers, and making nightmares come through others.

On the wall behind Arnie's head, someone had scrawled:

The Nightwatchman looked into the heart of the dreamers, and found their dark secrets.

Despite everything she'd seen that night, Alice could no longer hold back. She sat down beside the rotting corpse and began weeping. She didn't weep for herself or for Thad Allen or Sam Pratt or for those she'd seen who had died and those she had not seen who had died.

She wept for Arnie, who had died before any of this had begun.

Even dead, the house had taken him.

The house is unrelenting.

The house is pure fury.

Harrow is alive and insane, and it sucks the dreams and the souls.

It must be stopped now.

She got up after a few minutes of sitting with the corpse and went to the doorway, opening it to the hall. Then she returned to the dead boy's body, and lifted it up. She had gotten used to the stink of it, and no longer saw it as a putrefying corpse, but as a little boy who needed to be buried somewhere far from Harrow.

21

In the hallway, Alice saw that the house had somehow turned itself down. Images of stone and wood flickered a bit, as if there had been an energy drain. She didn't know what it meant, but she carried the boy along the corridor. When she came to a staircase, she saw Ronnie Pond and Dory Crampton and a little boy named Kazi who had a mummified dog's head in his hand.

"Thank God," Ronnie said. "Alice, you made it."

Dory glanced at the middle-aged woman with the braid and then at the dead boy in her arms. "What if she's part of the house?"

"No," Ronnie said. "She's not."

Alice laid the corpse on the floor. She looked at the others. "This is Arnie Pierson. Even after death, Harrow's kept his body."

She went over to Kazi Vrabec. A light around him shimmered with a whiteness that she hadn't seen in anyone in years.

He's got power in him he doesn't even know, she thought. *He may be a source.*

"We need to leave now. Right now. With you," she said to him. "Will you take my hand?" She offered her right hand to him.

Kazi looked down at the dog's head and then at her hand. He glanced over at Dory and Ronnie. He glanced at the corpse, as well, as if it would talk to him.

Then he put out his hand and let his fingers touch the edge of Alice's palm.

As he did so, Alice said to him, "We have to find the heart of Harrow."

22

Alice closed her hand around Kazi's fingers and felt a surge within her. Not a surge that brought her anything. Not the kind of surge she felt when she sensed another "sensitive" nearby.

This surge sucked at her. Took what she had within her and began to drain her of any ability she'd felt.

She looked at the boy, shocked. As she did, it was no longer Kazi, but Arnie Pierson himself, with metal knife-points for teeth that overbit his lips and sunken, hollow eyes. He parted his lips and said, "You will never find the heart of the house, Alice Kyeteler. I *am* the house."

The dog's head in his left hand began snapping as if alive, and the boy raised it up toward her.

23

Dory saw the look on Alice's face—her eyes widened and her skin had gone chalk-white as if she were being drained of blood. Alice still clutched the boy's right hand. The boy pressed the dog's head up to Alice's lips.

24

Ronnie lifted her hatchet, defensively, ready to swing at anything she saw, but all she saw was a little boy pushing the tattered dog skull at Alice's face.

25

Alice saw something entirely different.

26

Her eyes began to turn up into her skull, and she felt her breathing going too rapidly, but she could not control it. She tried to tell herself that what she saw was nothing, just another nightmare of Harrow, but she couldn't get it from her mind—

It was the other world that Harrow guarded, the doorway into something more fierce than Alice had ever been able to imagine. And when she tried to make sense of what the little boy showed her, she felt her throat clutch, and her heart begin to burst inside her chest.

27

As Alice fell, dying, Kazi Vrabec dropped the dog's head and turned to face Ronnie and Dory.

Alice's body twitched and spasmed as her face contorted into a rictus of pain. As she died, she did what she could to send a message to the others. But in her last seconds, she knew her mouth could not form the words.

28

Even so, Ronnie thought she heard a distant voice, weak, as if a phone signal were being lost even as the words were cried out. And then, a terrible silence.

But Ronnie had heard the words.

In flesh.

Kazi turned toward her, tears streaming down his face. "Please. Help me. Get me out of here. Take me somewhere safe."

He reached his arms up to Ronnie like a child needing its mother.

Superimposed over his face, she saw the other little boy with the knife teeth.

In flesh. What did it mean? What was it?

The house is in the flesh.

He is the flesh of the house.

Flesh is weak.

Flesh is corruptible.

He is the heart now.

"Please," the boy whimpered. "I feel sick. Something bad is happening. Please. Hurry. Take me. Take me out of here."

"Are you Harrow?" she asked, her voice full of calm even when she raged within her body.

He glanced up at her, his eyes flashing almost like a wild animal's. "You wouldn't hurt a child."

Without hesitating, Ronnie swung the hatchet around and caught Kazi Vrabec squarely in the chest.

Dory screamed, but she might've been screaming ever since Alice had fallen—Ronnie had blocked everything but her focus on the boy.

Kazi Vrabec looked down at the hatchet embedded in his chest and the blood that burst from it.

29

The little boy fell over, dead.

Ronnie went to draw her hatchet from his body.

Dory listened to the sound of what seemed to be a hundred doors slamming open and closed, and windows slamming shut, and the sound of breaking glass upstairs and down the hallway.

Above it all, she heard the man she knew was Mr. Spider screeching from some upstairs room as if he were being tortured to death.

30

From the open wound in Kazi Vrabec's chest, what looked like a swarm of flies came up, buzzing and humming in a small cyclone that grew until the room itself seemed blackened. The sound became deafening, and Ronnie covered her ears against it.

They flew toward the ceiling, and then up the stairs.

When the house went silent again, Ronnie looked back at Dory and said, "It's done."

31

"We need to take him far from this place," Ronnie said after several minutes had passed.

She and Dory had simply become numb from what they'd experienced in the house, and they stared at the bodies that lay before them for too long, bewildering thoughts going through both of their minds.

"We need to take him to some kind of sacred ground. Jewish, Christian, Muslim, pagan, doesn't matter. It has to be someplace where this house can't ever touch him again."

"But he's dead," Dory said. "Isn't he?" She went to kneel beside Kazi Vrabec.

"Not him," Ronnie said. She pointed to Arnie Pierson's rotting body. "Him. He's the one who set this in motion. I don't know how. I don't know why. I don't give a damn. But we have to take him out of here. Whoever dug him up from his grave knew that the ritual the night my sister and her friends were here put power in his bones and flesh. Woke something up, and put some to sleep. I don't know who Arnie Pierson was. I know nothing about the kid. But whatever was in his bones or body is still in them. And he can't be near this house ever again." She knew this must be true, and that the words she heard from Alice's mind had been an indication. "We all have some minor ability, Dory. Maybe a lot of people do. This kind of psychic bullshit. I don't really even believe it, but for Alice's sake, I'll play along for now. I wouldn't have believed everything we've seen tonight, either. But I can play along with it while I'm still scared shitless. So let's get Arnie out of here now. Then we'll see if we can get help, and if there's a way to burn this house down."

Dory nodded, and they both went to pick up Arnie Pierson's body. "Uh," Dory said, as she lifted his legs.

Ronnie had a grim look on her face. "Ignore the smell. We just need to get him out."

They carried him along the hall, past another door or two, but Harrow was completely ordinary again.

Nothing to fear.

The switch was off. The house was dead. Or if not dead, sleeping. Ronnie only felt a whisper of something lingering, like the smell of ozone after a machine that's been running too long shuts off.

Harrow's front door was open wide, and although it was still night, both she and Ronnie could see faint traces of purple light along the treetops as they brought Arnie Pierson out.

Dory looked at the corpse and let out a gasp.

Ronnie looked down as she carried him by his shoulders.

The face of the boy had plumped up when it met the outside air, and it was not the face of Arnie Pierson at all.

"How the hell . . ." Ronnie said.

It was Kazi Vrabec's face. Eyes closed.

They set the body down at the edge of the driveway, and looked back up at the open door of Harrow.

"Harrow's playing tricks on us," Ronnie said.

"You want to go back in there?" Dory asked, a tremble to her voice.

"No way in hell," Ronnie said. "I'd rather just go find explosives and blow it up."

"Does this mean it's still going?"

"Maybe. Maybe it's just a shred of something. A whisper. I think we shut it down. Even if it has a little energy right now, it would not have let us out," Ronnie said. "I guess objects in that house are closer than they appear."

Dory gave her a funny look, as if she didn't quite understand what Ronnie had meant.

And even if she didn't completely believe it, Ronnie Pond didn't care. She looked up at Harrow, with its towers and gabled rooftops and its stone and wood and glass, and she uttered a curse upon it as if curses could actually work.

"I feel like it's over," Ronnie said. "Maybe that's all that matters."

They carried the body down the driveway.

When the sun finally came up, they were still walking with the boy in between them, along the narrow unpaved roads back toward the village. Dory kept dropping his feet, until Ronnie decided that she'd just carry the boy and deal with the weight of him, but she too was exhausted. When they found an abandoned car with the keys in the ignition but the driver missing, they decided that they'd drive up to Parham. "We can tell the cops," Ronnie said. "We can get some rest. And they can deal with all this." She didn't want to have to mention all the dead. She didn't want to have to even remember all that she and Dory had seen the previous night.

She just wanted it to be over, and for the shock and numbness to begin.

She opened the back door of the car, and laid the boy's body down as gently as she could.

Dory got the car started, and said, "Well, at least whoever abandoned this one left us a little bit of gas."

32

They drove out along the bumpy roads as the sun broke from over the hills, and they ran over some chains that had fallen in the road from "No Trespassing" signs on each side of it. The roads that they took twisted through woods and across fields, and Dory was glad she'd taken the back way so they wouldn't even see the rooftops of the village again.

They soon found a rural route that Ronnie could identify as meeting back up with the main highway again. They took it and drove another three miles toward the main roads. But then the car coughed to a stop.

"Gas?" Ronnie asked, glancing over at the gauge.

"Maybe," Dory said, tapping at the dashboard as if it would tell her something. "Well, I guess if you steal a car, you get what you deserve. Want to walk from here?"

Ronnie glanced around at the rocks and the field and the distant woods behind them. "Sure."

33

By the time they'd reached the main highway, they had walked for more than an hour. The sun had completely risen, and a slight wind picked up. Ronnie sat down on the gravel shoulder, and when Dory joined her, Ronnie leaned against her, and then closed her eyes from sleeplessness.

34

Ronnie opened her eyes a few seconds later and knew she was back in Harrow, but it was only a dream. She knew the difference, and it didn't frighten her at all to be there.

You're out on the highway with Dory, and you're just sleeping. It's all right. The house is turned off now.

She lay on a bare mattress in a room of the house she hadn't seen. Above her head, a window was open, its shutters drawn back. A chilly wind came in. Outside, it was night.

She felt as if someone were tugging at the mattress. She glanced down along its edge by her feet. She saw him.

"It's all right," she said, softly. "Don't be afraid."

He crawled toward her on his hands and knees. He had a beautiful face, nearly radiant and cherubic. His hair had grown long, and so had his fingernails—so long that they curled a bit at the ends. She saw the scar just under his chin, and assumed that it ran all the way down his chest and little belly beneath his shirt.

"I know your name," she said, as she swung around to sit at the edge of the bed. She patted the place beside her. "You're Arnie, aren't you?"

The boy's grin widened, and small knifepoints in his gums shone in the morning light from the open window.

"Someone did something terrible to you," Ronnie continued. "But you don't need to be afraid, Arnie Pierson. I know all about you and how Harrow's inside you, just a little bit. I know you didn't mean for all this to happen."

The boy's smile faded and he shook his head violently.

"None of it's your fault," she cooed, and reached her hand out. "Please. Take my hand."

The boy waited a minute, glancing about the room as if expecting someone else.

His thick yellowed fingernails scraped her flesh when he touched her, but she closed her fingers around his.

"I don't have many friends, either," she said. She reached over with her free hand to stroke his hair. It was tangled and full of dried blood, but she combed it out with her fingers until it had a shine to it.

He drew his hand from hers and then spread his arms wide, making a bleating sound.

He wants me to pick him up, she thought. *He just wants love. He just wants someone to care for him.*

She bent forward, lifting him beneath his arms, raising him high and bringing him down on her lap. She kissed his scalp lightly. "I will take care of you, Arnie. I will never leave you alone. I promise. I promise you'll always have me here. I'll make sure you are never lonely or afraid. Never again."

Ronnie and the little boy lay down together on the mattress, her arms over him, his clawlike fingernails curved around her hands.

Somewhere far away she heard the sound of a tea kettle's whistle.

35

Ronnie awoke, her head in Dory's lap.

"You hear that?" Dory asked. "I can't believe it. I can't believe it."

Ronnie sat up. She did hear it, although the noise had seemed part of the tea kettle's whistling sound from her dream at first. It was the high-pitched squeal of sirens as a police car came around the corner from the direction of the next town to the north.

She pushed herself up from the gravel, feeling groggy and as if she were still half in a dream in a room in the house.

Over the sound of approaching sirens, Ronnie said, "I'm still dreaming about it. I think we need to go back. There may be a shred of it still going. Awake. A whisper of Harrow."

"I don't know where I'm going, but it's not back, that's for damn sure."

"Do you feel cold?"

"A little. Like my heart's an icebox."

"I guess that's to be expected," Ronnie said. "I feel shellshocked. I feel like the world just ended and we're still here."

"Well," Dory said. "With luck, some people just slept through it."

36

The sunlight came up brighter, but it was still October and getting colder as the day wore on. Golden and red leaves danced in little whirlwinds at the side of the road, and several birds dipped and rose along the telephone lines. The police car came around the bend, slowing down as the officer driving saw the two young women.

"Just when you think it's at its worst," Dory said. "The cavalry show up."

"Let's hope they always do," Ronnie said.

"You feel silly?"

"A little. I think it's the shock. And lack of sleep. I feel like laughing at everything right now. Do you?"

"Absolutely," Dory said, giggling a little. "Christ, I'd better not be losing my marbles."

37

"Miss?" One of the cops leaned out of the car. "Are you all right?"

Ronnie and Dory looked at each other. Ronnie had dried blood all over her clothes; and Dory looked as if she'd been thrown in a washing machine and left out to dry. Ronnie nearly grinned, but it was half-hearted and she couldn't manage more than a flat line of lips.

Then Dory started laughing and wouldn't stop until Ronnie got her to slide into the back seat of the squad car.

38

The red-haired guy driving was named Officer Phil, and the one next to him with the short dark hair said his name was Tappan, which seemed like a funny name. Ronnie wondered if he had been named for the Tappan Zee Bridge, but decided not to let him know she'd been thinking this. She felt light-headed all of a sudden, and chalked it up to the long, dreadful night of horror and to lack of sleep.

Dory began telling the two policemen all that had happened, from the moment the dogs had escaped the pound and she'd seen what had become of Benny Marais, all the way until dawn. She spoke in rapid-fire staccato bursts of words, and when it sounded too ridiculous she dropped certain things (like the squishy thing that had been about to rape her under the supervision of Mr. Spider). By the end of her tale, she could do nothing but laugh, and it became contagious until both cops in the squad car starting giggling, too, even as she described the worst of it. Ronnie laughed, and that's when she wondered if she and Dory hadn't gone insane. She shot Dory a look, and Dory seemed to understand. Dory nodded, chuckling. "I know it sounds crazy," she said, covering her mouth with her hands.

"Hysterical," Ronnie said, and she too had to catch her breath in between the maniacal laughing. She also told her tale as the cops listened patiently, laughing now and then in the contagion of Ronnie's and Dory's laughter.

When she finished up the last bit, she began to feel lightheaded and a little faint, and her need for sleep became overpowering (*No shit, Sherlock, you've been up for at least twenty-four hours and you're a nine-hour-a-night girl*) and that's when Officer Phil said, "Well, you two are okay now. It does sound crazy."

"Loony tuney," Officer Tappan said. "But we got some reports last night that had us calling some cops down here, and nobody made a lick of sense."

"That's why we're here," Officer Phil said. "You two have had it rough. I know we've all been laughing, but it's the shock, believe me. If even a quarter of what you've told us is true, well, you're lucky to still be 'all there.' "

"Let's just get going," Officer Tappan said. "The sooner they get settled in, the sooner we can clear this thing up."

Officer Phil turned the key in the ignition, and glanced in the rearview mirror. "You girls just relax. We'll run you back up to Parham and find you a place to sleep. We'll get some other officers down here to check out your story."

"Thanks," Dory said. As soon as she felt the car moving, she closed her eyes and leaned against Ronnie, who leaned against her. Ronnie smelled like death, which didn't bother Dory as much as she thought it would.

Sleep came so fast it was like a train hitting her from a dark tunnel.

When Dory awoke, it was because the car had come to a full stop.

39

Neither officer was in the car with them, and the doors had been flung open. Dory nudged Ronnie awake.

She pointed ahead, to Harrow. The police car was parked in the driveway of the house.

Harrow looked ordinary and dilapidated, with none of the grandiose overgrowth it had shown them the night before. It had shrunk back down to being a mere pile of a mansion.

Ronnie laughed.

"What's so funny?"

"Everything."

"Where'd the cops go?"

"Probably inside. They're probably working for the house. I guess I thought that might be the case. I was hoping it wasn't, but . . ."

"What the hell are we gonna do?" Dory asked.

"How're your legs?"

"What?"

"Your legs. Mine are good. We can take a lot of back roads and eventually find our way to Parham or maybe go south to Beacon. I don't really care as long as it's far the hell away from here."

"Won't they come after us?"

"I don't know. We need to be more careful. How much sleep do you think we got?"

Dory leaned over the back of the driver's seat to check the car's digital clock. "Looks like about ten minutes. Or less."

"Well, it'll have to do," Ronnie said. "Let's go."

40

The first hour, Dory kept looking back along the road as if expecting the cops to show up again, or someone in a car, or even people with pitchforks and hatchets to come wandering out of the woods, but none of it happened. By the second hour, Ronnie pointed down the gravel road they were following to a large street and a small building beyond some oaks. "I know that place. They make good pancakes. Pancakes would be good right about now."

"I think we should keep going," Dory said. "At least until dark."

"I'm hungry. Let's go. I have . . ." She took her left shoe off and reached into it, under the tongue and between the shoestrings. She drew out a twenty-dollar bill. " 'Always have a little cash tucked away,' my dad used to tell me."

"I don't know. What if . . ."

"What if we drop from hunger?" Ronnie asked.

41

The Wind Cliff Diner was nearly empty. Ronnie went in first and checked the few patrons at their tables to make sure none of them seemed as if they might suddenly rise up and attack them. Once she noticed that they all seemed fairly ordinary, and the guy with the baseball cap and the flannel shirt was scarfing down so many pancakes it made her mouth water, she stepped all the way in with Dory following.

They sat at the counter on stools, and when the waitress

with big blue hair and the cat's-eye glasses came by and asked them if they wanted blueberry or buttermilk, her eyes nearly doubled in size looking at them. "You girls look like you been through the wringer. Somebody hurt you?"

"I'd like blueberry, with extra butter and lots of syrup," Ronnie said. "And a side of bacon. And one egg, over easy. And coffee."

"Me, too," Dory said. "Instead of coffee, milk."

"I think you should go for coffee," Ronnie said. "You need to stay awake."

"Oh, right. Coffee's fine."

"Sure," the waitress said. Dory glanced at her badge: *Marjorie*.

"Marjorie," she said.

"Hon?"

"You live up in Watch Point?"

"Nope. I'm down in Beacon."

"I love Beacon," Dory said.

"Me, too," Ronnie said.

"You sure you're not hurt?" Marjorie asked Ronnie. "You look a little . . . well, dirty."

"Oh," Ronnie grinned. "It's nothing. Where's the wash-room?"

Marjorie pointed it out—at the end of the counter and to the right.

42

In the bathroom, Ronnie splashed her face with water. She squeezed some of the pink liquid soap into her hands and scrubbed at her arms and face until it was all clean.

She looked at her face in the cracked mirror.

"You're fine." She checked the cut in her shoulder from the previous evening. It felt a little sore, but was barely more than a scratch. "You're fine and it's over. There are

---

just little whispers still around. Shreds of Harrow. You shut it. But it's a little leaky."

43

After breakfast, they again used the bathroom to clean themselves and wash their hair and then dry it and then use the toilet. Dory went to get some Wrigley's Spearmint gum and a tin of Altoids, while Ronnie paid the check.

"You sure you girls are doing okay? Sometimes boys can be trouble," Marjorie said as she rang up the breakfast and the gum and mints.

"We're fine. We had a little accident. Nothing serious," Ronnie said. She gave up her twenty, and got the change, and thanked Marjorie for a wonderful breakfast. As she turned toward the door, she looked back toward the restroom and thought she saw someone she recognized.

44

Outside on the steps of the diner, Ronnie tapped Dory lightly on her arm.

Dory looked over at her, a question in her eyes.

"How do you destroy a house?"

"Burn it. I guess."

"I don't think Harrow burns well. Seems to me someone tried it already."

"I don't know," Dory said. "Demolish it."

"Got a bulldozer?"

"What about blowing it up?"

"Ah," Ronnie said, surveying the parking lot in front of the diner as if looking for someone. "If I had a bomb, that's what I'd do."

"You're actually thinking of going back there to *blow it up?*"

"I'm just keeping my options open," Ronnie said. As if it

were an after-thought, she added, "We never saw that man again, did we?"

"Who?"

"The one who put you upstairs. The one without pants on."

"Oh. I thought you got him. With the axe."

"I hit him. Maybe twice. But I don't think he died. I just got a good one in."

"You think he's still there?"

"I don't know. Maybe he wasn't even real." Ronnie shivered and put her arms around herself. "It's getting too cold already. I wish I had a good jacket."

"We could just stay in the diner today," Dory said, glancing back at the glass door with the news rack next to it.

"No. We need to be on the move. You know, I felt power in that house," Ronnie said. "I mean, real power. I had that hatchet in my hands and I felt I could . . . well, I could do anything. I felt like a *goddess* or something. I had this . . . *energy*. Out here, well, I'm just cold. No power whatsoever."

"Maybe if we told that waitress what happened, she'd help us. She seemed okay."

Ronnie glanced at Dory and then back to the parking lot. "Did you feel it? That surge of power?"

"In the house? No."

"Truth."

"A little. Just a little. But I didn't feel it all the time."

"Harrow wanted us because it's scared of us. 'You hold your enemies closer than your friends,' my dad used to tell me. You watch your enemies. It's afraid of us. I think we're going to have to go back there someday and make sure that house is brought to the ground. And then salt the ground so nothing grows. And then pour concrete over it or something. Get biblical on its ass. And I think it has to be you and me. It got everyone else it was afraid of, Dory. I don't think we even have a choice."

Dory looked at Ronnie, who watched the highway beyond the parking lot. Beyond that roadside, a dip in the hill went right down to the Hudson River.

Dory said, resignation and determination in her voice, "Okay. We'll do that. Someday. I promise."

"Good," Ronnie said. "We'll be prepared next time. We know what we're up against now. Because it's not over, you know that."

"It might be."

"See that Chevy Malibu?" Ronnie nodded to the far end of the parking lot. "Looks kind of dirty?"

Dory glanced over at a sleek but dusty car. "Sure."

"That's my car. I bought it from all my summer jobs. It breaks down all the time, but it runs most days. I let my sister drive it all the time. I loaned it to her that night—the one last summer when Arnie Pierson's body was cut up out at Harrow. It should be in the driveway at my house. But my mother's dead. And I'm pretty sure my sister's dead. So why is it parked here?"

Dory asked, "Are you sure it's yours?"

"I know my own license plate. See the cracked back window? It's mine. It's the one she drove that night. She drove it most nights when she had a date or a party. And I think I saw someone I know in the diner. From Watch Point. She was sitting at a booth near the restroom. I didn't see her at first. I noticed her when I was paying the cashier for our breakfast. Like she had come in to sit down just before we left."

"Jesus Christ. Who?"

Ronnie shifted uncomfortably. "Someone who should be dead. Or maybe I imagined I saw her. It's funny, isn't it? It *is* like a whisper, the way Harrow gets into you and stays with you. It's playing games with us now," Ronnie said. She fell silent a moment. Took a deep breath. "Let's keep walking. Ignore anyone you see. Don't stop until we get to Beacon. It'll be chilly, but we'll live. Harrow's still afraid of us. It's not being direct. Eventually, we'll get beyond its reach."

"What if—" Dory was about to ask: *What if we never get away from it?*

"For all I know," Ronnie said, "we're carriers. We may have Harrow in us just as much as that boy did. I guess if that's true, there's not a hell of a lot we can do. We may be spreading the plague wherever we go. Typhoid Marys on the run."

"Thanks for that thought." Dory grinned, shaking her head slightly.

"Glad you kept your sense of humor." Ronnie slapped her lightly on the back. "You know, it's good to make new friends."

As incongruous as the words were, Dory felt them, too. "Sure is," she said with a trace of sadness in her voice.

They began walking south on the highway, with the sun shining and the wind picking up. They heard someone calling them back to the diner, and at first neither Ronnie nor Dory wanted to stop to find out who it could be.

Dory glanced back, briefly.

"I told you," Ronnie said. "Ignore everyone."

It was Marjorie, standing out at the edge of the parking lot, waving her hands. The waitress shouted to them that she had given them the wrong change, but the two seventeen-year-olds ignored her call, and walked faster down the highway.

Epilogue

1

At sundown, the Nightwatchman had decided to take the back roads, the twisty-turny unpaved roads across the fields, between the patches of woods. His old Ford station wagon ran just fine, and he'd filled it with a mattress and some blankets so he could sleep in it, if need be. He no longer knew the name Speederman or Mr. Spider, and felt that he was truly the Nightwatchman, and always had been and always would be.

He asked directions, at a gas station in Peekskill, of a twenty-year-old with slicked-back hair whose face was covered with grease as he came to get paid for the gas.

"Where you going?"

"South, I think." Even when he spoke, the Nightwatchman saw the look in the young man's eyes. *He feels it. He knows what's inside me.* The Nightwatchman reached out and touched the young man on his shoulder, and the man flinched.

The Nightwatchman didn't know when it would happen, but he knew that the grease monkey's life would be over sometime soon. It might be in an accident at work, or he might fall down some stairs and hit his head on something hard and sharp. But he had passed a whisper of Harrow on to him. The Nightwatchman grinned as he saw the young man's reaction to his touch.

The gas station attendant's eyes widened with a slight, and perhaps imagined, fear.

It felt good to have that touch, to pass it so easily.

"Take care," the Nightwatchman said to the attendant as he got back into his car. He watched the young man in the rearview mirror as he pulled out onto the road—the attendant was staring at his hands as if they had been plunged into some kind of filth.

He drove along the byways of the Hudson Valley, and took a southerly route toward the city, taking hours to get there because he wanted to see the small towns and stop for coffee in Ossining and look at the prison there. He thought about Sing-Sing, and what a delightful place it would be for him, but the voices did not give their approval, so he continued toward New York City, waiting for a sign from within.

2

He slept most days in the car, parked under bridges down by the waterfront. By dusk, he arose, and went looking for a place to spin a web. One night in November, he found it—an advertisement in *The New York Times* for a nightwatchman. He applied for the job, and knew he would get it because he had managed to touch the woman who interviewed him, although she had seemed repulsed by him. He had gummed her up good with visions of love and lust for him, and he thought as he started his first night of work that she would make an excellent Mrs. Fly one day soon, and maybe they'd have a whole litter of shiny white maggots. She had even asked him out—right after hiring him—and he had said to her, "Sure. Maybe Friday. You can invite me to your place. We'll get something to eat."

She had nodded, a slightly confused grin on her face as if she didn't understand why she felt she had dreamed of this moment. But in her dream, she had seen the man standing in the doorway of a house that loomed against the sky as if it were a bird of prey, descending.

3

You can just see it sometimes, over the tops of the trees if you're on one of the hillsides or if you're out on the river in a boat. Not the whole house at once, but parts of it—the spires and the turrets, and the way the treetops seem like fingers clutching its uppermost windows.

Few venture up the road to it, to the long private drive, overwhelmed with brambles and grasses and the fences and "no trespassing" and "hunting not allowed" signs posted along the way.

Some overcome the fears and the legends and the stories and the signs and the fences.

Some go there, because there are always those people— usually very few—who are called to places like this house.

DOUGLAS CLEGG
NIGHTMARE HOUSE

There are places that hold in the traces of evil, houses that become legendary for the mysteries and secrets within their walls. Harrow is one such house. Psychic manifestations, poltergeist activity, hallucinations, and other residue of terror have all been documented in Harrow. It has been called Nightmare House. It is a nest for the restless spirits of the dead.

When Ethan Gravesend arrives to inherit Nightmare House, he does not suspect the horror that awaits him—the nightmare of the woman trapped within the walls of the house, or the endless crying of an unseen child.

Also includes the bonus novella *Purity*!